Christmas Revels V

FOUR REGENCY NOVELLAS

Kate Parker

Louisa Cornell

Anna D. Allen

Hannah Meredith

Singing Spring Press

This is a work of fiction. All names, characters, and incidents are the product of the author's imagination. Any resemblance to actual occurrences or persons, living or dead, is coincidental. Historical events and personages are fictionalized.

CHRISTMAS REVELS V : FOUR REGENCY NOVELLAS

Mr. Hunt's Christmas Caller copyright © 2018 by Anna D. Allen
The Christmas Gamble copyright © 2018 by Kate Parker
The Gnome and the Christmas Star copyright © 2018 by Meredith Simmons
A Perfectly Ridiculous Christmas copyright © 2018 by Pamela Bolton-Holifield

All rights reserved. With the exception of brief quotes used in critical articles or reviews, no part of this book may be reproduced in any form or by any means without written permission of the author.

ISBN: 978-1-942470-09-0 (Print)
ISBN: 978-1-942470-08-3 (E-book)

Published by Singing Spring Press

Table of Contents

Mr. Hunt's Christmas Caller
by Anna D. Allen...5

The Christmas Gamble
by Kate Parker..91

The Gnome and the Christmas Star
by Hannah Meredith..185

A Perfectly Ridiculous Christmas
by Louisa Cornell..307

Mr. Hunt's Christmas Caller

by

Anna D. Allen

Mr. Hunt's Christmas Caller

6 December 1816

The darkest days of winter descended upon the village of Upsbury at a most inopportune time for Mr. Matthias Hunt of Oakwood Hall. When snowflakes peppered the cold air, his neighbors, as was their wont, opened their merry homes to friends and family and even the occasional foe to brighten a gloomy season and warm the frigid nights. Companionship and good cheer would reign until Twelfth Night, with all its accompanying revelry and joy.

But this Christmas, Mr. Matthias Hunt wanted none of it, preferring instead to go home, sit before his own fire, and sulk in misery. Alone. As he might at any other time of year without notice.

For a moment, as he hovered at the drawing room doors, lights and laughter before him, he considered just that—rushing home before anyone spoke to him. The only thing worse than his neighbors' knowledge of his great humiliation was their genuine sympathy for his unfortunate situation—inevitably followed by the subtle shaking of their heads in shared dismay and the occasional clucking of tongues. Behind their words, he knew they thought him such a fool, pursuing a girl half his age... only to be rejected.

But he could not very well snub Lord Upsbury, or more precisely, Lady Upsbury, at this, their annual St. Nicholas Day party. He would simply stay long enough to be seen, give his regards to the host and hostess, and then slip away with none the wiser.

Considering it further, Matthias decided to partake of the Wassail bowl to warm himself before the short stroll home. He paused, though, to see what the guests' children had found in their boots and slippers left in the hall. Toys and sweetmeats, he imagined, but the youngest Upsbury boy sat crying on the floor over a bundle of switches, while the other children ran about with squeals of delight. Such a strange Continental tradition, Matthias thought, brought by Lady Upsbury's diplomat father when he returned home from the Bavarian court with a bride. Thankfully, the family had dispensed with all that nonsense about sap-laden trees in houses.

Familiar, unwelcomed laughter interrupted his short-lived respite from his misfortune. Mrs. Lancaster sat by the fire and held a usurpatory court in the Upsbury home, her jovial smile and twinkling eyes belying a malicious nature. She had caught poor Miss Blackwell in her snare, and Matthias—and half the house, no doubt—clearly heard the merry lady's carefully-worded compliment, as she fully intended.

"How splendid," she crowed with delight to the lady standing before her. "It always amazes me how well you dress on nothing but egg money."

Mrs. Lancaster never failed to strike where she knew it would hurt the most. Miss Blackwell lacked a sense of fashion—although Matthias suspected much the same could be said of him—and her dress depended on her own needle, despite her gentle birth. True, she did a splendid job with that needle, and were she his sister, Matthias would have no qualms about being seen in her company. But for Mrs. Lancaster to speak so snidely and remind everyone present of Miss Blackwell's diminished circumstances was unacceptable. The matron should be asked to leave... except, it was not his house. Why Lord and Lady Upsbury invited her to begin with, Matthias could not imagine. Mrs. Lancaster had no fears of her opinions on Lady Upsbury being known. She frequently proclaimed them aloud and found the current viscountess much too Popish for her taste. This, of course, did not stop Mrs. Lancaster from coming to celebrate a saint's feast day, not when food and gossip abounded.

"Or do you keep the dairy money as well?" continued Mrs. Lancaster.

Matthias felt the sting of Mrs. Lancaster's compliment, and he knew Miss Blackwell—a demure spinster near his own age—well enough to know she would be polite regardless of anything Mrs. Lancaster said to her. And Mrs. Lancaster would take full advantage of her captive audience by prattling on about nothing, and then some. No one deserved Mrs. Lancaster's attention, least of all Miss Blackwell.

He should rescue her, Matthias knew, but he had no desire to draw Mrs. Lancaster's fire. He dismissed the idea of a bit of Dutch courage and took the matter into his own hands. He glanced about the room to confirm his strategy would work, and then leapt into the fray.

"Miss Blackwell," he said causally approaching the pair,

"I believe your aunt is looking for you." It was not entirely a lie. In Matthias's experience, Miss Blackwell's aunt was usually looking for her.

"Oh, Mr. Hunt." Mrs. Lancaster's merriment took a downward turn as she spied him, and Matthias knew what would soon follow. She even shook her head. Miss Blackwell glanced up at him, only to avert her eyes before hurrying off, presumably in search of her aunt. Matthias had little time to consider her unusual reaction—no friendly greeting, no polite response, not even her customary shy smile—before Mrs. Lancaster said, "We have not seen you since the reading of the banns." *Touché.* Her barb hit its mark. "Such a surprise, Nerissa Merryweather and that Thompson boy...."

"Quite."

"They do make a handsome pair, but I never imagined, not with you in the running. I could hardly believe my ears when Reverend Ragsdale...."

Matthias didn't need a recounting of the moment he learned—along with the entire congregation—that his suit had been rejected. An audible gasp had filled the cold interior of the Norman church, followed by a silence soon broken by Mrs. Martin—Miss Blackwell's aunt—loudly asking, "Jonathan Thompson? But I thought she was going to marry Mr. Hunt?" before being hushed by her niece. Matthias could still hear the echo in his mind.

"If you will excuse me, Mrs. Lancaster." He gave the surprised lady a curt bow and turned to leave. He'd had enough and headed out into the hall. He would give his regards to Lady Upsbury and then leave this bright festivity for the solace of home where only his own thoughts could pester him.

"I have no idea where it is." Mrs. Martin's voice always seemed to carry—unintentionally... quite the opposite of Mrs. Lancaster.

"Perhaps you left it in Mr. Forbes's carriage," replied Miss Blackwell to her aunt, "I'll go see."

As she turned, Miss Blackwell nearly collided with Matthias in his progression across the hall. She easily sidestepped, but as she looked up at him and recognition covered her face, she faltered. The necessary niceties seemed to catch in her throat, and Matthias thought she blushed before looking down and continuing on her way outside. He found it all most peculiar but did not dwell on it.

He made his regrets to Lord Upsbury, thanked Lady Upsbury, and then departed the great house, leaving behind the laughter and gossip and raucous children. Outside, in the crisp, afternoon air, the sky grey with a stray snow flurry, Matthias breathed deep, feeling as if he'd held his breath during the entire short visit. The walk home along the footpath through the forest would revive his spirit, he knew. He did not need company; he needed time alone, away from prying neighbors, so that he might recover from yet another disappointment. He had been so certain this time would be different, that Nerissa would be the one to accept his proposal and accept him as her husband. It never occurred to him, when he asked for her hand, that she already belonged to another. She didn't even have the decency to admit as much. Instead, she asked for time to consider his offer properly. How everyone must have laughed about it, the middle-aged bachelor courting the golden-haired debutante.

As he walked down the drive, carriages and horses lining the way, he looked up to see Miss Blackwell heading toward him, back to the house. She carried a lady's wrap this time—the item her aunt must have mislaid—and walked with her eyes lowered.

"Good day, Miss Blackwell," said Matthias, tipping his hat to her. He never expected her startled response. She briefly stopped mid-step. A look of distress passed over her face and quickly faded before she resumed walking and continued past him.

"Are you all right?" he asked, turning to watch her.

"Yes. I'm quite all right," came her surprisingly terse response with only the slightest glance back.

Baffled by her behavior, Matthias felt as if she were snubbing him, something he knew Miss Blackwell would never do. She even managed to put up with Mrs. Lancaster. Clearly, something was amiss.

"Miss Blackwell," he called after her, "have I offended you in some way?"

She abruptly stopped and turned to face him, her face conveying shock over the suggestion.

"No," she said, adamant. But then her brow creased, and she seemed to reconsider. When she spoke again, it was with a determined voice, "Well, yes, if you must know." She took two steps toward him, and her words came at him fast and steady. "It grieves me to see you so injured by Miss Merryweather, but you were not engaged. Everyone knew you asked her to be your wife and that she asked that you allow her to think about it. Quite prudent with most proposals. A man can be all charm and kindness while pursuing a lady, but once he has her, once there is no way to escape, he reveals his true self, for good or ill. So I understand a lady wishing to think on marriage before accepting a man."

She took a deep breath, and Matthias thought he saw fear—or was it anger?—in her eyes, while he felt his own heart pounding fiercely for some inexplicable reason. "But with you?" she continued, "I've seen you happy, kind, and gentle. I've seen you full of anger. I've seen you at work in the fields on good days and bad, through deluge and drought. I've seen you at your worst. And any lady who would not say yes to you in the space of a heartbeat is not worth the having."

And then she gasped at her own words, a horrified look on her face. Before Matthias could even fully comprehend all she'd said, she turned and ran back to the house. He stood there, stunned, her words echoing in his head. Polite, demure, shy Miss Blackwell who rarely raised her voice in his experience had given him a thorough dressing down.

In the midst of his bafflement, a slow dawning occurred. And then he realized.

Miss Blackwell loved him.

ಸಿಂಡ

On the afternoon of Christmas Eve, Miss Constance Blackwell set a large basket down on the stiff, brown grass and glanced up the lane to Oakwood Hall—Mr. Hunt's home—and stretched her back. Sometimes, she thought herself a very foolish girl... although, hardly a girl anymore. At only thirty-four, she already had far too many grey hairs for her comfort, while her back ached much too often for one still deemed young by her elders. Only two stoneware jars of marmalade remained in the basket—Aunt Penelope's annual Christmas gift to her neighbors made from Mr. Forbes's hothouse oranges. Constance had, as usual, promised to deliver them, with the help of the scullery maid, Patsy.

But Constance had failed to anticipate the sudden turn in the weather, the temperature dropping, the wind picking up, the day growing bitter. As soon as Patsy's basket was empty, Constance sent the girl home and continued the deliveries herself. Now, dark clouds gathered, and stray bits of ice mixed with the intermittent drizzle.

She didn't particularly like the Christmas Season, and this was yet another example of why. On such a day as this, any sensible soul would be at home beside the fire with a good book in hand. But she had ventured out on a task not of her own making. Worse, in an imprudent act of procrastination, she avoided Mr. Hunt's house until last, and now a wet, frigid mile separated her from home. She should have delivered the two jars there first and been done with it. All the anxiety and embarrassment would already be over, and she would be hurrying home to tea and biscuits and the promise of an excellent dinner.

Instead, she still had to endure an encounter with Mr. Hunt. The first since the day of Lady Upsbury's St. Nicholas's Day party and that thoughtless tirade.

She never should have spoken to Mr. Hunt like that. She should have kept her thoughts—and feelings—to herself, and treated him with polite civility, as always. She should have smiled and lowered her gaze and acted as if nothing were amiss. But Nerissa Merryweather was not worth the suffering he endured, and it infuriated Constance to see that he had allowed that silly chit to break his heart. The moment he arrived at the party, it was writ plain for all to see there on his face—the hurt, the humiliation, the harm done by the girl's callous rejection in such a public manner. Then Mrs. Lancaster had to dig her claws in him, purely for the sake of her own entertainment.

Constance could *almost* excuse Mrs. Lancaster and Nerissa—everyone knew their true natures; wasps will sting—but Mr. Hunt was an intelligent man who knew better. Or at least, he should have known better than to pursue the likes of Nerissa. Of course, Constance reminded herself, he was a man. Reason tended to abandon a man at the sight of a pretty face, with folly arriving in its wake. Like most men, Constance concluded, he would rather have a pretty girl—no matter how poorly she treated him—than a plain, ordinary woman who treated him well.

Constance tucked the basket in the crook of her arm and walked ram-rod straight up the long drive toward the house, a multi-gabled red-brick Elizabethan structure surrounded by ancient oaks and, beyond that, vast fields asleep 'til spring. The massive trees even lined the drive, for which Constance was grateful; they blocked much of the drizzle and even some of the wind, the leafless old branches creaking overhead as she passed beneath.

She smelled the house before she reached it, pale grey wood smoke rising up from every chimney into a greyer sky. She saw no other signs of life, the house deceptively still and quiet, and she again thought of sensible people sitting beside their fires.

Constance rang the bell before the door and braced herself for the possibility that Mr. Hunt might open it. But then she scoffed at the ridiculous notion. Gentlemen didn't answer their own doors, especially on cold, winter days. Behind her, she heard the frozen mix pick up, the drizzle turning into a light but steady shower, pinging against the flagstones and gravel, but, for the moment, the portico protected her.

She breathed an inward sigh of relief when the door opened and she saw Mr. Wilkins, the thin, grey-haired butler, standing there. His face brightened at the sight of her.

"Miss Blackwell, good afternoon," he beamed, "I'll see if Mr. Hunt is at home. Please, come in." He stepped aside to allow her entry.

"No, no, Mr. Wilkins, that's quite all right," she replied, reaching into the basket. "No need to bother Mr. Hunt. I'm just delivering Aunt Penelope's marmalade." Constance held out the last two stoneware jars.

"How lovely, Miss Blackwell," said Mr. Wilkins, accepting the jars with a great smile, "Mr. Hunt is especially fond of your aunt's marmalade."

"Not just for Mr. Hunt, but for everyone."

Mr. Wilkins' face stilled, his eyes widening with wonder and delight. "Oh, bless you, Miss Blackwell. And Mrs. Martin, too. Please, thank her."

"I will," replied Constance, taking a step back. She began to feel anxious, fearing Mr. Hunt might make an appearance.

Mr. Wilkins again motioned into the house. "Are you sure you won't come in?"

"Quite sure, thank you." She stepped away, never turning her back on the butler but eager to make her departure. "Happy Christmas, Mr. Wilkins."

"Happy Christmas, Miss Blackwell."

She turned away, hurrying across the flagstones and down the single step. She heard the door close behind her, and she felt an immense sense of relief. Resisting the urge to break into a run down the drive, she walked with deliberate determination and dignity, head held high despite the precipitation. Soon, she would be home.

"Miss Blackwell!"

In that instance, when the voice called out to her, Constance recognized the deep resonance. Her heart sank, her stomach jumped, and her feet stopped in mid-step.

Mr. Hunt.

Once, before the rumors of his impending engagement to Nerissa Merryweather, Constance's heart would leap up at his mere presence. His voice would send warm ripples through her soul, and she knew then the world was better simply because he resided in it at this time. But after the rumors, she dreaded the presence of Mr. Hunt. Reverend Ragsdale reading the banns for the betrothal of Nerissa to Jonathon Thompson only made it worse, culminating in Lady Upsbury's party. The sight of him that day made her feel sick. And then angry. Not at Nerissa. But at Mr. Hunt. And then she had made such a fool of herself.

"A moment, Miss Blackwell, if you please."

Trembling—and not from the cold... well, maybe a bit—Constance turned to see Mr. Hunt striding toward her, a large black umbrella raised, the door open behind him with Mr. Wilkins standing there. She wanted to slink away, unseen, unnoticed, but instead, she pasted on a tight-lipped smile, and endeavored to appear pleased by Mr. Hunt's sudden arrival.

At such moments, quite irrationally and unfairly, Constance sometimes thought the universe, even God, conspired against her and endeavored to torment her. After all, Aunt Penelope had not *made* the marmalade. Oh, yes, it was her recipe, and it was her tradition to give a jar to each of her neighbors. But Constance had done all the work, by herself—not wishing to cause more work for Cook and Patsy—when Aunt Penelope expressed fatigue at the prospect, just as she had the year before. And the year prior to that. Constance didn't mind; she just wished Aunt Penelope could have delivered the marmalade instead. At least, *this* Christmas. Mr. Forbes would have loaned his carriage, Constance felt certain, had Aunt Penelope but asked. Then this embarrassing moment with Mr. Hunt would not be occurring.

Of course, with such thoughts in her head, Constance felt worse, chastising herself for being ungrateful and selfish.

"Happy Christmas, Mr. Hunt," said Constance, her feigned cheer firmly fixed. But Mr. Hunt didn't look the least bit happy. Concern and distress vied for dominance in his face, and it horrified Constance to know she was the cause.

"Happy Christmas," he replied by rote as he reached her and held the umbrella aloft over her head. She sensed no joy in the sentiment. "Please, come in and warm yourself. It's much too far for you to walk home on such as day as this."

"Oh, no. It's quite all right, Mr. Hunt."

But he took her empty basket. "Please. Mrs. Ivers has just made some scones. I'm sure she has some cake, too. Come in... at least until this passes over, and then we'll send you home in the carriage."

She would have said no and hurried on her way, but she had no wish to worry him further. Besides, her feet ached, and the sleet came down harder, and poor Mr. Hunt grew more drenched the longer she lingered there, until at length, she reluctantly nodded. His face broke out in a genuine smile, much of his unease dissipating.

They walked together toward the house, Mr. Hunt's

umbrella protecting Constance from the frozen downpour without regard for his own comfort. He slowed his gait to match hers, leaving Constance feeling flustered. She didn't like being fussed over, especially not by Mr. Hunt. Until she felt no choice but to lift her skirts ever so slightly and quicken her pace so that they might reach the door sooner.

Entering the house behind her, Mr. Hunt collapsed the umbrella and handed it off to Mr. Wilkins, along with her basket. The butler quickly closed the door, but it did little to lessen the cold damp of the vestibule. Mr. Hunt ran his fingers through his brown hair to flick off some of the water and then motioned Constance toward the great hall.

Constance had only been in the house twice before, but she remembered the way—a turn to the left and then a cautious step over a threshold. The great hall opened before her, long and immense, with high oriel windows on opposing ends to allow in the dull December light. As on her previous two visits, it reminded Constance of some medieval banqueting hall. Today, it stood empty, save for several chairs and side tables huddled about the burning fireplace.

Mr. Hunt motioned to the fire, and without any further prompting, Constance hurried over to warm herself. Her footsteps against the stone floor echoed throughout the vast space and mingled with the pinging of sleet pelting the windowpanes.

She pulled off her gloves, her finger red from cold, and held her hands before the fire. Savoring the warmth, she closed her eyes and breathed deep, grateful she had decided to accept Mr. Hunt's invitation. Her host strolled over in a more sedate fashion and took the place beside her, his hands outstretched toward the flames.

Constance heard Mr. Wilkins clear his throat and ask, "Miss Blackwell? If I may..." He held out his hands. "Your coat and bonnet will dry faster in the kitchen."

"Oh, yes, of course," replied Constance, and she began unbuttoning her coat.

"Here, allow me," said Mr. Hunt as she finished with the buttons, and he helped ease her out of the coat. She untied the ribbons of her wet bonnet and handed it to Mr. Wilkins. With a shiver, she moved closer to the fire.

As the butler's footsteps faded into the servants' portion of the house, Constance glanced over at her companion. Moisture darkened his shoulders. "You should find something dry."

"Yes," he replied, "but it would be frightfully rude of me to...."

"I assure you, Mr. Hunt, I will be perfectly all right until you return." She gave him a reassuring smile, and to her surprise, he exhaled, as if he had been holding his breath. His brown eyes lit up, and he returned her smile, a tension easing from his body.

He bowed to her. "I'll be but a moment."

Once he left the hall, Constance sat down and stretched out her feet to warm them. She wished she could take off her half-boots, but she would be home soon enough. Owing to the holy day, there was still much to do before the Midnight Service that night, as well as the Christmas festivities tomorrow. She had promised their servants the day off, beginning this evening. As a result, Constance would have to manage the late supper before leaving for church. Tomorrow, she and Aunt Penelope would dine with Mr. and Mrs. Forbes. But still, dresses needed to be ironed, baths needed to be drawn, hair needed to be dressed and curled. And then there were all those unexpected things bound to happen at the most inopportune moments.

Constance shivered again. She did not remember the hall being cold and drafty, but then, thinking back, she realized both previous occasions had been in summer. She wondered if Mr. Hunt spent his days before this fire or if it were lit for her benefit. Perhaps the fire burned always, simply to keep the edge off the chill.

The sound of footsteps foretold Mr. Hunt's return well-before Constance saw him. He had exchanged the blue coat for a black coat, and he looked so much more… No. She mustn't think such thoughts. Such things were impossible. Mr. Hunt was her neighbor, an acquaintance, perhaps a friend, but nothing more.

"Is this your usual fire?" She pointed—always rude according to Aunt Penelope—at the hearth and hoped she didn't sound impertinent.

"Heavens, no." He almost laughed. "It's not very practical, is it?" He stood with his hands behind his back and looked up at the timbered ceiling. "Too much space for the fire to warm, and besides, all the heat goes up the chimney. How the ancient lords of the land with all their retainers slept in here—on flag stones, no less—I can't imagine." Constance laughed. Mr. Hunt, a bemused look on his face, asked, "Why the laugh?"

"Well, since you've *thought* of those retainers sleeping on the floor in this hall, clearly, you have *imagined* it."

At that, Mr. Hunt, too, laughed. "You're right, of course." He glanced about again. "Well, then, what's it to be? Where shall we have our tea? There's the morning room, which isn't very comfortable in winter. There's the drawing room, where I usually receive guests—I suppose we should adjourn there. Of course, there's always the library."

"The library?" Her heart leapt up the way it used to leap up at the sight of Mr. Hunt, before she only felt mortification and embarrassment.

"Yes." His browed knitted together, and he inquired, "You have been here before, haven't you?"

"Only twice. Once when I was fourteen and your uncle gave a ball—I was allowed to attend. And then when you gave that ball several years ago." Constance remembered it quite well. They had danced. Mr. Hunt had danced with every lady that night. He had been joyful, in love with Miss Deveraux. Everyone expected an announcement of their engagement, but none ever came. Miss Deveraux went to London instead and married some younger son of a younger son with nary a penny to his good name, and that was that. "All I saw of the house then was the hall and the dining room." Constance did not mention the withdrawing room.

"Then I must show you more of it," said Mr. Hunt, just as Mr. Wilkins carried in the tea tray. "Wilkins, take that to the library. And ask Mrs. Reid if she could find a shawl for Miss Blackwell."

"Very good, sir."

Mr. Hunt led Constance from the public rooms of the house into the private portion reserved for family and their guests—although, the *family* did not extend beyond Mr. Hunt. He had inherited the house some years ago from his uncle, a titled gentleman who owned vast estates, including a home in London, properties in Sussex and Kent, and a palatial seat in Wiltshire—all of it entailed to his son... except for

Oakwood Hall, far to the north and largely ignored, an afterthought, the loss of which, no one begrudged.

Past the grand, carved staircase dominated by another oriel window they went, only to wander from one room to the next, in that archaic fashion of houses before someone now forgotten to history hit upon the idea of central corridors: the bright but frigid morning room, the formal drawing room, the cozy breakfast room—where Mr. Hunt took all his meals, he informed Constance—next to a small sitting room, and finally, the library.

Dark wood and drawn curtains left the room in shadow, and it took a moment for Constance's eyes to adjust to the dim light of the fire. Mr. Hunt pulled back a curtain, just enough to allow in a streak of grey light. It more than sufficed, revealing shelf after shelf after even more shelves of books, more than Constance had ever seen. More than both Mr. Forbes and Lord Upsbury possessed together.

"Do you read?" asked Mr. Hunt as she went forward and caressed the spines of the nearest books.

"Like a fish swims," she replied absently, imagining a lifetime of reading, in this room, before this fire. It felt like standing on the edge of a precipice, the unknown stretching far away to the horizon, yet perfectly safe and inviting, like a pond on a hot summer day. Constance looked up at Mr. Hunt. He stared at her, a spark of amusement in his eyes, and she feared he thought her rude, gallivanting off as she did, gathering wool. "Mr. Forbes and Lord Upsbury allow us to borrow books from their libraries." She inwardly gasped at the sound of her own words. They came out without her realizing the implication, that she wished to borrow Mr. Hunt's books. Or worse, that she coveted his books. "I'm so sorry. I didn't mean it the way...."

"Nonsense." He smiled, moving toward the tea tray Mr. Wilkins had left near the fire. "I'm grateful to find a fellow bibliophile. You must come and borrow to your heart's content. Any time you wish." He picked up a teacup and poured. "I insist."

Constance felt certain she blushed and was thankful for the dim light. She moved before the fire and sat down, the dark room so much warmer than the bright hall. "Were these all here when you inherited the house?"

"Most of them, yes, but I had my own collection as well. Sugar?" he asked. When Constance nodded, he continued speaking. "My uncle—Lord Hunt—knew I loved books, and it appears, in his latter years, he shifted much of his collection about until most of it was here. All so that I would inherit it with the house." He held out a cup of tea to her. She accepted it and took a soothing sip.

"I remember your uncle," she said, settling the cup in her lap as Mr. Hunt poured a cup for himself. "He came here infrequently, but he was always kind in my experience."

"Mine, as well." He sat down opposite her. "What are you reading now?"

"*Mansfield Park.*"

"Do you like it?"

"Not one bit."

Mr. Hunt laughed. And she was laughing with him. And she realized how she had longed for a moment like this with him, to sit and talk and laugh with ease. She had known him for seven years, ever since he arrived to claim his inheritance. And she had loved him for most of that time, despite always knowing it was impossible. He favored young ladies like Miss Deveraux and Nerissa Merryweather.

Constance couldn't fault him that. Handsome gentlemen of property naturally gravitated toward attractive females. And he was handsome—or at least, Constance thought so. But she had to admit, she didn't at first. It was only after she had been acquainted with him for some time that one day, quite literally, she noticed it, much to her surprise. Oh, yes, his hair was thinning, despite his efforts to hide it with the fashionable Brutus cut. His brown eyes—appearing amber in the firelight—were too small. His face had grown somewhat craggy over the years, with fine lines about his mouth and eyes, from laughing and smiling with frequency. Without those smiles, he tended to appear stern with a saturnine air lingering about him. The dark eyes and locks, the firm, pressed set of his lips fostered that false view, until laughter erupted, his eyes flashing with amusement, his lips parting to reveal strong white teeth—although a tad crooked—as his true spirit escaped.

And in that moment, her heart seemed to lodge in her throat, and she remembered all the reasons she loved him. It wasn't because he was handsome or because of his wealth. It was because....

Wilkins entered carrying another tray, along with a grey, woolen shawl draped over his arm.

"At last," said Mr. Hunt standing up as Wilkins set the tray down on the library table, "I feared Mrs. Ivers had forgotten us." He raised his eyebrows at Constance, a hint of mischief in his eyes. The mature man disappeared, replaced by a boy, eager for cake and biscuits. But he delayed satiating his appetite and presented the shawl to Constance first.

The variety of food sent by Mrs. Ivers—the cook at

Oakwood Hall—impressed Constance: cake, biscuits, and sandwiches, as well as the scones Mr. Hunt had promised. And she realized she had not eaten since breakfast.

"Scones first?" he asked, handing her a plate.

She gave him a crooked grin and replied, "If we must."

And so, there in the warmth before the fire, they indulged themselves in scones laden with thick, sweet cream and strawberry jam tasting like summer days almost forgotten in the cold depths of winter. Perhaps that was why they failed to notice the grey world outside the windows growing ever greyer. Perhaps the steady pinging of sleet against glass lulled the pair as conversation flowed between them, a hum broken only by bouts of laughter. Time slowed. Or perhaps it sped up.

Either way, they didn't notice the hours passing amongst the cups of tea and plates of fruitcake. They didn't notice the darkening shadows amidst their literary recommendations—*Have you read this one?*—and testimonies—*Oh yes, we are well-acquainted with Mr. Scott; surely he must be the author of* Waverly, *don't you think?* From *The Lay of the Last Minstrel* to *MacBeth* to Reverend Ragsdale's recent sermon on covetousness, they traversed subjects and topics seamlessly. And the world went by without the least bit of regard from the two friends ensconced together among books and teacups.

For friends they were. Or so Constance believed. She loved him dearly, but she also knew such things were impossible. At least, they were impossible for old maids who lived with their widowed aunts.

Somewhere in the house, a clock chimed.

"Good Heavens! Is that the hour?" Mr. Hunt took out his

watch to confirm the sound fading in a distant room. "You'll have missed your dinner—please tell Mrs. Martin the fault is purely mine."

A pang of disappointment and regret rose up in Constance. She didn't want to leave yet. She simply wasn't ready to part from Mr. Hunt's company. And then she felt selfish and guilty; he had better things to do than entertaining the village spinster, and Aunt Penelope would be worried by the long delay.

Mr. Hunt rang the bell. Whereas he had been all smiles and laughter a moment before, now he looked stern and unhappy. But when he spied Constance looking at him, he flashed a quick smile, just as Mr. Wilkins entered the dark library.

"Have the carriage readied," said Mr. Hunt to his servant.

Confusion covered Mr. Wilkins' face as he glanced from Mr. Hunt standing before the fire to Constance still seated. "I beg your pardon, sir?"

Realizing something must be amiss—and before Mr. Hunt could respond to the butler—Constance asked, "What is it, Mr. Wilkins? What's wrong?"

With a slight gesture of his hand, Mr. Wilkins took two steps toward the window before stopping. "Have you not seen...?" he asked without hiding his incredulous tone.

The light from the window crept in, dull and grey, unchanged since Constance's arrival at Oakwood Hall—unchanged, in fact, since her rising that morning, although, perhaps even greyer. But now, she realized... the sound... she no longer heard the pelting against the glass but silence. Along with Mr. Hunt, she hurried to the window.

And stared in wonder at the sight before her.

Ice covered the wide world, all the way to the horizon, like sugar glaze on a cake—the ancient trees, the fallow fields, the forest beyond. It all glimmered and drooped, encased in a vast cocoon of ice.

"How beautiful!" she said.

"Yes," replied Mr. Hunt, "but dangerous, deadly even." He briefly turned away from the window to address Mr. Wilkins. "Have Mrs. Reid prepare a room for Miss Blackwell."

"Oh!" Constance gasped, the full impact of his words hitting her. She knew he meant nothing untoward, of course, but she had no desire to put anyone out, not for her sake.

"Very good, sir," replied Mr. Wilkins before Constance could protest.

"And inform Mrs. Ivers to expect another at dinner."

As soon as the butler departed, Mr. Hunt returned his attention to his stunned guest. "I can't very well send you out in this." When Constance opened her mouth to speak—unsure of what she might say—Mr. Hunt shook his head and assured her, "Mrs. Martin will know you found shelter with a neighbor. We'll see how it is tonight, and if it's safe to attend Midnight Service, I'll return you home then. Otherwise, there's plenty of room here. One of the maids can stay with you."

"I'm dreadfully sorry to cause this inconvenience to you and everyone."

Constance thought he blushed as he quietly replied, "I'm not." He moved away from the window and returned to the fire. "We need more tea, I think." He seemed distracted, as if embarrassed, and he avoided looking at her, instead focusing all his attention on the cooling teapot as he picked it up and clutched it to his chest. But then he grinned, that boyish smile that always captivated her, and he almost laughed—at himself, at his own unknown thoughts. She couldn't help but smile with him.

"What is it?" she asked.

He glanced over at her, his smile fading, as if she had caught him unawares in a private moment. Growing solemn, he turned to face her and, after a moment's hesitation, asked, "When did you see me angry?"

Oh, no. Constance felt her heart plummet as she realized he was thinking of Lady Upsbury's party and all those things Constance had said to him. The mere memory of that day mortified her. "Oh, please, not *that*."

"No, no." He set down the teapot abruptly and took a step toward her, his hands raised to placate her. But then he stopped and lowered his hands. After a moment's pause, he shrugged, a pained expression of resignation on his face. "You were right, of course. I am apt to dwell on my misfortunes, despite having little cause. God has given me so many blessings." He glanced about the room, as if taking in all his possessions, and he gave a small, deprecating laugh as he continued speaking. "I daresay I'm something of a joke about the parish. I simply have a terrible propensity for courting ladies who have no desire for my attention." Sorrow crept into his voice. "Or at least, they ultimately choose another over me. Why is that, do you think?"

Constance couldn't be certain his question pertained to his choice of lady or the fact they preferred another. She decided the latter. "'The Heart has reason that Reason does not know?'" It was a pathetic, clichéd attempt at an answer, but sometimes, she found, clichés were alarmingly accurate. "It is an inadequate explanation, but I don't know any other reason females accept one man when others are so much more worthy."

"Perhaps," ventured Mr. Hunt, "your earlier assessment is the most accurate—such females are not worth the having."

It was certainly her assessment of Nerissa Merryweather. And Miss Deveraux, for that matter, but Constance was not about to point that out. Instead, she wished to offer Mr. Hunt words of comfort, words of wisdom, anything to ease his spirit. But she little understood the hearts of females. Or men, for that matter. Except they never chose as she thought they should.

Wilkins returned and—once he discreetly caught Mr. Hunt's attention—announced, "The fire is lit in the blue room for Miss Blackwell."

"Splendid," replied Mr. Hunt, his spirits rising and dispersing his spell of melancholia. He turned to Constance, "If you wish, you may rest a while before dinner. Mrs. Reid can have hot water sent up to you."

Constance welcomed the idea. She particularly wished to take off her half-boots.

Mr. Hunt handed her a book. "Here, take Miss Austen with you. She can lull you to sleep."

෨෬

A few hours after Miss Blackwell retired to the blue room, Matthias opened his eyes to the darkening twilight. Rubbing the sleep from his eyes—he couldn't believe he'd fallen asleep, as if already in his dotage—he rose from his snug chair and stoked the fire. Then he made his way to the window to see if the weather had improved at all. Via the vestiges of fading light, he saw a blanket of snow covered the world, a thin curtain falling steadily.

It was the turning of the blue—the white and grey landscape bathed in blue as evening crept on, changing, not to black of night, but to a stunning shade of cobalt. A trick of the light, Matthias knew, but still exquisite.

Miss Blackwell would not be returning home that night. He had spoken the truth when he told her he didn't mind. Her presence, here at Oakwood Hall, made him happy—a selfish kind of happiness, he supposed, as it was most inconvenient for her and Mrs. Martin.

He felt he owed Miss Blackwell an apology—not for her confinement to the house on Christmas Eve. That could not be helped. But for the fact that he'd never really noticed her. He had taken her for granted—the niece and companion of a neighbor. Kind, thoughtful, ever-present in their gatherings, but nothing more. How shameful he felt never to have considered her further. She was surprisingly pretty—why had he never notice that? True, bits of grey now threaded her hair, but he could condemn no one on that account. She had only the finest lines about her blue eyes, whereas his face was growing rather rugged.

How strange it had been to converse with one his own age. Everyone, of late, had seemed so much older than he, or so much younger. It was awkward, forever the older, but hardly wiser gentleman among the ladies he courted, especially Miss Merryweather. He had never shown her the library. He rather suspected she had never willingly opened a book in her life, with only thoughts of frocks and parties filling her head. It was certainly all he recalled of their conversations. And now he couldn't explain for the life of him why she had so captivated him. If not for Miss Blackwell's thorough dressing down, he never would have viewed the matter in such a light. He never would have realized it wasn't love.

He'd never loved Miss Merryweather. Instead, he'd been a magpie fascinated by a shiny object and wished only to possess it. It had been much the same with Miss Deveraux. Oh, he'd never admit that truth to anyone, and it still felt like love—or, at least, akin to love—but it was never real.

Two narrow escapes, he now realized. How miserable he would have been with either of the ladies. He needed to thank Miss Blackwell for helping him to realize that. Not that he ever would.

He checked his watch and went up to change for dinner.

By the time he came down half an hour later, eager to see Miss Blackwell again, the wind had picked up and now began to roar. The house seemed even colder as a result, and he feared his houseguest might lack appropriate nightwear. But then he assured himself that Mrs. Reid would find something for Miss Blackwell. And the blue room faced away from the prevailing winds.

Standing at the foot of the grand staircase, Matthias glanced up to see Miss Blackwell descending. As expected, she wore the same simple day dress of black, draped in the grey shawl, but she looked rested, refreshed, with a healthy color in her cheeks. She wore her hair swept up, with soft stray ringlets framing her face. Before, when he had rushed out to bring her back, he had feared for her well-being. She had appeared pale and tired, her coat and bonnet bedraggled from the freezing rain, her hair limp. Now, he could not take his eyes from her.

"Good evening, Miss Blackwell," said Matthias, offering

his hand to her.

"Good evening, Mr. Hunt," she replied, accepting his hand.

He tucked her hand into the crook of his arm and motioned toward the breakfast room. "If you don't mind, the breakfast room is much more comfortable than the dining room, especially in this weather."

"Of course," she replied without any apparent hesitation. She didn't appear the least bit offended by the informality of the meal. In fact, she smiled and seemed pleased.

And in that moment, her blue eyes gazing up at Matthias, a thought occurred to him. A wonderful but strangely frightening thought. And before it frightened him too much, he took a leap of faith. He took a step back from her.

"Tell me, Miss Blackwell, might I...," he asked, stumbling over his words like a school boy, "Might I, when this is all over... I mean, when this weather has past and Christmas is over... Might I call upon you?"

Her smile faded. She blanched. And Matthias knew he had presumed too much; she had taken offense at such an impertinent question, particularly as she was a guest in his home and under his protection.

But then, after a hard swallow, she replied, "Yes. Yes, of course."

With nothing further needing to be said—at least, not until after Twelfth Night—Matthias bowed low over her hand. After all, dinner awaited. And the whole of the evening, alone with her, and talk of books.

A pounding at the door, loud and reverberating through the house and hall, made them both jump.

ଛଠଓ

"Good God—oh, pardon me, Miss Blackwell—but what blasted fool is out in this?"

Constance barely had time to recover from the shock of Mr. Hunt's question—*Calm yourself, it's not a proposal, he's merely asking to call upon you*—when the pounding at the door overtook the pounding of her heart. Mr. Hunt's blasphemy and profanity hardly fazed her after that.

By the time they reached the hall, a snow-crusted figure stood before the fire, with both Mrs. Reid and Mr. Wilkins helping her—it was a female, Constance could see, a rather round one at that—divest herself of coat, muffler, gloves, and hat....

"Mrs. Lancaster!" cried out Mr. Hunt by way of greeting.

Constance, for her part, felt slightly ill at the sight of her neighbor, an inward groan bemoaning the loss of her tranquil evening with Mr. Hunt. But as always, she likewise felt ashamed for such thoughts. Mrs. Lancaster was clearly in need of the same shelter and protection Constance had found at Oakwood Hall.

"Mr. Hunt, there you are," replied the lady before the fire, "I'll have you know I walked all the way up that drive of yours, I did."

"Surely you are not out alone in this?"

"Certainly not," pronounced Mrs. Lancaster, clearly astounded by the mere suggestion, "Sam is with me."

"But where is he?" asked Constance coming up beside Mr. Hunt. Mrs. Lancaster seemed to notice her for the first time and turned her steely eyes on her, making Constance wish she'd remained quiet. Or better yet, slunk away to the warmth and solitude of the library.

"I sent him 'round to the servants' entrance."

Oh, poor Sam. The boy had enough troubles employed as Mrs. Lancaster's footman, groomsman, page, and all-round whipping boy without adding this weather to it.

"And Spenser, too," added Mrs. Lancaster.

"Spenser?" asked Mr. Hunt. Constance did not know a Mr. Spenser, either.

"My sister's coachman. Knee-deep in his cups, if you ask me. Drove us into a ditch." Mrs. Lancaster plopped down in the nearest armchair—the best, as well—and stretched out her wet feet toward the fire. "Thankfully, I soon surmised where we were and saw the lights of Oakwood through the darkness."

"But where is Spenser?" asked Mr. Hunt.

"Oh, he unhooked the horses and is taking them 'round to your stables."

Merciful Heaven. Without any ceremony, Constance left Mrs. Lancaster prattling on about the state of Mr. Hunt's drive and his dangerous oaks—*They really ought to be cut down; someone could be killed if a branch fell on them*—and made her way to the servants' wing of the house and specifically the kitchen. She arrived just as Sam dragged himself through the back door, snow and wind billowing in with him.

After apologizing to Mrs. Ives for entering her domain, Constance informed them of poor Mr. Spenser, still out in the storm. A groom and a footman were sent out to find the man and assist him, while Mrs. Ives had hot wine prepared to fortify them all. Dinner would keep.

There were still the sleeping arrangements to consider, when Mr. Wilkins came striding in with Mrs. Lancaster's half-frozen belongings. He appeared worried and distressed, but

Mrs. Lancaster tended to have that affect on people.

"Forgive me, Miss Blackwell." He spoke in a low voice to Constance. "This is a rather inappropriate topic to discuss with a lady, but I had already ordered the staff to double up for the night, for purposes of warmth, you see."

"Yes, of course. An excellent plan given the circumstances, Mr. Wilkins."

"Only now, with the arrival of Mrs. Lancaster, there is an odd number of females in the house."

"Have no concern on my account, Mr. Wilkins," replied Constance, quickly accessing the scope of the problem. "The maid assigned to me can stay with Mrs. Lancaster." *The poor girl.* "I can sleep alone. I only require a good fire and plenty of coal should I have need in the night." Then she smiled at the butler. "But of course, you don't need me to tell you this."

"No, indeed not." He matched her smile.

Constance returned to the hall to find Mrs. Lancaster firmly ensconced before the fire and holding court, with Mr. Hunt as her only subject, in his own house, no less. She droned on about her visit with her sister in Winchcomb, some four miles away, as if the small village were London with all its diversions and entertainments. "I waited as long as I could for this to pass but could wait no longer. There is so much to do—the pudding, the goose, the greenery—with Lord and Lady Upsbury promising to call tomorrow." Her eyes suddenly lit up, "Oh, and your Miss Merryweather was there. Although...," she shook her head and clucked her tongue, "...she's not *your* Miss anything, now, is she? She and Mrs. Merryweather have returned from Town. Buying wedding clothes, no doubt."

In that moment, Constance decided she hated Mrs.

Lancaster. But then, with that familiar pang of disappointment in herself, Constance realized, no, that was not true. And it was unkind and unfair of her to judge Mrs. Lancaster so. Constance hated Mrs. Lancaster's words and actions and how they hurt people, the way they hurt Mr. Hunt right now. Constance vaguely remembered a younger lady, before her marriage to Mr. Lancaster. What a mistake that had been. A liar and braggart who frequented houses of ill-repute—Constance was not supposed to know that—and now spent all his time in Bath because of his gout, but everyone knew that was not the disease from which Mr. Lancaster suffered.

Too much of him had rubbed off on his wife, and now she poked and prodded for her own amusement because it was preferable to the disappointment of her own life. Be that as it may, that did not make her tongue less sharp nor her barbs less pointed, but still, Constance could mourn for the girl she had been, full of hopes and dreams, if not the lady seated before her now. She was, in the very least, worthy of pity, even if Constance couldn't stand to be in the same room with her.

But then Mr. Hunt rose with Constance's appearance again in the hall, and Mrs. Lancaster turned her attention on her. "Oh, poor Mrs. Martin. How very worried she must be about you, Miss Blackwell, believing you lost in this tempest. Most distressing."

On second thought, Constance reconsidered, perhaps she had been too hasty in her assessment of Mrs. Lancaster.

Thankfully, Mr. Wilkins entered, bringing the mulled wine, a horn cup for each of them. Mrs. Lancaster exclaimed with delight, "Thank you, Wilkins," as she took a cup; but upon tasting it, she said, "It's good, but tell Mrs. Ivers not so much orange peel and more cinnamon. That will make it excellent."

Constance took a cautious sip... and found it perfect for her taste, with exactly the right amount of orange peel and cinnamon. Of course, she would never say so in Mrs. Lancaster's presence.

Mr. Wilkins lingered a moment longer and said, "Dinner will be ready momentarily in the breakfast room, sir."

Mr. Hunt turned to Mrs. Lancaster. "You will be joining us, won't you, Mrs. Lancaster?"

"Oh, yes, thank you. I'm quite famished. That walk up your drive."

"Thank you, Wilkins," replied Mr. Hunt.

"But the breakfast room?" gasped Mrs. Lancaster as Mr. Wilkins departed. "Well, I never heard such thing. Dinner in the breakfast room? Surely not."

"It's more... intimate," said Mr. Hunt.

"That may be, but your dining room. It's magnificent. And you have the finest table in the district. If it were up to me—and of course, it isn't—I'd take every meal there, I assure you."

Without a word, Mr. Hunt rose and rang the bell. Wilkins appeared in the space of a few heartbeats, and Mr. Hunt informed him, "We'll dine in the dining room."

"Very good, sir."

"Oh, no. Please, Mr. Hunt," protested Mrs. Lancaster, "There's no need to go to any trouble for my sake. Really, it's not necessary."

"Nonsense," Mr. Hunt assured her, "It's no trouble, Mrs. Lancaster."

But Constance suspected Mrs. Ivers felt differently. The extra mouths to feed were little trouble to a cook of her skill. But having the dinner delayed not once—due to Mrs. Lancaster's arrival—but now twice, all in order to prepare the dining room for the pleasure of the unexpected lady. Having every dish ready on time was pressing at the best of times, but tonight, undoubtedly, everything would be overdone. Worse, in quick order, everything would turn cold in the dining room of Oakwood Hall.

The wait until Mr. Wilkins would return to announce dinner seemed interminable, Mrs. Lancaster recounting—again—the journey from her sister's home and the crash into the ditch. At last, Mr. Wilkins returned and announced dinner. Mr. Hunt escorted Mrs. Lancaster in; it occurred to Constance that, had Spenser the coachman not driven Mrs. Lancaster's sister's carriage into the ditch, Mr. Hunt might now being escorting her in to dinner.

Once in the great dining room, all dark wood paneling with a much too small fire, Constance half-expected Mrs. Lancaster to take Mr. Hunt's seat at the head of the table. Instead, she took the chair to the right of Mr. Hunt's place, while Constance sat opposite.

"Really. This is quite a treat," proclaimed Mrs. Lancaster, running her hand over the polished surface of the table. And when Mr. Wilkins and the footman removed the lids from the various blue china dishes and revealed a fish course, she exclaimed, "Oh, I so love fish, but it always makes my feet hurt." Constance imagined Mrs. Lancaster's poor little feet in their oh so tiny slippers supporting her round figure, and Constance suspected those feet always hurt.

The main course, however, was a roasted chicken with

boiled potatoes and sprouts with chestnuts and onions in cream. And it all smelled so delicious. Constance hadn't realized until that moment that she was hungry, despite the earlier scones and tea and cakes and biscuits.

"Chicken?" With a bemused smile, Mrs. Lancaster shook her head. "I would not have thought of serving poultry two days in a row... except for nuncheon, of course."

"I beg your pardon?" asked Mr. Hunt, rising to carve the chicken.

"Well, surely, you are serving goose tomorrow? Oh, a thigh, please."

Constance tried not to listen to the conversation, instead spooning up potatoes and onions in cream onto her plate—avoiding the sprouts, which Mrs. Lancaster piled onto her own plate—and patiently waiting as Mr. Hunt carved the chicken.

"Gracious, Mr. Hunt," suddenly exclaimed Mrs. Lancaster as her host handed back her plate, "That's far too much chicken for me. My needs are little. Nothing so much as all that." She held the plate out to Constance. "Here, Miss Blackwell, trade plates with me."

And without thought—but with a sinking feeling in her stomach—Constance handed her plate to Mrs. Lancaster and discovered before her a dish with a thigh and a mound of sickly green sprouts, neither of which she wanted. She had so wanted a bit of breast, perhaps with some of that perfectly roasted skin.

Constance pasted on a smile and dished up more potatoes and onions in cream.

"We always have beef on Christmas Eve," continued Mrs. Lancaster between bites, "but, Heavens, Lady Upsbury serves oysters! Can you believe it? Oysters. How they manage to arrive still fresh, I cannot fathom." She shook her head. "Some popish tradition, no doubt."

Constance wished Mrs. Lancaster would be quiet so they could enjoy the meal in peace. Not that Constance was enjoying it at all. At home, she would pick apart the chicken with her fingers—much to Aunt Penelope's horror—but now, in front of Mr. Hunt, she endeavored to cut it, in a genteel way, so as not to call attention to herself.

"Miss Blackwell," asked Mr. Hunt, "what does Mrs. Martin serve on Christmas Eve?" She could sense his effort to expand the conversation.

"Oh," replied Constance, "we were to have beef for dinner today."

"See there? Beef!" Directing her words to their host, Mrs. Lancaster pointed her knife at Constance and crowed with delight, but then she turned her sights on Constance and narrowed her eyes in a manner that Constance suspected was meant to be sympathetic. "How fortunate you are to have such a kind aunt, otherwise you might have nothing but drippings and bread for Christmas Eve." Mrs. Lancaster shoved another bit of chicken in her mouth, but it did not slow the flow of words from her mouth. "Why, Miss Blackwell, you're not eating your sprouts. You can't have any pudding if you don't eat your sprouts."

Constance stared down at her plate, the mound of sprouts still there. She had eaten all the chestnuts from among them but wished nothing more of the dish.

"Pay her no mind, Miss Blackwell," said Mr. Hunt, "You will still have pudding whether or not you eat your sprouts."

"Of course, Miss Blackwell. I am only teasing." Mrs.

Lancaster gave a little laugh. Everyone was silent for a moment, a welcoming sound after all Mrs. Lancaster's chattering. But then she broke the peace and said, quite pensive, "I always worry about the poor of the parish, particularly on days like this, and at this time of year. I worry they do not have enough to eat."

Constance took a bite of the sprouts.

And instantly confirmed why she hated them so much.

She pushed the rest aside. Mr. Hunt's pigs could have them.

ஐα

Sleet no longer pelted the leaded window panes. Now, a fine but audible spray of wind-blasted snow collided against the glass instead. Matthias believed this qualified as a blizzard. The wind howled outside, with wails and moans echoing on drafts through the house. Cold seeped through every crack, every crevice, whorled on eddies, chilling the house and driving the inhabitants closer to the fires.

Unfortunately, Matthias and Miss Blackwell sat before a fire with Mrs. Lancaster.

After dinner, despite Matthias's suggestion they adjourn to the small sitting room—it was warmer and more comfortable than the larger rooms in the house—Mrs. Lancaster insisted that ladies withdrew to the drawing room after dinner. He did not argue with her. And now they sat in the over-large room with an inadequate fire, as Mrs. Lancaster rattled on more incessantly than the wind outside.

And poor Miss Blackwell sat through it all, quiet as usual, a captive to the verbal onslaught, as Matthias supposed he was as well. At length, however, Miss Blackwell rose, far too early in the evening, by his standards, but understandable, and bade them goodnight. As soon as she left, Matthias excused himself for a moment and hurried after her.

"Miss Blackwell, a word, please," he called to her as she reached the stairs. She stopped and turned to him. "I am so terribly sorry."

"Whatever for?"

"Mrs. Lancaster. The sprouts. You do not care for them, do you?" When she did not respond, he continued, "I should have been more forceful. I saw no harm in allowing her to have her way about the dining room. It was an insignificant matter, but for her to browbeat you about the sprouts...."

"She is your guest," she simply said, as if that excused him, "And you are not responsible for her words."

But he felt like a coward, unable, unwilling to go up against the woman, for fear she would turn on him those slings and arrows she used with startling proficiency. And he didn't have the skill to dodge them or even defend Miss Blackwell from such a volley. He suspected that was Mrs. Lancaster's goal—strike first and leave one's opponent defenseless.

Matthias shook his head. "Mrs. Lancaster has a terrible habit of putting people in their place."

"When there is no need," responded Miss Blackwell, "I know perfectly well my place—I am a servant in my aunt's house."

As sad as that statement was, he could not argue with it, because, for all intents and purposes, it described Miss Blackwell's place in this world perfectly. And he wondered if that was the reason he never really paid her any real notice; she blended into the background, like a servant. With a small sigh, Matthias added, "And I am just a farmer."

"There is nothing *just* about you."

If she had physically struck him, Matthias would not have been more astounded. She didn't even give him a chance to recover from the shock. Without so much as the pause of a heartbeat, she said, "Goodnight, Mr. Hunt," and headed up the stairs.

He wanted to follow her up, not for any depraved reasons—*Heavens, the lady was under his protection!*—but just to avoid Mrs. Lancaster. After all, he couldn't very well retire for the night and leave his guest alone in the drawing room, a lady at that. But then it occurred to him, with all her vast knowledge of gossip and rumor, and given her long history in Upsbury, perhaps he should take advantage of the opportunity and put Mrs. Lancaster to good use.

When he returned, Matthias offered Mrs. Lancaster a brandy—not really to be polite but in the hope it might put her to sleep. *Good God*, all the older people he'd ever known fell asleep after dinner, but she didn't exhibit the slightest sign of fatigue. And sadly, she declined the offer of brandy. Well, he was bloody well going to have one.

Slumping down in the armchair before the fire, filled glass in hand, Matthias asked in the most nonchalant manner he could muster, "Why do you suppose Miss Blackwell never married?"

"Oh. Well. *That.*" Mrs. Lancaster appeared to ponder the matter for a moment and then, with a half-shrug, said, "I suppose it was just decided. One of those things." Before Matthias could query further, she continued, "Not intentionally, of course, but every family has one—the child who stays to care for the old ones. And then there's no need for a dowry."

"Miss Blackwell had no dowry?" *Had?* Why not *has*, he wondered. Even he dismissed her chances for marriage without meaning to. He vaguely remembered that her father had died shortly after his arrival in the district, and something about the lands being sold off. So he couldn't understand Miss Blackwell not having something.

"Her grandmother did leave her 50 pounds a year," explained Mrs. Lancaster, "but any money the family had went to buy her brothers' commissions and degrees and whatnot. The land and house went to the eldest brother, but it wasn't entailed, so he sold it off and went to London to live a life of..." She whispered the final word as if it were a secret. "...debauchery."

"Which house? Who purchased it?"

"Mr. Forbes. The land adjoins his property. And the house is let to Dr. Vance."

Matthias couldn't believe he didn't know this. How could he not know something so fundamental to Miss Blackwell, let alone integral the community? It made him feel so very selfish, wrapped up in his own petty troubles and blind to others.

Mrs. Lancaster wasn't finished, raising her forefinger. "Now, she once had an impressive array of furniture—the sort of thing common girls collect for their trousseaus. Not that a gentleman would have found it impressive, but it would have sufficed for a farmer's bride—that, and the 50 pounds."

Matthias, however, had ceased listening some time ago and was oblivious to her words, his thoughts focused instead on Miss Blackwell. And the possibilities he might find with her.

❧❦

A maelstrom of ice and snow roared around the house. But Constance had a good fire, with plenty of extra coal, so she felt snug and secure, with Mr. Hunt's copy of *Mansfield Park* and a blanket. Usually, the book put her to sleep; now, though, she sat wide-awake, curled up in the armchair by the fire, although dressed for bed in the nightrail Mrs. Reid had found for her. She had heard the others retire for the night, Mr. Hunt's solid footsteps passing her door, while Mrs. Lancaster chattered to the poor maid stuck with her all the way to her chamber on the back side of the house.

Constance wondered if it were the same maid who had kindly sought and provided her with a lantern to place in the window—Constance didn't want to burn down the room by placing a candle there. After all, despite the weather, despite the strange company, it was still Christmas Eve, and there was room at this inn.

It occurred to her that it would have been kinder to the maid to have volunteered to share with Mrs. Lancaster rather than to forego a bedmate entirely. Perhaps she would ask Mr. Hunt to give the maid a bonus for service above and beyond the call of duty.

The wind wailed and pushed against the leaded windows, as if a sentient force trying to gain admittance to the room, only to moan more in its failure. Constance listened and felt the house shudder but never yield. And then, in the midst of a moment of stillness...

Something felt wrong. Constance couldn't put her finger on it. It was akin to that absurd feeling that one has failed to bolt the door or forgot to bank the fire or left a candle burning in the dining room. Perhaps that was it; someone failed a final duty and Constance simply sensed it, the way she would at home.

As if she were lady of this great house.

Oh, stop it. He had only asked to call upon her. Nothing would come of it. Nothing ever came of anything. There was always a strange sense of unfulfilled serendipity to her life, as if everything had a purpose and a point, but then someone failed to do their small part. They were supposed to go to the shop at that moment but changed their mind, preferring to have another cup of tea instead. Or they were supposed to invite another person to the party but then realized the gentlemen would outnumber the ladies and that just wouldn't do.

A lifetime of experience told her not to hope. Disappointment always followed. But somehow, when a light shone in the darkness, she always found herself following it. And hoping... this time might be different.

The house creaked and shook with every blast of wind, while outside, the wailing....

Constance threw the blanket off. Something was wrong in the house. This time, she *heard* it. Or at least, thought she heard it. With no dressing gown at her disposal, she tied the great shawl about her, picked up the single burning candle at her bedside, and crept barefoot out into the dark-as-pitch passageway.

She carefully plodded in the direction of the staircase, with only the limited light of the candle to guide her way.

"Miss Blackwell!"

Constance jumped, her heart pounding, and she nearly screamed. Thankfully, she did not, because it was only—

only—Mr. Hunt standing there in his dressing gown.

"Mr. Hunt. You gave me a start."

"I'm frightfully sorry, Miss Blackwell. I thought you could see me by your candle. Mine has gone out, you see." He lifted the smoldering candle helplessly.

"Here," said Constance, holding out her candle, and he quickly relit his own. Now they had two candles by which to see, but it was still abysmally dark, the house creaking about them with every blast of the wind.

"Why are you out of bed?" asked Mr. Hunt.

"I heard something. It didn't sound like the wind," she replied, without elaborating on her vague feelings regarding the matter.

"Then it wasn't my imagination."

"Unless we both imagined it."

"Stay behind me," ordered Mr. Hunt. A modicum of relief washed over Constance; she had feared he would send her back to her room. But then, as he turned to lead the way, she saw he carried a pistol pointed toward the floor. Surely, he didn't expect real danger, not on a night like this. Not on Christmas Eve.

The pair crept down the stairs, slowly, cautiously, aware of every movement. Each tread creaked loudly in the stillness of the house, unnoticed at any other moment, while trees and shrubbery and snow flew against the windows. After reaching the foot of the stairs, Mr. Hunt led the way, first this way, then that, with nothing amiss, until finally, Constance followed him into the vestibule. She realized they were now under the chamber she occupied, and the wailing wind sounded loudest here.

Mr. Hunt set down his candle and lit a lantern. He

handed it to Constance, and then, he pulled back the bolt and opened the door.

The wind extinguished both candles in an instant, with only the lantern light remaining as Mr. Hunt stepped out under the portico. Constance saw nothing; neither, it seemed, did Mr. Hunt. She peered out into the darkness, the swirling snow brightened by the dim lantern light. But then, the light sputtered, and they plunged into darkness.

Yet in that instant, before the light vanished, Constance saw something. A moment later, she realized she could see, faintly. The light cast from the upper room where Constance left the lantern burning allowed sufficient light for her to see. There, huddled against the portico wall, Constance saw a snow-crusted figure cowering against the onslaught.

"Mr. Hunt!" she cried out, "There's someone here!"

He moved so quickly. In a heartbeat, he had the poor wretch safe inside the vestibule, the door slammed and bolted against nature's ferocity, all of them safe. With his pistol forgotten on the vestibule table, he endeavored to light the candles, while Constance struggled to remove the frozen outer garments from the figure and reveal the soul hidden beneath. And then she saw the pale face with those familiar golden curls and terrified blue eyes staring up at her.

"Oh, Constance!"

It was Nerissa Merryweather.

And she clung, sobbing, to Constance like a drowning sailor clinging to a lifeline. "I thought I was going to die!"

"It's all right, Nerissa, you're safe," replied Constance, holding the girl close, "We found you."

"Let's get her to the fire," said Mr. Hunt, and without another word, he lifted Nerissa up and carried her into the great hall. Constance followed as fast as her cold bare feet allowed, her mind racing, wondering, *How did Nerissa Merryweather come to be here, of all places, on such a night as this? Where, for that matter, was her betrothed, Mr. Thompson?* And while she considered the possibility that he might be lost somewhere in this, as well—*They should send men out to search about the house to make certain*—Constance had the most horrible feeling that Mr. Hunt would not be calling on her after Twelfth Night. Or any other time.

"Oh, Matthias," Nerissa cried out as Mr. Hunt set her down in the chair before the banked fire.

Matthias?

"It's all right, Miss Merryweather, you're safe now." Mr. Hunt rang the bell. Fiercely. And then turned to build up the fire. Constance continued her efforts to remove Nerissa's outer garments and began working on her half-boots.

When Mr. Wilkins appeared in his nightcap and dressing gown, Mr. Hunt ordered, "Brandy. And wake Mrs. Ivers."

But as the butler turned to do as ordered, Constance called out, "No," stopping Mr. Wilkins. "Some of the hot wine from earlier. And ask Mrs. Ivers for any hot broth she might have. Then put on the kettle. We need hot water, and a basin, but also for tea. Towels and blankets, too."

Mr. Wilkins glanced at Mr. Hunt, who nodded once, but as the butler turned again to do as ordered, Constance remembered her earlier thoughts. "Wait." Then looking at the half-frozen refugee from the storm, she asked, "Was anyone else with you?"

"No," replied Nerissa, "just me. And Daisy."

"Daisy?"

"Her horse," replied Mr. Hunt with clinched jaw. He

motioned Mr. Wilkins to be on his way and then said, "I will return presently." And he followed the butler toward the kitchen.

"I knew Matthias would be angry," said Nerissa, "He's always so grim, don't you think?"

"He's not grim. Or angry. He's concerned."

By the time Constance managed to get off Nerissa stockings, Mr. Wilkins returned with the hot wine and a can of hot water. A maid with a porcelain basin accompanied him.

"Oh, I fear I've awakened the entire house," said Nerissa, accepting the horn cup of hot wine. But despite the words, there was a noticeable gleam in Nerissa's eyes. Now that the danger had passed, she was clearly enjoying this. Well, thought Constance, as long as she didn't also wake Mrs. Lancaster. Kneeling at Nerissa's feet, Constance poured the hot water in to the basin, the maid assisting her while Mr. Wilkins again disappeared. He returned shortly with the blankets, and soon, they had Nerissa bundled up, her feet soaking in hot water, and a cup of wine to warm her insides. And something about her reminded Constance of a satiated cat curled up before a fire.

Mrs. Ivers arrived with a tankard of broth—and promising tea shortly—and as they all hovered about the invalid, tucking in blankets and plying her with more wine and broth, Nerissa repeated her miserable tale. "I didn't know where I was. I just saw a light and followed it. I thought I was going to die."

And then the irony of the situation struck Constance. Nerissa found her way there because of the light Constance left in the window. No, Constance didn't wish Nerissa harm—

she just wished she'd found her way to another house.

☙❧

Blast that wretched girl!

Mrs. Lancaster was bad enough, but now Miss Merryweather, too? When all he wanted was to be alone with Miss Blackwell. Not in some lurid way, but as in the library that afternoon, when he found himself wishing that it might be like that always. Always Christmas. Always alone. The two of them in the library with books and tea and cakes.

He had selfishly hoped the storm would not abate for a few days and that they might spend Christmas together. Well, now it seemed they would spend Christmas together, but with Mrs. Lancaster and Miss Merryweather in tow. Between those two, Miss Blackwell would not get a word in edgewise.

Worst of all—well, perhaps not *the* worst—Miss Merryweather's presence in his house reminded him of what a fool he'd been.

Ah, Miss Blackwell. The sight of her there in the passageway with a single candle, in nothing but her nightrail and a shawl about her, with her dark hair plaited into a long braid… regardless of his oblivious nature in the past, he certainly noticed her now.

He had thought in that moment that she had awakened him with her slight movement outside his chamber door, but her statement that she, too, heard something, confirmed Matthias's sense that something was wrong and he needed to investigate.

And she had followed him without question, without discussion, and most of all, without fear. She had stood there in the vestibule, potential danger on the other side of door, and held the lantern while he stepped out. She had seen the figure—Miss Merryweather—and only when they were once again safe and the candles lit, did he notice her bare feet. In all that snow and ice, all that wind, across the cold stone floors of the house, Miss Blackwell walked on bare feet! He wanted to sweep her up and put her by the fire, but Miss Merryweather needed his help; all other matters came second.

With Tom the footman and George the groom helping, Matthias found Daisy on the backside of the stables—he supposed she knew where she was and remembered the way. With the horse safely installed and George seeing to her, Matthias returned to the house and ordered hot wine for everyone involved. But he was most anxious to get back to Miss Blackwell. Instead of tending to Miss Merryweather, she should be tending to herself. He feared *she* might become ill. And furthermore, he didn't want anyone else to see her in a state of undress.

Before he even entered the hall, he could hear Miss Merryweather's voice drifting through the house. "It's such a dreary place, don't you think. He should tear it down and build something modern. Or better yet, move to London." She spoke with such glee. Miss Blackwell, on the other hand, in her usual fashion, said little beyond murmurs of acknowledgement.

When Matthias entered the hall, he saw Miss Blackwell sitting in an armchair close to the fire, her bare feet tucked under her, and the shawl wrapped tight about her. Matthias returned to the kitchen, retrieved a blanket from Mrs. Reid, and with Wilkins following in his wake with a tray carrying hot wine, reentered the hall. Without a word, Matthias draped the blanket about Miss Blackwell and handed her a cup of wine before taking one himself.

After a long draw of wine, he turned his stare on the invalid and demanded, "Now then, Miss Merryweather, what were you doing out in all this?"

"Oh, please don't scold me, Matthias. Not now." She pouted so very prettily, as if that would soften his disposition. "I feel dreadful and just want to go to sleep."

"Well, how unfortunate for you, then. For I fear we are out of beds right now. Unless you want to sleep in a cold bed in a room that hasn't been aired since summer."

"You're angry with me." She frowned, her blue eyes gazing up at him in a puppy-dog fashion. In fact, he half-expected her to bat her eyelashes at him. He couldn't believe these manipulative efforts had once worked on him.

"Not angry. Frustrated. I can't believe…."

"Let's wait until morning for this. My head is pounding."

"Be that as it may, there's no bed…."

Miss Blackwell interrupted. "She may sleep with me."

Both Matthias and Miss Merryweather turned as one to look at her. Matthias felt an unfamiliar sense of relief. The matter was settled. Miss Blackwell had settled it, had taken it from him, as it were. And he was grateful. But still, he felt sorry for Miss Blackwell. Now she would be stuck with Miss Merryweather until morning.

ഔ

Christmas morning.

Between the weather and his unexpected houseguests, Matthias slept poorly and woke early. Well, at his usual time, but given the night he'd had, he had expected to sleep late. He didn't. He felt out of sorts. And lazy. So after dressing, he put on his Banyan and retreated to his library before anyone above stairs rose. He found himself wishing Miss Blackwell would somehow make her way there, to eat breakfast together and spend the day hidden from the rest of the world.

He barely noticed the stillness, the storm having subsided shortly before dawn. Now, a foot of snow—in some places, more—blanketed the landscape. No one would be going anywhere for a few days. He couldn't decide if that was a blessing or a curse.

Mrs. Ivers—*bless her*—sent him coffee and sweet buns for breakfast, with Mrs. Martin's marmalade and butter.

"Happy Christmas."

Matthias looked up to see Miss Blackwell standing in the doorway. He immediately rose and, filled with joy at the sight of her, replied, "Happy Christmas."

"May I come in?"

"Of course." He motioned her to the armchair opposite him. "There's coffee, or I can ring for tea, if you prefer."

"Coffee sounds wonderful."

Thankfully, Mrs. Ivers had thought to send extra cups, and as Matthias poured, he asked Miss Blackwell, "Did you sleep well?"

"Yes."

He wanted to laugh. "You're very kind."

"I beg your pardon?" she asked, accepting the proffered cup.

"With all due respect," he said with raised eyebrow, "I find it hard to believe you slept well having to spend the night with Miss Merryweather." He shook his head and imagined the girl taking all the bedclothes and pushing her bedmate to the opposite edge. Perhaps she even snored.

"It was no great hardship," Miss Blackwell assured him.

Dreading the answer, Matthias cautiously ventured, "Is Miss Merryweather awake?"

"She woke long enough to tell me to inform Mr. Wilkins that she would be breakfasting in bed." Then Miss Blackwell motioned toward the window. "I see the snow has stopped."

"Yes," he replied, holding out the basket of still-warm sweet buns to her, "but I fear we shan't have you home in time for Christmas dinner."

"You needn't concern yourself about it," she replied, waving away the basket. "While I know Aunt Penelope will be disappointed by my absence, I am not particularly fond of Christmas."

"Not fond of Christmas?" He failed to hide the shock from his voice. He had always loved the day and much of the season—until this year, with the disappointment of Miss Merryweather. He'd wanted nothing to do with good cheer and making merry. But to state one was *not particularly fond of Christmas* seemed such a sad comment. "Why ever not?"

"There's too much to do, too much to worry over. It's supposed to be a celebration of the birth of Christ, a time of great joy, but it never is."

"You can't mean that?" Truly, he found it so very hard to believe. While he cared little for the revelry and tomfoolery of Twelfth Night, he loved Christmas—the food, the family, the friends, the greenery, attending church at Midnight, singing carols, dancing. It was always such a happy day for him, such happy memories.

"I do mean it." She sat back and sipped her coffee. "Always something amiss. Always some disappointment."

"Such as?"

She sat silent for a long while, until Matthias began to believe she would not reply, but then she bluntly said, "My father getting angry with my mother over the quality of the goose. It wasn't bad. It was just overdone and... not perfect. She had cooked it herself rather than leave it to the cook. My father was furious—although one couldn't tell without knowing him. He was silent. The look he gave her—I'll never forget it. It made me sick. No one spoke all through the dinner. Nothing was ever said of it. But to this day, I dread sitting down to Christmas dinner, and I cannot eat goose without experiencing those feelings again, as if I were in that moment again."

He reached out and took hold of her hand. "Surely, there were happy times, too?"

"Oh, undoubtedly. But bad things always dominate one's memories."

He gave her hand a gentle squeeze in an effort to reassure her. He wanted to give her a truly happy Christmas. And as they were stuck with each other for the holy day—much to his delight—he decided he'd start now.

"Well, you'll be happy to know, then, that Mrs. Ivers is preparing roast beef for our Christmas dinner." He grinned, and Miss Blackwell almost laughed.

"There you are!"

Matthias jumped with a start at the sound of Miss Merryweather's voice, dropped Miss Blackwell's hand, and stood up. "Miss Merryweather. Happy Christmas." But he did not feel the sentiment. He didn't want her here, in his library, with Miss Blackwell sitting quietly with him. It felt like an intrusion.

"I thought I'd never find you," said Miss Merryweather,

glancing about the room, "My, you own a lot of books. Have you read all of these?"

Matthias ignored her question and said instead, "I expected you to sleep late this morning."

"I was hungry, and no one would bring me breakfast." She plopped down in his vacated armchair and seized a sweet roll. "Oh, Constance," she said as if only just seeing her—how the inappropriate use of Miss Blackwell's Christian name grated on Matthias—"Mrs. Lancaster needs your help with something. I'm not sure what."

Miss Blackwell gave a resigned little sigh and said, "Of course." She rose and left quickly, leaving Matthias alone—and quite annoyed—with Miss Merryweather. Whereas once the mere thought of the lady seated before the fire left him anxious and excited and overjoyed all at once, now, her presence made him painfully aware of how little he cared for her.

"There isn't a single sprig of mistletoe in this entire house," announced Miss Merryweather, abruptly, "I should know; I looked."

"We will have to rectify that, then," he replied without any real conviction or concern for the matter.

"How marvelous." She smiled up at him. "Because I would very much like to kiss you."

Disgusted by the idea, Matthias deliberately moved further away from her. "I suspect your betrothed would object. You do remember him, don't you? Mr. Thompson?"

"Yes, I remember him." She pressed her lips together, lifted her chin, and looked away, as if snubbing the very thought of her betrothed. Then she gave a little smirk. "But it's no concern of his now. I've cried off."

"Cried off?"

"Yes. I don't want to be his wife." She turned slightly toward him and leaned forward, like a cat about to pounce. "I want to be your wife."

Now seeing why Miss Merryweather made her way to Oakwood, Matthias crossed his arms over his chest. "That, I am afraid, is not going to happen."

"Of course it is." She practically purred. "You see, well, as they say in French, *je suis enceinte*. You are going to be a father."

A loud, horrified gasp issued from the open doorway. Matthias turn to see Mrs. Lancaster standing there. "Well! I never!"

Behind her stood a wide-eyed Miss Blackwell.

༶

Constance had lied to Mr. Hunt that Christmas morning. Well, perhaps not *lied*, per se, so much as neglected to inform him of the whole truth, which amounted to much the same thing.

She had awakened to find Nerissa sitting on the window ledge, her feet tucked under her, while golden curls cascaded down to her waist. She looked like a fairy tale princess within a blue bower, silhouetted against the snowy landscape outside. Upon hearing Constance stirring, Nerissa had turned to her and said, "If you knocked down that line of trees, it would improve the view significantly."

Horrified by the mere thought of such a thing, Constance rose and hurried to the window to see which trees Nerissa referred to. And was further shocked to see the girl meant the line of ancient oaks shading the lane up to the house.

"And a lake could be added there," continued Nerissa,

pointing to a nearby field where Mr. Hunt grew corn in summer. "If you pulled down those cottages, the lake could be expanded even further and a nice folly added on that rise there."

Nerissa appeared oblivious to the fact that those stone cottages with columns of grey smoke gently rising from their chimneys housed Mr. Hunt's tenants, each well-known to Constance by name and character.

"People live in those cottages," said Constance, none too delicately.

"They can live somewhere else."

"And what do you propose Mr. Hunt do to make up for the loss of those rents?"

"Oh, that." Nerissa gave a little smirk and shrugged. "I'm sure he would make up for it somehow."

As Constance dressed, Nerissa climbed back into bed. "Please inform Wilkins that I will breakfast in bed," she said, pulling the covers up to her chin.

"You do realize there is a bell pull just there, don't you?" And without another word, Constance left, appalled by Nerissa's covetous plans for Mr. Hunt's lands. However, the moment she arrived in the library, the sight of Mr. Hunt drove all such animosity from her mind. Nerissa was simply being Nerissa, as usual, nothing more.

But now, Constance stood behind Mrs. Lancaster in the open doorway to the library and heard Nerissa's damning words.

Je suis enceinte.

Constance felt sick, something inside her screaming, her throat tightening. Tears threatened to fill her eyes, and she wanted to slink away, unseen, unheard, but Mrs. Lancaster opened her mouth and added her two cents to the scene before them. Mr. Hunt turned—his face a reflection of her own internal dismay—and his eyes met hers. She thought she saw pain in those brown eyes—or perhaps she imagined it. Either way, she couldn't stay, and as Mrs. Lancaster charged into the room, Constance fled.

Mrs. Lancaster's voice echoed in the wake of Constance's retreat. "Upon my word, Mr. Hunt, I never thought... You, of all people..."

"Now see here, Mrs. Lancaster...," followed Mr. Hunt's voice, but Constance did not stop, the words fading further away with each step, until they disappeared altogether. She found herself standing in the midst of the great hall, the light blinding from the sunlight off pristine snow. It did nothing to lessen the chill, and she pulled the grey shawl tighter about her body.

Constance hurried on, past the fire, into the dining room, and on to the servants' wing of the house. She didn't know why; she just wanted to get away. She couldn't bear to witness Mr. Hunt finally winning the woman he loved.

The light in the window—the light that guided Nerissa to Oakwood, the light Constance had put in the window. She had lead Nerissa through the storm. Serendipity. Constance had done her part to bring Nerissa and Mr. Hunt together. She had served her purpose. Now, she just wanted to go home.

"Miss Blackwell, is something amiss?" asked Mr. Wilkins.

Constance stood there, dumbstruck, and realized she was in the servants' hall. They were in the midst of their breakfast. The men quickly rose, and everyone stared at her, Mrs. Reid with a look of concern on her face. Constance glanced about, wondering *What to do?* when she noticed the windows... and the snow-covered yard beyond... and the stables with the groomsmen shoveling snow.

"I should like to go home," replied Constance, realizing there was no reason she could not. Only the deep snow prevented her from doing so, and she knew how to get around that.

"Oh, no, Miss Blackwell, that's not possible. Not in this."

Why not? If that silly Nerissa could make it here in the midst of a blizzard, there was no reason she could not make it home. It was only a mile, and Constance did know how to ride—although, it had been many a year since she last had. Having half a dozen brothers did have some advantages.

"Have one of the Shires saddled," said Constance, deciding one of the farm's large work horses would have little difficulty getting through a foot of snow. Romantic dashing would not be involved. In fact, on further consideration, it might be clumsy and awkward for her, but a Shire horse would get her home. "A gentleman's saddle, if you would, Mr. Wilkins."

"I beg your pardon?" asked the flabbergasted butler.

"It'll be much safer," she calmly replied to him and then addressed Mrs. Reid, "I'll need a pair of trousers."

"Trousers?!" That was one of the maids.

"I'll wear them under my skirts." After all, by riding astride, her skirts would ride up, leaving her legs visible *and* exposed to the cold, and Constance didn't want that. "Preferably wool trousers, Mrs. Reid."

When Mrs. Reid shook her head, Constance expected more reasons against her purpose, but instead, the housekeeper said, "Oh, Mr. Hunt wouldn't like you going home on your own."

"I suspect Mr. Hunt will hardly notice my absence. More important matters concern him now. Undoubtedly, you'll hear all about it soon enough." When no one moved to do as she asked, she added, "Please. There is nothing keeping me here." Then she remembered the day. "And I would like to be with my aunt for Christmas."

With that, everyone set about to do as she wished. Then, when one of the maids hurried past her, Constance asked, "Kitty, I need sewing scissors. Could you find me a small pair?"

"Of course, miss," the maid replied and soon presented Constance with a delicate silver pair, perfect for her requirements. Then, with Mrs. Reid's permission, she settled herself in the housekeeper's sitting room and went to work tearing the seam out of her skirt. She could repair it later, but this way, the skirt wouldn't hinder her from riding astride. As for her coat, she would only button the upper most buttons and leave the skirt open.

By the time Mrs. Reid returned with several pairs of trousers for her to try, Constance had finished with the seam, all the way to the top of her thigh. Rather shocking, she thought, seeing her white stocking topped by bare flesh.

After several tries and the realization that she had to remove her half-boots first, Constance managed to get a pair of the trousers on under her skirts. She didn't like the things, found them confining and irritating against her skin, even worse than scratchy wool stockings.

"What do you think?" asked Constance, turning about with a decided frown.

The housekeeper looked her up and down. "It almost

looks respectable." But then she blanched. "Oh. Beggin' your pardon, Miss Blackwell."

"Nothing to forgive, Mrs. Reid. Please thank whomever contributed them. I promise to return them as soon as possible."

"They're Mr. Hunt's trousers."

Oh! Constance felt sure she blushed at the revelation. The very idea.... "Well, then. Perhaps it's best we keep this our secret."

"Yes, miss."

When Constance exited the housekeeper's sitting room, she discovered Mr. Wilkins waiting in the passageway, her coat in his hands. Kitty stood beside him with Constance's gloves and bonnet.

"Are you certain, Miss Blackwell, you want to do this?" asked the butler.

"I'm afraid it's for the best, Mr. Wilkins," she replied, putting on her coat and accepting the gloves and bonnet.

"Then the horse is ready for you."

Everyone followed her out into the snow-covered yard where George the groomsman waited with the massive Shire horse. Thankfully, he'd brought a box so that she could at least manage to reach the stirrups—with some help. *Gracious*, Constance couldn't even see over the horse, and once upon the box, George still had to hold out his hands for her foot so that he might fling her upward into the saddle. It had been much easier to climb up on these beasts when she was a child playing with her brothers, perhaps because they had no qualms about pushing her posterior. But in the end, Constance managed to settle onto the saddle, astride, with her coat and skirts awkwardly spread about her.

She wished everyone a happy Christmas and headed off across the frozen fields toward home, the Shire plodding through the deep snow with all the grace and ease of a four-year-old child through a mud puddle. It was only a mile, she reminded herself, the cold nipping her. But the sun shined, bright and glorious. *How very appropriate*, she realized with a growing warmth inside her, *For He has come!*

ଞଠଓ

The moment Matthias's eyes met Miss Blackwell's in the doorway, he felt sick. And then she turned and fled the abysmal scene of deceit. He took a few steps in a futile effort to go after her, but then Mrs. Lancaster's booming voice stopped him.

"Upon my word, Mr. Hunt, I never thought... You, of all people..."

Good Lord, the woman was mad if she thought.... "Now see here, Mrs. Lancaster...."

"Yes, Mrs. Lancaster," interrupted Miss Merryweather, "my relationship with Matthias is hardly any concern of yours."

Matthias spun on Miss Merryweather and saw the smug look on her face. He knew exactly what she was doing. "*We* do not have a relationship."

"Well, you certainly have some kind of relationship," countered Mrs. Lancaster, "or Nerissa wouldn't find herself in such a sad state."

"Yes, Matthias, how can you say such a thing to the mother of your unborn child?" She produced a handkerchief and dabbed at the corner of her eye—hardly a performance worthy of even an amateur theatrical.

He didn't have time for this. His immediately concern

was for Miss Blackwell. Surely, she didn't believe this lie? But any chance he had of going after her was further thwarted by Mrs. Lancaster.

"There, now, Nerissa," Mrs. Lancaster soothed the little performer and put her arm about her shoulder, before glaring again at Matthias. "What do you intend to do about this?"

"I don't intend to do anything, as it is no doing of mine."

Miss Merryweather let out a shriek.

"Christ Almighty!' continued Matthias, "the girl...."

"Mr. Hunt!" bristled Mrs. Lancaster, "such language. And on Christmas Day, too!"

"...is lying. I've never touched her. Not even a brotherly kiss."

Miss Merryweather burst into tears, and this time, Matthias believed they were real. But it didn't soften him one bit. She was lying, and not some little white lie about the fit of a dress, but bearing false witness, literally against her neighbor and potentially doing irreparable harm. He would not stand for it.

"Mr. Hunt!" cried Mrs. Lancaster pulling the sobbing Miss Merryweather into her ample arms, "Have you no shame?"

"With all due respect, Mrs. Lancaster, would you please shut up!"

A loud gasp emanated from Mrs. Lancaster, and Miss Merryweather abruptly ceased crying to stare in shock at Matthias.

"I don't know who the father of Miss Merryweather's child might be," continued Matthias, "but it is most certainly not me. Now, I have more important matters to deal with, so if you would please get out of my library." And he pointed toward the door.

"Mr. Hunt, this is really most...."

"Yes, yes. I know," he said, herding the two ladies out, "Hell and damnation and the recrimination of my neighbors. Oh, my, what is the world coming to? Happy Christmas." And he slammed the door closed behind them. *Now*, what had he been doing before he was so rudely interrupted? *Ah, yes.* Miss Blackwell.

Oh, dear.

She must think the worst of him. After all he'd said to her—that he wished to call upon her after Christmas—and given how she felt about him, Miss Blackwell must surely feel betrayed in some way. He must find her and explain. But first… he poured a brandy for himself—a bit of Dutch courage.

That done, he hurried off in search of her, passed the ladies in the breakfast room, and continued up the stairs in the certainty Miss Blackwell had retreated to her room.

Upon reaching the door to the blue room, Matthias took a deep breath and attempted to figure out exactly what he would say to her. The truth, of course, but he had no idea how best to go about it. That did not stop him from tapping on the door.

"Miss Blackwell, please," said Matthias in the softest tone he could muster, "Please, allow me to explain. It's not what you think. Miss Blackwell? If you would, open the door. We must speak. Miss Blackwell?" He stopped and listened. After a moment of nothing but silence, he pressed his ear to the door. He expected the sounds of movement or sobbing or something, but still, he heard nothing. He tapped on the door again and then tried the handle. And as he slowly opened the door a mere crack, he said, "Miss Blackwell, I'm coming in."

He expected words of refusal, demands that he get out, but still, nothing. And then, he stood before the empty room—he felt very foolish having been speaking to nobody but himself—and saw she wasn't there.

"Blast!"

He ran from the room with a shout, "Wilkins!" and rushed down the stairs. And as he passed the windows there, he heard voices outside, the shouting of *Happy Christmas* from a voice he longed to hear more. With a pause to gaze out the window, he saw Miss Blackwell *on a Shire horse* in the yard! And she was riding away! Riding astride! Was she that determined to get away from him?

"No! No! No!" he shouted at no one in particular. Why didn't someone stop her?

He continued his rush down the stairs, all the while shouting, "Wilkins! Wilkins! Stop her! Someone stop Miss Blackwell!"

But by the time he reached the yard, it was too late.

Miss Blackwell was gone.

ಸಂಖ

Constance left the great Shire horse with the blacksmith and trudged on foot across the village green to the cottage she shared with Aunt Penelope. Stomping her half-boots and brushing the snow off her skirt and trousers, Constance entered and looked up to see her aunt descending the stairs.

"Oh, there you are," said Aunt Penelope, her voice filled with surprise, "I wondered what had become of you. I've been looking for you since yesterday afternoon."

"I was left stuck at Oakwood Hall," replied Constance,

tugging off her coat. "Wasn't it a frightful storm?"

"Yes, indeed. I hope they took good care of you." Aunt Penelope shook her head upon reaching her. "Poor Mr. Hunt. He'll probably never really recover. One doesn't, you know."

"Yes," said Constance, knowing full-well the truth of that.

"Constance?" Aunt Penelope scrunched up her nose and gave her a queer look. "You're wearing trousers."

Constance glanced down at her skirt, one trousered leg exposed. "Well. Look at that. Can't imagine how that happened."

"You shouldn't tease like that. Someone might take you seriously."

"I'll tell you all about it after I've changed into some dry clothes…"

"Some *proper* clothes."

"…and had a cup of tea. And then…." But before she said another word, Constance thought she heard something—the happy sound of bells. "Do you hear that, Aunt Penelope?"

"Hear what?"

"Sleigh bells."

"Oh, someone probably out for a ride. Such a wonderful thing, to have a white Christmas. Although, I missed going to church."

But Constance had seen almost no one as she rode home, everyone snug and warm in their homes. And then she jumped as someone knocked on the door—pounded, in fact.

Constance unlatched the door and opened it to see Mr. Hunt standing there.

"Miss Blackwell," he said, removing his beaver hat. And then he held out the basket Constance had carried the stoneware jars of marmalade in just the day before. "You left your basket."

"Thank you, Mr. Hunt," she replied, accepting the basket. "Would you care to come in?"

"Thank you, yes."

And as he stepped inside, Constance saw the conveyance that had brought him all the way from Oakwood Hall; a sleigh decorated in Christmas holly stood on the opposite side of their gate, another Shire horse hitched to it and arrayed in tiny bells.

"You have a sleigh, I see."

"Yes. Hasn't been used in years. Wasn't sure it would still work." As Constance closed the door, he caught sight of her aunt. "Oh, Happy Christmas, Mrs. Martin."

"Happy Christmas, Mr. Hunt. Won't you come in to the sitting room? We were just about to have tea."

"Oh, no, thank you. I won't take much of your time. Just a moment if you please." He turned to face Constance and said, "Miss Blackwe...," before pausing with his eyes lowered to her skirts. He furrowed his brow in confusion. "You're wearing trousers."

"So I've been told."

"Are those... are those... mine?"

"They are."

"I see." He seemed unconcerned with the fact that she stood there in his trousers. Instead, after a brief hesitation, he took a deep breath and looked her directly in the eye. "It's not true. I'm not the father of her child."

"Yes, I know."

That seemed to baffle him even more than the trousers, and he leaned in closer to her. "You know?"

"You would never do such a thing," explained Constance

in the most straightforward manner she could muster, but she could feel herself trembling ever so slightly. "You're an honorable man. No matter how silly of a girl Nerissa might be, no matter what liberties she might allow, you would never take advantage of her, or anyone else, for that matter."

He stood up straighter, his eyes widening in surprise. "Then why did you leave?"

"It is because you are an honorable man, I know you will always endeavor to do the right thing... and Nerissa's announcement, false as it may be, provides you with the chance to... to have what you have wanted all along... to have the woman you love." Constance swallowed hard and feared she might turn into a watering can. "And I couldn't be party to that. I couldn't be witness to that. I'm sorry to be so selfish, but I had no wish to witness that."

"Miss Blackwell, you don't understand." He smiled, took her hand, and shook his head all in one motion. "I don't love Miss Merryweather." Constance felt her stomach turn over, a small gasp almost escaping from her but leaving her mouth open. "I came here to tell you that," continued Mr. Hunt, "And to invite you..." He turned to Aunt Penelope. "...and Mrs. Martin, to Christmas dinner at Oakwood Hall."

Constance demurred, uncertain, not wanting to see either Nerissa or Mrs. Lancaster, but Aunt Penelope piped up. "Oh, but I managed to get a goose. We were supposed to dine with Mr. and Mrs. Forbes today, but owing to the snow, well, I got a goose for us."

"That settles it," said Mr. Hunt, "You both *must* dine with me today. After all, Miss Blackwell doesn't care for goose."

"Really?" asked Aunt Penelope, "I had no idea."

"Nor does she care for sprouts."

"Now that I knew. Perfectly understandable."

"I can't promise sprouts won't be on the table, but I happen to know Mrs. Ivers is preparing beef for our dinner."

"Beef?" That raised Mrs. Martin's eyebrows, her delight at the prospect apparent. "Well, then. I suppose we could have the goose tomorrow."

"Or Cook and Patsy and Bess can have it," suggested Constance. "They can invite Mrs. Howes and Sally and maybe Mrs. Landry. Their own lovely Christmas feast." At these words, Aunt Penelope hesitated, no doubt concerned about the expense of such a plan.

"Splendid!" Mr. Hunt clasped his hands together and smiled before Aunt Penelope could change her mind. "Pack a few things and expect to stay the night."

"The night?"

"Given the inconveniences you suffered last night, Miss Blackwell, it's best to be prepared. Besides, with my plans for the evening, well, it may be very late and simply easier for you and Mrs. Martin to stay at Oakwood." He turned to Mrs. Martin. "Be sure to bring your dancing slippers."

"Oh!" exclaimed Aunt Penelope, and hurried off with a twitter.

"What is this?" asked Constance, wondering what Mr. Hunt was up to, "What are you planning?"

"If I have any say in the matter, I plan a happy Christmas. As simple as that." He gave her a warm smile, the lines in his face deepening. "Now, hurry along. We mustn't keep Wilkins and Mrs. Reid waiting."

"And what about Mrs. Lancaster and Nerissa?" Constance could hardly imagine a happy Christmas with those two ensconced at Oakwood.

He reached over and gently enveloped her hand within his grasp. "I fear we must endure Mrs. Lancaster. But Miss Merryweather? We'll take that one as it comes."

It took half an hour for Constance to quickly wash, change, and pack a small bag. Even then, she found Aunt Penelope waiting for her with Mr. Hunt. A moment more, and they were bundled in coats and mufflers and bonnets and even a veil for Aunt Penelope.

Then, with a "Are you ready for your sleigh ride, Mrs. Martin?" from Mr. Hunt, they were off, only pausing briefly at the blacksmith's to retrieve the borrowed Shire and tying her behind the sleigh.

It was not a fast drive over the snow and down the lanes. It was slow, steady glide, while bells jingled and holly fluttered and cold kissed their cheeks. Mr. Hunt drove from the seat in front, and the ladies snuggled behind under mounds of lap blankets. And they all laughed—at the Shire attempting to prance, at the far-flung snow flying up with every stomp of her feet, at Mr. Hunt's humorous promises to have them to Oakwood by Twelfth Night… and then by Lady's Day. Constance felt like a giggling schoolgirl, as, too, she suspected, did Aunt Penelope.

Until they turned and Oakwood Hall came into view at last. Then the memory of Nerissa's presence there came foremost to mind, and all the joy Constance felt evaporated. She didn't want to see the girl who had caused her so much pain with a lie, even though that lie was not directed at her.

But for Aunt Penelope's sake—and Mr. Hunt's—Constance pasted on a smile and prepared to face Nerissa again.

Mr. Wilkins stood waiting for them inside the vestibule

and welcomed them into the hall, as Tom the footman took their bags. To Constance's amazement, she found the hall transformed, no longer a dreary font for medieval musings. Still chilled as before, now it glowed in the array of green boughs of holly and pine, all trimmed with red ribbons. Servants busied themselves assembling a table at the far end of the hall, while in the fireplace burned...

"No Yule log, I'm afraid," said Mr. Hunt, "Next year, maybe."

"Next year," whispered Constance, almost afraid to hope. And she hadn't seen Nerissa yet, the one person who could still ruin it all, despite Mr. Hunt's assurance to the contrary.

"A room has been prepared for you, Mrs. Martin," said Mr. Wilkins.

Mr. Hunt turned to Constance. "You may share, if you prefer, Miss Blackwell." He leaned in closer to her and quietly added, "Or Miss Merryweather can share with Mrs. Lancaster." He gave her a mischievous grin, and for a moment, Constance could see the boy hidden beneath the middle-aged man.

"We are happy to share, thank you," replied Constance, "Aunt Penelope, perhaps you would like to go up and settle in?"

"And put on your dancing slippers," added Mr. Hunt.

With a shy glance backward, Constance and her aunt headed toward the great staircase, Mr. Wilkins leading the way, and they made their way upstairs. All the while, she dreaded the possible sighting of Nerissa. Or Mrs. Lancaster, for that matter. Given the quiet stillness of the family wing of the house, Constance wondered where they might be. Mrs. Lancaster's voice usually announced her presence long before she arrived, but now, only silence filled the house, save for the faint babble of servants preparing the hall for Christmas.

Constance followed Aunt Penelope into the room and stopped with a gasp.

"Oh, my," said Aunt Penelope, confirming for Constance that she wasn't imagining things. "It's your furniture."

My furniture.

Sold several years ago by her father. To whom, she never knew. Yet, here it was before her, or at least, some of it: the two green brocade armchairs Constance purchased when Lady Upsbury changed the color of her drawing room; the clothespress Mrs. Walker gave her after Mr. Walker died; the Pembroke table bound for Mr. Forbes's fire due to a broken leg but saved by Constance and repaired by the late Mr. Martin's groom for only half a shilling; and most of all, her grandmother's tester bed. Constance thought it long-lost, but there it was, grand as always. She remembered how her parents hated the black wood, probably two-hundred years old, but it went so well in this room, with its Elizabethan wainscoting and windows. It didn't quite match the more modern clothespress, though, and she wondered if the matching coffer—or any of the other pieces—might be somewhere in the house.

It didn't matter, of course. They were here, with Mr. Hunt.

"Is everything all right, Miss Blackwell?" asked Mr. Wilkins.

"Yes. Yes. Everything is fine," she assured him with a smile, but she felt her throat tighten, her eyes stinging as tears threatened to form. Despite her words, she hurried from the room and went in search of Mr. Hunt—how had her furniture come to be at Oakwood?

Constance found him hovering about at the foot of the stairs. He appeared restless, moving this way, then that, checking on the preparations then turning away. But when he glanced up the stairs and saw her there, he brightened, only to frown and furrow his brow.

"What's wrong? Does the room not meet with your approval?" he asked, coming toward her as she descended the final step.

"My furniture...," she managed to say.

"I beg your pardon?"

They stood quite close, and Constance looked up into his eyes. "The furniture... in the room... where did you get it?"

"I purchased it when I arrived," he explained, "My uncle, in sending books here, took some of the better pieces of furniture in exchange. As a result, some rooms were empty. Is it not to your liking?"

"Yes. It is. Very much so." She held back a sob and nearly choked on her words. "It's my furniture. Or at least, it once was. My father sold it all, a little while before his death. Do you have any other pieces?"

"Oh, yes, I purchased quite a bit for the house. Or, I should say, Wilkins purchased it at my behest. There is a commode with a basin set in my bedchamber—I think those came with that lot. The table in the breakfast room..." *The breakfast room?* How did she miss that? But then she remembered it was covered with a cloth. "...It didn't have any chairs; I thought that very strange."

"No, it didn't. That's how I got it so cheap." When Mrs. Gilbert died, Constance recalled. She stifled another threatening sob and remembered her father scolding her for lamenting the loss of mere possessions, which, he had added, she would never have need of. They were just things, of little value at that. She had felt foolish, and even now, she felt foolish, for being so happy at having found them again. But in truth, the pieces of furniture weren't merely *things*. Each piece was the memory of a neighbor, still living or now dead, and a reminder of their time on earth. It was a tribute to the craftsmen, now forgotten, who'd built it, of their skill and the work they had endured to learn that trade. And it was a testament to Constance, as well, of her vigilance, foresight, and economic acumen at obtaining treasures on such scant funds. Most of all, they were a physical manifestation of her hope for the future.

Mr. Hunt continued, "There's a settee—it eventually ended up in the upstairs sitting room—and a coffer in one of the other bedchambers, I think. There are a number of odd chairs in the attic."

"Yes. I had a habit of finding odd chairs."

Without any warning—and without meaning to—Constance burst into tears.

༄༅༄

The sight of Miss Blackwell crying nearly broke Matthias's heart. He couldn't possibly imagine what had caused it—certainly not a discussion regarding the household furniture. Acting purely on instinct—yes, that must have been it—he pulled her into his arms and held her close. As she sobbed against his waistcoat, he slipped a handkerchief into her hand.

"It's all right, Miss Blackwell," he attempted to assure her, "Whatever it is, I am sure we can find a solution. It can't possibly be as bad as all that."

Between sobs, she managed to say, "How mortifying."

"What is?"

"To be crying over furniture."

Furniture? Well, yes, they had been discussing furniture, but he couldn't believe that was the cause of her distress. But then he vaguely recalled Mrs. Lancaster's words only the night before, of Miss Blackwell's *impressive array of furniture* and 50 pounds from her grandmother, the sort of thing that would suffice for a farmer's bride.

Matthias smiled and suppressed a laugh. Instead, he pulled her closer and rested his cheek against her head.

He was a farmer.

"It's all right," Matthias repeated and then hit upon an idea. "We'll have the chairs brought down, and we can use them in the hall tonight. They're perfect for the occasion."

But as he glanced over the top of Miss Blackwell's head, he saw Miss Merryweather standing there.

"Oh, Constance," she said the moment Matthias spotted her, "whatever is the matter? Did the Christmas pudding fall?"

He lowered his arms so that he no longer touched Miss Blackwell, but he did not move away from her. "That's *Miss Blackwell* to you." He ground out the words without intending to.

Miss Merryweather tilted her head and fixed a smile on her lips. "I'm sorry, Matthias, it's just that I've known Cons…"

"*Mr.* Hunt," he informed her.

Her smile faded. "I beg your pardon?"

Matthias heard someone on the stairs, and with a quick glance, discovered it was Mrs. Martin standing very still. At the same time, he became aware of the silence in the hall and that several servants now lingered in the doorway. Beyond Miss Merryweather, he saw Mrs. Lancaster emerge from the drawing room.

"You are too familiar," he responded to the girl. "It is neither appropriate nor desirable."

He could see the growing anger in Miss Merryweather's eyes as she looked from him to Miss Blackwell, and then she raised her brows with a dawning realization. "Is she the reason you...? How can you choose her over me?"

"Because I love her."

All eyes turned on him, but Matthias sought only Miss Blackwell's eyes, raised to him in amazement.

"How can you love *her*?" continued Miss Merryweather, "She's old."

Matthias, however, no longer cared what she had to say. His entire focus was on Miss Blackwell. "I do love you." A single tear trailed down her cheek, and Matthias took her hands in his. "I have loved you since the moment of your most thorough dressing down. But the things I love about you I've always noticed. How you treat everyone with respect and kindness. You don't scold or fuss. You're not full of righteous indignation. You take people as they come and accept them for who they are, not who you want them to be or who you think they should be. You are thoughtful and kind and hold others in your heart the way others hold selfish desires. You walk into the room and I am always happy to see you. And what's more, I am a better man with you. That is just the start of why I love you."

He exhaled, realizing he spoke rapidly and wondering where all those words came from and questioning whether he had drawn breath even once.

"Well!" exclaimed Mrs. Lancaster—*of course, it would be her*. "That was certainly a declaration."

Miss Blackwell seemed to become aware of their audience and quickly glanced around. She withdrew her hands from his and dabbed her eyes with his handkerchief, before asking, "Mr. Wilkins, would it possible to have some tea? My aunt could probably use some after..." She hesitated before continuing. "...after the drive here."

"Of course, Miss Blackwell," responded Wilkins, "Where would you like it served?"

Miss Blackwell looked at Matthias and asked, "The small sitting room?"

He nodded, with a growing fear that perhaps he had been wrong; perhaps, yet again, he had chosen the wrong woman. He leaned in closer to her and whispered, "Have I offended you?"

"Oh, no. No, not at all," she replied, adamantly. She gave him a small smile and continued in a low voice, "I'm simply overwhelmed, that's all, and need to sit down."

"Of course," replied Matthias, then searched about for Wilkins and quickly ordered, "Tea. Sitting room."

And with a natural ease, he slipped his hand to the small of her back and guided her toward the sitting room. Only as they reached the room did he notice Miss Merryweather was nowhere to be seen, much to his relief.

Of course, when Wilkins brought the tea, Matthias quietly inquired about her whereabouts—he still had some degree of responsibility for her while she was under his roof—and Wilkins kindly reported she had retired to the blue room with a migraine.

That settled, he put the lady in question out of his mind, and determined to enjoy the company of Miss Blackwell, Mrs. Martin, and even Mrs. Lancaster, who did most of the talking. For once, he was thankful; he just wanted to sit with Miss Blackwell. Of course, in truth, he wanted to sit quietly with her before the fire in the library, as they had only the day before. But he knew there was time to do that—years and decades, God willing, to do just that.

As the early darkness of winter fell, they adjourned to their various rooms and reassembled a short while later in the breakfast room for Christmas dinner. Miss Merryweather did not join them. Matthias had offered to take Mrs. Lancaster home in the sleigh, but she had declined, stating her rheumatism wouldn't allow such a venture. Matthias knew, in truth, the events of the day would provide her with gossip for years and she surely didn't wish to miss a moment of it.

Matthias had Miss Blackwell seated opposite him, as if they were already married—although, he mustn't get ahead of himself; after all, he hadn't even proposed to her yet. She could still refuse him.

He especially asked that the cloth be left off the table, so that Miss Blackwell might see the polished sheen of *her* table. It suddenly occurred to him that, when he proposed, she might accept him only for the sake of the furniture. Well, so be it, if it took stray bits of furniture to commend him.

And so they dined on rare beef and roasted potatoes with not a sprout in sight. And more. All followed by Christmas pudding, until Mrs. Lancaster announced they'd have to roll her out of the breakfast room. To which, replied Matthias, there was still the dancing to be had.

"Dancing?" asked Miss Blackwell.

"Oh yes," said Matthias, "I promised you a happy Christmas, and I intend to keep that promise." He rose from the table, moved to the opposite end, and held out his hand to her. "The festivities await."

He led her from the breakfast room, Mrs. Martin and Mrs. Lancaster following close behind, and as they entered the hall, the assembly gathered there burst into applause. It was, most decidedly, not a squeeze, as they would say in Town, but a welcomed gathering of Matthias's servants and tenants and nearest neighbors, all collected, at his request, by sleigh and horse, to celebrate Christmas. He smiled at them all, thankful so many had come, nearly thirty, he imagined. One of his tenants, Frank Eliot, stood in the corner with his violin ready, beside him the pianoforte with Miss Rogers—she was not even out yet—seated before the keys.

Matthias turned to Miss Blackwell. "Shall we lead the first dance," he asked, "or would you prefer a cup of punch instead? I can lead Mrs. Martin out. Or Mrs. Lancaster."

"Oh, no. I would be happy to dance with you."

Matthias shouted to the musicians, "Play a waltz."

A gasp went up from the assembly, followed by giggles and laughter of delight, with couples quickly pairing off. Miss Blackwell, however, looked quite shocked.

"You do know how to waltz, don't you?" asked Matthias.

"Yes. Well, no. I know the steps but I've never danced it in company. Or with a partner."

"Then I am honored," he said, taking her into his arms, "Have no fear. We will go slowly."

The music started, and they began the steps of the dance, awkwardly at first, with Miss Blackwell glancing down at her feet every so often. But soon, they managed to glide quite well together across the ancient floor. And despite being surrounded by a dozen other couples, it felt as if they were alone, in their own little world.

"Am I right?" asked Matthias at length. Despite his courage at asking the question, he feared the possible answer. "Do you feel the same about me?"

"Oh, yes." She gazed up at him, her eyes softening and filled with moisture. "I love you dearly. I have for several years."

"Years?" That surprised him. "But how… when?"

She smiled shyly and looked away, her steps never faltering. "Mr. Forbes organized at picnic at the abbey ruins. We were all piled in the carriages and about to depart, and someone asked, 'Are we all here?' and you replied, 'Wait. Where's Miss Blackwell?' I simply said, 'Here I am,' and we departed. But I felt so much… more." Her gaze returned to his eyes. "To be thought of. To be held in another's mind. *Your* mind."

"Miss Blackwell, please, this is not the right time or place but I must know. Would you do me the great honor of becoming my wife?"

She abruptly stopped, and probably would have stumbled had Matthias not held her about the waist. And then, most unexpectedly, she threw herself into his arms and clung to him.

"Oh, yes. Yes, I will be your wife," she cried against his waistcoat as he held her close.

The music stopped, and Matthias became aware of everyone staring at them there, in the midst of the dancers.

"It's all right," he announced without releasing her, "Miss

Blackwell has just consented to be my wife."

A great applause arose from those gathered, interspersed with shouts of *Huzzah*! After a moment, he released Miss Blackwell, and still holding her hand, stepped back and bowed to her, his blushing bride-to-be. The clapping grew even louder when he lifted her hand to his lips and kissed her knuckles.

"No!"

Matthias looked around for the source of that single word, Miss Blackwell doing likewise.

"No!" it came again, "You can't!"

A few of the dancers parted to reveal Miss Merryweather standing there. "I am your betrothed. You proposed to me and I accepted."

Matthias drew Miss Blackwell closer, as if to protect her, and replied, "You never replied, and you accepted Jonathan Thompson instead."

"Well, I am accepting you now."

This was becoming intolerable. Matthias was ending it now. "The offer is withdrawn. I won't have you."

"I'll have her."

A new, masculine voice rose from somewhere in the hall. As the crowd parted, Matthias saw Mr. Thompson, still in his coat and hat, his boots covered in snow. "I'll have you, Nerissa."

"But I don't want to marry you, Jonathan. You're poor."

"I'm not poor. I own a farm."

"You're a farmer! I don't want to marry a farmer."

"*I'm* a farmer," said Matthias.

"Yes, but unlike you, Matthi... Mr. Hunt, Jonathan can't afford a house in London."

In the stillness of the hall, Mrs. Lancaster finally put in her two cents. "But Nerissa, you have to marry Jonathan. After all, you're...." She raised her eyebrows and tilted her head. "Everyone will know soon enough, especially once I get home and tell Mrs. Landry and she tells Mrs. Howes. She's such a gossip."

It seemed to take Miss Merryweather a moment to grasp Mrs. Lancaster's full meaning, her eyes widening with the horror of it. "You wouldn't!"

"In a heartbeat. Such a mischief maker, even when you were small. Well, you've made enough trouble, so, I'm afraid you've made your bed and now you must lie in it."

"But, it's not true. I made it all up." It was probably the first truthful thing Miss Merryweather had said since arriving there the night before. "I just wanted to accept Mr. Hunt's proposal, instead of Jonathan's. That's all. I wanted to live in London."

"Not true?" Mrs. Lancaster tsk-tsked, her entire body slumping with the disappointment of Miss Merryweather's confession. "Well, that's that, I suppose."

"No." Everyone turned at the startling sound of Mr. Thompson's voice once again echoing through the hall. Matthias thought he could see gears working in the boy's head. "It's true. We..." He blushed and stared down at the floor, all the while nervously turning his hat. "We... We have to marry."

Miss Merryweather squealed in protest, while Mrs. Lancaster proclaimed, "Well, I just knew Mr. Hunt could never be party to such an indiscretion. Honestly, the very idea. But that Thompson boy...." And she wandered off, shaking her head, toward the punch bowl and a gaggle of gossips waiting to hear the tale.

Matthias motioned toward Mr. Eliot and Miss Rogers to play something, anything, to distract everyone from what had just happened. It was futile, of course. It would be the talk of the village and half the district before noon tomorrow.

He turned to Miss Blackwell, still at his side.

"Are you all right?" he asked, leaning in close to her.

She nodded and gave a sideways glance toward Miss Merryweather and Mr. Thompson. "Do you think she's done?"

"With us? Yes, I expect so. But I think she is going to cause that boy a lifetime of troubles and he'll regret having ever stood up for her." He gazed down at Miss Blackwell and thanked God for sending her to him, for her words that day of the party. Otherwise, he might have found himself stuck with Miss Merryweather on some foolish pretext of honor.

Matthias gently took her arm and guided her to one of the chairs—her chairs—positioned around the perimeter of the hall. He sat down beside her and took her hand. "Would you like a cup of punch? Or maybe another dance?"

"In a little while."

"I'm sorry."

"For what?"

"I promised you a happy Christmas, and this is hardly turning out that way."

"The evening is not over yet."

She gazed up at him, in a way he'd never known, a mingling of love and respect and admiration. And without thinking about it, he leaned in and kissed her. A simple, chaste kiss. A promise of more to come in the days and weeks and years ahead. The hall fell silent, and when Matthias opened his eyes, he realized Mrs. Lancaster stood before them, a sprig of mistletoe dangling over their heads. Miss Blackwell smiled and blushed, reflecting, Matthias suspected, his own face. The hall erupted in good-humored cheers and laughter. As if to give their audience an encore, Matthias leaned in and kissed Miss Blackwell—Constance—again.

Pulling away, he whispered, "Happy Christmas."

Constance slowly shook her head. "Oh no," she said with a smile, "*Happiest* Christmas."

"Ever?"

"Yet."

And he kissed her again.

About Anna

Anna D. Allen is essentially half-Finnish and half-Southern, which means she has no sense of humor and will shoot you for wearing white shoes after Labor Day... unless you are attending a wedding and happen to be the bride. She holds a Bachelor of Science and a Master of Arts in Language and Literature. She is a recipient of the Writers of the Future award and a member of Science Fiction and Fantasy Writers of America, but she also has a great passion for Regency Romances. It is generally acknowledged that she spends way too much time with the dead and her mind got lost somewhere in the 19th Century. Case in point, her website:

http://beket1.wix.com/annadallen

Along with her contributions to the five *Christmas Revels* Regency anthologies, her available works include the Regency Romance novel *Miss Pritchard's Happy, Wanton Christmas (and the Consequences Thereof)*; the Regency Romance novelette "A Christmas Wager;" the novel *Charles Waverly and the Deadly African Safari*; and three short story collections: *Mrs. Hewitt's Barbeque*, *Lake People*, and *Lady de Kiernan's Headache*; as well as some boring scholarly stuff about dead people. Currently, she is writing a Victorian mystery novel, which she freely admits is Holmes and Watson fanfiction... but then, Sir Arthur was writing Edgar Allan Poe fanfiction, so Anna is in good company.

In the virtual world, she can be found on Facebook.

The Christmas Gamble

by

Kate Parker

Chapter One

Lizzie Hancock pressed her nose to the window of the carriage as she and her guardian rolled through the streets. An entire city lay before her, a world she could explore once she was rid of her loathsome guardian.

Her pulse sped at the sight of so many buildings, smoke rising from every chimney. Dozens of people hurried along, their breath making little clouds as they greeted each other. She couldn't wait to join them. The possibilities that living here would bring seemed as endless as the streets.

She could hear bells on the harnesses of carriages as they passed. Carolers sang in front of a huge stone church. Children, laughing and calling to each other, marched hand in hand down the sidewalk under the gaze of their minders.

This city, Heverwell, might really be only a large town, not as sizable as London or even Bath. But it appeared grand enough to have books and music and art. A host of lively people. And all this would mean a joyous Christmas season. Her guardian's estate lacked these advantages. These things she enjoyed.

"Doesn't make a promising aspect," her guardian, Lord Grambling, sneered.

"It's much cleaner than I expected. And the roads are in decent shape, considering the snow we've received," Lizzie replied. She would have preferred to walk the rest of the way rather than listen to her guardian's belittling remarks. They were the only type he made, and she'd grown weary of them years before.

"Hope the earl has a fire laid and a meal prepared for us," Lord Grambling said, rubbing his hands together.

He couldn't possibly be cold. He'd hogged the coals in the brazier the entire trip. It had to be anticipation. Lizzie knew Lord Grambling enjoyed any treat he didn't have to pay for.

"Is it much farther?" She found she was nervous at the thought of meeting the man she'd spend the rest of her life with.

"No. Now, don't get your hopes up, Lizzie. The marriage market for a lady with no title and no dowry is small."

"But I don't understand. My parents left me a legacy."

"I explained it to you," he said, using his falsely patient voice. "There was little, and now, with the costs, there's nothing." They turned a corner and he brightened. "There it is. On the left. Stonebrook House."

They stopped in front of a house that was large and well-proportioned. Three stories and an attic with large Georgian windows. Corinthian columns held up the porch roof. Two steps led to the porch from a walkway through a small garden. The house and grounds were separated from the road by a wrought-iron fence. More extensive grounds spread out toward the houses on either side.

Lord Grambling's footman climbed down from the carriage and walked up the shoveled path to the front door. In a moment, two footmen emerged from the house to assist Lizzie and her guardian inside.

Once out of the imprisoning carriage, Lizzie looked around. This was the largest, prettiest house on a street of large, imposing houses. And that meant neighbors. Something else she'd lacked in the country. She couldn't wait to meet them.

As she looked around she noticed the other houses had festive greenery attached to windows and doors and gates. There was nothing at the earl's house marking the approach of the Christmas season.

She'd been told her betrothed would make few demands on her and would often leave her alone. That would suit her well. But she would not be content if he were as cold and as cheap as her guardian.

Lord Grambling escorted her inside in a rush. "Blastedly cold out," he groused, as if it were someone's fault.

She entered to find a man of about forty and a woman of about fifty waiting to greet them. Both wore the plain clothes of upper servants. The man bowed and said, "We're sorry his lordship isn't here to greet you, but he's had to travel to London on business. He plans to return as soon as he is able. In the meantime, he has instructed us to greet you in his name and serve you."

The butler was Lizzie's height with sharp, dark eyes that appeared to overlook nothing.

"Thank you," Lizzie said. "What is your name?"

"Jenkins, miss. And this is Mrs. Thompson, the housekeeper."

Mrs. Thompson dropped a curtsy.

"Where's a fire? And food?" Lord Grambling demanded and walked across the black and white tile floor to open the double doors to one side. Beyond the doors, Lizzie saw a lovely blue drawing room. And no fire.

Lord Grambling banged the doors shut as Jenkins said, "If you'll come this way, my lord. Miss." He led them to a double doorway on the opposite side of the two-story entry hall. Inside was a large formal dining room with a table that could seat two dozen. The fireplace at one end held a warming fire. "I'll have luncheon brought in immediately, my lord."

Lord Grambling sat down at the end of the table closest to the fire, not waiting to see where, or even if, Lizzie sat. She chose a seat on one side, leaving a chair between them. Soon, she promised herself, soon I'll be free of him.

"Too bad Waters isn't here. I have business with him. Oh, well, a few days in Heverwell at Christmastime can't go amiss. There must be a card game going somewhere in this town," Lord Grambling said.

A card game where his unpaid debts weren't legendary, Lizzie thought. She knew why she was betrothed to George Waters, Earl of Stonebrook. Her guardian owed him a fortune. She was the repayment.

No one had told her directly, but she'd heard murmurs when they'd gone out in company. She'd seen the silver disappear. Her small inheritance had vanished almost as soon as he'd gained her guardianship upon the death of her equally irresponsible father.

At least the earl was willing to marry a penniless orphan. Even if her guardian had sold her for the price of his gaming debts.

The earl was nearly forty. She hoped he was a young forty, not gouty or corpulent or sickly. She'd dreamed of a loving husband. He didn't have to be handsome, but she wanted to be a wife, not a nurse.

Jenkins returned with two steaming bowls of stew and fresh, crusty bread and butter.

"Stew? We're not the help, man. Get us something better," Lord Grambling snapped.

"This is hot and fresh and quite nice, Jenkins. We're sorry we traveled without sending word of the exact date of our arrival. Thank the cook for us," Lizzie said.

"I will, miss. I'm afraid this is all we have for now. Tonight, there will be food more to your liking, my lord," Jenkins said and walked out of the room.

"He's getting above himself. Sack him," Lord Grambling said.

"I most certainly would not, if I had the authority, which I don't." Lizzie tasted her stew. It was hot and well-seasoned, and the meat was more tender than she was used to eating in Lord Grambling's household. "The cook is a treasure."

"Good." Lord Grambling fell on his bowl, gobbling as if he hadn't seen food for days. Finishing first, he rose and began to pace around the dining room as he appraised the paintings and draperies. "Aren't you finished yet?"

"There's no rush. We don't have to get back into the carriage and travel farther. We're here and I'd like to catch my breath."

"We have a house to explore. Hurry up."

Lizzie smiled, knowing she'd soon have a new master and hoping he'd be kind. She savored each bite.

As if he had second sight, Jenkins returned the moment she finished. "If you're ready, I'll show you to your rooms. I've taken the liberty of putting the young miss in the countess's room, since that's what she'll be soon."

"Thank you, Jenkins." Lizzie rose and swept out of the dining room, following her guardian who'd already stalked out.

The countess's room was done in pink and beige. A maid had already unpacked for her. And the stately four poster bed looked inviting. Tired from four days of travel, Lizzie wondered how soon she could climb into the bed and sleep through the night without the noise of a tavern keeping her awake.

"Since Waters isn't here to tell us, who are our neighbors?" Lord Grambling asked from the hallway.

"You and Miss Hancock will meet them tomorrow night at a Christmas ball next door in the direction of the church. Lord and Lady Wallace are hosting the party."

"Will the earl return in time to attend the ball?" Lizzie asked, walking to the doorway of her room.

"I fear not," Jenkins said.

"Is there some reason the house is not decorated for Christmas? Does the earl not like garlands and ribbon?" Lizzie pressed.

"I think his lordship was waiting to let you decide how you wanted to decorate."

At Jenkins' words, Lizzie's face lit up. "Oh, I'd like fir garlands along the fence with a wreath on the gate. And another wreath with a large red bow on the front door. And garlands running along the banister in the front hall with more red ribbon. Could that be done tomorrow morning? I'd like to surprise his lordship."

Lizzie couldn't tell if Jenkins was smiling because he liked Christmas decorations or found her enthusiasm amusing, because he answered, "Yes, miss."

"That's rather extravagant with only the two of us to see it," her guardian said.

"But this will be my home now, and I'd like to begin as I plan to go on," Lizzie told him. She didn't add it would cost him nothing. She hoped the earl wouldn't pay only for his own pleasures, like her guardian.

Holding in a sigh of exasperation, she added, "Will you escort me to the ball tomorrow?"

"Of course. I'm sure they'll have a card room." Lord Grambling followed Jenkins to see his room.

Lizzie went back to admire the countess's room. The view out the windows was of a Georgian mansion decorated for Christmas and the street between them. As she watched, a man rode up to their gate on horseback. A footman went out to get the beast and the man walked up the path. She lost sight of him when he climbed up the steps onto the porch.

Hearing footsteps pass her door, Lizzie looked out to see Jenkins go downstairs, followed by her guardian. She trailed behind hoping, and fearing, it would be the earl.

The man in the hallway took off his top hat, gloves, scarf, and heavy coat as if he belonged there. "Is George here?" he asked Jenkins.

"George, sir?" Jenkins asked.

"George Waters. My brother. Is he here? I'm Gabriel Waters. You must be new since I left England. Where is he?" The stranger glanced around the entrance hall, examining it as if for any changes. He appeared to be just past thirty, fit, and, judging from the laugh lines on his smiling face, with an easygoing manner.

"I'm afraid the earl isn't home. He's gone to London on business," Jenkins told him as a footman took his outerwear.

"I just came from there. We must have passed on the road." The man turned twinkling brown eyes on Lizzie. "Hello. I'm Gabriel Waters, at your service." He gave her a deep bow.

She curtsied in return. "Elizabeth Hancock, the Earl of Stonebrook's fiancée."

"My brother is well-blessed. His taste is outstanding."

He gave her such a wide smile that she blurted out, "I've never met your brother. My guardian, Lord Grambling, arranged our betrothal."

"Then my brother is lucky to have a friend in you, my lord." The stranger held out his hand.

Lord Grambling shook it. "Nice of you to say. Do you play cards?"

"On occasion." Gabriel Waters turned to Jenkins. "Could my bags be taken upstairs?"

"They already have, Mr. Waters, and put in the room I was told was yours as a lad."

"Good. What time does George have you serve dinner?"

"The same time it's always been served, sir." Jenkins tried to hide his surprise as he watched Gabriel. His tone was more guarded and suspicion flickered in his eyes. Lizzie knew the telltale signs of mistrust. She'd seen it in the eyes of those dealing with her guardian.

"When I was a boy, dinnertime seemed to change constantly. Perhaps it was my inability to tell time except with my stomach," Gabriel said, still cheerfully grinning.

"Harper, the butler when you were a lad, told me it was always served at seven while the family was in town," Jenkins said in a stuffy tone.

"How is Harper these days?" Gabriel asked.

"Dead these two years, sir."

Gabriel's face fell. "I'm sorry to hear that. I'd hoped to see him again." Then he looked straight at the butler. "I didn't ask your name."

"Jenkins, sir."

Gabriel nodded and then turned to Lizzie. "I hope to have the honor of escorting you into dinner tonight."

Lizzie took in the square line of his well-shaved jaw, his battered-looking nose, the smile on his lips, and the copper sheen of his skin that complemented his brown eyes and sun-streaked hair. He was pleasant to look at and it appeared he would make an agreeable dinner companion. She returned his smile. "I'd like that very much."

"When is the wedding? I'm glad I made it back to England in time to see you and George wed."

Lizzie realized with a shock she hadn't asked that question. The servants should know as well as her intended. "I don't know. Jenkins?"

"His lordship thought to get a special license before he left for London, miss. It only needs his return."

If only he is like his brother, she thought. Gabriel was vigorous, pleasant, and exotic, all at the same time. Lizzie wanted to get to know him better, but there wouldn't be much time before his lordship returned.

Chapter Two

"We'll have three at dinner tonight, Mrs. Robbins," Jenkins said as he entered the kitchen.

"That's all right. We can make it stretch," the old woman said, wiping her hands on her apron. "They'll just have to be happy with what I fix them."

"You'll never guess who has arrived," he said.

"Who? The earl, I'd imagine." She lifted her brows.

"Gabriel Waters."

"Master Gabriel. Well, I never expected to see him again in this life. He swore he'd never return." The cook smiled as she gave the pot a stir.

"Why was that?"

"He and his father never got on. The countess died giving birth to the boy, and the old earl never forgave him for living. Finally, his father gave him passage to foreign shores and they agreed they'd not meet again in England."

"How many of the staff remember Mr. Waters as a boy?" Jenkins asked, not looking the cook in the eye.

"Only me, both here and at the estates. The rest have left or died. I'll be glad to see him though. The boy had quite an appetite. And a winning manner." Mrs. Robbins smiled, looking back over the years.

Jenkins turned away, frowning.

☙❧

Dinner was more suited for Lent than Christmastime, but the food was well cooked. "The cook should be sacked," Lord Grambling said, cleaning his plate.

"It was well prepared, and I didn't send warning ahead of my arrival," Gabriel said. "I think you should blame me for any lack."

"Don't concern yourself. We didn't either," Lizzie said. She wouldn't blame him for anything. The food was better than what they ate at Lord Grambling's. "Only that we were coming, but not the day. As it was, we would have been wrong because the carriage broke an axle and we were forced to wait a day for it to be repaired."

"In winter? The trip must have been harrowing for a young lady," Gabriel said.

"Not at all." Traveling with Lord Grambling was worse than being stranded in a blizzard. "We were fortunate that the axle broke just outside of a town. We were never in danger of freezing to death in a snow drift." Lizzie gave him a broad smile.

She and Gabriel had talked the entire meal. He'd been in the Far East, making his fortune only to lose it and make it again. The second fortune he'd made now resided in a bank in London.

His adventures were fascinating. Even better, he never gave a word of complaint. A great deal of laughter, mostly at himself, but no whining.

Her guardian would have complained constantly. He certainly had about the broken axle.

"It sounds like you're very brave. Not many young women of my acquaintance would risk traveling in this weather."

"And how many young women are you acquainted with, living in the Far East?" she asked with a raised-brow smile.

He grinned back. "Admittedly, not many. But if I were, they wouldn't be as brave as you."

"You're flattering me." Lizzie couldn't hide her pleasure. No one had ever complimented her before. At least, no one who had played cards with her guardian and then tried to collect. "Are there many European women where you were staying on Penang Island?"

"Very few, all of them well chaperoned, and all of them in George Town. I spent too much of my time on the high seas between the Malay coast and India, where there were no women on board."

"Why did you choose to return now?" She wanted to know more about him. He would be her brother by marriage. It would be a shame if his brother, her unknown fiancé, wasn't as daring, as handsome, as dashing as Gabriel.

"George wrote me, asking me to come home. Telling me that our father had died and he was now the earl. Telling me he wanted my help in running the estate."

"You're his brother. I'm sure he missed you."

"And I missed him. We're the last of the line of Waters. Previous generations had few children, most of them female." He grinned at her. "You and George will have an obligation to continue the line and produce healthy male children."

"If we fail, it will be down to you," Lizzie replied.

"Elizabeth. This is not a proper conversation for a young woman to have," Lord Grambling said. Then he looked at Gabriel. "Where do you think I might find a card game tonight?"

"I have no idea. I've not been in Heverwell in ages."

Lord Grambling rose. "Perhaps one of the servants might know." He left the room without saying goodbye.

"How long ago did George send you the letter?" Lizzie asked.

"Nearly three years. It went first to Egypt, where I'd originally gone, then India, and finally found me in George Town on Penang Island. I was suffering from a tropical fever and it was weeks before I gathered the strength to think about traveling home."

"You faced so many dangers. Malay pirates, the French, and fevers."

Gabriel's face fell. "The fevers were the worst. I had a partner in my shipping business between India and George Town. We were as close as brothers. Shared everything. I would have left him the business, but we shared the fever that laid me so low. It killed him as it does so many. I lost heart, sold the business, and traveled back." He roused himself to drain his glass of wine. "And here I am."

"Will you give half the profits to your partner's family?"

"He was an orphan, sent to sea as a youngster because there was no one left to care for him." Lizzie could hear anger in his voice on behalf of his dead partner.

"He had a hard life."

"He did." The room fell silent for a moment except for the crack of the fire. Finally, Gabriel said, "Enough of me. Tell me about the life of Elizabeth Hancock."

"Prepare to be bored."

ಸಿಂಚ

When Gabriel came downstairs the next morning, the hall was filled with the long-forgotten scents of pine and fir coming from the twin wreaths on the parlor and dining room doors. He breathed deeply as he walked to the dining room in search of coffee.

He stopped in the doorway as Lizzie came in the front door followed by two footmen. The sound of her laughter surrounded him. Her cheeks were rosy from the cold. Her auburn hair was windblown. The two young men listened to her every command to decorate the stair railing with looks of rapt devotion on their faces.

George had better be up to the challenge.

For that matter, he wouldn't mind challenging George for her himself.

"Mr. Waters, come see how we've decorated the front of the house."

He couldn't resist her command. With nothing but his jacket and boots to protect him from the cold, he went out onto the front steps. A rope of greenery ran along the front fence, stopping for the gate where a large wreath with a red bow held pride of place.

"Miss Hancock, you've outdone yourself," he said as he returned to the relative warmth of the front hall.

"Do you remember how the greenery was held on the banister when you were a boy?" she asked him.

"Magic?"

Her smile lit up her face. "I was thinking of something more practical."

"There's a big storeroom in the attic where some Christmas decorations used to be kept. We could look up there and see what we can find. After breakfast."

"Excellent suggestion." She turned to the two young men. "We'll work on the railing later."

Gabriel gave her his arm and they went into the dining room. When Jenkins entered the room moments later, Lizzie immediately put the question to him.

"I don't know, miss. We haven't decorated the indoors since I came here, both in the old earl's time and the current earl."

"Who would know?"

"Mrs. Robbins, the cook, has been here the longest. Should I send her to you, miss?"

"I'll go to her after breakfast, while I thank her for this delicious meal. It smells wonderful." She served herself from the sideboard and sat before looking at the place at the table for her guardian.

Gabriel reached out and patted her hand. Her skin was not as soft as it appeared. Had her guardian put her to work around his manor house? She didn't seem flighty like so many closeted young women. Maybe it was good training. "Perhaps he'll be down later."

She nodded, looking worried. Then she appeared to shrug off her downcast mood and gave him a smile.

Gabriel looked toward Jenkins as he was leaving the room. "Any word from my brother?"

"No, sir. We're hoping to hear from him today."

"Not a good letter writer," Gabriel said.

"Oh, no, sir. He wrote you at least once a month, contacting everyone he could think of or anyone else suggested. He tried very hard to reach you, sir."

"And then I finally return and he's not here." He wasn't certain he wanted the Earl of Stonebrook to return. But it had been so long, perhaps… "Have you sent word to let him know he has company?"

"I sent word by messenger when the young lady and Lord Grambling arrived. I expect to receive word back at any time."

"Did he travel with only his valet for a companion?"

"No, sir. He let his valet go a few weeks ago. Not satisfactory. He hoped to return from London with a replacement."

"You mean he traveled alone? In this weather?" Gabriel was surprised. He had, and while he was used to hardship, it had been a difficult trip. He had the coin an earl would to make his trip easier, but he'd learned frugality at a young age as a necessity.

Jenkins didn't respond for a moment as if he hadn't heard. Then with a jerk, he said, "Yes. He didn't feel London was that far. He only took a driver for the carriage with him. He plans to have a valet on the return journey."

"Oh." It sounded like an adequate reply. "I'll worry about getting a valet in time. I'm so used to doing for myself that I'm finding your occasional help sufficient, Jenkins."

"Very good, sir." The butler left the room.

After they enjoyed their breakfast, unencumbered by Lord Grambling's presence, Lizzie said she'd go down to ask the cook how they used to hang the greenery from the banister.

Gabriel leaped at the chance to go with her. "If it turns out there is some fetching to do, I'll be your footman."

"Hardly a footman," she said, "but I'll be glad of the company."

They went downstairs toward the back of the house where the clatter and smells directed them to the kitchen. When they walked in, everyone stopped their tasks and stepped back.

"Please," Lizzie said, "don't stop on my account. Mrs. Robbins?"

A short, rotund woman with white hair stepped toward her, bobbing a curtsy. "Yes, miss?"

"Breakfast was excellent. But I've not come to talk about the food. As the longest serving member of staff, you must remember when they would decorate the front hall for Christmas with greenery."

"Indeed, I do, miss."

"How did they attach the greenery to the banister?"

"There were these metal clamps with rings to run the red ribbon through. The metal clamps were attached to the banister with leather straps. Then the ribbon was wound through the branches of fir and holly."

"It sounds like a well thought out plan."

"That it was, miss. The head groom when I was a girl, just a scullery maid, dreamed it up from the bells on the harness. They haven't been used in years."

"You don't know where they've been stored, do you?"

"Let me think. It's been a long time since anyone has seen them."

"If anyone can remember, I'm sure you can, Mrs. Robbins," Gabriel said.

"Thank you, sir. I'm trying my best. And who are you, sir?"

"You've forgotten me? I'm Gabriel, all grown up."

She peered at his face. "My goodness. You look so different from the youngster who left us nearly twenty years ago. You were still a child then."

"The years have changed me," he said with a smile,

returning her stare.

She continued to stare at him, and he grew nervous. What was she seeing that no one else had? It had been a bad idea to accompany Lizzie down to the kitchen, but Mrs. Robbins wouldn't have seen much of the young masters, George and Gabriel. And it had been many years.

Then her face changed to a look of determination. She gave a nod and said, "It's good to have you back, Master Gabriel, and that's a fact."

He'd passed a test. He would like to know what the test was.

Chapter Three

Mrs. Robbins finally remembered where the old metal rings and leather straps were stored. "In the cellar. Under the front part of the house. The old earl had wanted every trace of Christmas removed. He told the servants to throw it all into the rubbish heap, but we couldn't stand the thought of it. We knew he'd never look in the cellar."

"Why did he hate Christmas so much?" Lizzie asked.

"He was engaged to be married a second time. When Master Gabriel was a boy. The wedding was to be New Year's Day. The lady he was to marry called off the wedding at Christmas."

"Why did she end things with him?" Lizzie felt sorry for the couple, but she'd learned from living with her guardian that she often discovered important details when she asked prying questions. Especially when the questions had to do with her inheritance.

She felt she needed to know, in case the reason had some bearing on her own wedding. If the family was hiding some ominous secret, she would be wise to flee.

As if her guardian would allow any sign of independence that might interfere with his plans.

"We heard rumors, miss, but I don't know. And rumors are just as likely to be wrong as right." Mrs. Robbins turned back to her stove. "I'm afraid I can't help you. I need to work on dinner."

Lizzie followed Gabriel out toward the cellar.

"I'm finding I get turned around in this old house. It's been so long since I've been here." After opening the door to the laundry and another that led to the root cellar, Gabriel opened a door that led down to a dusty cavern-like area.

A couple of unpolished lanterns sat on one side, and lighting them both, he led the way.

Lizzie was fascinated with the castoffs she found in the cool, dry cellar. The splintered remains of a chair. Half of a butter churn. A traveling case.

"Seems like a strange place to store a small trunk," Gabriel said. "Here are the metal rings and leather straps for the greenery." He held them up in triumph.

"I wonder what old treasures are hidden in here," Lizzie said, her gaze going back to the traveling case.

"Only one way to find out." Gabriel set down their original goal and walked over to her. Reaching out, he undid the clasps and opened the top of the case.

Inside were men's clothes badly folded and obviously packed in a hurry. Lizzie lifted a shirt and shook it out. It still smelled fresh from the laundry and was barely wrinkled.

Gabriel lifted a small box from inside and opened it. Inside was a signet ring as well as wax and a seal with the same design. "These belong to the Earl of Stonebrook. These are his coat of arms."

"What would they be doing down here?" Lizzie asked.

"Hidden while the earl was traveling," came a voice from the entrance to the cellar.

Lizzie jumped at the surprise of another joining them.

Encircled as she was by the lantern light, the figure in the doorway was in shadow. She shivered as a man stepped forward.

"Jenkins, you gave us a shock," Gabriel said. "Why are my brother's signet ring and wax seal down here in a trunk of old clothes?"

"To hide them while he was gone."

"Wouldn't he need them?" Lizzie asked.

"He was afraid of highwaymen whenever he was traveling, and especially this trip since he was venturing out in his carriage alone. He hid them down here in the cellar rather than his room because your guardian, I'm afraid, miss, doesn't have an unblemished history," Jenkins told her.

"Oh." The part about her guardian's reputation was certainly true. But why hide fresh clothing down here?

Before she could ask, Gabriel said, "How can he conduct business in London without them?"

"He is known to everyone he needs to speak with, Master Gabriel." Jenkins stepped to the side and picked up the rings and straps. "I believe this is what the young lady was looking for."

Gabriel put the small box back together and set it inside the trunk. Then he closed and clamped the trunk shut. Taking the greenery holders from Jenkins, he walked out of the cellar.

Lizzie hurried after him, handing the lantern to Jenkins on her way.

Once in the hallway, where she no longer felt as if she were trespassing, she saw the cellar go dark and then heard the metal base of the lantern clink before Jenkins came out.

"Mrs. Robbins must have told you where we were,"

Gabriel said.

"Indeed she did, Mr. Waters. Shall I send the footmen up to help with the greenery?" Jenkins said.

"That would be good," Lizzie said, hurrying away to the steps heading up to her world above stairs. She couldn't shake the feeling she'd been trespassing into places and matters where she wasn't wanted.

ଔଔ

Lizzie's guardian appeared for dinner with a black eye and a swollen nose. "What happened, Lord Grambling?" Lizzie asked.

"I slipped and fell on the snow last night. Banged myself up." He took another sip of wine before carefully taking another small bite of meat.

Lizzie found the meat almost too tender. "Did you hurt your mouth, too?"

"My jaw. The whole side of my face aches."

"Will you want to attend the ball with us tonight?" Gabriel asked.

"Of course. I don't want to miss it."

Lizzie had heard that tone of voice before. It told her he'd found a card game the night before, had lost, and wanted to win back his undoubtedly hocked or stolen assets. He either decided the other man cheated and wouldn't call him on it at the ball, or he'd found another angle he could work to his advantage.

Not the way she wanted to meet her new neighbors.

"I'll be glad to escort Miss Hancock to the ball. It's only next door," Gabriel said, an innocent smile on his face.

Lizzie didn't believe the smile any more than she believed her guardian had been injured falling in the snow.

Snow drifts provided a soft landing.

"No. We'll all go together." Lord Grambling sounded adamant.

"Will you be all right walking next door? Don't want you falling in the snow again," Gabriel said. His smile widened.

Lizzie felt certain Gabriel had her guardian's measure, at least as far as the story about his injuries went.

They finished dinner and went upstairs to ready for the night's entertainment. Lizzie, with the help of the maid acting as her lady's maid, put on her best ball gown, a pale green, which accented her auburn locks and emerald eyes. She knew she didn't have fashionable coloring. Blonde and simpering seemed to be in style the one season her guardian allowed her. No offers had come her way since word soon circulated that she had no money, and her guardian thought of her as a useful commodity.

The maid was quite good at curling and styling Lizzie's hair, and with a green ribbon woven through her locks like greenery on the banister, she looked presentable. But without jewelry, she looked like a poor relation, not the fiancée of an earl.

Lizzie searched the looking glass for a countess, but the woman who stared back at her looked like a fraud. Not an aristocrat.

She thanked the maid and left her room, only to run into Gabriel in the passageway.

"You look beautiful," he said. "My brother is indeed the most fortunate of men."

"Thank you."

"So why don't you wear the countess's emeralds?"

Lizzie looked at him and blinked. "I'm not the countess."

"You will be. And she has a necklace of emeralds that is lovely. The color of your eyes. Come on. It must be in the dressing table." Gabriel led her by the hand back into her room.

"But I'm not the countess yet. These must have been your mother's jewels," she protested.

"They were, and now they will be yours." He started rummaging through the drawers.

"May I help, Mr. Waters?" Jenkins said, walking into the room.

"Yes. The countess's emeralds. Wouldn't they look magnificent on the next countess tonight?" He waved one arm toward her as if a magician.

"They are locked up in your brother's room. No one has worn them since your mother's time." Jenkins looked slightly scandalized.

"Well, let's get them out, Jenkins."

Lizzie thought Gabriel looked masterful. Tall, still rugged from his hard life in the Far East, and expecting to be obeyed. His hair was well-trimmed, his evening clothes bore the shine of newly made fabric, and his boots reflected the glow of the candles. His chin was up and his eyes held a light that defied anyone to disagree with him.

After a moment, Jenkins gave him a bow and stepped out of the way. Gabriel left, and after a moment's hesitation, fearing Lord Grambling's first thought on seeing them would be to gamble them away, Lizzie went after him to her future husband's chamber.

Lizzie looked around as she walked in. The room was gloomy with dark paneling, dark blue draperies, heavy furniture. The safe had pride of place near the bed.

When Gabriel unlocked the safe, he pulled out a jewel case and handed it to Lizzie. She opened the case and gasped.

The emerald necklace was exquisite. She held it up in front of her and looked at the two men for approval.

"Breathtaking," Gabriel said and moved behind her to fasten the necklace. "My brother would be so pleased."

"You look like a countess," Jenkins said, approval in his tone.

Lizzie nodded to them with what she considered aristocratic grace, but her dazzling smile displayed her joy at being admired.

"Shall we go down?" Gabriel said, giving her his arm.

She took it and they left the earl's room. Then they separated to retrieve their cloaks and gloves. As they walked arm in arm down the staircase past the fir branches along the banister, they saw Lord Grambling waiting for them in the front hall.

"Are you ready? Good. Don't want to be late," he said.

"Do I look all right, Lord Grambling?" Lizzie asked, holding open her cloak so he could see her gown and jewels.

His eyes gleamed as he looked at her throat before he gave her a glance. "Yes. You look presentable. Let's get going."

"The footpath has been shoveled the whole way to the Wallace's path, which has been shoveled by their people. You should go dry shod the whole way and not meet with any accidents," Jenkins said, glancing at Lord Grambling.

"Good. Good. Now, let's go." Lord Grambling slammed his top hat on his head and barged out the door.

Gabriel again offered his arm to Lizzie and she gladly took it. She'd never had such a handsome, interesting escort before and wondered if she ever would again. She still had no idea what the earl was like and little idea beyond a painting from a few years ago. He had piercing blue eyes in a narrow face and an unfortunately long nose.

The air outside was cold and clear, but with all the lights from the surrounding houses, Lizzie discovered she couldn't see all the stars she could at her guardian's manor.

It was as if Gabriel was reading her mind when he said, "I can't see nearly as many of the stars as I could at sea. We used them to find our way from India to Penang Island and back."

"At least on land we have familiar landscapes to mark our route. At sea, you didn't have that comfort." She looked up at him and smiled, holding his arm a little tighter.

"No. It can be pretty bleak. At least topside, you have the wind and stars to the horizon. Below deck, all you have to hold on to is timbers rising and falling without end."

"It sounds terrible." Lizzie couldn't imagine willingly undergoing such an ordeal.

"You grow used to it. My younger self hated it, but you can get used to anything if you have to."

"You could have stayed in Egypt and not gone to sea," she reminded him.

"Perhaps. But that wasn't my path." He looked up. "Ah, here we are. Your guardian seems to have gone inside already."

"In search of the card room," Lizzie said. She didn't bother to hide the bitterness in her voice. She barely managed to hide the fear of what he could do to embarrass her in front of her new neighbors before he went back to his manor.

Chapter Four

Gabriel puffed up with pride as he reached the Wallace's front door and was admitted. He would never grow tired of being admitted to a grand house for a ball with a beautiful woman by his side. And that it was Elizabeth Hancock, bright, charming, and intelligent, was even better.

George was lucky.

George was probably used to these things, being an earl. Gabriel had spent over fifteen years at sea, building the business, fighting storms and pirates and the French. There hadn't been much time to escort delicate, delightful European women like Lizzie, and little in the way of European society to enjoy.

Gabriel realized he was lucky, too. He'd survived to reach this point. And had a small fortune tucked away in a London bank from selling his ships.

A shiver ran down his neck. What would happen when George returned?

He kept mostly silent, watching Lizzie charm everyone as their hostess introduced her to the other guests. Was it her curiosity about everything around her? Her genuine interest in other people? Her easy laughter?

Whatever it was, it held him spellbound. As soon as the wedding was over, he would have to leave. Maybe George needed an estate manager someplace far away.

And what was Lord Grambling up to?

Gabriel wandered off, around the ballroom and then to the side rooms. There was Henry Grambling, seated at a table, eyes only for his cards, his opponents, and the growing pile of cash on the table.

"Mr. Waters, would you care to join them?" his host asked.

"No, thank you, my lord. I prefer to bet on a sure thing." Even as he said it, Gabriel knew it wasn't true. He'd gambled plenty of times in his life. And right now, he was living the biggest gamble of all.

"Not him, Wallace. He'd rather squire my ward around," Lord Grambling said without looking up.

"She certainly is prettier than you, Grambling," Gabriel said with easy confidence. It was a technique he'd used many times in his life. He needed it to work tonight.

"I'd have said you didn't have the courage for taking risks," Grambling said. "Not even for a friendly game of cards."

The men's faces, studying their cards, looked anything but welcoming. The pile of coin on the table was creating a contest as deadly as any he'd fought with pirates. Gabriel smiled. "I prefer to take my risks on things like ships. I'm a younger son, remember?"

"How could I forget? And what will you do when Waters returns?" Grambling wore a smirk.

"You mean Lord Stonebrook. I'm also Waters." Gabriel kept the edge out of his voice only by effort.

"You two don't look alike. *Stonebrook* is tall and thin..."

"Skeletal," someone muttered.

"While you are built like a peasant, although you do have his height," Grambling continued.

"It's all the years at sea. It makes a man strong, and hard, and quick with a blade." The threat was implied, but Gabriel was glad to see Grambling's eyes widen with fright when he finally looked at him.

With a bow to Wallace, Gabriel left in search of Lizzie. Grambling wouldn't bother them this night.

He found her in the ballroom, dancing a reel and laughing, her reddish curls bouncing. She was a happy sight. Gabriel found he hoped she'd continue to be happy as Lady Stonebrook.

He watched her, soaking in her beauty, until the dance eventually came to an end. He walked up to her and gave her his arm. "Would you care for something to drink after that amazing display of footmanship?"

"You're teasing me," Lizzie said good-naturedly. "Yes, I'd like a cup of the fruit punch, and then I want to get you out on the dance floor."

"The fruit cup is easy to procure. This way, my lady. Getting me onto the dance floor may prove to be more of a challenge." Gabriel favored her with a smile that wasn't forced like the one he'd shown her guardian.

"You must remember the country dances from your childhood."

"There wasn't much time for dancing," he said, looking back over the years.

"Why no time for it?"

"My father saw to that. He was unhappy with me. Unhappy with life. And so, we didn't dance." He handed her a cup of fruit punch. "However, I did some dancing in India among the European community."

Her face lit up. "I'm glad to hear it, because you are going out on the dance floor with me, Mr. Waters."

"As soon as you're ready. In the meantime, cool off so you don't get overheated."

"Everyone at Stonebrook House has been so solicitous of my health. Why is that?" Lizzie asked, suddenly sounding suspicious.

"George's health has always been fragile. Mine was too, as a child, but years at sea have hardened me." He shook his head. "It wouldn't do for both the Lord and Lady to be sickly."

"If we do both die, or just your brother, he's the important one, I'm sure you're capable of continuing the line. You've relieved the servants' minds," Lizzie told him.

Gabriel frowned. He hadn't been concerned with the thoughts of George's servants. "Why is that?"

"You're the end of the line. Until you arrived, they thought George was the end of the line, and as you say, he's always been sickly. If he died without heir, the land would revert to the crown. And that would mean Prinny would sell the estates to one of his buddies, who wouldn't want to keep a house in Heverwell."

"So?"

"So, the staff would all be out of work. And with all these unemployed soldiers coming back from the war with France, they'd have trouble getting another position. It would mean starvation for some of them." Lizzie looked at him with an anguished expression.

"These people have come to mean something to you." He knew she was bright. He hadn't realized she was also sympathetic.

"Yes, they've been very kind to me. I know no one here, my fiancé is in London, and they've accepted me as mistress of the house. I feel I have a duty to them."

Gabriel was suddenly struck with a thought that made him smile. "How do they feel about your guardian?"

"They're counting the silver and keeping an eye on valuables, just in case." Then she smiled. "I told them that would be prudent on their part."

"I'd keep a close eye on your necklace, if I were you."

"I plan to give it to you to put back in the safe in Lord Stonebrook's room when we return."

"And you and Jenkins will watch me put it back," Gabriel said.

"What are you saying? Don't you trust Jenkins?"

"I'm sure he's as trustworthy as the next man, but something isn't right. He keeps watching me from the corner of his eye. Popping up at every opportunity. He's too vigilant."

"He's probably just a very diligent servant. It must be why your brother puts so much trust in him." Lizzie set her cup down. "And now we must get you onto the dance floor."

☙❧

Gabriel enjoyed dancing with Lizzie, swinging her around, holding her hand. She seemed to only have eyes for him, and his pride knew no bounds.

When everyone adjourned to the supper room, Lizzie chose Gabriel to fix her plate and bring it to her, apparently a sign of favor if he read the signals correctly between other young men and women.

They spent a lovely time together. He saw Lizzie was already making friends with the local aristocracy. Her guardian and the other card players didn't make an appearance.

Then there was more dancing. Gabriel enjoyed the dances where Lizzie and he were in the same group, but often, he had to dance with people he didn't know. They either didn't remember him, being too young, or remembered him as a child, being too old.

That was all right with Gabriel.

Finally, the musicians put away their instruments and the crowd gave signs of leaving. Gabriel went over to the other side of the dance floor where Lizzie was fanning her face and talking to two other young women.

"Are you ready to leave? I don't see Wallace anywhere to thank him," he said when he reached Lizzie's side.

"I saw both Lord and Lady Wallace head toward the front hall. Probably to direct us all out the door," Lizzie replied.

"Do I dare try to round up your guardian?" Gabriel asked.

"Not if you're smart. The card game is Wallace's problem," Lizzie said. "Let's find our cloaks and go."

That was easier said than done, but a quarter of an hour later, they'd finished saying goodnight to all and sundry, thanked their hosts, and headed next door. Jenkins opened the door at their arrival.

"Lord Grambling isn't with you?" he asked as he handed off their cloaks to a footman.

"No, and I wouldn't expect him for a while. He's playing cards," Lizzie told him. "I'd like to have this necklace put back into the safe."

"A wise idea, miss." A look passed between Lizzie and

Jenkins. Gabriel was certain the servant and the future countess had discussed Grambling's card playing and his methods of paying for it. Did Lizzie fear Grambling would steal from his host?

Gabriel led the way upstairs to the earl's bedroom and again opened the safe with the easy to remember birthdate of the old earl. After a moment to admire them, the emeralds were locked away.

Lizzie turned to him, a smile in her eyes. "I want you to know I had a wonderful time at the ball. And despite what you say, you are a good dancer. Several of your partners told me so."

He stepped toward her. "What do you say, Miss Hancock?"

Jenkins tactfully withdrew.

"You are marvelous." Then she blushed and stepped back, looking down. "At—at dancing."

Just as he began to puff up with pride, it hit him. Why hide the seal and the ring in the basement in a suitcase full of clothes if there was a trusted safe in his bedroom? "It's late. Let me escort you to your room."

As soon as he told her good night, Gabriel hurried to his room. Changing into work clothes from his sailing days, he waited for the house to settle into silence and then slipped quietly out of his room. Moving stealthily was a necessity for survival in the rough and tumble world of the Far Eastern colonies.

He froze when a stair tread squeaked behind him. He spun around, slipping his knife from its holder, to see Lizzie, her hair in a long braid and wearing a robe over her nightgown, following him downstairs.

She joined him on his step, her eyes wide. "I couldn't sleep. I thought I'd look for a book. Where are you going? And why are you dressed like that?" she whispered.

He might as well tell her the truth. "There's something wrong in the cellar."

"What do you mean?"

"The jewels are valuable, and they are left in the safe in the earl's room. The seal and signet ring are also valuable, but you'd expect the earl to travel with them. Instead, they are hidden in the basement. It makes no sense."

Her eyes and mouth rounded. "You're right. It makes no sense to hide one valuable thing in the cellar but leave another in the safe."

Then he told her the other thing that was bothering him. "I think there might be a clue down there as to why the earl took off for London when he was expecting your arrival." If Gabriel were the earl, he certainly wouldn't have been absent when his betrothed arrived.

"I'd love to know. It is rather embarrassing," she admitted, "meeting the local gentry without him by my side."

"I'm more than happy to escort you anywhere you'd like to go." He smiled, thinking just how much he enjoyed the honor.

She returned the smile, until a squeak from the upstairs hallway hurried them along. Using his acquired skills, he had soon silently led them to the cellar and was lighting a lantern.

The traveling case was where they had left it, and the box containing the seal and signet ring were in place amid the clothing. Why?

Holding the lantern high, Gabriel began a methodical search of the dirt-floored cellar. There seemed to be no rhyme or reason for the cast-offs left there. Nothing appeared to be disturbed, nor did anything suffer from rot or mildew. The supporting walls and beams looked to be in good shape.

She looked around the dimly lit space. "Have you found anything?"

He shook his head. "There's still half a cellar to inspect."

She smiled at him. "After you."

Gabriel held the lantern high, deeply aware of Lizzie close to his back. He ducked under another beam and the light shone on something in the far corner. "There's something there."

Lizzie slipped under the beam, barely needing to lower her head. "Where?"

He walked toward where he'd seen the reflection flicker, ducking under two more beams and passing shattered glass bottles and broken boards. Half buried in the dirt, he found a shovel. A shovel in good repair. "Why would someone want to dig down here?"

When Lizzie didn't reply, he turned to look at her. She was pointing at a trench in the dirt and beyond, a hump near the supporting wall. In a weak voice, she said, "Gabriel, that's the right size to be a grave. A human grave. What have your ancestors been doing down here?"

Chapter Five

"Do you want to go back upstairs?" Gabriel asked.

"And leave you down here alone with who knows what? That wouldn't be fair," Lizzie said. She had a bad feeling about this. *Murder* rang in her brain.

"Very well. Hold the lantern." With a grim expression, Gabriel picked up the shovel and began to work on the dirt pile.

In a matter of moments, he hit something solid. Brushing away the dirt with his hand, he found a wooden board. Carefully shoveling the top layer of dirt, he soon uncovered a narrow plank about six feet long. Prying the board up at one end, he found it was the lid of a coffin. Inside, laid out with dignity, was a body.

He quickly shut it again.

Lizzie was at his shoulder with the lantern. "Raise the lid again. I want to make sure."

He put one hand on her shoulder. "You don't want to see. It's not a Christmas gift."

"Don't try to protect me, Gabriel. We're in this together."

He studied her face while she tried not to shiver as she held his gaze. He gave a nod and did as she asked.

She studied the well-preserved corpse with pity and curiosity. "He certainly looks like the painting of the earl upstairs." And then she had a terrible thought. "Oh, dear."

He dropped the lid in his hurry to grab her.

"I'm not going to faint," she assured him. "I just realized I came here to marry a man who is already dead. My guardian is not going to be happy about this."

"It's not your fault." In the lantern light, did she see a moment of relief on Gabriel's face?

"Nor yours," she told him. "But Lord Grambling came here to bring me to be wed and to exchange me for something. I don't know what the something is, but I can guess. You can be sure if you don't hand it over to him right away, since you inherit the title, he will be sneaking around looking for it."

"Knowing your guardian, I suspect it's an object that's worth a great deal."

"Knowing Lord Grambling, I'm sure it would be an object that is worth a vast sum of money. Enough to finally trade me for. Most of his vowels, perhaps?"

Gabriel nodded. "We'll have to check the safe. There are no papers in the case."

"What are we going to do about—him?" Lizzie asked. It didn't feel right to leave him in the cellar like this.

"I'm going to look him over and see if I can see the cause of death. Hold the lantern, please. You don't have to look," he added.

"There's never been room in my life for squeamishness. Who do you think takes care of organizing the autumn slaughter and preparing the meat for the winter?" She moved next to him and held up the lantern.

He smiled down at her. "A lady after my own heart. Let's see what we have." He lifted the coffin lid again. "He's been dressed. The head shows no wounds and very little decomposition."

"It's the cold, dry air. It preserves flesh and is great for winter foodstuffs."

"Ah!"

Pulled away from her thoughts on winter foods, Lizzie asked, "What?"

"From the front he looks dressed. But everything is open in the back. We can check him over quickly this way." He peeled the clothes back in a single motion. "No sign of gunshot or stab wound. No obvious broken bones or wounds or signs of a struggle on his hands. His body looks like he wasted away. He looks like he was frail. I've seen starved sailors who looked like this."

"He starved to death? How awful." She shivered from the thought and not the cold that was working its way through her slippers.

"Probably some sort of wasting disease. Or poison."

She came to a decision. "We're going to have to talk to Jenkins. If anyone knows what happened, he does."

"No point in waking him up at this hour. Let's leave everything and go to bed. We can talk to him first thing in the morning. But remember, if the earl died of poison, Jenkins was probably involved." Leaving the corpse's clothes disheveled, Gabriel replaced the lid.

"And if the earl was poisoned, you could be next." She wouldn't allow it. Gabriel was too caring, too brave, and too good a dancer to lose.

They tiptoed out, shutting the door quietly and sneaking up the stairs. At the door to her room, Lizzie whispered, "Good night, my lord."

He blinked and then looked at her with a shocked expression. "Oh, no." Hadn't he realized before what the death of the current earl meant?

☙❧

Lizzie came down the next morning to find Jenkins handing Gabriel a cup of coffee. "Tea, miss?" he asked.

"Thank you, Jenkins."

As he poured that for her, Lizzie said, "Gabriel, have you asked Jenkins about what we found?"

"I was waiting for you." He then turned to Jenkins. "We found the earl, we found George, in a coffin in the cellar. Care to explain?"

Lizzie wondered how he could be so calm.

"I believe you're mistaken, Mr. Waters. Your brother went to London just a few days ago."

"Leaving the jewelry in his room in a safe, but his signet ring and seal in a case in the cellar with the clothes he would have taken on a trip? A trip taken with his fiancé arriving, and Christmas just around the corner? Doesn't make any sense." Gabriel sat back, arms folded.

"If you'd care to check, I believe you won't find any coffin or your brother in the cellar." Jenkins sounded equally unruffled. Lizzie watched, amazed at both of them.

Gabriel bolted upright and dashed to the cellar, Lizzie and Jenkins following at a slower pace. The new earl had a lantern burning and was looking at the spot where they'd found the coffin the night before. All there was now was a hole in the ground.

Lizzie looked around. No other spot in the cellar appeared to be disturbed. There was no coffin, no body, nothing.

"As I was saying, Mr. Waters, your brother is on a visit to London. He should arrive in the next few days, if the weather doesn't worsen," Jenkins said.

"No. Corpses don't get up in the middle of the night and change graves. Where is George's body?" Gabriel demanded.

"I told you, he went to—"

"I saw him, too, Jenkins," Lizzie said in a quiet voice. The two men were starting to shout. "And I am not prone to hysteria."

Jenkins shook his head and walked out of the cellar.

"What do we do?" Lizzie asked.

"Search the outbuildings. Anyplace cold enough to keep a body fresh. If that doesn't work, we start to follow Jenkins and find out how he seems to know where we are all the time."

"We'll start after breakfast."

"No. We'll start now. I don't think he'll expect that." Gabriel walked to the door of the cellar. "Coming with me?"

"Yes." She was used to getting up early and beginning her work. "Let me get my boots and outerwear. I'll meet you by the garden door."

Gabriel was waiting when she came downstairs. He wore his heavy coat and boots for riding and was well muffled up. She doubted she'd be as warm as he looked. Wrapping her scarf once more around her head, she stepped outside as the footman opened the door.

"There's one of the reasons Jenkins knows where we are all the time," Lizzie said. "The footman will immediately report to Jenkins that he let us out the garden door."

"Do you feel like we're living in a household of spies?" Gabriel asked.

"With so many people begging for work since the war ended? No. I see a group of people fearful for their jobs," Lizzie said.

"Has it been that bad? I've just returned to England." Gabriel searched her face.

"Yes, it's been that bad." In truth, it had been worse. Lizzie followed Gabriel, or the new earl as she was beginning to think of him, into the barn and other outbuildings.

They had finished their search when Lizzie realized they'd missed one building. "The curing shed where they keep meat throughout the year. They should have one. Look for a structure that's partially underground."

Gabriel found the easily overlooked building, half covered in snow, behind the cowshed. The snow had been crushed by the entrance. He led the way in, lighting the lantern by the door. As Lizzie entered, shivering from the cold, she saw he was pointing at the far side of the shed—at a coffin on two trestles.

"I can't believe there are two bodies stored on these grounds," Gabriel muttered as he walked over and pried off the lid. Lizzie stepped forward and peeked over his shoulder. It was indeed the earl, her promised bridegroom.

"I think Jenkins owes us an explanation," she said.

"Why move the body? Why hide it again after we found it?" Gabriel replied.

They stared at each other, and Lizzie knew she looked as confused as Gabriel. He put an arm around her shoulders. "You're chilled, and no doubt upset to see your wedding plans thrown into disarray. Go find Jenkins and send him out here. I'll wait so we don't have any more surprises."

She nodded, feeling cold and sad that their discovery the

night before wasn't a nightmare. "I'd be happy to never have another surprise, Mr. Waters."

"Have you had a lot of surprises? Ones as gruesome as this?" He sounded curious. "And please, call me Gabriel. Anyone who goes hunting for the same corpse twice with me should call me by my Christian name."

"I'm Lizzie, Gabriel." She gave him a sorrowful smile. "I've had some sad surprises. Being told both my parents had died. The first time I walked into the home, the very slovenly home, of Lord Grambling. Discovering my legacy from my parents had gone to pay Lord Grambling's gambling debts. And now my prayed for deliverance is dead." She shook her head and tried to erase the bitterness from her tone. "I'm sorry. You don't need to be subjected to my self-pity."

"Don't be. You've already suffered enough to knock anyone low."

She looked into his eyes and saw a fellow sufferer. "You were sent away from your homeland at a young age. That had to be difficult."

He smiled grimly. "If only you knew."

"How could your father do that?" She put a hand on his shoulder.

"It wasn't..." He leaned slightly toward her as he began to speak, then stopped and straightened. "Never mind. Go get Jenkins."

She gave one last glance at the coffin, then pulled her cloak more tightly around her and hurried out into the cold. She'd taken only a few steps before she saw Jenkins rushing toward her around the corner of the cowshed.

When he saw her, he came to a halt and began to back up.

"Too late, Jenkins. Come here. The earl wants you," she called.

His shoulders slumped. Then he raised his head and walked toward her. "The earl hasn't returned from London yet, miss."

"Into the curing shed. Now." She'd learned a fierce tone worked well on men when they were in the wrong. And Jenkins certainly knew he had failed his new master.

With a sigh, acting as if he were walking toward the gallows, Jenkins plodded toward the door to the cold storage shed. He opened the door and held it for Lizzie to enter before he walked in.

"Jenkins was coming this way when I went outside," Lizzie said to Gabriel. He had set the lantern on the lid to the coffin which he had shifted so the light would illuminate both the shed and inside the coffin.

"You wanted me, Mr. Waters?" Even now, with the evidence of Jenkins' deceit in front of them, he was holding on to his illusion.

"Yes. Come over here, Jenkins. I want you to explain something to me." Gabriel's voice was low and cold.

Jenkins inched forward like a whipped dog.

"Come here, man."

Jenkins finally made it to Gabriel's side, but he didn't look at or in the coffin.

"Would you say it is possible to be in two places at once, Jenkins?" Gabriel's quiet tone was lethal.

"No, Mr. Waters."

"And we are in agreement that this is the body of the earl? The earl who is supposed to be in London?"

Jenkins glanced down at the body in the coffin and shut

his eyes as he nodded his head.

"I can't hear you, Jenkins."

"Yes, Mr. Waters. That is the body of the late earl."

"Did you poison him?" Gabriel asked.

"No!" Jenkins shook his head. "He was a gentle soul. None of the servants had anything to complain about. None of us would kill him. Why would we? Why would I?"

Lizzie believed his firm denial. "When did he die?"

"He took a turn for the worse and died the night before you arrived. We knew you were coming. We'd hoped to get him married to you, so there would be someone to inherit the unentailed properties while the crown and Parliament decide what to do with the title."

"But I didn't get here in time. So why hide his body in the basement? And once we found him, why hide him out here?" This made no sense to Lizzie. Having someone in place while the various forces decided what to do with the estates, the title, and her made good sense for the servants. But they weren't married. And now there was a legitimate heir.

So why hide the body?

"We needed time to decide what to do," Jenkins replied.

"Why, when you have a legitimate heir to take over. He isn't going to let anyone go, are you, Gabriel?" Lizzie said.

"He's not a legitimate heir," Jenkins said.

"What?" Lizzie said.

Gabriel reddened but said nothing.

"When Gabriel Waters left for the colonies, he, like every member of the Waters family, had blue eyes. Now they are brown." Jenkins turned to Gabriel. "Who are you, sir?"

Chapter Six

Lizzie looked at Gabriel, her eyes wide with shock. "Tell me this isn't true."

He wished he could. He and Gabriel—the real Gabriel Waters—had looked so much alike, except for their eye color, that the other Europeans in India and the Malay Islands were forever mistaking the two partners for each other.

When he remained silent, Lizzie turned to Jenkins. "Are you certain about this?" There was hurt in her tone.

"Everyone in the family has blue eyes. She spotted it right away."

"Who?" Lizzie was persistent. Gabriel admired it, even as he was regretting every moment of this encounter.

"Mrs. Robbins, the cook. She remembers him from the old days, before young Mr. Waters left."

Gabriel nodded. He had gambled and lost. "I could see in her expression that something was wrong. Why didn't she or you say something earlier?"

"It's not pleasant to be thrown out of your position and home at Christmas," Jenkins said with a worried frown. "And all the gentry around here now believe you are Gabriel Waters."

Lizzie faced Gabriel again. "Who are you? And where is Gabriel?"

"Gabriel Waters, the real one, is buried on Penang Island under a headstone marked Thomas Morton. We were both delirious with the fever, and when Gabriel succumbed, people assumed he was me. I don't know why. And then George Waters's letter came, asking Gabriel to come home. I read the letter while I was convalescing. Everyone expected me to go back to England. They believed I was Gabriel and my brother the earl wanted me home."

If only he could explain how close knit the two of them were. "It was eerie how much we resembled each other. How much we thought alike. And then Gabriel told me his father had a sister who ran off with a farm worker and was cut off by the family. My mother died when I was born, and I came to hope, almost believe, that she was Gabriel's aunt. That we were cousins. My father and other family members have died, so there is no one to tell me whether this is true."

"Did you think you could fool his brother?" Jenkins sounded angry.

"I didn't plan to. I came here expecting to meet George and tell him about Gabriel. Ask him for a job as a farm manager. And then I arrived and George wasn't here. I had no desire to be thrown into the street, so I kept up the pretense."

"Can you prove any of this?" Jenkins was unmoved.

"Write to the British officials in India about Waters and Morton Shipping. How two young men, called twins by all who knew them, worked hard and built up a shipping company. Best of friends. Spent years in each other's company. How when one man died, the other sold out and returned to England."

"I believe him," Lizzie said in a quiet voice.

"What did you do with the money you got from selling

the ships?" Jenkins asked.

"Your first question concerns the sale of the company? Where did you get such a clever head for business?" Gabriel responded.

"My father was a mill manager. He taught me to look at things through the lens of a businessman." Jenkins watched him carefully.

"You were lucky," Gabriel said as he crossed his arms. "My father was a tenant farmer, and when most of the family died, the estate manager sent me with a man to Bristol to work on a merchant ship. I was six."

Lizzie gasped.

"I was lucky in that the captain was a kind man. He discovered I was quick and started teaching me reading and figures. There's a lot of math that goes into sailing the right course and figuring at what price a cargo becomes worth carrying."

"How long were you with him?" Lizzie's voice was gentle, and Gabriel would have liked to curl up in the dark with only that sound for company.

But he'd learned life wasn't like that. "I was nearly twenty when we were hit by a storm. I washed up, half drowned, on Penang Island. The captain and most of the crew were lost at sea. I worked as a seaman for a year. That's how I met Gabriel."

He couldn't hide his smile. "What a stroke of luck that was. What I didn't know, he did. He taught me to read, really read, contracts, while I taught him about the value of ships and cargoes. We were the perfect partnership."

"Was he nice?" she asked.

"Yes. A real gentleman. A true friend. Honest and brave."

He felt his eyes dampen at the thought of the friend he'd lost. He blinked the tears away.

"What are we going to do?" Jenkins asked, his voice full of misery.

"For the moment, nothing. Tomorrow is Christmas, and it is impossible to carry out business until after Twelfth Night. By then, the four of us will decide on a plan," Lizzie said with assurance.

"The four of us? You don't mean to include your guardian, do you?" Jenkins sounded horrified.

"The three of us and Mrs. Robbins. She's the one who originally discovered Gabriel's—weakness. She needs to be part of whatever solution we work out," Lizzie said.

"What about your guardian?" Gabriel asked.

"Not a word to him. He'll drain this house dry to pay for his gambling if he knows there's a secret, and that will limit our choices." Lizzie gave him a big smile.

Gabriel realized he wore the same scowl as Jenkins. Lizzie was way ahead of them with some idea, and until the men knew what it was, there was no way to know if the idea was good or bad.

෴

They returned to the house and Gabriel escorted Lizzie to the dining room to have their missed breakfast. She gave a small gasp when she found her guardian sitting at the table. "I didn't expect to see you so early, my lord."

"I've been banned from the card games of the aristocracy in this two-penny town," he said, fury in his voice.

"What happened?" And how would they keep him busy and out of the way, Lizzie wondered.

"A man expected me to pay up at the end of the evening

without giving me a chance to win back my losses. I've been banned until I cover my debts." He frowned, his chin on his chest.

Lizzie picked up a cup and added tea, grateful for the warmth and normality it brought. "Have some breakfast. It will make things look brighter. And tomorrow is Christmas. Perhaps if you apologize to the man you owe, he'll forgive you in light of the season."

"Who was the man?" Gabriel asked.

"Lord Glenshaw," Lord Grambling mumbled.

"I'll keep an ear out, see if I hear anything of purpose." Gabriel seemed relaxed despite what had happened in the outbuilding. As Jenkins came in bearing the breakfast platters, he added, "Oh, good. Mrs. Robbins has done well again today, Jenkins."

"Oh, Jenkins, see to our packing. Miss Lizzie and I shall return home today," Lord Grambling said.

"What? And spend Christmas on the road? That's a terrible idea. Besides, I expect the earl to return any day," Lizzie said.

"When he gets here, we'll return. If I can't play cards here, why should I stay?" Lord Grambling said.

"But what about Christmas?" Lizzie was horrified at this turn of events. She didn't want to go anywhere. She wanted to be lady of this house. Countess of Stonebrook. With Gabriel as the earl. Freed of her guardian. That was the Christmas she desired.

"The weather hasn't been bad lately. We can celebrate Christmas on the road home." Lord Grambling rose and filled his plate from the dishes on the sideboard.

"And then have to turn right around and head back?

That's an expensive proposition," Gabriel said as Jenkins poured coffee into his cup.

"But not as boring as these Christmas balls without cards." He glanced at Lizzie as he sat down.

Lizzie rose. "No."

Lord Grambling stopped, fork halfway to his mouth. "No?" Then he boomed out, "No?"

Lizzie put food on her plate, paying no attention to what she took. She was too worried that her guardian would see her hands tremble in fear over defying him. "Tomorrow is Christmas Day. I want to go to church and feast on Mrs. Robbins' good cooking. After that, there are balls and parties almost every night through Twelfth Night, and the earl will return long before then."

"I'm leaving today, and you are going with me." Lord Grambling nodded once sharply with finality.

"You can leave. I'm staying. Lady Wallace has a poor relation, a most respectable widow, staying with her. I'll ask her to come over here and chaperone me, if you'd like. It won't be long until the earl returns and we are wed and I will no longer need a chaperone or a guardian." Lizzie saw Gabriel quirk one brow as he tried to control a smile.

"There will be no gambling anywhere tomorrow," Gabriel said as he stared at her guardian. "You might as well stay through that blessed day. And I know my brother will want to see you as well as your ward."

"Very well." Lord Grambling turned his attention back to his breakfast.

Lizzie and Gabriel exchanged a glance. That gave them two days to decide what to do about the earl.

೮೦೧೩

After breakfast, Lord Grambling decided it was warm enough to go for a walk and insisted Lizzie accompany him. She agreed willingly, and after bundling up, they set off to see the town.

As soon as they left, Gabriel called Jenkins into the dining room. "If I'm going to participate in this charade, I want to see the accounts. I want to see if the title is worth protecting, along with your jobs."

When Jenkins paled, Gabriel knew there was more to this than he'd guessed.

"The accounts. Both for the household and the estate."

"Estates, Mr. Wa—sir. There are two. I suspect neither is well managed. My lord has never had the strength to straighten out any difficulties."

"He hadn't visited either lately?"

Jenkins shook his head. "He didn't visit either as earl. That's been three years. And the old earl hadn't been to either place in at least a year before his death."

"Do you know these estates, Jenkins?"

"Yes. My father managed the mill on the larger of the two. I know most of the people there." He set his body as if expecting to take a blow, took a deep breath, and said, "The estate manager is either taking more than his due and stealing from the earl, or is so lazy that the people there are running the estate with little interference and growing rich themselves."

Gabriel knew how to read people. Now to find out if he read Jenkins correctly. "Do you know the estate manager?"

"Only from what people have told me."

"Which is he?"

Jenkins took another deep breath. "He's rumored to be a

hard and greedy man."

"If I take over the title, do you want to go there as my estate manager?"

"No, sir. I've never liked life in the country. I'd much rather work in a town."

Gabriel was surprised. An estate manager was a step up from a butler in pay and social standing. "Show me the account ledgers."

Jenkins led him to a small office in the back of the ground floor. A quick glance told Gabriel the books were up to date. "Who's been keeping these ledgers?"

"Lately I have, sir."

That answer surprised him. "Have you had bookkeeping experience?"

"For my father and others on the estate. More recently, for the earl when his man of affairs quit."

"Quit? Why?"

"The earl is—was unable to keep up with his duties. Finally, the man of affairs was so frustrated with the blatant cheating he could do nothing to stop that he quit. The earl's been in poor health for years. That's why he wrote to his brother, telling him to come home."

Gabriel nodded. "I need a bright lamp and solitude. If Lord Grambling and Lizzie ask, I've gone out. I'll join them for dinner."

By the time Gabriel finished, he realized it was full dark outside. He also realized there was clear evidence of both mismanagement and thievery. The underlying estates appeared to be valuable properties, at least as long as the old earl had been in power. Shortly after George had taken over, the slide began.

He stared at the darkened window and considered his options. He'd love to have a title and the estates to go with it, but would he be able to pull it off? The cook had spotted the deception. Who knew who else would?

The earl had been dead a few days. Surely someone would notice the changes in the body and start asking questions that could cause any plan to unravel.

And while he had experience running a shipping company, would those skills translate into the ability to run estates?

He'd need a lot of luck to pull off something this audacious. More than that, he'd have to have the complete agreement of everyone else involved in this deception or he could end up in jail.

Worse, did he want to fight hard enough to bring around these properties so they'd be profitable, if there was a possibility that they could be taken away from him?

Chapter Seven

Once out of the house with her guardian, Lizzie spent the morning visiting the shopping district and exploring the local church. She'd spoken to the vicar. She'd asked a portrait artist with a studio in town and who displayed paintings she liked to paint her portrait for the earl. She'd visited a shop that sold books and sheet music.

Despite Lord Grambling suggesting that they take a walk, after ten minutes he no longer wanted to brave the chilly air. Lizzie knew it fell to her to keep him away from the house. She was determined to learn as much as possible about the town while keeping her guardian out of the way of both Gabriel and Jenkins. She knew they had planning to do, and they had to learn to work together if any audacious plot could succeed.

Lord Grambling could turn their plans, and hers, upside down. While he'd never discover the corpse on his own, he'd tear the house apart looking for any record of his debts if he learned the earl was dead.

"I'm going to turn into a block of ice," her guardian complained for the hundredth time.

"Nonsense. Isn't that fabric lovely? May I go inside and take a look," she asked, stopping to gaze in a shop window.

"No. I'm cold, I'm tired, and I want to go back to the

house," he grumbled.

"Miss Hancock, isn't it? And Lord Grambling. How nice to see you again," the older of two ladies said as they crowded each other on the pavement.

"Lady Mercer. And Miss Mercer. I'm pleased to see you, too. I was just telling Lord Grambling that is beautiful fabric. Living in the country, I don't often have a chance to visit shops." Lizzie smiled, hoping to find a way to delay her guardian a little longer.

"But you'll soon be our neighbor and can enjoy shopping any time you like. Has the earl returned home yet?"

"He's expected at any time." His death would have to happen soon. Already a doctor would be able to tell he'd been dead a while, she guessed. Living on an estate, she knew from fishing and autumn butchering that the eyes would give away how long he'd been dead.

Hopefully Jenkins and Gabriel were now ready for the earl's arrival and demise.

"You must be lonely," Miss Mercer said. She was a pretty blonde who'd talked at length about her London season at the Christmas ball. It sounded a great deal more fun than Lizzie's had been.

"I am. But I'm glad to know I'll soon be able to count you as my neighbor." Lizzie hoped that wasn't laying it on too thick. Lord Grambling was getting louder with his grumbling.

"Why don't you return with us for tea?" Miss Mercer said, glancing at her mother.

"I'd love to. Lord Grambling, would you—?" Lizzie wasn't going to give Lady Mercer a chance to halt the invitation.

"I saw a hotel back there. I think I'll go get something to warm me up. Find out what news has come in with travelers.

I'll see you at the earl's."

He lumbered off, and Lizzie took a deep breath. It looked like the type of hotel that would have a card game discreetly tucked away inside the pub.

Lizzie turned to the two ladies. "Shall we go?" she asked with a bright smile. She planned to learn all she could about the town, those in power, and the families that held influence in the area. Who knew what might be useful in the next few days?

The two Mercer ladies pointed out every shop as they walked along, telling Lizzie which gave good value for money and which had shoddy goods. As they passed the church, they told her which pew was the earl's, and how much they hoped they'd see her at the Christmas service. Then Lizzie was treated to a description of each family as they passed houses on their way to the Mercer's.

They went into the drawing room and Lady Mercer ordered tea from the maid who took their wraps. Lizzie glanced around at the well-stuffed chairs and the patterned rug on the floor. Not as opulent as the earl's home, but the Mercers were wealthier than her guardian.

As they sat, Miss Mercer asked, "Have you heard from the earl?"

"No. I hope nothing's wrong. I'm anxious to see the earl, but I'm sure not as much as his brother is." She tried to put enough concern into her voice to plant a seed in the minds of these two ladies.

"He probably thinks he can travel as fast as any message," Lady Mercer said in a soothing tone. "Still, it's an odd time of year to travel."

"I'm sure you're right," Lizzie said with a faltering smile.

What an idiotic reply. Don't overplay your part, she warned herself.

Lady Mercer poured the tea from a lovely silver service when it arrived. "Have you known the earl for a long time?"

"We've never met. The earl knows my guardian and the two of them made all the arrangements." At least that much was true.

"Some of the most successful marriages have been arranged," Lady Mercer told her.

"Please tell me about the earl. Did you know the two brothers when they were children?"

"They were my playmates," Miss Mercer said. "George was always the paler of the two, although Gabriel is darker than I remembered."

"No doubt from being out in the jungle sun. I hear it browns the Europeans until they look like the natives," Lizzie replied. Would that be enough to divert attention from Gabriel's coloring? "What were they like as boys?"

"They were close, although Gabriel was the one protecting George, and not the older protecting the younger. I suppose this was because George was so often kept in bed with one illness or another. In fact…"

Lady Mercer interrupted her daughter. "It's true. He was a sickly child, while Gabriel was hearty like his father. And his father could never forgive Gabriel for being healthy while his mother died giving birth to him. His father was just as angry that George, the heir, nearly died twice of influenza."

"How sad, that Gabriel was not well-loved like his brother. Their father's poor treatment doesn't seem to have turned Gabriel against his brother, though," Lizzie said and then took a sip of tea. It was warm and welcome.

"Perhaps the boys both realized how incompetent their physician is," Lady Mercer said, adding more tea to her cup.

"Is?" Lizzie asked weakly. This might be too good to be true.

"Oh, Doctor Clifford isn't incompetent. He's just blind," her daughter said. "The next time the earl is sickly, call Doctor Porter. He's quite capable. And he can see."

Shortly thereafter, Lizzie thanked her hostesses as she prepared to leave. She'd learned all she thought she could when two other ladies, Lady Wallace and her penniless cousin, Miss Grace, were announced. Christmas greetings were exchanged, and then Miss Mercer said, "We've been telling Miss Hancock about the family she's marrying into."

"Has the earl returned yet?" Lady Wallace asked.

"Not yet," Lady Mercer said, "and Miss Hancock has yet to meet him."

Lady Wallace gave her thoughts on how good arranged marriages were. The conversation was going in circles. Gabriel was darker than remembered because of the tropical sun. George had always been sickly. It was a shame... On and on they went until Lizzie thought she'd scream.

"I need to get back," Lizzie said, rising from her chair. "The earl may have returned and be wondering where I am. It was so lovely of you ladies to tell me about my fiancé. I feel like I've met him already."

"Too bad you're not marrying Gabriel," Miss Mercer said. "He seems much more likely to live to an old age and produce children. George has been growing weaker for months."

"Really?"

"Oh, dear. You've grown pale. We didn't mean to frighten you," Miss Grace said.

"You might as well know the truth," Lady Mercer said.

They didn't know how very close to the truth they were. Lizzie smiled weakly and hurried away, a little faster than was seemly.

When she reached the front door, darkness was beginning to descend. Jenkins opened it for her immediately. "Has my guardian arrived yet?" she asked as she removed her hat, gloves, and cloak.

"Not yet, miss," he answered as he took her outerwear.

"He stopped in at a hotel that was certain to have a card game going," Lizzie told him. "The ladies I spoke to were aware that the earl had been sickly all his life and had become worse in the past several months."

"They, at least, will believe the earl arrived home late tonight and died shortly thereafter. Did they believe Gabriel is...the earl's brother?"

"They commented on how much darker he is and wrote it off to spending years in the tropical sun. That and how much healthier than his brother he's always been were the only two comments made about Gabriel."

"That's good." Jenkins walked away.

"Is Doctor Clifford really blind?" Lizzie asked his retreating back.

"I'm counting on it," Jenkins said. As he disappeared through the doorway that led below stairs, he called out, "Mr. Waters is in the small office in the back of the house."

Lizzie made some false starts before she found Gabriel. He looked tired and rumpled, but when he glanced up and smiled at her, her heart fluttered. She knew she wanted his ruse to succeed.

She also wanted to convince him that the only way this

would work was if he married her. She needed a husband to escape her guardian, and this imposter was the calmest, smartest, and handsomest man she had ever met.

Hopefully, someday she'd meet the real man behind the thrilling stories and not the frightened pretender watching every step.

"Looks like we're running out of oil in the lamp," Gabriel said, turning the wick up higher.

"How long have you been working here?"

"All day. The good news is the estates make money. The bad news is the earl hadn't visited them in the three years since he succeeded to the title, and others are syphoning off the profits. It'll take a big effort to get the right people in charge and to improve all the things that are going wrong." He snapped the ledger shut.

"I know you can handle it. You ran a shipping company. Estates can't be much different, besides being on land."

"Will I be allowed to?"

She saw heartache in his eyes. "This means a lot to you. Beyond the title and the money, you want this. Why?"

"I want a home. I came here hoping to obtain a position as an estate manager."

"And you will be. Just on a grand scale." She gave him a big smile. He could do this.

"Even the cook knew I wasn't Gabriel."

"The neighbors believe you are Gabriel. Just darker from spending time in the sun."

"It wouldn't change my eye color. There are paintings in the house showing me as a young boy with blue eyes."

"Paintings can disappear." A simple enough matter to hide the evidence.

He smiled at her then. "You believe we can pull this off."

He said we. Her heart soared. Then, settling down to practical matters, she said, "Yes, I know we can."

"I wonder if Jenkins would like to be our man of affairs. He's kept up the ledgers since the last man of affairs left."

"Ask him," she said. "Before the earl returns tonight."

He frowned. "If we can fool his physician."

Lizzie told him all.

Jenkins came into the room when she finished and said, "Lord Grambling has returned and is demanding his dinner."

"Is he in a foul mood?" Lizzie asked.

"Yes, miss."

"Then he must have lost at cards again. Ask Cook to send dinner up as soon as it's ready. And Jenkins, Gabriel has something to ask you."

"You said you don't want to live in the country and be an estate manager. Do you want to be a man of affairs?"

Jenkins's eyes lit up before they shuttered. "I don't have the required knowledge."

"Neither do I. We'll learn together." Gabriel held out his hand and Jenkins shook it with both of his.

"Now, we just have to have the earl arrive tonight and go to bed," Gabriel said.

"We'll take care of that, Master Gabriel."

He frowned. "Who is we? How many people in the household know about this?"

"I called in two of the footmen and swore them to secrecy before we dressed and moved the earl's body the first time."

"So, the whole household knows now." Gabriel ran his hands through his hair.

Jenkins looked him in the eye and said, "I told them their jobs depend on it. If the estates revert to the crown, they could be given to a friend of the Prince Regent. In which case, this house would be shuttered and we'd all be out on the street. Not a happy Christmas."

"Let them know that their continued silence is needed to keep their positions," Gabriel said in a grave tone.

Lizzie held up a hand when she heard a sound in the hall outside the door. Jenkins looked at her and then pulled open the door. Lord Grambling stumbled into the room.

"Were you listening at the door?" Lizzie demanded.

He tugged on the waistcoat covering his girth and said, "I thought you and the earl's brother were having a clandestine meeting. I was protecting your honor."

"Well, you won't have to protect me much longer. The earl is due to arrive home tonight. He'll be home for Christmas."

Behind her, she heard Gabriel and Jenkins make faint noises of dismay. It would be all right. She had a plan.

Chapter Eight

Dinner was a long, tense meal. Gabriel couldn't imagine why Lizzie had told her guardian about the earl's impending arrival. Grambling was now rising from his chair every time he heard noise out on the busy street. People were traveling from one house to another, wishing their neighbors a joyous Christmas or visiting family, giving him plenty of opportunities to rise.

Grambling wanted to get to the earl first. That much was clear. Gabriel was afraid his deception had been found out and Grambling wanted to use his lie as a bargaining chip to boost his own position with the earl at the expense of Gabriel's wellbeing.

The only clue Gabriel had to Lizzie's plan was her frequent refilling of Lord Grambling's wine glass. Lord Grambling, oblivious to the tension in the room, talked about the men he met at the hotel and their card game, the weather, and how soon the earl might arrive.

Lizzie played with her food more than she ate, but Gabriel found he had a good appetite. He'd not stopped going through the accounts for the estates to take time for lunch and he was hungry. Also, he felt exhilarated. Finally, for good or ill, they'd bring this to a conclusion.

Once the meal ended, Lizzie directed Jenkins to serve the

coffee and port in the drawing room away from the street. "What would you be doing on Christmas Eve if you were at your estate, Lord Grambling?" Gabriel asked, swirling the port around in the glass without drinking. He'd need a clear head for what was coming.

Grambling would need to be well foxed before the earl's appearance. Or bound and gagged, but that might raise a few questions.

He went on and on about card playing and eating for the entire Christmas season. When Gabriel glanced at Lizzie, she gave him a faint smile.

"How close is the church to your manor?" Gabriel asked.

"It's in the village. Not far if the snows don't keep us at home," Grambling told him.

"I've never missed because of snow," Lizzie said.

"I hope your brother likes a bit of piety in his women," Grambling said to Gabriel with a wink.

Gabriel felt his blood run cold. Grambling would sell Lizzie to the highest bidder. Gabriel had seen what disdain her guardian had shown that magnificent woman. Lizzie deserved better.

He hoped Lizzie would settle for an imposter like himself. She deserved better, but he wouldn't be selfless enough to find her a better man. If she'd marry him, he'd be as joyful as a child at Christmas.

"Are you going to church in the morning?" he asked her.

"Of course. I'd be happy if you would escort me," she told him.

"No, the earl should escort you. He'll be here then," Grambling said.

Lizzie paled. She must have forgotten that they were

waiting on the earl's arrival. Gabriel had, too, but fortunately no one had said anything to give them away. "My brother and I will both escort you," he told her.

"Thank you," she said, looking relieved.

Time drew on. Gabriel found a book in the library to hold his attention, or at least to hold in his hands. Lizzie went to her room and returned with her knitting. Grambling kept lowering the level of the port decanter and making boorish comments.

When Jenkins came in and took the decanter to refill it, Lizzie said "I want to give you some instruction for breakfast after church in the morning." She rose and started to follow the butler.

Grambling wordlessly held out his glass to her.

Lizzie took it and followed Jenkins out of the room. She returned a minute later and handed her guardian his refilled glass. "Jenkins will be back with the bottle in a few minutes."

By the time Jenkins returned, Grambling's glass was nearly empty and his chin was beginning to bounce off his chest.

"Perhaps you want to wait in your room, my lord, where you'll be more comfortable," the butler suggested.

"I should wait up for my host," Grambling mumbled.

"You've had a trying day. Go upstairs. I'll be there in a moment myself," Lizzie told him. "The earl is probably safely asleep in an inn along the way and we are staying up for no reason."

"You come upstairs, too." He waved his glass.

"I'll be along in a minute."

"No. Now." He swallowed the dregs in his glass and tried to stand. He made it halfway up before he fell back onto the chair.

"Jenkins, if you'll call a maid for me and some footmen to assist Lord Grambling, I think we can say goodnight."

Lizzie rose gracefully and remained standing until two footmen arrived a moment later. They helped Grambling to rise and then out of the room.

In the meantime, Gabriel was already on his feet and standing by her side. "I think the port has done its job, along with something extra," he whispered to Lizzie.

"Laudanum. Do you need me for anything else this evening?"

"No. Just get up and dress for church early for the next part of this production where you may need to be present."

A mumbled "Lizzie" echoed in from the hallway.

She nodded, a serious expression on her face. "Good luck." Then she followed her guardian out.

Gabriel sat down and idly leafed through the book as he waited for Jenkins to come and either ask him for help or tell him the earl was put to bed.

It was nearly a half hour later before Jenkins reappeared. "We're ready to bring the earl in and put him to bed."

"And Grambling?"

"Snoring fit to shake the house apart."

Gabriel nodded, rose, and followed Jenkins outdoors to where two footmen were carrying the earl out of the cold storage building. A third carried a lantern. Evergreens and outbuildings blocked the view for any neighbors who might happen to look outside.

"Up the back staircase," Jenkins told them.

They banged and thumped their way up the stairs with

the dead weight between them. Jenkins led the way with one lantern and the third footman followed behind with the other. Gabriel brought up the rear of their little funeral procession.

Jenkins stopped and looked out into the hall before he signaled the rest of them to head for the earl's room. They made it down the hall quietly, without stopping Grambling's snoring or causing him to cry out in his sleep.

Once in the earl's bedroom, the two tired footmen dropped their charge onto the turned down bed. Then Jenkins sent the footmen to their rest and gestured to Gabriel to help with the last, disagreeable task. They undressed the earl and put away the funeral clothes before pulling a nightshirt over his limp frame.

Gabriel straightened and as he did, looked at the painting on the far wall. "Blast," he murmured.

Jenkins jerked upright. "What?"

"The painting of the two boys. They both have blue eyes."

"Help me get it down. I'll hide it in the cellar."

Once the covers were in place, they tiptoed out and went down the back staircase. Jenkins went first, the painting in his arms.

After they hid the painting where the earl's body had once rested, Gabriel followed Jenkins to the drawing room, where Jenkins poured them both a stiff brandy. "He's starting to smell, even though you've kept him cold," Gabriel said.

Jenkins took a large swallow. "I think we can pull it off tomorrow morning. All of official Heverwell will want to sleep or go to church or sit down to a big meal with family. They won't spend time on more than a basic examination before they notify the crown."

"Sit down, man." Gabriel said to his conspirator. "The staff is on board with this?"

Jenkins wearily dropped into a chair. "Yes. Every one of them want this to work. They want to keep their jobs."

"And they shall if we can pull this off. We may have to employ Miss Hancock to keep her guardian out of this until the officials have come and gone." Gabriel took another sip from his brandy.

"Do you think Lord Grambling will try to block you gaining the title? Why would he?" Jenkins frowned into his snifter.

"Who knows why that man would do anything?" Gabriel shrugged and then said, "I'll head him off by asking for her hand in marriage."

"That's taking things a bit far, isn't it, my lord?"

"I want to marry her. And if it makes life simpler for all of us while we try to prove my right to the title, so much the better."

"Do you love her?" Jenkins asked.

"Why do you ask?"

The butler studied the floor. Then in a soft voice, he said, "I've grown fond of Miss Hancock in the short time that she's been here. I know her guardian won't look out for her. I feel as if I should."

Gabriel grinned. "Yes, I love her. Have no worries. She'll be my countess."

"And a fine countess she'll make, my lord."

The newest earl in the realm rose and said, "We need to get some sleep. Wake me at dawn and we'll go into the earl's bedroom together."

※※

Lizzie rose the next morning and, hearing noises in the hall, put on a wrap over her nightgown before she opened the door of the countess's room. "Happy Christmas," she greeted Gabriel and two strangers.

"Happy Christmas, Miss Hancock," Gabriel replied. "May I present Doctor White and Sir Percy Leamond, the magistrate for the city. Miss Hancock is, was, the fiancée of the earl."

"Was?" She hurried toward them, hoping she wasn't overdoing her expression of shock and dismay. She looked in to see a man-sized lump in the bed under the covers. Bringing the back of one hand to her mouth, she gasped and looked away.

"Our sympathies on the loss of your fiancé, Miss Hancock. How did he appear when he arrived home yesterday?" This man had a gentle voice and eyes that seemed to gaze at the far distance.

"It was quite late, but he said he was relieved to have arrived home before the weather turned worse. He was glad to be home for Christmas and pleased to meet me." She looked from one stranger to the other. "We'd not met before. My guardian arranged the marriage. We talked for just a few moments. Then he said he was chilled and needed to lie down and we'd talk more in the morning."

"And where is your guardian?" The other man's tone was gruff.

"Still asleep, I'd imagine. He had quite a bit of port last night."

"Have the butler wake him," gruff voice said to Gabriel.

"Lord Grambling, my guardian, didn't see the earl last

night. He'd already been helped to bed," Lizzie said, putting on her most innocent expression.

"Who saw the earl return home?" the man seemed annoyed, although that might have been from being woken early on Christmas morning.

"Just myself, Miss Hancock, Jenkins, the butler, and the groom who took care of the carriage horses," Gabriel told the two men. "As I said, Sir Percy, it was quite late."

"Who removed the painting?" Sir Percy asked, pointing to the empty spot on the wall where the wallpaper was brighter.

Lizzie saw a flash of panic in Gabriel's eyes and grabbed for the first explanation she could think of. "Jenkins told me the earl had it removed before he left. He-he wanted to have my portrait painted when I arrived and hung where he would see it first thing every morning." She warmed to her tale. "It was such a romantic gesture." Lizzie glanced at Gabriel. From the look of relief in his eyes, she guessed she was doing well.

Sir Percy turned to Gabriel. "I shall send word to Westminster of the earl's death. You are Lord Stonebrook now, my lord. Get that body coffined as soon as possible. He's beginning to smell already. Died of a wasting disease, did he, White?"

"Yes. Most sad."

"I'd thought I'd have more time with my brother. Life's nothing like what we plan, is it, gentlemen?" Gabriel said as he ushered both men toward the stairs.

Lizzie rushed back to her room and dressed hurriedly. She ran down the front staircase still pinning up her hair to say good bye to the two officials. They bowed. She curtsied.

They said a few more words to Gabriel and then were gone, Jenkins shutting the door behind them.

"Jenkins."

"Yes, my lord?"

Gabriel grinned at the formal response. "Could you please have my brother's body coffined and stored in the cold storage building until it can be properly buried in the spring?"

"I'll see to it." Then in a quiet voice Jenkins said, "Is that it? Have we passed all the hurdles?"

"I hope so," Gabriel said.

At that moment, there was hammering on the front door. Lizzie looked from one man to the other and found she was holding her breath.

Jenkins straightened his spine and opened the door. "Yes?"

"Where's Grambling?" a man demanded, forcing his way in. "He owes me money." Then he paused and said, "This is the Earl of Stonebrook's house, isn't it? I knew the family once."

Chapter Nine

"I'm afraid, sir, you'll find Lord Grambling owes everybody money," Lizzie said, deliberately ignoring the rest of his words. "Could you have someone wake him, Jenkins, and tell him to get dressed and come downstairs immediately?"

"Are you Lady Stonebrook?" the man asked.

"And you are?" Lizzie asked, not wanting to answer his question.

"Miles Penderidge, third son of the earl of Hoping," he said with a bow.

"Were you in the card game at the hotel yesterday?" Lizzie asked. He spoke like an aristocrat, but his clothes were limp and worn in spots like a traveler down on his luck. "Jenkins, could you have coffee served to Mr. Penderidge and Mr. Waters and myself?"

"You know about the card game?" Penderidge looked sheepish.

"It was an easy guess," Lizzie said.

The stranger then turned to Gabriel. "Mr. Waters? Gabriel Waters? Is that you? Last time I heard, you were in the East."

"My brother wrote me to come home. And not a moment too soon."

"Is something amiss besides having Grambling under your roof?" Penderidge asked.

"My brother, the Earl of Stonebrook, died in the night." Gabriel sounded stunned by the loss, although Lizzie suspected he was more upset by the arrival of a person who knew him.

"Good grief. You're the earl now?"

Gabriel nodded.

"My condolences on losing both your father and brother."

"Thank you."

"Your father must be spinning in his grave." Penderidge laughed.

"If only you knew," Gabriel said with a dry grin. Lizzie could tell he was worried, not knowing who this man had been to the real Gabriel.

"You must come in, have some coffee, and tell me all about Gabriel as a boy," Lizzie said, while Jenkins helped to remove his outerwear.

"We were in the same boarding school near Banbury for two years. The next year, Gabriel didn't return. What was that about? Fall afoul of the pater?"

Gabriel nodded. "Something like that."

Lizzie asked the stranger, "How old were you when you two were in school together?"

"Twelve or thirteen. We were in the same room in the dormitory. Gabriel, me, Honeycutt, and Thackery. We got into scrapes almost daily. Do you remember putting the frog in the soup?"

"It needed more meat," Gabriel said.

"That was Thackery's reasoning. He got an extra

slippering for saying that," Penderidge said.

"I recall." Gabriel's smile was weaker than Lizzie was used to seeing.

"Where did you go next?" Penderidge asked.

"A monastery."

"You're kidding." Penderidge's surprise hung in the air while Lizzie suggested to the men that they move to the dining room and to Jenkins that he bring up coffee and the breakfast platters.

Once they were seated at the table, Gabriel held his coffee cup in his hands as if savoring the heat. "I wish I was joking. I spent two years there. I got a good education, but it showed me how much I like warm fires and warmer blankets. Living in the East for several years finally thawed me out."

"The East was all right? Even during the war?"

"Yes. What did you do during the fight with Napoleon, Penderidge?"

"Served in the cavalry with Thackery." His voice became muffled. "Saw him die."

The two men stared at each other in silence until Gabriel looked down.

"Hey." Penderidge scowled as he peered closely at Gabriel. "I thought you had blue eyes."

Lizzie held her breath.

Gabriel shook his head. "No. Brown. Thackery's were blue."

"I remember that. But I remember yours were blue too."

"Show's how tricky a memory can be. I was always the dark horse of the family," Gabriel said. "So why are you in Heverwell for Christmas?"

"Avoiding my father. He wants me to become a solicitor. All I want is to manage an estate. Live in the country. Spend my days outdoors. My time in the cavalry showed me I was best suited for a farming life. Dealing with the weather."

Lizzie watched as Jenkins simultaneously carried in a breakfast platter and caught Gabriel's eye. She waited as staff carried in the rest of the platters and Gabriel and Penderidge helped themselves. What was going on? Did it concern her guardian? She hoped she hadn't given him too much laudanum.

She put a little on her plate, not having an appetite while she wasn't sure what would happen next. The two men, she noticed, tucked in like schoolboys.

"Will you still be here after Twelfth Night?" Gabriel asked the shabby looking aristocrat.

"Depends on the weather and my finances. Why?" Penderidge replied.

Before Gabriel could reply, Lord Grambling walked in, bleary eyed and disheveled. "Good mor—oh, it's you."

Penderidge set down his fork. "Yes. I believe you forgot to pay me what you owe from yesterday."

"It's Christmas. Can't this wait until tomorrow? I have such a headache. Coffee," Lord Grambling growled as he dropped into the closest empty chair.

Lizzie quickly poured a cup and passed it to him. She felt guilty, but at least she hadn't overdosed him.

"We need to discuss business," Gabriel said, "especially since I am the new Earl of Stonebrook."

"What?" Lord Grambling's hand shook, spilling coffee over the rim of the cup.

"My brother died in the night."

"Where?" Lord Grambling demanded.

"In his bed."

Lord Grambling rose so abruptly he knocked over his chair. "Impossible. I want to see him."

Jenkins neatly blocked his way as he spoke to Gabriel. "Excuse me, my lord, but the late Lord Stonebrook is in his coffin in the cold room out back until the thaw so we can bury him properly. The sheets and mattress are currently being burned, per your request."

"Very good, Jenkins. What time does the Christmas service start?"

"In a half hour, my lord."

"Then I suggest we eat up and head to church on this blessed morning. I'll speak to the vicar about prayers for my brother after the service. Will you join us, Penderidge?"

"I'd be glad to, my lord." It was clear to Lizzie that Penderidge hoped to keep Grambling in his sights.

"Grambling?" Gabriel put the weight of his new position into his tone.

"I don't feel well this morning." He was pale and kept squinting his eyes as if his head hurt.

"All the more reason for you to be in church," Lizzie said when no one else refuted his words. He didn't need to be alone here snooping around while everyone else was gone.

"Women," he snapped.

"Are usually right," Gabriel said. "Jenkins, have one of the footmen tidy up Lord Grambling."

"Of course, my lord."

Lord Grambling only managed another sip of coffee before a muscular footman came in and assisted him out of the room despite his protests.

"If you gentlemen will excuse me, I need to freshen up and get my prayer book." Lizzie rose from the table and the men rose with her. She hurried away and met Gabriel and Penderidge twenty minutes later by the front door.

"Where's your guardian?" Gabriel asked with an aggrieved sigh.

"You two aren't wed?" Penderidge said with dawning understanding.

"I was the late earl's fiancé. As of this morning, I suppose I'm a houseguest." And once more subject to the whims of Lord Grambling. She turned to Gabriel. "I heard my guardian arguing with one of the servants when I came down."

"He's going to make us late," he grumbled in reply.

She gave him a bright smile. "No, he won't. I had a word with Jenkins, and we really have another fifteen minutes. I've grown used to Lord Grambling always being tardy. He'll be down here shortly."

They all turned to the staircase when they heard plodding footsteps. "I suppose it's too late for church. How about a hand or two of cards before dinner?"

Lizzie couldn't hide her smile. "We have plenty of time to walk to church. It'll do you a world of good." After the footman helped Lord Grambling on with his coat and hat, Lizzie linked her arm with his and headed him out the door.

Gabriel and Penderidge followed them along the frosty streets to the church, the servants all trailing behind. To Lizzie, it sounded like the bells of a hundred churches were pealing in the crisp, clean air of Christmas morning. The reins of every passing carriage had small bells attached, and they added to the merriment of dozens of voices greeting their neighbors.

When they reached the church, it was obvious word of the earl's passing was spreading through the congregation. Men weighed down by fur and dignity came up to Gabriel and spoke consoling sentiments. Women she'd met at the ball came up to Lizzie and commiserated with her on losing her fiancé. A few of the braver women glanced at Gabriel and said, "There's still an earl. Perhaps this will work out well for you in the end."

Her thoughts exactly, although she couldn't admit it. Yet.

To all words of sympathy, Lizzie said, "It is such a tragedy. He only arrived home last night, so we had little time to get to know each other. He was looking forward to spending Christmas at home with his brother and me. And now he's been cheated out of it."

Lady Mercer said, "You didn't know him well, so you won't grieve him much. Look to the future, child."

Lizzie almost wondered if Lady Mercer could read her mind. But it was a shame that no one seemed to mourn the late earl. She would try, even though she'd never met him and it was mere chance that their paths had crossed at all.

Her guardian came up to her in the snowy church yard. "You have to convince Gabriel to marry you," he muttered in her ear. "He has the title now, and he owns the majority of my gambling vowels which are hidden in the earl's room. Or his study. I need to get them back."

"How much are they for?" Lizzie asked.

Instead of brushing her questions away, for once her guardian told her. It was a fortune. "You can never repay that."

"You were the price with the former earl. Perhaps you can be once again with this new earl."

Lord Grambling wasn't looking at Lizzie. Otherwise, she was certain he would have seen what she thought of him. Determined to hide her feelings, she walked away.

The service was joyful, with the congregation joining the choir in familiar hymns. The building smelled of beeswax and fir, although it was nearly as cold inside as out. And once the service was over and the crowd made their way outside to spirited cries of "Happy Christmas," Lizzie found herself warmed by good wishes and genuine sympathy for her unenviable position.

Gabriel slipped next to her in the throng. "I think I have the perfect solution for Penderidge, but first we need to get rid of your guardian. And to do that, we need to get married."

When she turned her head to look into his eyes, he continued, "This isn't much of a proposal, Lizzie, and I'm not getting down on one knee in the snow, but will you marry me?"

It was now or never to put their partnership on a good footing. "Will you always treat me with honesty and fairness?"

"Honesty, fairness, and love." His expression was somber.

"It will still take us three weeks for reading the banns. Three weeks Lord Grambling will be with us." Could she put up with her guardian that long?

"No, it won't. Jenkins said George obtained a special license a couple of weeks ago. It only says G. Waters, Earl of Stonebrook. Now, that is me. We could marry tomorrow if you and the vicar are willing."

Her smile should have lit up the churchyard. "I'm willing."

His eyes glowed with excitement. "Is that a yes?"

She squeezed his hand. "Yes."

"Come on," he said, pulling her along against the tide of parishioners. They found the vicar by the church door. After he said there would be a special prayer service for George, Lord Stonebrook in the church before vespers, he immediately agreed on the next day at eleven for the wedding, provided Gabriel produced the special license.

Frightened, Lizzie hoped Gabriel was could find it.

They met up with Lord Grambling, Penderidge, and a few of the neighbors as they walked back to Stonebrook House. The neighbors greeted Gabriel with the respect due a peer, giving him words of comfort on the loss of his brother. Lord Grambling jerked Lizzie to one side away from the knot of people.

"I want my vowels from Lord Stonebrook, whichever one he might be."

Lizzie told him in a murmur what they had decided with the vicar. "You'll get your vowels. Be content."

"I will be when I get them and get out of this town." He dropped her arm and stomped off toward the house.

Penderidge waited for Lizzie to catch up, and the two entered the house together. At that moment, Gabriel came down the stairs and told Jenkins and Penderidge about the church service that evening and the wedding the next day.

"We'll decorate and fix a wedding feast," Jenkins said.

"With the last earl just dead? No, we'll do something small for just the wedding party and delicacies for the servants' hall." She couldn't see celebrating when the man she was supposed to marry lay in a coffin in a storeroom.

"Are you sure? It's Christmas, Lizzie, and our wedding,"

Gabriel said. "I want to make you happy."

"Next Christmas, we will have a ball and a celebration. This Christmas is too soon. Too close to George's death," Lizzie shook her head.

Gabriel took her hand in a strong but gentle grip. "You're right. We should have a quiet wedding. And a very happy marriage. You'll be content?"

Lizzie smiled. "Yes, but right now, let's have a joyous Christmas dinner." She led the way into the dining room, followed by Lord Grambling, Penderidge and Gabriel.

Once they were seated, toasted Christmas, and Gabriel carved the roast, he said, "Each of us came here looking for something. As it is Christmas, I will try to give us each what we've wanted this yuletide that brought us together."

"What about you, Gabriel?" Lizzie asked.

"Even me, but I'll get to that last."

Chapter Ten

Gabriel eyed Grambling. "You, Lord Grambling. What would you like most for Christmas?"

He looked around the table. "Why, to see my lovely ward married."

"Why to my brother? Why not someone closer to your home so you could see her more often?"

"He saw a miniature of her and asked for her hand in marriage." Grambling turned his attention to his meal.

Gabriel had been ignored by better men but never at his table. "When was this?"

"I don't see a need to answer all these questions."

"Was it perhaps at a card game?" Gabriel tossed Grambling's betting markers on the table where he could see them.

As his eyes widened, Grambling reached for the papers, but he was too slow. Gabriel snatched them back in his fist.

Lord Grambling looked up, swallowed, and then smiled. "Why yes, I believe it was."

Gabriel tapped the edge of the papers on the table. "You believe it was?"

"Yes," Grambling said, defiance in his tone. "All right. It was."

"Tomorrow at noon after the wedding, you will leave

here and ride home in your carriage. If I never hear from you again, you will never be bothered by these vowels." Gabriel stared hard at the pudgy dandy.

Grambling appeared to wilt under Gabriel's gaze. Finally, he nodded.

"Wait a minute, Waters. He owes me, too. Money I can ill afford to ignore," Penderidge said, leaning forward as he looked from one man to the other.

"I have a choice for you, Penderidge, after dinner. For now, please enjoy our feast." Gabriel smiled and then turned to Lizzie. He'd been gambling since he arrived at Heverwell, and he'd been lucky. He prayed his luck held.

"You said you'd make me your countess. That is the best Christmas surprise I could hope for." Lizzie gazed at him with love in her eyes.

Love he willingly returned. He pulled out the paper with the archbishop's seal from his jacket. "Here is the special license. We shall be wed at eleven tomorrow morning here in the parish church."

"I shall be ready, my lord," Lizzie said.

"I am to see her wed and then leave immediately?" Grambling asked. "What if the weather is bad?"

"You'd better hope it's clear or your vowels won't be quickly forgotten." Gabriel had taken his measure and would bet that Grambling was a man who lived for two things: gambling and his own comfort.

The meal continued in near silence. Grambling shoveled food in as if storing it up for the travels ahead, and Penderidge ate with a puzzled frown. Gabriel could hear his mind running through possibilities.

Lizzie started conversation again by asking Penderidge

what part of the country he came from. He was soon telling them about the country estate in Lancastershire where he'd grown up, the youngest of three mischievous boys.

"Is your oldest brother now earl?" Gabriel asked.

"Yes."

"My condolences on the death of your father."

"Thank you."

"And your other brother?"

"Still in the navy, captaining his own squadron."

"You didn't want to stay in the army?" Lizzie asked him.

"No. I went home. My brother was earl, so I asked him to take me on as estate manager. I have the book learning for the job and love the work. Physicking animals, finding the best mix of crops, keeping up the workers' cottages while turning a profit." His eyes glowed as he talked of what he wanted for his home estate. Then his face fell as he added, "My brother found the thought too embarrassing."

"You never wanted to go into law or medicine or the clergy?" Gabriel asked. He knew that was where younger sons often went. His business partner, the real Gabriel, had spoken of where he might have ended up many times.

"No. It's a curse being born a younger son. I should have been born a farmer," he grumbled. Then he looked around the table and said, "Who am I to complain when I'm at the table of an old friend enjoying the bounty of Christmas?"

"And we're honored to have you," Lizzie said.

After they finished the meal, they went into the music room where Lizzie was encouraged to show off her talent on the pianoforte. Neighbors dropped by to give their Christmas wishes to the new earl.

Gabriel took all their greetings gravely, looking for a sign someone knew his terrible secret. Everyone appeared convinced he was Gabriel Waters, Earl of Stonebrook.

Pulling this off would be the second greatest miracle of this and every other Christmas. He was not deserving, but he'd take it. And in the spirit of Christmas, he'd do well by others.

Several of the neighbors joined them at the church for the prayer service where all thoughts were on the late earl. Gabriel gave leave for all the servants to come to the service, and he suspected that those who knew the truth gave thanks that their gamble would allow them to keep their positions.

ಸಂಟ

Late that evening, Gabriel met Penderidge in his study. "I have a proposition for you. I'll either pay you what Grambling owes you or make you my new estate manager."

As a joyous light shone in Penderidge's eyes, Gabriel held up a hand and added, "It will be a tough task. There are two estates, both badly run. I'll have to throw out the old manager who was either lining his pockets or too lazy to do a decent job."

"I've always liked a challenge. And I imagine the job comes with a nice cottage?"

"It should. We won't see it until the roads improve a little."

Penderidge held out his hand. "We'll see the estate together."

As they shook hands, he added, "I appreciate you taking a chance on me. Especially as I remembered the color of your eyes wrong."

Gabriel grinned, even as he knew Miles Penderidge was letting him know he knew the truth. "Nothing wrong with making a mistake, as long as you don't repeat it."

"Never," Penderidge said. "We both have what we truly want."

As Penderidge left the room, Jenkins came in. "Shall I close up in here?"

"Not just yet. Are you ready to take on the position of man of affairs for me? You will need to be discreet about everything that has or will happen under this roof. And in the spring, you'll travel with Penderidge, who'll be my new estate manager, and me to take stock of the land, the buildings, and the people on the estates. This will be a large undertaking. Are you prepared?"

For the second time in a few minutes, Gabriel shook on what would become a lifelong agreement with loyalty on both sides.

※

The wedding the next morning was everything Lizzie wanted. Not because it was elaborate or attended by the mighty, which it wasn't, but because she was now married to a man she trusted. A man with a sense of humor and a generous streak.

And because her guardian was being packed off and sent on his way.

Gabriel had asked Lord and Lady Wallace to witness the ceremony along with Penderidge, and they were pleased to perform this function. Now they had gone home, Penderidge had discreetly taken himself off to the inn for a day or two, and once the servants had served the wedding breakfast, they disappeared below stairs.

"Lizzie, are you satisfied with our bargain? I'm not upstanding or noble like George," Gabriel asked, reaching for her hand.

"Very satisfied, Gabriel. You must believe me. You are every bit as noble and upstanding as I hoped George would be."

"You know what I mean." He kept his head down, but he clung to her like a drowning man to a raft.

"Yes, and you're wrong. It doesn't matter where you were born in this situation, but who you are now and how you act."

"How well I can act."

She made her voice hard. "Are you going to admit everything to everybody?"

He jerked his head up and stared into her face. "No. That would not only mean ruin for me, but for you."

"Then forevermore, you are Gabriel Waters, Earl of Stonebrook. Hold that to your very soul and never let it go." She knew if he could make himself believe it, everyone else would too.

"I wonder what Gabriel would have thought of this?"

"What was he like?" she asked as she squeezed his hand.

He stared off into the distance. "He cared about people—me, the crew, the people in the harbor. And he had a wonderful laugh."

"He sounds like you."

"We were very much alike."

"And by taking care of me, Penderidge, Jenkins, and the servants, you are doing what he'd want done. Don't worry about it anymore."

"What if someday, someone comes along who knows. What if all of this is taken away?" He looked panicked.

"The longer we go on as Lord and Lady Stonebrook, the

less likely anyone will be able to come along and prove anything." Still holding his hand, she used her other hand to stroke his face. "And I have a bit of insurance. I spoke to a portrait painter in town the day before Christmas about painting my portrait. I could ask him to repaint your eyes in the portrait of the two boys."

"What reason could you give?"

"Your father was angry with you for causing your mother's death in childbirth. He never forgave you, and he always tried to make you into a different person. One he could love. That seems suitably romantic to tell a painter, don't you think?"

Gabriel chuckled. "You think of everything. And I have a perfect place to hang your portrait when it is finished. In the front parlor where everyone can gaze at your beauty."

Her tone was serious. "If this doesn't work, and it all falls apart someday, we'll still have each other."

"You'd stick by me?" He stared into her eyes.

"Yes. Will you stand by me?"

"Of course. I love you."

"I love you. I love your intelligence, your sympathy for other people, your wonderful laugh. I love you, Gabriel. And I am sure you'll go on doing good things for your tenants and your servants and everyone you meet for the rest of your life. No woman could ask for more than to be loved by a man like you."

He grinned. "And if I go wrong, I know you'll set me on the right course."

She smiled back, her heart overflowing with love. "Count on it, my lord."

"Then I, as Gabriel Waters, have gambled everything I

have and now want to claim my Christmas winnings from you, my lady wife." He pulled her into his arms and gave her a long, cherishing kiss that sealed their two hearts together for eternity.

About Kate

Kate Parker considers herself the most fortunate of people, with a loving family and a profession she adores. After many years of commuting in horrible traffic, she now only needs to walk across the house to her office to begin a new day plotting murder and mayhem. After work she simply has to remember not to poison anyone with dinner. That part is easy - it's the unburned and tasty part she has trouble with.

This past year, Kate began a new series, the Milliner Mysteries, with *The Killing at Kaldaire House*. A young milliner in Edwardian London, Emily, is trying to raise the money to send her younger, deaf brother to school. When her aristocratic customers don't pay her for their hats, she uses the skills taught her by her father's larcenous family to encourage them to honor their debts — with disastrous results.

Next up will be the fourth in the Deadly Series, *Deadly Deception*, in which our intrepid reporter, Olivia, finds herself caught between rival spies as Hitler menaces Europe.

Follow Kate and her deadly examination of history at:

http://www.KateParkerbooks.com

http://www.facebook.com/Author.Kate.Parker

http://www.bookbub.com/profile/kate-parker

The Gnome and the Christmas Star

by

Hannah Meredith

Chapter One

London
November 1809

Sophia, the Dowager Viscountess Lyndon, knew the minute her stepson Henry put the pieces together. The look of anger on his face was unmistakable.

She stifled a sigh, seeing all her careful preparations coming to naught. She'd chosen the small dining room for its friendly ambiance and had the leaves removed from the table so the three of them could have a convivial discussion. She'd chosen Henry's favorite wine. And she'd devised a clever menu that didn't require cutting anything into bite-sized pieces. But they'd only gotten to the fish course, and now the bulk of the dinner might never be served. She hoped Henry didn't go stomping out of the room like a child, as he was lately wont to do.

"I thought this was supposed to be a family dinner." Henry placed his fork on his plate with a decisive clink. "But I see now that it is an ambush."

"Ambush might be a bit harsh," said Alexander, Henry's oldest brother, the present Viscount Lyndon, and Sophia's co-conspirator. Alexander, bless him for good intentions, sounded a bit too hearty.

Henry shook his head in negation. "Harsh, perhaps, but undoubtedly true. I can see you two are going to start picking at me again to *get on with my life*." Uncomfortably, Sophia silently acknowledged that the last emphasized phrase did seem awfully familiar. Henry then turned to glare directly at her. "Fee, you're the one I'm most disappointed with. I thought you'd given up trying to fix everything that isn't perfect in our family. Well, *I'm* imperfect, and that's the end of it!"

Henry threw his napkin on the table and placed his hand next to it in the process of rising. Sophia covered his hand with her own.

"Henry, sit!" She used the tone she'd honed rapier sharp when he was in his rebellious teens and which, on occasion, still seemed to work. "Alexander has come up with an interesting idea. You need to hear it, and if it doesn't fit your needs, you may continue to..." wallow in self-pity would be the truth, but to say this would simply make Henry withdraw further into himself, so she amended her first thought to... "investigate other possibilities."

To her relief, Henry subsided into his chair, and she nodded at Alexander to continue.

"Commons," Alexander said with an emphatic nod. "You should stand as a Member of Parliament." He held out his hands to forestall any comments. "While you were studying at Grey's Inn, you often complained about the stupidity of many of the current laws, and you've had some scathing things to say about the focus of the current war since your return from the Peninsula, so a seat in the House of Commons should appeal to you."

Alexander's pronouncement was met by an uncomfortable silence. Then Henry made an odd, choking sound. Sophia clutched his hand in alarm. Good heavens, was he crying? Henry had been sullen and angry and self-pitying, but she had never seen him cry. Alexander's idea had seemed like such a good one. They had hoped to give Henry some direction for his future, not upset him.

Then the sound changed, and she recognized it as laughter. Laughter? The plan she and Alexander had arrived at with such hope was to be met with derision? Irritation threatened to force out any sympathy she'd felt.

"I have no doubt I'd make a better MP than the majority who pretend to govern," Henry got out between chuckles, "but as I recall, you have to run for a seat, and I can't imagine the voters would find me appealing."

"I have no idea why you think that." Even piqued with his behavior, Sophia rose to Henry's defense, just as she'd been doing since she married his father when Henry was nine and needed an advocate. Alexander and the middle brother, Ralph, had already been men grown with families of their own, but Henry had still been a boy in need of love and guidance. The ten years difference in their ages wasn't enough for Sophia to feel motherly, but Henry had become the beloved younger brother she'd never had. She'd often stood between him and his father's wrath.

"You've been trained in the law and are a war hero," she said with conviction. "There isn't a constituency in the entire country that would not be glad to support you."

He turned his hand over and gave hers a quick squeeze. "Oh, Fee, how I love you. But Alexander can tell you that political campaigning is a cutthroat business. It isn't as if we control a nomination borough where I would be unopposed, and anyone running against me would be quick to point out that I left the Inns of Court before I completed my studies. As for being a war hero—I was in Portugal for all of three weeks and fought in two battles before leaving most of my left arm in Vimeiro and coming home."

"Being admitted to the bar does not indicate your understanding of British law and length of time fighting does not a hero make," she countered.

Henry gave her a weak smile. "While we got away with acting as if it was father's gout rather than his confusion that kept him in Somerset for the ten years before his death, I don't think we can pretend I'm anyone other than a man who can't put on his own boots or cut his own meat."

"You lost your arm, not your wits. And your wits are what voters care about." Sophia insisted Henry look realistically at what he had to offer. Oh, she knew his enthusiasms to be changeable. He'd been adamant about becoming a barrister and then after years of study, had suddenly been consumed with buying a commission and becoming a soldier. But she felt Henry just needed to find his passion, and she thought Alexander had come up with a future that would hold Henry's interest.

"I still doubt I have a chance to be elected, if and when the next general election takes place." That Henry said this pensively gave Sophia hope that he was indeed considering this path.

"What if I knew of someone who controls a pocket borough that will soon have a by-election—and this person is willing to meet with you and see if you're philosophically compatible?" Alexander asked, looking rather smug.

Sophia and Henry both swiveled toward Alexander like moored boats caught in a strong current. "You never mentioned such an opportunity," Sophia said.

Simultaneously, Henry asked, "Where?"

"Northumberland," Alexander answered.

"Who's the sponsor?" Henry's apparent interest pleased Sophia.

"The Earl of Marle."

"Bloody Hell!" Henry immediately looked embarrassed by his oath. "I apologize, Fee, but the Gnome of the North..."

"Is a political power to be reckoned with," Alexander supplied. "He controls nine pocket boroughs and influences the political ideas of MPs from a dozen more."

"But to be tied to a gnome who's all wizened and hunchback—"

"He doesn't look like that," Sophia said quickly. "You're describing a caricature from political cartoons."

"You've met the Earl of Marle?" Alexander looked skeptical. "He hasn't been to London for years."

Sophia laughed. "And until I bought this house last year, neither had I. My acquaintance with the Earl of Marle was brief and in the past. I met the earl the year of my come-out, 1791. He had just made his maiden speech in the House of Lords and was invited everywhere. I found him..." charming came to mind, but she chose, "nice."

What she most distinctly remembered was that the earl had kind eyes. He'd been older than she was and married, but in the anxiety laden atmosphere of her introduction to society, the memory of his intrinsic kindness had lingered.

"He's not misshapen and dwarfish?" Henry asked.

Sophia remembered thinking the Earl of Marle was quite

handsome, but that wasn't something a woman of thirty-seven admitted to her stepsons. "Well, nearly twenty years ago the earl was perfectly normal looking. Not terribly tall, maybe a few inches over my height, but on the whole, pleasing in appearance. I think all else is legend and imagination, since he has eschewed society and stays in the north."

Then the oddness of Alexander's knowing about this specific parliamentary vacancy hit her. "Since the man is a recluse, how are you in contact with the Earl of Marle?" she asked.

Alexander looked uncomfortable. "When I took my seat in Lords after Father died, I was surprised to get a note of congratulation from him. We were both at Eton at the same time, although he was a couple of years behind me, and I really didn't know him well. But I must admit I was flattered that someone who was known to be so politically astute had taken note of my maiden speech. We've continued to correspond. I've kept him abreast of the prevailing attitudes in the House of Lords and he's given me some helpful suggestions. At any rate, when I heard of the borough vacancy and upcoming by-election, I suggested Henry, and the earl said he'd like to meet him." Alexander grinned as if he'd explained all.

"How and when is this meeting supposed to take place?" Henry asked.

"Well, the earl would like you to present yourself at Norsham Castle the second week in December. There will be a large gathering then, a house party, if you will. Most of those present will be involved in politics. You would stay about a week and then everyone will leave to enjoy

Christmas with their respective families. The earl did mention something about your remaining in residence if—"

"Wait! I'm supposed to travel to Northumberland in December?" Henry's face exhibited horror at the thought.

Sophia tended to agree with his reaction. She could think of nothing worse than traveling nearly to the Scottish border in winter. But this also might be Henry's best chance to discover a vocation at which he could excel. He needed to find his life's work. Something that allowed him to see that there was fulfillment available for a man with one arm.

"Yes, it's a long journey," she said, "but it's not too far considering what might come from this visit. It would take about what, a week to get there?

Alexander nodded. "That would be my guess. The Royal Mail can make it in two days—although going by mail coach would not be particularly comfortable. Instead, you can use my new traveling coach, which is very well sprung. You'd be on the Great North Road for all but the last few miles, so you'd have excellent inns all along the way. All in all, it should be a pleasant trip."

"The north of England in December? This sounds *pleasant* to you?" Henry's incredulity dripped from every word.

"Henry, you need to weigh what might be a slight discomfort against what such a trip could mean to you. *If* you think being an MP is something you would do well and *if* you want to pursue the idea, then you couldn't do any better than have the Earl of Marle as a sponsor." When Henry looked thoughtful but still unconvinced, Sophia added, "If I were in the position to effect change in this country, I'd certainly be willing to take such a trip."

"See, Sophia is willing to go with you. And you'd be doing her a favor by taking her to an interesting house party during this boring part of the year." Although he spoke to Henry, Alexander beamed at her as if she'd saved the day.

Sophia, however, was trying to quickly review the conversation to discover at what point she'd agreed to go on this trip. Which was never. Alexander had purposefully misconstrued her comment. She was *not* willing to spend a miserable week going to Northumberland and another miserable week returning. Not to mention what a *political* house party would be like. Dear Heavens. It had been years since she'd attended any sort of house party. What if she put her foot wrong and hindered Henry's chances at finding preferment?

But she kept her seat and smiled back at both of her stepsons as if she really wanted to trek to the north. She owed a debt to their father and felt it would not be repaid until all three of his sons were comfortably situated in life. Henry was the last to be settled. Once she'd accomplished this task, she could get on with the rest of her own life.

"Fee, would you really be willing to go to Northumberland with me?" Henry's hopeful look eliminated anything other than a positive response.

"Of course," she said. "It would be an adventure. I've never had the opportunity to travel any distance, and I've certainly never been to Northumberland. I look forward to going with you... if this is something you'd want to do. Neither Alexander nor I want to force you into something that is not to your liking."

Henry sat immobile for a long minute, his attention seemingly turned inward. Then he smiled and his shoulders relaxed. "I think I want to do this." The smile he turned on Sophia was an expression she'd not seen since before he'd left for Portugal.

"Wonderful," Alexander said. "I'm pleased you want to take advantage of this opportunity. And Sophia, I hope you too see this as an opportunity to meet some new people and to visit a section of the country you've never seen." He beamed at both of them, as well he should. They'd both fallen in with what he'd planned.

Sophia suspected she had been manipulated along with Henry. She was somehow set to embark on a trip she'd had no intention of taking. And Alexander seemed delighted with the fact.

The next day, her suspicions were reinforced. A large box was delivered with a note from Alexander that said, *For your journey.* Inside was a soft wool cape lined with fox. It was an expensive gift and one that could not be ordered overnight. When Sophia tried it on, it fit perfectly.

Chapter Two

Northumberland
December 1809

Duncan Ashe, the eighth Earl of Marle, leaned back in his chair, luxuriated in the heat of a well-drawing fireplace, and enjoyed the blessed sound of silence. He would grant himself a half hour of solitude before once again entering the fray. In an establishment as large as Norsham Castle, it should have been easy to find a place to be alone, but the addition of thirty guests meant the public areas were crowded—especially when no one wanted to leave the few rooms that were comfortably warm.

At a time when many peers were building crenellated houses and calling them castles, Norsham was the real thing. Sitting on a basalt outcropping in an otherwise relatively flat area of the North Sea coast, fortifications had been built here since the Viking era. The big square keep that now centered the massive walls had been constructed in the Twelfth Century to show Norman domination of the area.

Duncan smiled. He used the cold and inconvenience of the castle to judge how the various candidates for his political support handled discomfort and adversity. But even he was not cruel enough to house anyone in the keep in winter. While it was structurally sound, no modernization had taken place in the last three hundred years.

By comparison, Duncan's grandfather had spent a small fortune to upgrade the Great Hall and the adjacent large building, now referred to as the palace. Windows had been enlarged and glazed. Fireplaces had been added or reworked. The entire palace had been furnished with comfortable, modern pieces.

The sixth earl had made Norsham a showplace, a perfect location for the family to summer. But it was not conducive to winter habitation, which made it ideal for Duncan's gathering. He'd discovered that a man had to be willing to undergo personal challenges if he wanted to pursue a political career, and a visit to Norsham in December was an excellent test of a man's character.

A soft knock on the door brought him out of his reverie. Only his daughter, Amelia, would dare poke the lion in his den. He looked at the clock on his desk and sighed. He'd only enjoyed half of his allotted time, but Amelia would not bother him if she could handle a problem herself.

"Come," he called.

Amelia entered with a cheeky grin. "I know, I know. You wanted to hide for a while, but I need to know where we are going to come up with a new room for Henry Phillips' mother.

"I thought you'd put her in Geoffrey's room, next to St. Clare's daughter."

Winter-worthy accommodations were one of the reasons Duncan discouraged the men looking for his support from bringing their wives or other family members.

Discouraged, but not prohibited. He did prohibit additional servants, valets and the like. Everyone had to make do with the footmen he provided.

The occasional lady was often an interesting way to evaluate the man, however, and the addition of the fairer sex kept the evening from being a continuation of the day's discussions. This year there were two ladies attending. Their planned accommodations were the two unused bedrooms in the family wing, since these rooms were well-furnished and most importantly, warm.

"Since we expect Henry Phillips and his mother to arrive this afternoon, I had the staff set a fire this morning so Geoffrey's room would warm. All seemed in readiness, and then, just a while ago, one of the maids noticed smoke seeping out around the door. Not to draw this out describing all the dashing about involved, I'll just say the room is filled with smoke and uninhabitable."

Duncan ran his fingers through his hair. "I'm assuming it's a bloody jackdaw nest."

"So it would seem. We had all the chimneys swept this autumn, but evidently, they missed something."

"The fireplace is now unusable?"

"Most definitely. So, where are we going to put *the mother*?"

Duncan chuckled. "Amelia, you're going to have to call the poor woman something other than *the mother*, especially in that tone of voice. She's the Dowager Viscountess Lyndon."

Amelia answered his laugh. "As I well know. What I can't figure out is why a grown man would bring his mother with him."

"Perhaps Henry Phillips' disabilities are more severe

than we'd reckoned. From what I've heard of the man, I doubt he's still tied to his mother's apron strings."

"Well, regardless of the reason for her arrival, we have to figure out some accommodation for her that will be comfortable. The obvious choice would be the countess's suite. But since Mr. Phillips is in his middle twenties, his mother must be what…? Mid-forties? Anyway, that's your age—which makes putting her in the room next to you problematic." Amelia wiggled her eyebrows in a suggestive manner. "The connecting door and all."

"Is the suite kept ready for visitors?" Duncan couldn't contain his surprise. In the fifteen years since his wife had left, he'd never opened that connecting door. Once he'd found her note, it was as if she had taken her personal space with her when she departed. Oh, he knew the rooms were there. He wasn't delusional. He just chose to ignore that part of his life and focus on his four children. It seemed odd to think that all these years, the staff had held the rooms ready for someone to arrive.

Amelia looked equally surprised. "Yes. It's cleaned weekly. Of course, it would need a fire started and a quick dusting, but it could be ready for Lady Lyndon. I was concerned about the perceptions of the other guests. House parties are notorious for people scuttling between rooms in the dead of night and even with our politically oriented gathering, others might wonder what is going on in the family wing.

"They could wonder that anyway, since Miss St. Clare is just down the hall."

"Not likely. Katherine St. Clare is my age."

Duncan didn't know whether to be offended or amused.

His daughter obviously thought there could be no attraction between a man of forty-five and a young lady in her early twenties. Lord, Amelia must think he was in his dotage and uninterested in sex. He wondered if his sons would come to the same conclusion. There were certain areas of his life, however, he would just as soon not have his grown children speculating about.

But in this case, Miss St. Clare was totally safe from his sneaking down the hall to visit her. Although she was attractive and vivacious, and her father undoubtedly intended to troll her past the eligible men at this gathering, Duncan would not be rising to the bait. The chit truly was too young and intellectually unformed to be of interest.

Duncan decided to be amused. "Well, since age appropriateness seems to be a deciding factor about who sleeps where, I think we would be safe in putting Lady Lyndon in the room next to mine. Henry, the son she's coming with, must have been a late in life surprise. Her eldest son was a couple years ahead of me at Eton, so she is undoubtedly in her late sixties."

"Wonderful." His daughter's suddenly relaxed position told him he'd solved her immediate problem. "I'll have the room ready before Lady Lyndon arrives. And until then, I'll leave you to your contemplation."

Duncan looked at the clock. "Alas, that time has passed. I need to go haunt the billiards room and see if any of the gentlemen present seem to be dedicated gamblers. But before you go, have any of the candidates struck you as particularly deserving?"

Amelia was the only one of his children interested in politics. She'd proved herself an astute judge of character and kept up to date on the latest laws and bills. Duncan regretted she was not one of the boys, since she would have made a fine Prime Minister.

"It's too early to tell, although I like what the footman assigned to David Marsh had to say. The man had his room totally in order, even made his bed, and was completely dressed when the footman went to wake him, so he is obviously used to doing for himself. And then the boot boy said his boots were old and worn, but well cared for with a good shine... and a new half-sole. So, without really talking to him, I'd judge him to be poor but ambitious."

"We both know ambition is essential to success, so long as being poor hasn't made him grasping," Duncan said.

"I'll watch for that. But now I need to get the countess's suite ready for Lady Lyndon... and you need to determine for yourself which of our guests are best suited for the tasks you set before them." She leaned over and planted a quick kiss on his forehead before sweeping across the room and out the door.

Duncan smiled at her retreating figure. Amelia was a young woman to make any father proud. She had her mother's height but carried it with more confidence and grace. Poor Jane had always seemed embarrassed by her height and had slouched, particularly when she was standing next to him. Sadly, he hadn't realized she'd thought being married to him was such a trial until she'd left.

Jane Armstrong had been chosen as his wife to add stature, literally, to the succeeding generations of Ashes, and she'd done that. Three of his children significantly overtopped him. All but the youngest, Marcus, who was brilliant and currently studying to be a physician. Duncan suspected Marcus would attain stature that had nothing to do with his actual height.

He stretched his shoulders and went to see what other men's sons had to offer the nation. They were all clumped in four rooms, driven indoors by the rain, wind, and cold. In one room, the less-than-thrilling debate was about the weather, a large contingent confident a good solid freeze and snow would be preferable to the current frigid sogginess. In another room, Duncan found a more heated discussion about the relative merits of Wizard, who had won the 2000 Guineas Stakes, and Pope, the winner of the Derby Stakes. A third more raucous group was gathered in the billiards room where a match was underway. Only two men had found their way to the library, where both were comfortably seated before the fire, reading the latest editions of *The Quarterly Review*. Duncan thought their activity was the one he'd choose on such an inclement day, but he was always willing to make allowances for different personalities.

The location of the library and its relative silence allowed him to hear a carriage approaching. He excused himself and went to greet the late arriving Phillips party. Amelia, also hearing the coach, met him in the entry next to the medieval Great Hall. Two footmen stood ready with umbrellas and dashed out the door when they heard the horses come to a stop.

Duncan and Amelia stood in the broad doorway. As soon as the coach steps were dropped, a hatless, brown-haired, young man swung out of the door, his right hand grasping the side bar. He gracefully pivoted to face the open carriage door, showing his left side and a jacket sleeve that had been pinned up to end above the elbow. The young man then extended his right hand to help a petite woman descend.

At first, all Duncan could see was the top of the dark blue hood that covered her head. But when she was securely on the ground, she looked up toward the door—and Duncan's breath caught in his throat. A face, which could have been used as the model for the fairies in the illustrated books he'd read to his children years before, now stared up at him. Blonde almost white hair nestled inside a circle of red fox. Her face was a delicate heart shape, her eyes a surprising dark blue that matched her cape.

"If this is *the mother*, she is certainly not sixty," Amelia said softly.

Duncan gave a quick nod of agreement, and then his face broke into a smile and he walked partway down the steps in the rain, extending his hand.

Chapter Three

Sophia hadn't realized how strange this house party was until she walked into the drawing room prior to dinner. Except for two much younger women standing near the fireplace on the far side of the room, the assemblage was all male. And there were a lot of them—all ages and sizes and shapes, and every one of them was deeply involved in whatever their particular conversational cluster was discussing.

Good Lord. It had been almost twenty years since she'd stood at a door and felt so out of place. And then she'd been a green girl making her come out. She no longer had that excuse, but she still felt adrift.

Attending gatherings after she'd married Viscount Lyndon had been simple. She'd just acted like a moon to his planet, stayed in near orbit, and looked at him adoringly. When his condition had worsened and they'd moved to the country, they avoided society altogether. She was out of practice at entering a room full of strangers.

When she'd agreed to come to this house party, she'd imagined a small intimate group of three or four congenial couples where she would have something in common with the ladies involved and enjoy getting to know them. This room, full of intense men, made her feel an outsider with nothing to contribute.

Alexander, who must have known what to expect but still had maneuvered her into making this ridiculous trip, would be getting the sharp edge of her tongue when she returned home.

She attempted to locate Henry amid the mass of men who looked identical, dressed as they were in dark evening coats and white linen. Henry must have been watching for her, however, since he suddenly appeared to her right, striding toward her with a wide smile on his face. He looked more energized and happier than he'd seemed since his return from Portugal. If this were the case, she might forgive Alexander his manipulation.

"Fee, you look radiant." Henry kissed her hand. "Come and let me introduce you to some interesting gentlemen I've met."

He placed his hand on the small of her back and began guiding her through the throng. He stopped before three men, all of whom smiled at her approach. Sophia felt herself relax. This would not be so difficult for all that she was out of practice.

"Lady Lyndon," Henry began, "may I present Mr. St. Clare? He is the MP from Slocolmbe. Mr. St. Clare, the Dowager Viscountess Lyndon, my esteemed stepmother." The oldest gentleman in the group gave her a polished bow. He was a handsome, square-faced man with a receding hairline. Sophia judged him to be a few years beyond her age.

Henry then introduced Mr. Harding, a dark, narrow faced gentleman with the look of a hunting hound straining to be loosed, and Mr. Marsh, who was closest in age to Henry and had a shy, quiet manner.

"Gentlemen," she said, "I'm delighted to make your acquaintance. I must admit this gathering is larger than I had anticipated, so it's nice to put names to faces. It's all a bit overwhelming."

"I think Marle's purpose in holding this gathering at Norsham Castle is to overwhelm," Mr. Harding said. "It's a reminder that we are all here as supplicants."

The man's sarcastic tone surprised Sophia. Judging from the other men's reactions, they were similarly taken off guard.

"I believe Norsham is the largest of the earl's properties," Mr. St. Clare said in an even voice, "so it makes sense to house this large a group here. Norsham has been in the Ashe family since the Twelfth Century, although then it was only the keep."

"I find it impressive, but I wish it were not quite *so* historical," Mr. Marsh said, but his tone was humorous rather than derogatory. The other gentlemen chuckled and nodded in agreement.

Sophia had the uncomfortable impression that she was missing the joke. She thought of the beautifully appointed suite to which she'd been shown. While there was a feeling of antiquity about the space, the huge bed with its elaborate hangings, the plush Wilton carpet underfoot, and the breathtaking view of the North Sea from three large windows made her bedchamber spectacular.

"My accommodations are lovely," she said.

"My daughter said the same thing," Mr. St. Clare said. "But you ladies are housed in the family wing, while we gentlemen are in a… eh… less improved wing."

Henry laughed aloud. "Very diplomatically stated, St.

Clare." He then turned to address Sophia. "Our rooms are perfectly satisfactory, but they do tend toward the medieval. Arrow slit windows, stone floors, and rather miniscule fire places."

"In a word—cold," said Mr. Marsh.

"Bracing," corrected Henry, eliciting laughter all around.

Dinner was announced, and Henry offered Sophia his arm. "Lady Amelia told me there will be place cards on the table and our positions will change nightly, so may I take you in?"

"Please," she said. "Four eyes trying to read a distant place card will be better than two."

He leaned toward her and lowered his voice. "What do you think of Mr. St. Clare?"

"He seemed quite affable and levelheaded, at least from such a brief meeting. Why?"

"He's a widower. The second son of Lord Ridley and well-respected in Parliament with a good possibility of becoming a Minister at some point. I thought perhaps..."

As the direction of Henry's conversation suddenly became clear, she stopped dead. "No." They were now blocking the flow of the crowd and a number of people had turned toward her when she uttered the one word, perhaps too loudly. She pulled on Henry's arm and started them moving again. "Henry, I do not want your matchmaking. I have avoided pressing available young women on you, and I expect the same courtesy."

She was relieved that she found her place quickly and let Henry seat her without either of them saying another word. How could he think she would want to remarry? As if once had not been enough.

She'd married Lyndon because there had been no other choices. Otherwise, she would not have chosen a man thirty-seven-years her senior. But Lyndon had been good to her. And she had done her duty to him. She'd been the beautiful, young woman on his arm when he wanted to impress. She'd been the one to guide him through a world that became progressively more confusing. She'd stayed by his side when he no longer knew who she was, and she'd remained during all the time he did not know who he was.

By being here with Henry, she was still doing her duty. Her fondest hope was that Henry would find a satisfying life—and then she could move on and find one for herself.

But this new life, whatever form it took, would not include another man who would control all her choices and monopolize her time. She had finally gotten the independent life promised in her marriage settlement. Her wonderful little townhouse on the edge of Mayfair was in her name. She was in the process of decorating it completely to her tastes. She would choose friends whose company she enjoyed, caring not a whit about their importance or influence.

Forty was still a few years distant, and she knew that while she was not in the first flush of youth, she was not repugnant and was attractive to men. She might decide to take a lover. But it would be on her terms. She had earned the right to be selfish.

Mr. St. Clare seemed like a nice man and was attractive in a solid sort of way. He would be comfortable, like a well-worn chair next to the fireplace. He would make a good friend. And definitely nothing else.

Her table partners filled in around her. Both were men since the three ladies present were scattered around the table. Both were pleasant and once it became obvious she was not well-versed on political topics, talked to her about their children. Sophia was relieved when Lady Amelia indicated it was time for the ladies to retire, and she happily made her way to the drawing room.

Sophia had met Lady Amelia when they arrived. A personable young woman with her father's chestnut hair and sparkling gray eyes, Lady Amelia was attractive without being beautiful. The other lady present, Mr. St. Clare's daughter, Katherine, had dark hair and eyes and a long face that would be called arresting rather than pretty. She and Lady Amelia were of an age, probably in their early twenties.

"I've ordered tea," Lady Amelia said as they settled into the seating group closest to the fire, "but I've never understood why only men should enjoy a digestive drink, so I'm going to have a glass of port. Miss St. Clare?"

"Oh, I'll also have port." Miss St. Clare's face flushed at her announcement. Sophia surmised that port was not her usual drink and she was being daring.

"Lady Lyndon?"

"Port, please." Sophia chose not to confess she preferred a nice, smoky whisky to see her to bed. After a day of minding her late husband as if he were a three-year-old, she'd needed a tot to help her relax and the Lyndon cellars held a stash of whisky. The nightly ritual had become habit. She owed it to Henry, however, to present a picture of a staid matron. She was very glad her hostess had offered the port.

Lady Amelia signaled a hovering footman and they were soon each holding a glass of the ruby wine.

"Is this the first politically oriented house party you've attended?" Miss St. Clare asked.

Sophia smiled, wondering if this were polite conversation or an attempt to judge Henry's fitness to run for Commons. "Most certainly. The previous house parties I've attended all seemed to revolve around some sort of hunting."

"So, you and your family are more interested in sporting pursuits?" Lady Amelia queried.

Sophia took a sip of her too sweet drink. It seemed ridiculous to just hold it, especially when she was to be subjected to an inquisition. "My late husband enjoyed riding to the hounds and tromping about shooting at almost anything with wings. I generally was not included in either activity, although I do enjoy riding. I was left to enjoy garden parties with the ladies where we would have in-depth discussions on the type of sleeves that were most popular on ball gowns that year. But my husband was very ill for the last ten years of his life and we stayed in the country and did not socialize."

Not wanting to always hold the answer position in a question and answer session, Sophia decided to take the offensive. "I assume you ladies are well acquainted with the political scene, however, and could, therefore, give me some direction on how to answer the question posed by both of my dinner partners—what do you think of Perceval, the new Prime Minister?"

For a moment, the two younger women were nonplused. Apparently, they'd been intent on examining Sophia's merits and had not anticipated she would question them.

"I think it is too early to tell how he will govern. His positions seem to have no consistent center," Miss St. Clare said.

Sophia was surprised the opinion was offered by Miss St.

Clare. She would have guessed Lady Amelia would be the more politically oriented of the two. But that lady did not disappoint, and the two of them were soon engaged in a lively debate, during which their glasses were magically refilled at least once. Perhaps in response to this development, the two younger women took on the task of acquainting Sophia with some of the current political notables by making pronouncements in those worthies' imagined voices.

The gentleman arrived in the midst of the hilarity.

"I suspect someone is being lampooned," Lord Marle said as he approached. He was smiling, but he gazed intently at his daughter. "I hope it is no one present."

"No, Father," Lady Amelia said, trying to look contrite and utterly failing. "Katherine and I were trying to familiarize Lady Lyndon with some of the current ministers, in this case First Lord of the Admiralty. I was reciting part of Lord Mulgrave's 'Ode on Trafalgar.' It isn't my fault that it is terrible poetry."

Sophia had to look down at her lap to keep from laughing. Lady Amelia had been *singing* the ode, with comedic results.

"I hope, then, Lady Lyndon, that you have been well entertained." Since Lord Marle spoke directly to her, Sophia had to raise her eyes—and immediately met his own gray ones. She remembered thinking he had kind eyes all those years ago. She now acknowledged she'd been wrong. His eyes were compelling, like the moon on a foggy night when it is the only light discernable in the sky.

"Lady Amelia and Miss St. Clare have been most kind in helping me untangle the various positions held by some of those in Parliament. I've discovered there is much to learn."

"You could not have found two more knowledgeable ladies," he smiled with pride at Lady Amelia. "British politics is a labyrinth more confusing than most ancient buildings. Both have been cobbled together over time, and architecture that was necessary in one period becomes useless and needs to be abandoned in another." He suddenly laughed. "I fear I have made myself unpopular by suggesting the demolition of some outdated ideas in our government. I think it a mistake to try to patch cracks in unstable structures."

She smiled back at him, wondering how anyone who had actually seen him could call him a gnome. He was one of the most handsome men she'd ever met. "To continue your metaphor," she said, "I think I would have a much easier time navigating some crumbling building than finding my way through the constantly changing halls of politics."

"Would you like a tour of part of my crumbling building? The Great Hall, perhaps? I, for one, would enjoy an after-dinner stroll."

The earl looked at her expectantly and she felt something long frozen inside of her begin to thaw. "I think that would be lovely."

"Good," he said. "I'll send someone to get you something warm to wear. We keep a fire burning in the hall, but it cannot comfortably heat so vast a space. The blue cloak you arrived in would be ideal."

"Thank you. That sounds like an excellent choice." She was proud she could speak sensibly since all that swirled through her mind was that the Earl of Marle remembered the color of her cloak.

Chapter Four

Duncan ignored Amelia's glare. She knew he was acting out of character and couldn't figure out why. Hell, *he* had no idea what had motivated him to ask Lady Lyndon to walk with him in the Great Hall.

No, that was a lie. He knew exactly why he had. Something about her enchanted him, and he wanted to spend some time alone with her. Or as alone as they could possibly be and remain socially acceptable.

These yearly gatherings were always difficult. Some established MPs like Roland St. Clare came looking for support for specific bills, but most of the attendees hoped to begin a Parliamentary career. Some came looking to represent one of the safe boroughs he controlled; others wanted his far-flung influence in contested elections elsewhere. But whatever the reason, everyone desired something.

He went to bed every night exhausted, feeling as if a mob with grasping hands had hung on him throughout the day.

When he started having this winter gathering, he'd seen it as a duty to those who didn't have their own voices in governance. He'd never anticipated he would find anything satisfying for himself until an unexpected fairy woman stepped out of a carriage. And then he had wanted—Lord, he wasn't sure exactly what. But the need overwhelmed him. It had been years, maybe forever, since he'd felt his interest so engaged by a woman.

When the footman arrived with their outerwear, he draped Lady Lyndon's cloak over his arm and went to where she sat, talking to her stepson. He held out his hand. "My lady, would you care to take a stroll through the middle ages... and see that while it is picturesque, it is much nicer to live in the nineteenth century?"

She gave him a dazzling smile. "With pleasure." Her small hand nestled in his as comfortably as a bird in its nest. He slipped the soft cloak onto her shoulders and moved her toward the door.

They received some curious looks, which he purposely ignored. They walked down the hallway until they arrived at the broad door leading into the Great Hall.

"This door was put in to connect the Great Hall to the newer residential section, which was built in the late seventeenth century and rather grandly called *the palace*." He chuckled. "I think my ancestors had delusions of being the kings of their own domain and tried to live in that manner. We surmise the Great Hall wasn't demolished during the construction of the palace, as so many of the other older structures were, so it could eventually function as a ballroom. Improvements were never made, however, and my earliest memory of it as a boy was of a large, dusty storage area."

He pushed open the door, made sure it would remain open for propriety's sake, and looked around. He was pleased to see the staff had followed his instructions. Candles were alight throughout the massive room. Colorful tapestries covered the lower half of the walls, and the flickering flames made the scenes on the hangings move as if alive.

"Oh, my," Lady Lyndon said in a breathy voice. "This is a store room no longer." She turned to him. "It's magical."

He refrained from saying it was not as magical as the face that looked up at his. He felt himself flush with embarrassment. Dear Heavens, where were these aberrant thoughts coming from? He was not a fanciful man, particularly when it came to women. And yet, ever since Lady Lyndon's arrival, he'd behaved atypically.

"My father completely refurbished this room while I was away at school. Since the hall had originally been built in the fifteenth century, to make the space useable, he needed to add more modern comforts like glass for the windows and the large fireplace at the far end of the hall. Fortunately, the building hadn't been allowed to deteriorate, so the wonderful hammer beam ceiling just needed cleaning. Since the original heat source was a central fire pit, there was a louvre in the middle of the roof. That was permanently closed… and the large octagonal table in the middle of the room can't be moved, even when the hall is used for dancing, or people would stumble into the original pit."

Since Lady Lyndon seemed frozen in place, he took her arm and urged her forward. "Come, let me show you the tapestries. They came from France right before the Revolution and are beautifully done."

They strolled down the right side of the room, Lady Lyndon making appropriately appreciative comments. "May I touch them?" she asked.

"Of course. They're designed to last for centuries. Their only enemies are moths. And to combat those, the panels are regularly beaten, so touching them will be gentle by comparison."

Her hand appeared from beneath her cloak and gently touched the heavy fabric. "Why do they shimmer?"

"They were woven with a combination of wool and silk. It's the silk that catches the light."

"Beautiful."

She now seemed to pet the wall hanging. Duncan stifled a groan. He had a visceral image of her hand doing the same to his naked body. It would be soft and warm and... Hell, how had he gotten so off balance?

"Let's go warm ourselves in front of the fireplace." His voice sounded rusty to his ears. "This is the only area where the man in charge of the renovations errored. There is no way a single fireplace, regardless of its size, can heat this large a space, particularly with the ceilings so high. But standing directly in front of it is quite toasty."

Just because he was heated didn't mean she was, and he suspected she might be getting chilled. This contention seemed supported when, upon arrival, she held her hands toward the flames with a sigh and said, "Lovely."

"The only problem is we're going to have to turn like we're on a spit," he commented, "or we'll cook too much on one side. But putting our backs to the flames will give you an opportunity to find a watcher."

"A watcher?" She rotated and looked down the length of the hall.

"In the rafters," he said. "My father added two carved men peeping down, and this is the easiest one to find."

She immediately looked up. "Where?"

"Now if I told you, it would take all the fun out of it."

She scanned the beams. He finally took pity on her. "On the far left," he said.

"Oh, I see it." Laughter boiled up. "A little face is peeking over the edge. Where's the other one?"

"In the middle of the room, but it's hard to see without light coming in the windows. You can come find it tomorrow."

"Why did your father have them placed so they are hard to find?"

"Because they're watchers and they're trying to be sneaky. Not everyone wants to be watched. And I also think it was my father's version of whimsey. The idea is surprising since he was, for the most part, a very pragmatic man."

She turned around to look at the fire again, and he joined her in facing the flames. His back had been getting uncomfortably warm. "Whether whimsical or pragmatic, your father certainly created a wonderful room. But it must have cost a fortune."

"It did," he said dryly, "but we have a fortune—in case you're checking out my financials with the idea of compromising me."

He'd meant his comment in jest, but he was very much out of practice in teasing a lady, if he'd ever known how. Instead of laughing, Lady Lyndon looked horrified.

"Oh, I'm so sorry," she said. "I didn't mean to be invasive. I know talking about money is not done. I just remembered the expense of reroofing part of the Lyndon estate and the thought simply popped out of my mouth. I apologize—"

Duncan managed to stop the flow of words by placing his index finger on her lips. "Enough. It was meant as a joke. Evidently a joke that wasn't funny. I would estimate that over half of the men here this week know my total worth to within a few pounds, since many of them want some of it. I spoke without thinking as well."

"I still apologize."

"But your comment was legitimate. The cost of the Gobelins' tapestries alone was astronomical. But my father saw this room as an investment meant to awe the people who would become my in-laws. I'm an only child, as my father was an only child, so he was not going to leave the succession to chance. For my wife, he carefully chose a lady from a family with a history of having a lot of children, most of whom were males."

He looked up at the Ashe family crest that was carved into the fireplace surround. "Perhaps more importantly, the members of the family he selected, that of Baron Armstrong, were tall. My father always felt uncomfortable with his height, and hence, with mine. According to him, male Ashes for generations kept choosing women who were shorter than they were, so it was not surprising we were successively shorter than our progenitors."

"So, your wife was tall?"

"Oh, yes. Very. Her whole family was. My children still refer to their four maternal uncles as *the trees*."

This time she laughed as she was supposed to. "I guess height isn't any worse reason to marry than most peoples' concerns, and you said it was of paramount importance to your father. Of course, your marriage could have been a love match, as well, which would have satisfied everyone."

"Was your marriage a love match?" Duncan suspected his question was pushing the boundary of proper discourse, but he truly wanted to know.

"No, but I came to have affection for my husband. He was nearly forty years my senior and was looking for..."

"For?" he prompted.

She rotated to look back over the hall, perhaps to avoid having to look at him. "Oh, it sounds egotistical to say so, but Lord Lyndon wanted an attractive, younger woman for his arm. I met that need, and he met mine."

"And what did you need?"

She laughed again, but this time the sound held no humor. "Someone to marry me before the end of the season."

She seemed to steel herself and then looked at him directly. "Growing up, I'd been oblivious to the fact that my father was not a good steward of his estate. When he died and my cousin Bertram became the new baron, it was immediately obvious that Bertram had inherited debts far beyond what the income from the barony could pay.

"My cousin attempted to do what he could to guarantee I had a good life. The entire family scrimped to give me a come out after the year of mourning for my father was completed. But Bertram was very clear that this would be the only season he could afford and that there would be no dowry. My cousin is a dear, but I'm afraid he is a bit delusional. He was sure I was beautiful enough that some worthy man would overlook the lack of a dowry. The only one who did was Viscount Lyndon."

"But you said you came to care for him."

"As I did," she said. "We each did our duty to the other. I was not unhappy in my marriage."

Not unhappy didn't sound like a ringing endorsement of her marriage to Lyndon. But she had just made a long journey in support of his youngest son, and if her behavior was any indication, the relationship she had with her stepson was one of affection, even if it was not one of blood.

Could he go as far as say his own marriage had been *not unhappy*? For years he'd thought it was, and to discover this was not the case had exposed the greatest failure of his life.

"I remember meeting you at some unremarkable musicale the year of your debut," Duncan said, hoping to stave off any examination of his own marital relationship. He did not add that she'd been pointed out to him as the Pauper Princess, and he'd thought she did look like a princess, sitting in isolation during one of the intervals. Her aloneness had called to him, and he'd gone over to keep her company until the program recommenced.

"I can't believe you recall that," she said. "Although I, too, remember you. I thought you had kind eyes." Her dark blue eyes sought his and held. "Your eyes are still kind, although I think they are now more discerning and warier."

And there, caught between the heat of the flames and the cold of the empty hall, Duncan Ashe, who considered himself a rigidly controlled, political manipulator, felt an almost overpowering desire to kiss this woman. His arms actually moved to gather her to him, as if she held a warmth that promised to keep the coldness of his life at bay.

He managed to stop himself and change the motion into one indicating the hall at large. "Shall we go? I fear it is getting late."

She nodded and took his arm, almost with relief, as if she, too, needed to regain the persona used to face the world at large. They didn't speak again until they'd returned to the drawing room, surrounded by the noise of conversation. He relinquished her to her stepson, who seemed to be awaiting her return. She thanked him for his tour.

He made some sort of comment about needing to check on the guests who would be in the library and billiards room, and then he fled. Oh, he made his retreat look like it was something purposeful, but he could not fool himself. He did not stay long in either location before seeking the isolation of his bedroom.

His valet, Hocking, was ready for him. The brandy decanter and glass, the pen and ink, and his journal for recording the day's impressions sat on the table next to his favorite chair by the fire. His quilted banyan lay waiting on the bed. Duncan felt stress begin to seep from him.

"An early night?" Hocking asked as Duncan toed off his shoes and rubbed his feet on the carpet.

"Long day," Duncan replied, beginning to shed his formalwear.

Hocking knocked Duncan's hands away and began working on his coat and waistcoat buttons. Duncan was perfectly capable of disrobing on his own, but there was something comforting about being fussed over. Maybe all men wanted to return to the nursery.

"Does it look like a good crop of men this year?" Over time, Hocking had become as much a political animal as his employer.

"Some seem excellent at first glance, and others…" he shrugged, "not so impressive, but I've yet to do individual interviews."

Hocking whisked away his coat and waistcoat, and Duncan pulled his shirt over his head. He'd just held it out to his valet when the connecting door opened.

Lady Lyndon, clad in her night robe, stood in the door,

the light from the candle in her hand turning the pale blonde hair that flowed across her breasts and down her back into a river of silver.

"Oh, oh, wrong door," she said, immediately disappearing back into her room and rapidly closing the door.

Both Hocking and Duncan stood frozen for a few seconds, Duncan still holding his shirt out to the side. Then Hocking dryly asked, "Were you expecting company?"

"Hell, no." Duncan threw his shirt at Hocking, but an open piece of material did not make a good weapon, and it fluttered to the ground. "I suspect Lady Lyndon is about to expire of embarrassment. She probably meant to go to her dressing room and chose the wrong door, as she said."

Hocking chuckled. "She looked like the bird that hourly comes out of the clock in the servants' parlor. The one that pops out, chirps, and then pops back in again."

Duncan smiled at the apt description. "I agree, but I'd appreciate if you didn't mention anything about what happened to anyone."

"Of course not, milord."

Duncan realized he'd offended his valet. He knew Hocking was the soul of discretion, and he shouldn't have suggested the valet would divulge anything. Hocking finished his chores in a bit of a snit but became more normal at his departure.

"Should you like coffee in your room before going down tomorrow morning?"

"That would be excellent," Duncan said, and then he was blessedly alone with his brandy and his journal and his thoughts—thoughts that kept drifting to the intriguing woman in the next room. He stared at the closed door, willing it to open.

It never did.

Chapter Five

Sophia heard the maid enter to refresh the fire. The house was slowly awakening around her. But the last thing Sophia wanted to do was greet the day. Instead, she slid deeper under her covers and closed her eyes. Perhaps she could plead illness and stay in bed until it was time to leave for London—a realistic impossibility.

The list of those she did not want to face today, or ever, for that matter, was remarkably long.

Last evening, her stepson Henry, the only reason she was here, had quickly let his displeasure with her become known. He'd been waiting for her when she returned from her tour of the Great Hall and suggested they play chess. Before she could object, he'd seated her at a table in a corner that boasted a lovely carved chess set.

"Henry, what is this about?" She'd been completely confused. "You've always said you found chess boring in the extreme."

"I do." He took the seat opposite her. "But I wanted to talk with you privately, and privacy is something that is hard to find here. Unlike the earl, I can't take you to some unused section of the house, so this will have to do."

He made the opening move she had taught him when he was a boy.

"What is so important that we have to indulge in this charade?" She countered with the second move in the set piece that was designed to teach the game. At least they could look like they were playing without having to use any thought.

"You've put me in an uncomfortable position, Fee." She looked up quickly from the chess board. "Wait," he said, raising a hand to forestall the comment that hovered on her lips. "Before you say anything, I know it was unintentional. But I've already gotten comments from the likes of Isiah Harding that suggest you're being eh, *overly friendly* to Lord Marle in an effort to push my advancement."

"What?" The concept was so foreign she had no idea how to respond. "Is this gathering some sort of contest to get the earl's preferment? Are *all* these men vying to become the candidate for the safe borough's by-election?"

Anger flamed through her for Henry's sake—and for her own. What sort of man would invite others to participate in what was basically a medieval tournament? Did Marle expect these men to bludgeon each other for the right to run for office? No wonder they called him the Gnome of the North. He sat up here like a cruel troll, deciding who could pass over the bridge to political office and who could not.

She didn't realize she was clutching a pawn as if ready to fling it across the room until Henry laid his hand over overs. "Fee, it's not like that. Yes, there are some who try to make this a contest, who will start gossip if it is to their advantage. But that isn't Lord Marle's intent. From what I understand, we will each have individual interviews to determine if the earl wants to support us. This support comes in many different forms, and, oddly, he doesn't seem to care if a man is a Whig or a Tory. His concern is that those who govern consider what would be best for the country at large instead of what would be best for their particular group or class."

Sophia let her hand relax. "If there is no contest, then in what way have I put you in a poor position? Lord Marle was kind enough to show me a fascinating room—one that I'd hoped to show you tomorrow. The time I spent with Lord Marle was totally innocent. I would like to know who has suggested that I am in any way being *overly friendly*. Was it that Harding man? I will certainly correct his mistaken assumptions."

Sophia was filled with righteous indignation, which was rather ironic since there had been a moment before the fire when she thought Lord Marle meant to kiss her. That wouldn't have been innocent—yet, when the moment passed, she wished they'd shared a kiss. She would admit, if only to herself, that there was something about the Earl of Marle that called to her. She suspected she would have enjoyed kissing him very much.

"No need for you to confront anyone," Henry said quickly. "I don't want to look like the cripple who needs his stepmama to fight his battles for him—just as I didn't want anyone thinking I needed you influencing Lord Marle's decision. I apologize for my overreaction. But when I overheard some comments, all I could think of was to ask you to be more careful. It was a stupid reaction, which I now regret."

Sophia had a similarly stupid reaction. She immediately wanted to find and verbally flay the asses who had placed such doubts in Henry's mind—and to do so *would* look like she was trying to fight Henry's battles for him. Ever since he'd been injured, she'd probably been helping him too much. He needed to know that whatever he accomplished had been by his own merit.

"I will try to be more circumspect in my behavior toward Lord Marle," she said. "I had not thought of how my going off alone with him might reflect on you. I just saw him as a nice man whose company I enjoyed."

She stood, bringing Henry to his feet as well, "It's been a long day and a long journey, so I will wish you a good night."

She quit the room, acknowledging a few people with nods but avoiding any conversation, and happily found her bed.

Where sleep would not come.

And after a night of tossing and turning, she felt battered rather than rested. Of course, the real reason keeping her awake was her later, inadvertent, less-than-circumspect behavior involving Lord Marle.

Now there was someone she definitely didn't want to see. But how did she ignore their host? She gave a quiet moan and pulled the pillow over her head.

But even buried in darkness, her mind remained active, and she couldn't forget what she'd already seen. The image of Lord Marle's naked torso must have been burned into the undersides of her eyelids, since every time she closed them, that was what she saw.

If she could see the printed word half as well, she would not have ended up in her current difficulty.

When she couldn't get to sleep for worrying about Henry's reaction, she'd decided to read. Her book was on the table by the bed, but not her spectacles. Assuming a maid unfamiliar with her needs had left them in the dressing room, she got up to retrieve her eyeglasses, opened the wrong door, and beheld the arresting sight of a man's naked chest. Specifically, Lord Marle's naked chest... and oh, my!

She didn't need spectacles to see at a distance and so had stood transfixed for what seemed an hour, but which probably encompassed only the few seconds she needed to mumble some sort of apology. She really had no idea what she'd said.

Sophia had fled—shocked, mortified, and intrigued. The first two reactions made her want to hide in her room for the rest of the visit. The last reaction, however, urged her to return for another look.

She had never seen a naked man. Well, mostly naked. She'd seen nude sculptures, of course, but usually from a distance since a closer examination would have been scandalous. But they had not elicited the response created by her glimpse of Lord Marle. She didn't think embarrassment had everything to do with her breathlessness.

A three-branch candelabrum had well illuminated the scene, the angle of the light accenting his musculature with shadow. Even the veins in the left forearm he'd extended toward the other man were obvious. The tops of his broad shoulders were bunched with muscles as was his chest. His abdomen looked ridged and hard.

Unlike any of the carved torso she'd seen in museums, a T of short, bronze-colored hair had crossed Lord Marle's chest to disappear into the top of his trousers—trousers pulled low on narrow hips by hanging braces. And in that split second, she'd wanted to touch his body, to feel the movement of his skin across those intriguing ridges, to see if the arrow of hair was soft or crisp.

It had taken thirty-seven years for Sophia to discover she was wanton. That might have been the biggest shock of all. Oh, she might have a harmless fantasy about taking a lover, since that was what she'd heard widows did. But she very much doubted she would have followed up on the idea—or at least that had been the case before she blundered into Lord Marle's room.

She had never felt such a compulsion to touch and discover. In the first few years of her marriage to Lord Lyndon, he'd come to her in darkness, always wearing his nightshirt. When he'd stopped coming at all, her only regret was that she would never have any children of her own. But the process of getting those children had been easily dismissed.

She now suspected that would not have been the case had the Earl of Marle been the other half of the equation.

Had she even looked at his face? To her chagrin, she thought not. Her eyes had been riveted on his body. But her memory conveniently supplied this missing part, so Lord Marle in his totality was the picture that persistently scrolled through her mind.

Putting her head under the pillow had in no way diminished this inner vision. In fact, the complete darkness may have made everything more vivid. In disgust, she pitched the pillow across the room and uttered the crudest of the oaths Henry had shouted during his period of pain and anger when he'd returned home. Sophia normally never said such words, but this particular one now seemed appropriate, and she felt surprisingly better for its use.

Her outburst was immediately followed by a knock on the door. The young maid assigned to Sophia must have been hovering in the hall, ready to prove her competence.

"I'm still abed and need nothing now," Sophia called, hoping to discourage entry.

The door opened, nonetheless. Only it wasn't the door to the hall—it was the door of her shame, the one that led to Lord Marle's room. And in the man walked, thankfully fully clothed and acting like he was the master of all he surveyed. Well, of course, this was his castle and...

She jerked her mind back from the confused path it was taking and pulled the covers up to just below her eyes. "You can't be here. I said I was abed."

"Which gave me confidence to enter," Lord Marle said. "I was sure I wouldn't find you in the process of dressing."

He raised his eyebrows in a suggestive manner and Sophia felt herself flush since she had barged into his room while he was undressing.

"You must leave," she said. "It is unacceptable for you to be in my bedchamber. If a maid should enter, neither of our reputations would recover."

Instead of departing, he strolled over and sat in the chair by the fire. At least he was half the room away. "We will not be discovered. It is still early, and the staff has finished with the fires in this wing and has gone elsewhere. So, unless you decide to begin screaming, no one will ever know I was here." He looked at her very seriously. "You're not going to scream, are you?"

"Of course not."

He gave a curt nod. "Good. We have some things to discuss and this seemed the simplest way to clear the air. First of all, I realize your arrival in my room last night was a complete mistake. If it is agreeable with you, we will pretend it never happened. This way, there is no reason for either of us to be embarrassed. We can meet downstairs without any discomfort, since, if we were to avoid each other, some in the party might take note. Can we act as if it never happened?"

"Of course," she said quickly, hoping her agreement would remove him from her room.

"Good." Another curt nod. But instead of leaping to his feet and departing, Lord Marle settled back into the chair. "I have a confession to make. I've mulled over the wisdom of addressing this and decided, in the long run, it would be for the best."

He sat forward, placing his elbows on his knees. "I'm attracted to you. Now this should not be unusual, since you are a beautiful woman... and I admit to enjoying the company of beautiful women. But I have never felt so... well, spellbound is the only word that comes to mind, as much as it embarrasses me to use it."

Sophia sat up straight with the speed of a ferret sighting prey. "Oh, my lord—"

"No, this is my confession and there is no need to comment. Before I came to bed last night, my daughter took me to task about escorting you to the Great Hall. She said it smacked of impropriety. I wanted to let you know that I meant no disrespect and will try to be more careful of your reputation in the future."

He abruptly stood. "If this discussion was unnecessary, please excuse me. I seem to have difficulty in figuring out what the fairer sex is thinking, and I wanted to assure you that I will in no way importune you."

He was across the room and through the door before she could stop him.

What a curious conversation, if it could be called that. It had been more of an announcement of intentions, or perhaps, non-intentions. But he found her spellbinding. She certainly didn't think anyone else had ever felt that way. And yet, he'd said he would make no improper advances. What a depressing declaration!

Chapter Six

Duncan Ashe never had second thoughts. Once he'd made a decision, he would live with it, no exception. That was how he'd always structured his life.

But now he was having second thoughts.

This was not a productive way to spend the time before the first of seven interviews he'd scheduled for the day. He needed to be clear headed and ready to weigh the positives and negatives of each man with whom he'd talk. But instead, his mind kept reviewing the discussion he'd had with Lady Lyndon in the early hours of this morning. Or perhaps it had been more a pronouncement than a discussion. That fact by itself left him in a quandary.

He'd thought it best to clear the air. It would avoid any embarrassment when they met later in the day. Her arrival in his room had, after all, been a simple mistake. And once he'd realized she had not locked the connecting door—that fact determined at some point in the middle of his sleepless night and caused by a compulsion he chose not to examine—going to her room had seemed the simplest solution. That decision didn't require any reexamination.

He'd not planned to blurt out that he found her appealing but would not act on the attraction, however. That idiocy had just tumbled out of his mouth while his mind was otherwise occupied... probably thinking how charmingly like a startled owlet she looked, peering over the top of the covers. Hindsight suggested his brain had not been involved at all.

Dear Lord, he'd used the word *spellbound*. He hadn't known that was even in his vocabulary. But he'd had sense enough to assure her he would not pursue this odd compulsion. After the disaster that had been his marriage, he wanted to make sure he and Lady Lyndon were very clear that there would not be any sort of relationship at all.

And therein lay the cause of his second thoughts. Why was he not willing to see if this unexpected attraction was mutual? Lady Lyndon was a widow—a mature widow at that. Perhaps she occasionally formed liaisons. She would be here for five more days, and during that time, perhaps she would be interested in a brief affair with him.

He'd indulged in mutually satisfying physical connections from time to time, and he thought both he and his various partners had found them enjoyable. He might be known as the Gnome of the North, but he'd never been called the Monk of the North. Oh, not a philanderer or a skirt chaser, to be sure, but still...

It made no difference. He'd told her he would not act on his admitted attraction. It would make him a man without honor to now do so, unless, of course, she gave him some sort of sign. But if she did, he doubted he would read the sign correctly. Past experience had shown he lacked the ability to discern what a woman felt.

It was irritating that he could so easily read a man's character. In the last fourteen years, he had yet to support a man who didn't have what was best for the country in mind when he cast a vote in Commons. Oh, sometimes Duncan disagreed with the way the man voted, but he knew his candidate truly thought he was doing what was right for all his constituents.

But in his relationship with his wife, the emotional connection that should have counted the most, he'd been oblivious to any signs she might have given. He'd known theirs was not a great love match. Had always known it. But he thought they rubbed along well. He thought they were both content. They had four healthy children to love. They had their own interests, which the other supported. On the whole, he thought his marriage a good one.

And then, fifteen years ago, he'd returned home at the end of the Parliamentary session to discover a house in chaos and his wife gone. Two days before his arrival, Jane had departed with the son of the squire who lived next door to her childhood home. She left Duncan a note—*I have always loved him.*

He'd put the note in his top bureau drawer—he still took it out about once a week to remind him of his failure—but he did not go after her. How could he when the fault was his? He'd thought they'd built a life, and they had built nothing. *I have always loved him.* And he had never known, had never suspected.

He vowed to never again subject another woman to his obtuseness, for that was what it had been. Consequently, his later relationships had been brief and based solely on physical gratification.

And then Lady Lyndon appeared and for the first time he wanted something more. A dangerous situation... perhaps for both of them. Unless she too would be satisfied with a short-lived affair, something ephemeral, but of a long enough duration for him to purge his system of this ridiculous desire. And then they could both return to their regular lives, and he would have regained his balance and his perspective.

She had not come to breakfast before he'd had to leave to begin the interviews, but he would possibly see her at lunch, definitely at dinner, and he would watch for a sign that she was willing to have something develop between them.

If this sign were not blindingly obvious, however, Duncan feared he would miss it.

There was a knock on the study door and Winthrop, his butler, announced Mr. Pierce, a possible candidate for a borough in Cumberland that was not one of those under Duncan's control. Mr. Pierce wanted to oppose the incumbent, a man who had proved himself to be both incompetent and unwilling to support any bill that would aid the miners in his district.

It was a need for competent opposition to the current MP that had caused Duncan to welcome Mr. Pierce to his gathering. If the man proved to have the good of the local inhabitants in mind, Duncan would see he also had the money to buy the gifts and the liquor needed to woo the local voters. Perhaps it was a sad commentary on British democracy that such enticements were necessary, but that was the game as it was currently played.

"Mr. Pierce," he said, coming around the desk with an extended hand.

The duty of his day had begun.

༺༻

Duncan sat with his pen poised over his journal—and watched another ink blob land on the page. There were now so many random drops, the page was beginning to look like he was copying runes from a standing stone. He could not focus his mind on his normal pre-sleep activity. Even an extra glass of brandy had not made his bed look inviting.

He finally gave up fighting himself, laid the quill on the side table, and stood up. He retrieved his glass of Dutch courage from the table and marched to the connecting door. If the damned thing was unlocked, it was *a sign*.

It had to be. He'd waited in vain for anything—sign, portent, acknowledgment, whatever—from Lady Lyndon for the entire day, and she'd managed to elude him. Even after dinner, she'd hunkered over the chess board with her stepson until it was time to retire. But if the door was unlocked…

He turned the knob and the door swung in with a slight groan of hinges.

The room was in darkness. The fire in the grate had burned low. Bloody Hell, the woman was asleep. He took a step back to return to his own room.

"Yes?" came a question from the bed.

Duncan froze. What did she mean? *Yes*, as in "come in"? *Yes*, as in "what do you want"? *Yes*, as in "yes, yes, I want you"? He shook his head. That last scenario, despite its appeal, was highly unlikely.

"What do you want, milord?" she asked.

Well, that solidified the meaning of "yes." Rather disappointingly.

"I was restless," he said. "And I hadn't had the opportunity to talk with you all day, so I thought if you were awake, we could perhaps, eh, talk." That explanation sounded lame to his own ears, but he allowed it to propel him into the room.

"Lord Marle, you can't keep popping into my bedroom. It's highly inappropriate."

He stopped, ready to retreat if she said she wanted him to go. He would behave as a gentleman, regardless of how improper the situation.

She sighed. "Since you're here..." From the deep shadows of the bed, her arm motioned toward the chair by the fire.

Even Duncan couldn't miss that sign of... well, welcome might be an exaggeration, but it was acceptance at least. "Thank you," he said, crossing to the chair, which he repositioned to face the bed before sitting down.

"Did you have anything specific you wished to discuss?" she asked.

"Not really. My day was hectic and has left my thoughts swirling. I usually write down my impressions, but tonight the writing was slow, so I was hoping that talking would help put my thoughts in order."

There was a rustle of bedcovers, indicating she was sitting up. Duncan wished he could see more than deep shadows. "How was your day hectic? You were absent from the general areas most of the time."

"I was having individual interviews with some of the men who are here. I know these men find the process onerous, but they each talked with me for less than an hour. Today I talked with seven—and believe me, that *is* onerous."

Her chuckle was soft and in some way comforting. "And yet you want to talk some more."

He stretched out legs and took a sip of his brandy. "This is hardly the same thing. When I talk to these men, I have to be alert to every nuance. I have to constantly evaluate. All in all, it is exhausting."

"So, why do you do it?"

He appreciated that she waited in silence as he marshalled his thoughts. "When I attended the House of Lords, I was appalled at the haphazard way the country is governed. So many peers are there only to protect their privilege. There's little consideration for the good of the country as a whole or for what would be best for the general populace. Initially, I thought it was a reaction to the atrocities of the French Revolution. But after all these years, the attitudes of many haven't changed. And I think that change will come from the Commons, and so this is where I'm putting my effort."

"But as one of the Lords Temporal, you've blithely abdicated your responsibility in the upper house. I'd think that would be the place to put forth your ideas, but you haven't attended Parliament in years."

"A just criticism," he acknowledged, surprised she had so unerringly gone to the weakest part of his argument for change. "But I discovered I was getting in the way of my own agenda. Once I was designated the Gnome of the North, it became too easy for those who draw political cartoons to make fun of the changes I was trying to make." If she did not know, he wasn't going to further explain that once Jane had left him, he became the gnome whose wife had fled to the continent with a lover, making him even more a figure of fun. Even her death ten years ago hadn't change others' perceptions of him, since she'd never returned to England and her gnomish husband.

There was more rustling from the bed and another soft

sigh. Lady Lyndon must have settled back. She was probably tired, and he was keeping her awake. Also, the idea of snuggling down in the bedcovers with her now vividly presented itself. It was more than past time for him to leave before he said or did something inexcusable.

"I'm sorry," he said, standing. "I have kept you from your sleep for too long."

"No, don't go yet. I need to ask about something that has bothered me for some time. Wherever did the term Gnome of the North come from? Especially when the term gnome is so patently untrue."

He subsided back into the chair, inordinately pleased she didn't find him gnomish. Oh, he knew he was short, but not unduly so, and he wasn't in any way misshapen. He generally tried to pass the gnome sobriquet off as a joke. That was one of the reasons the walls of his study here at Norsham were filled with beautifully framed cartoons in which the Gnome of the North figured prominently. But deep inside, it still bothered him that others would see him as the caricature in the illustrations.

"My late wife coined the term," he said. "It was the only time she joined me in London. I think she meant it to be witty. Jane was never particularly sophisticated, but she wished to be. We were at a rather stuffy dinner for many of the Tory hierarchy and one of the other ladies asked her if she knew the short man with the radical ideas, and she replied, 'Oh, yes. That's the Gnome of the North, my husband.'

"Well, by the end of the evening, the phrase was in common usage, much to Jane's chagrin. I now see she was always embarrassed that she overtopped me by a good six inches. I didn't recognize her discomfort at the time. But a few days later, when the first caricature appeared in which I was shown as bent and wizened and identified with her words, she chose to come back to Northumberland and never returned to London."

"I'm sorry." The words held such sympathy that for a moment he could not get his breath.

Then he stood, knowing this time he would depart. "I'm sorry too… about many things. But not about a derisive nickname. Good night, Lady Lyndon."

"Good night, Lord Marle."

He'd nearly made it to the connecting door when she said, "I, too, had to learn to ignore an unattractive appellation. When I made my come out, some wags referred to me as the Pauper Princess, since I had no dowry."

He didn't say he'd heard the term. Instead he said, "And like most malicious identifiers, the phrases used for both of us held a germ of truth. I am definitely from the north, and you, Lady Lyndon, do look like a princess."

And then he entered his room and softly closed the door behind him.

Chapter Seven

Sophia hummed as she made her way to the family wing. It had been years since she'd felt so lighthearted. Today had been an exceedingly good day.

Henry had had his interview with the Earl of Marle. He'd been nervous about it at breakfast. Nervous but steadfast. Perhaps that was how he had behaved when he'd been in the army in Portugal, but she hadn't seen such maturity before.

And then after the interview... he'd been filled with enthusiasm and plans. Lord Marle had given his support and Henry was now anxious to visit Clavermoor, the borough that was soon to hold a by-election. He even talked about living there when Parliament wasn't in session, so he could better determine the needs of his constituents.

It had been a long time since Sophia had seen Henry so happy and filled with purpose. It made her heart sing. She did a few waltz steps to the tune she hummed and then a long, flowing turn. She laughed at herself and quickly looked around to see if anyone had spied her silly behavior, but the corridor was blessedly empty.

She was still humming when she entered her room. Nan, a sweet-faced country girl who'd been assigned as her maid, turned from where she'd laid Sophia's nightwear on the bed. "Good evening, Lady Lyndon," she said, executing a bobbing curtsey. "Are you ready to retire?"

"Yes," Sophia said. "The rest of the evening belongs to those younger than I. What started as a few friendly games of whist has now become a hotly contested tournament and I was quickly eliminated. So I decided to take my tattered dignity and quit the field."

The maid had the good grace to chuckle at what Sophia said, and they began the nightly ritual. Sophia continued to smile when she thought back to the competitive whist games, which, joy of joys, her stepson had taken part in.

Henry had always been a good whist player. His ability to remember what cards had already been played was truly amazing. But since the loss of his arm, he'd been uninterested, saying it was impossible to both hold the cards and discard with only one hand, which, unfortunately, was true.

But tonight, when Lady Amelia had offered to hold his cards for him, to Sophia's delight, Henry had agreed. When she'd left the drawing room, Henry and Lady Amelia were seated side by side, laughing. Yes, Henry was showing interest in more than one aspect of his life and happiness seemed possible. It was all any parent, even a surrogate one, could hope.

After washing up and changing into her nightrail and quilted dressing gown, Sophia sat at the dressing table and sighed with pleasure as the maid released her hair from the pins and combs and brushed it out. She tilted her head back to aid Nan with forming her night braid and saw something odd reflected in the mirror.

"Wait," Sophia said, turning to face the fireplace. What had seemed out of place suddenly became clear. There were now two chairs in her room, one on either side of the hearth.

Last night there had been only one. She was sure of it. She distinctly remembered Lord Marle sitting in the chair on the right. He'd worn a heavy, dark colored banyan with a large geometric pattern embroidered down the front and around the bottom, and she'd thought he looked like an Eastern potentate.

A powerful, sexually appealing potentate.

Sophia could not help but envision the muscular physique that lay beneath the princely robe. From the bed, his form had been attractively backlit. But his face had been cast into shadow, and she'd been unable to see his expression. She remembered wishing he were sitting on the other side of the fireplace, where the light would have illuminated his features. But there had been no other chair...

"Oh, you've noticed," Nan said. "A footman came in shortly before you arrived and built up the fire rather than banking it. He said you were chilled last night, and this should keep the room comfortable for some time."

"How thoughtful." Sophia couldn't think of anything else to say. Her mind was busy adding up the evidence and concluding that Lord Marle would pay her a visit again tonight. A *planned* visit.

And this would mean? Oh, Lord, she didn't know exactly what. Was he expecting more than a mid-night conversation? While he'd admitted to an attraction, his behavior last night would seem to prove that he would not act on it, as he'd said.

If she left the connecting door unlocked, was she indicating she was open to a different type of visit? She'd seen the key in the lock, but she hadn't touched it. Yes, with one turn of that key, she wouldn't have to worry about what these obvious preparations meant.

But she knew she wouldn't lock the door. She wanted to see where Lord Marle's visits would lead—even if she wasn't sure where she wanted them to go.

Should she go to bed and act surprised at his arrival or wait for him in one of the available chairs? Or would that make her look overly eager, perhaps wanton? No, her being in bed was much more intimate. Sitting in a chair would be less suggestive. But he'd already had two conversations with her while she was abed. Indecision made her pulse accelerate.

"Since the staff has been so kind as to refresh the fire, I think I'll sit up and read for a while," she said. "It will be more comfortable than reading in bed. I'll just move the candle stand next to one of the chairs."

"Oh, no, milady," the maid said. "I'll change it for you."

Nan was already moving in that direction. Sophia hurried after her. "The least I can do is clear the top." Sophia picked up the candle holder along with a pretty, little, inlaid box and trailed the maid as she effortlessly relocated the table next to the chair on the right.

Sophia replaced the items. "That's perfect, Nan. I can get my book, so that will be all for this evening. I hope you have a restful night."

The young woman looked scandalized. "Let me get you a lap robe and light the candle."

"Oh, yes. Please do." Sophia retrieved her book and spectacles and settled into the chair. She hated being fussed over, but she'd learned she only sowed confusion if she objected. She was certainly capable of lighting her own candle. There was a container of spills on the mantel, for heaven's sake, and if she were chilled, she knew there were additional covers in the chest by the window.

She had never been able to understand why others assumed she was incompetent because she was petite. She easily could have moved the candle stand by herself but had refrained in consideration of Nan's sensibilities. For years, her late husband would become agitated, sometimes violently so, by the proximity of anyone other than herself and his valet. She had learned it was simpler to do what was needed herself.

But Nan wouldn't depart until she had Sophia settled, so Sophia put up with the fussing with good grace until the young woman finally took her leave—at which point Sophia collapsed back into the comfortable chair and wondered if she was doing the right thing.

Her mouth twisted into an ironic smile. She would certainly feel like a dolt if Lord Marle didn't make an appearance. And there wasn't any reason to be sure that he would. It was possible the earl had nothing to do with the arrival of the additional chair. The staff could have realized the chair had been removed some time in the past and had simply replaced it.

Perhaps she was looking for signs of Lord Marle's interest where there were none.

But, oh, how she wanted him to be interested, to spend time alone with her. She'd enjoyed their late-night talk. She felt there was a communion there in the darkened room that drew them closer to each other, and it had been an appallingly long time since she had felt close to anyone other than those to whom she was bound by the threads of responsibility.

With a flash of uncomfortable insight, she realized she was lonely—and had been for a long time. It had taken her years and a great deal of adversity to become self-reliant. Like all young women of her class, she'd been reared to believe she needed a male authority figure to guide her. When her husband had slowly lost his hold on the present, however, she'd been forced into the position of making decisions that effected the direction of his life as well as her own.

And she'd discovered she liked to be in charge. She liked making decisions. After she'd completed her year of mourning, she'd enjoyed choosing her own townhouse in London and decorating it in her taste. She'd believed she didn't want to ever again be subjected to a man's dictates and choices.

But she now saw that self-reliance couldn't take the place of an intense connection with another human being, such as the one she felt developing with the Earl of Marle. This desire for connection seemed very different from the brief affair she'd imagined she wanted. Somehow, an affair now seemed incomplete. She wanted affection as well as independence.

She felt torn between two desires… and was left, like an idiot, pretending to read and hoping the door would open and some answer to her quandary would walk in.

As if she'd willed it, there was the soft knock she'd anticipated. "Come in," she said quietly, pleased her voice didn't betray her excitement and anxiety.

The earl appeared around the open door, once again in his embroidered banyan. She'd been uncertain last night what he wore beneath, but tonight it was obvious he was in his shirt sleeves and trousers. She realized he was still dressed, while she awaited him in her bedclothes. That might have been acceptable while she was abed, but now she felt he might see her behavior as lewd.

There was no look of distaste, however. Instead his face held a welcoming smile. "I was hoping the second chair would lure you out from behind the bed hangings," he said. "It will be much easier to converse when I can see you."

"I was reading." She held up the book as if in proof, felt silly doing so, then remembered she still wore her spectacles and whisked them off. Heavens, after all that, he would think she was a complete ninny.

"I thought you might enjoy a nightcap." He held up two glasses filled with an amber liquid. "Amelia said you enjoyed port, but all I had was brandy, so if it is not to your liking, don't feel like you have to imbibe."

"I'm not really all that fond of port. I'd prefer brandy, although I must admit, my favorite drink is whisky."

He laughed and walked over to hand her a glass. "You do know that whisky is generally not considered a lady's drink." He'd removed his cravat and his shirt was open so she could see the strong column of his neck. The firelight glanced off the beginning of a light-colored night beard. The sight was so arresting she nearly fumbled the glass.

"Thank you," she said and then returned his laugh. "But I'm not sure brandy or port is considered a lady's drink either."

He raised his glass in a salute. "According to my daughter Amelia, everything that is considered a lady's drink is terrible."

"Terribly sweet, anyway, particularly ratafia and orgeat,

the twin curses of Almack's."

"If that's the case, then I don't feel badly about never receiving a voucher," Lord Marle said. "From what I understand, my maiden speech in Lords blotted my copy book, since the Patronesses considered it radical."

"And do you expect my stepson to become a radical? He was enthusiastic about your support this evening, and I was pleased for him, but I hope you don't demand he always vote a specific way."

Sophia was very serious. If she thought Lord Marle's patronage would injure rather than help Henry, she would actively campaign against the earl. As much as she liked the man, her first loyalty belonged to her stepson.

"I don't require anyone to vote any specific way. I want to support a man who will vote for the betterment of those he represents. And I think Henry is such a man. I was impressed by his sincerity. I suspect much of his character came from his upbringing and that you had much to do with rearing him. So you are to be congratulated in making him the fine young man he seems to be."

Sophia could feel herself blush. People seldom complimented her since her accomplishments weren't ones that drew attention. "If I'm to judge from your daughter, I'd say you, too, have done an excellent job forming your children's characters. She was so kind tonight when she offered to hold Henry's cards. She did it in such a way that he didn't feel as if she were pitying him."

"And they seemed to have a wonderful time together," he said. "I don't recall Amelia's laughing as much in a social setting as she did tonight. Of all my children, I think she will have the most difficult time finding her place in life. Perhaps because she's the most like me."

Sophia laughed. "I don't think you've had a hard time finding your place in life."

He gave her a wry smile and shrugged. "Tell me about the two older boys you inherited when you married. What have they made of their lives?"

She raised her eyebrows in acknowledgement of his topic shift but went on to describe Alexander and Ralph. He added comments about his three sons, two of whom were married with families of their own. "I have three grandchildren," he mused. "How did I ever get so old?"

"You're younger than my oldest stepson, so I would hardly consider you old. But if grandchildren are a prerequisite of old age, I have seven."

The earl sat forward. "Seven? Good Heavens, how did that happen?"

Sophia laughed again. The man could say the most absurd things. "I'm quite sure it happened in the usual way. Ralph is a committed vicar and has taken the admonition, 'Be fruitful and multiply' to heart."

Lord Marle raised his empty glass. "Well, seven grandchildren, step or otherwise, deserves a toast, and my glass is empty, so if you'll excuse me, I'll retrieve the brandy."

At Sophia's nod, he was out of the chair and through the door, only to return in a matter of seconds holding a cut crystal decanter. He looked so pleased with himself that Sophia could imagine the same smile on his face when, as a boy, he'd filched his father's liquor. He filled both their glasses and tucked the decanter next to his chair.

"To progeny," he said, "and all the joy and pain they bring."

Sophia joined him in the toast. Then they began comparing their lives as only children, which led to a broad and diverse range of topics. By the time he refilled her glass again, she was Sophia and he was Duncan. The intimacy of first names felt comfortable, since in a short period of time, they had become old friends.

Sophia let some of the conversation wash over her. She felt a pleasant dislocation from the brandy and enjoyed watching Duncan speak. The firelight danced along the sharp lines of his brows and cheekbones as he made a point. His eyes seemed a luminous gray. He was quick to laugh, most often at his own actions and foibles.

She thought him the most handsome and intriguing man she'd ever met. The latter was a reaction to his personality more than his physical appeal. His mind was quick and his interests broad. Many of his attitudes had been formed by working at the family mining operations, since his father had insisted he become familiar with each type of job by doing it. She thought him everything that was admirable.

"Sophia, I think I've just about managed to put you to sleep," he said, a smile in his voice. He leaned forward and placed his glass on the floor next to the decanter. Then like water returning to an estuary as the tide rose, he flowed from his chair to lean over hers. His hands were braced on the chair arms. His face lowered to hers. And with the gentleness of an evening mist, his lips touched hers.

As kisses went, his was hardly lascivious, but it did strange things to Sophia's mid-section and constricted her breathing. "Good night, my Sophia," he said, and before she could respond, he was gone.

Sophia sat in the chair, touching her lips with her index

finger and staring at the now dying fire. She wasn't sure what had happened, but this seemed to be a magical night. She finally got up, dropped the lap robe onto the floor, and made it to her bed before falling asleep.

Chapter Eight

Hocking awakened Duncan at the usual hour, which felt damned early, especially since his head was throbbing. But Duncan arose with a smile. Last night had been worth any amount of discomfort. He'd used drinking brandy as an excuse to sit and talk to Lady Lyndon—no, she was Sophia now, a much more appropriate appellation—and he would suffer the torments of Hell to continue watching the ever-changing features of her face.

He'd discovered a shy dimple would occasionally flirt with her left cheek. When she was skeptical, her eyebrows would raise in the most becoming manner. Her laughter comforted him like a warm bath after a cold day of travel. She made him feel lighter and younger. Well, mostly she just made him *feel*, which was something he realized he'd long been missing.

She'd been waiting for him. He was sure of it, although she pretended to be caught reading. He grinned as he remembered how quickly she'd removed her spectacles. Women were so odd about such things. He'd thought she looked like a studious pixie.

But she'd definitely been waiting.

That *had* to be a sign. Especially taken with the fact that she'd not suggested he leave when he rambled on and on about things that probably were of no interest to her. Heavens, he had no idea what he'd said. He'd just been making sounds so he could stay with her.

He looked forward to the time he'd spend with her tonight. Perhaps he could then figure out what the sign of his welcome meant. Did she want to pursue this... this... something? Or was his conversation just a filler for the night's empty hours? Why in blazes was he so adrift when it came to Sophia?

And then there was that kiss. Hell, it hadn't even been a proper kiss. He'd done a better job of kissing when he was a callow boy. He'd purposely throttled down the passion that surged though him, since if he hadn't, it was possible he would have tumbled her into bed. Yes, it wasn't much of a kiss, but it still seemed to tingle on his lips.

Maybe tonight he could tell if she would be open to something a little more adventurous. But could he be adventurous without being ravenous? He shook his head at his own distraction. He needed to get his mind on the interviews he would have today. Even those individuals he'd already mentally eliminated deserved the courtesy of being heard and given the reasons he could not support them.

But before he became immersed in the work of the day, there was one detail he wanted to take care of. "Hocking, can you get me some whisky and leave it in my room?"

Hocking, in the midst of holding out his coat, looked surprised. "Whisky, my lord?"

"Yes, I feel like a change."

To Duncan's amusement, Hocking was still looking perplexed when Duncan left the room.

There were only a few gentlemen in the dining room at

this hour, two of whom had the early appointments with him. Duncan was cordial but noncommittal. He would see them both soon enough.

He quickly finished his breakfast, escaped to his office, and leafed through the information on the gentleman with the first appointment. When there was a knock on the door, he called "Come," and the work of the day had begun.

Two hours later, in the middle of his third interview, the door to his office opened without any warning. Duncan glared at the interloper, who, to his surprise, was Amelia. He immediately felt alarm. There had to be something amiss for her to barge in like this.

"Father, I'm sorry to bother you, but if Sir Paul would not mind leaving for a few minutes, I really do need to talk with you," Amelia said.

Duncan nodded to Sir Paul and the man immediately got up and left. "What's the matter?"

He thought she'd take the chair just vacated. Instead she marched right up to where he sat behind his desk, bringing him to his feet. He'd believed her upset, but he now recognized she vibrated with anger. "I'm assuming you're going to announce your betrothal to Lady Lyndon tonight at dinner."

"What in the blazes are you talking about?" Duncan was unconcerned about his language. Maybe it would shock Amelia back to making sense.

"I'm talking about the tale that you spent the night with Lady Lyndon in her room. The story is sweeping though the staff and will undoubtedly soon make it to our guests."

"How would anyone know where I was last night? I haven't been sneaking around the halls." As soon as the words were out of his mouth, Duncan realized they hardly offered a ringing denial.

"Of course, you haven't been sneaking around where anyone could see you. You have a connecting door. And before you start on this being a baseless rumor caused by proximity, you should know your crystal decanter, two glasses, and a blanket were found in front of the fireplace in Lady Lyndon's room."

The vilest words he knew immediately shot through his mind, none of which he'd use in front of any lady, especially his daughter. But they were the only words that would express his horror and anger. How could he have put Sophia in this position? Their meetings had been completely innocent. But he was the one who'd brought a recognizable decanter and two glasses into her room and stupidly left them there.

It was that damned didn't-really-count kiss, that soft brush of lips, which had left him unbalanced. He'd been befogged by brandy, but the real reason he hadn't thought about the evidence was his desire to get out of Sophia's room before he acted on a multitude of dishonorable impulses.

"*Merde*," he finally said, flopping back into his chair. "Who's the originator of this tale?"

"You're not denying it?" Amelia asked.

"Denying what? That I left the brandy decanter and two glasses from my room in Lady Lyndon's room? I can't deny that, because I evidently did. But I can and will deny there was any impropriety, since there was none. Lady Lyndon and I enjoyed an after-dinner drink, with her sitting in one chair and me sitting in another. Good Lord, Amelia, we talked about our grandchildren."

His daughter looked skeptical. "A blanket spread before the fire. The brandy decanter available. This doesn't sound like a situation where one would discuss grandchildren."

Duncan reined in his temper. "This wasn't a scene of seduction," he said with clenched teeth. "This wasn't the wild, out of control passion of a cowherd discovering a comely milkmaid in the barn. This was two sensible, mature people sharing a drink. Nothing more. And so, I want to know who below-stairs suggested otherwise."

Amelia slumped against the edge of his desk. He couldn't tell if her posture suggested dejection or exhaustion. "It was one of the young men from the village who'd been newly hired to act as an extra footman while this crowd is here. He went into Lady Lyndon's room very early this morning to replenish the fire and found what looked like evidence of tawdry behavior among the upper class. This was a heady discovery for a village boy. He hotfooted it back to the kitchen, bringing as evidence the engraved decanter you got when the Halmere Canal was opened. He found a ready audience in the rest of the other temporary staff. By the time the cook had informed the butler, the damage was done."

"I want the bastard fired. Those who work at Norsham don't carry tales."

"It's already been done. The temporary people have been warned that if they spread this gossip, they'll follow the footman out the door. The permanent people know better, but the uncomfortable part is that they also think they know what happened. Silence is no proof against knowing looks and sly smiles. So, it's only a matter to time before our guests conclude something is amiss."

Duncan looked closely at his daughter's averted face. A

shiny trail on her cheek, that might have been a tear, was followed by a drop that could be nothing other. "Amelia, darling, this is containable. You have no need for embarrassment."

"Oh, Papa," she said in a miserable voice, "the problem is I *like* Henry Phillips. Like him more than any man I've ever met. He's good and kind and honorable. And I'm sure when he hears—and he will hear about this—he'll be angry on his stepmother's behalf and he'll take our whole family in disgust."

As soon as Duncan recognized Amelia's distress, he'd reached out and gathered her to him, so the final words were said to his chest as she stood within his embrace, her head on his shoulder. It had been much easier when the children were young and hadn't grown taller than he was, but in the end, he was still Papa, the man who could fix the problems in their lives.

"Amy," he said, her childhood name sneaking out, "no man who is good, kind, and honorable could ever take *you* in disgust. I made an error in judgment. The fault is mine. The truth is I wanted to spend time alone with Soph... eh, Lady Lyndon. I've discovered I care for her more than I have any lady—" He paused, since what he said was the truth, but he felt it might make Amelia resent Sophia if she thought another woman had supplanted her mother in his affections. "—lately," he added.

She straightened, his own gray eyes looking back at him. "You do? Care for Lady Lyndon, I mean."

"Of course. How could I not? Like her stepson, she's good and kind and honorable."

"And beautiful," Amelia added.

He smiled. "Well, yes, there is that."

"So, it's not beyond the realm of possibility that you will announce your betrothal?"

"Amy, love, there's probably little chance of that happening."

"But why? You said you cared for her. The boys and I have waited a long time for a lady to catch your eye. We've hoped it would happen. We want you happy above all else. Papa, I know I was a baby when mother left, but I do know she left with another man, so there is no need to pretend undying love for our mother."

"Yes, she went to Denmark with an old friend. It was her choice and one for which I will never fault her." *I have always loved him.* No, he would not tell his daughter of his greatest failing—and now his greatest fear. "But you need to realize that people who have lived as long as I have, and as Lady Lyndon has, to some extent, have pieces of their past they carry with them. While I very much like Lady Lyndon, I have no idea if she returns my affection."

"Good Heavens, Papa, ask her."

"Would you ask Henry Phillips how he feels about you?" The appalled look she gave him answered his question. "Well, since it would be wrong to force someone else into some sort of declaration," he said, "I've been waiting for her to give me some sort of sign of her feelings."

"Waiting for a sign? What kind of sign? Like what I wanted when I was a child and dragged you to the barn two years in a row to see if the animals would speak at midnight on Christmas Eve?"

"Well, maybe not something like that." Duncan frowned. Why did Amelia's imperfect understanding make his idea sound ridiculous?

"Oh, I know. You're looking for something like the Christmas Star. You always contended the Magi weren't all that perceptive, since anyone could have figured out there was something going on in that stable with a bright beam of light coming out of the heavens to illuminate it."

Actually, that was exactly what he needed, but he certainly wasn't going to admit it. "Amelia, has no one told you it is not wise to poke fun at one's father? Especially when this does nothing to alleviate the problem at hand."

Amelia suddenly became serious. "Right. What can we do to avoid a scandal that will tarnish both you and Lady Lyndon?"

"I'm still trying to figure that out," he said. "But the first thing that needs to happen is for Lady Lyndon and her stepson to be alerted to the potential problem. It would be unfair for the gossip to get out without giving them fair warning, and for this, I'm relying on you."

"Me?" Amelia's voice was unnaturally high.

"If the word does get out, everyone will look less guilty if we all followed our anticipated schedules. I need to complete my daily interviews. And it would not be out of the ordinary if you chose to take Lady Lyndon and her stepson to see the watchers in the ceiling of the Great Hall in daylight."

"But what do I say?"

"Just give them the facts of the situation but approach it knowing that nothing dishonorable took place. Because it didn't. I have every confidence you can keep Henry Phillips from smacking a glove in my face."

Amelia's look of shock told Duncan that Amelia had never considered the possibility of Sophia's stepson challenging him to a duel. But Duncan considered it a real possibility. He, nonetheless, hustled Amelia on her way and got on with his day as planned.

Chapter Nine

Sophia stood by her bedroom window and looked out over the North Sea. The steel gray water was covered with wind-whipped whitecaps, and the surf threw spume into the air as it pounded on the beach. What seemed to be rain clicked against the windowpanes, suggesting it was changing to sleet.

She took a sip of her cooling tea and turned to Nan, who was laying out her clothes for the day. "Is it ever not rainy and cold here?" Sophia asked.

Nan gave her a quick smile. "You're seeing Norsham at its worst. Winters are always cold and damp, but most Decembers are not this bleak. Usually, rainy days are interspersed with days of bright sun, but that hasn't happened this week. And after the new year, we can expect snow, which covers the world in white and brings out the sleighs." She laughed. "I'm particularly fond of the sleighs. In early spring we go through another muddy period, however, and then everything turns green. Summers here are glorious."

"Then I wish Lord Marle had scheduled this gathering for summer," Sophia said.

"I think Lord Marle chose this time to help the village. In winter the fishing boats seldom go out and his hiring extra workers for the castle gives needed employment to many. The additional income helps cover the lean times."

Sophia nodded. This sounded exactly like something Duncan would do. Most landlords wouldn't take the needs of the local village into account. But as admirable as the idea was, she still wished for a bit of sun.

She placed her cup on the breakfast tray. Embarrassingly, she'd slept so late that breakfast service in the dining room had stopped by the time she'd gotten out of bed. Nan's arrival, tray in hand, had been a godsend.

Now Sophia had to wash and dress and get on with her day—a day when she would again be housebound. How she longed to take a blood-stirring walk or a pounding ride with the wind in her face. But even the allure of fresh air wasn't enough to make her want to venture out into the freezing rain. Fortunately, there were always people interested in playing either cards or chess, and she'd found Katherine St. Clare to be a wonderful conversationalist as well as a wicked caricaturist. Sophia often laughed at how well Katherine caught the character of some of the men with just a few strokes of the pen.

Sophia wished she had more of an opportunity to spend time with Lady Amelia Ashe. Henry seemed to have some interest in the young lady, and Sophia wanted to make sure she was a worthy candidate for his affections. She smiled at her own reflection as Nan put the finishing touches to her hair. She was acting as any mother would, foolishly thinking a grown son would care about her evaluation.

She'd just picked up her reticule to leave her room when there was a knock on the door, which opened to reveal a smiling Lady Amelia. "Oh good. You're still here," the younger woman said. "I'm going to show Henry the watchers in the roof beams of the Great Hall, and my father said you'd only seen one of them. I was wondering if you'd like to go with us."

The request seemed odd until Sophia remembered Henry and Amelia, heads together, smiling at each other over the cards, and then it dawned on her... she was the chaperone whose presence was needed to make sure there were no snide remarks such as those made when she and Duncan had visited the Great Hall. "I'd love to," she said.

"Don't forget your cloak."

Sophia turned to get it and the ever-efficient Nan was already removing the cloak from the wardrobe. Sophia would miss the cheerful maid when she returned home. Her spirits plummeted on the realization that Nan was not the only person she would miss.

She threw her cloak over her arm and followed Lady Amelia to the drawing room where they pried Henry from a heated discussion about duties on Irish spirits.

"I never knew there was so much to consider about goods going to and from Ireland," Henry said, looking flushed but happy. "I naively thought the Act of Union made us one country, and all tariffs would be dropped. But I see I have a lot to learn."

Amelia gave him a bright smile. "At least you're willing to learn. I think that's why my father was so enthusiastic about your candidacy."

"I hope he's not the only one who's enthusiastic." Henry winked at the young woman.

My Heavens, Henry winked! Sophia felt joy suffuse her. She and Alexander had been so right in suggesting this to

Henry. He seemed to be stepping out from under the cloud that had followed him from the Peninsula and was becoming the happy young man she remembered.

This feeling stayed with her as she followed the couple into the Great Hall, again being caught by the beauty of the room. Amelia didn't linger by the tapestries as her father had and seemed to push them rapidly through the room to the fireplace. When Amelia set Henry to the task of finding the watcher, Sophia took a good look at the little face gazing down. Perhaps it was the pale, gray light from the windows that made the watcher look less benevolent than he had with just firelight illuminating him. Today he was, indeed, a watcher, someone hidden and sneaky who sought others' secrets. His frozen stare chilled Sophia.

"I found him," Henry said, pointing up. "He looks like a rather sinister fellow."

Amelia nodded. "Today he does. I don't know how the artist did it, but the expressions on the faces seem to change with the light."

"Let's find the other you spoke of." Henry would have started moving off had Amelia not put a hand on his arm.

"In a minute," she said. "I brought you both here where we could be private to tell you something disturbing."

Sophia felt colder, as if Henry's impression had turned the watcher's grin into one that was malevolent and evil. She didn't want to hear that Duncan had withdrawn his support. She couldn't believe that of him and hated to think how crushed Henry would be.

"There is the rumor circulating among the staff that my father spent the night in Lady Lyndon's room," Amelia blurted out.

"What?" Sophia and Henry spoke simultaneously, hers a word of shock, his one of incredulity.

Henry turned to look at her, his shock now shading into anger. "Fee, please tell me there is no truth to this rumor."

"Not as Lady Amelia stated it. No. Lord Marle and I had a late-night drink in front of the fire where we talked about our children and grandchildren and…" Sophia's words ran out at the look of fury that was gathering in Henry's face.

Amelia obviously saw a coming explosion, since she interposed, "It is just as my father described it. Two older people nattering about their offspring late at night."

Sophia didn't know how she felt about being described as a babbling old gossip. It made her sound as if she were in her dotage. But if would defuse the situation, she would willingly find a cane and begin tottering around.

But as Amelia went on to describe the scene that had been found by the now-dismissed footman, the evidence did, indeed, seem damning. And if it got out to the guests in residence, the tale would not stay in Northumberland. When they returned to their homes throughout England, the scandal would spread. She would become a pariah. She would not make the friendships she'd imagined. She would be alone in the lovely little jewel box of a house she was creating. The only guests arriving at her door would be gentleman seeking to entertain a merry, wanton widow.

Sophia felt nauseous. The room spun around her in a kaleidoscope of colors. She had to reach over and grip a chairback to keep from crumpling to the floor.

"Are you all right?" Henry was suddenly beside her, his one arm circling her waist, supporting her. "Amelia thinks the rumor can be contained."

"Yes," the younger woman said. "I wanted to alert you to the situation. Not alarm you. Winthrop, our butler, has made it clear than anyone carrying tales will be summarily dismissed, so we are hopeful that it will spread no further."

"And if it should, that too can be repaired." All three of them jumped at the sound of Duncan's voice. They'd been so involved in their own discussion they hadn't heard him enter and walk the length of the long room.

"If possible, I'd like to speak with Lady Lyndon." Duncan looked at Henry as he said this.

Henry returned a stare that wasn't friendly. "Feel free to do so."

"Privately."

"As things stand, I don't think that would be advisable." Henry had pulled himself to military straightness. Sophia could see he was digging his feet in as he had when he was a boy. She knew if she let him take a stand, he was difficult to move.

"Henry, Amelia," she said to the younger couple, "I think it best for both of you to leave. Lord Marle and I need to talk, and as Amelia pointed out earlier, we're mature and hardly in need of a chaperone. Leaving the door open should take care of propriety."

Henry didn't move. "Fee, I think this is ill-advised."

Duncan opened his mouth to speak, but Sophia beat him to it. "Henry, I appreciate your concern, but we've spoken before about my not interfering in your life and you not interfering in mine. At this point, you're interfering. Please leave."

The two younger people looked at each other, but at a nod from Henry, they exited together.

Duncan and Sophia watched their progress until they'd disappeared through the door, then he stepped closer and took her hands in his. "Sophia, I am so sorry this has happened. I was at fault for leaving suspicious looking evidence in your room. I don't know what I was thinking... No, the problem was I didn't think at all."

"And obviously, neither was I." Sophia was loath to admit his gentle kiss had chased every logical thought from her mind. "But I don't believe either of us was at fault. Since we'd done nothing wrong, we weren't thinking about not leaving glasses or a decanter out of place. We had nothing to hide."

Duncan's smile was slow and a little sad. "Unfortunately, we live in a world ruled by perception rather than reality. And we left evidence that gave the perception of impropriety. We can proclaim our innocence to the rafters, and it will do no good."

The truth of his words made the cold, which had dissipated at his arrival, return. It chilled her skin and caused her to tremble. He evidently felt her slight tremor, for he dropped her hands and pulled her into an embrace. Her head rested comfortably on his chest. His arms warmly encircled her.

"Oh Sophia, I don't want to see you suffer for this. If the worst happens and the rumor becomes common knowledge, we'll marry."

"What? No!" She pushed back from him and his comfortable warmth.

"The idea is so repugnant to you?" His arms now hung loosely at his sides, as if in defeat.

She tried to gather her thoughts. The idea of marrying

Duncan was *not* repugnant. The thought of doing so made her breath catch in her throat. Had his offer occurred all those years earlier when she made her come out, had he then appeared as a suitor, she would have leaped at the chance to be his wife.

But that time had passed. She was now a thirty-seven-year-old widow. During all the years she devoted to taking care of her late husband, she'd promised herself that if it were ever possible, she would live an independent life, responsible only for herself, needing to please only herself.

And yet, after just a few days of acquaintance with the Earl of Marle, she'd come to question these intentions. She suspected being married to Duncan would bring more fulfillment than she'd thought was possible. She was physically attracted to him. She didn't think she'd ever seen a more appealing man. But more importantly, she was attracted to his humor and his kindness and his basic goodness.

He'd said he was physically attracted to her—but she suspected sexual desire was both the beginning and the end of what he felt for her. He'd certainly never suggested he was interested in marriage. However, this debacle was putting him in the position where he obviously felt he had no choice but to offer for her hand. She found this forced situation distressing. Marriage under these circumstances wouldn't be fair to either of them.

"No, the idea isn't repugnant to me," she said, striving for honesty. "But you must admit that neither of us *wants* to marry. And I hate the idea that you would only marry me because your honor demands you do so to avoid scandal. We can hope that such extreme measures aren't called for."

"Well, I'm not willing to admit I have no desire to marry you." To her surprise, Duncan sounded adamant, angry.

"You would want to marry me, even if we were not in this situation?"

"What man with half a brain would not? You have beauty and grace. You're witty and kind and... I like myself better when I'm around you. No, marriage to you would not be a hardship."

He reached out and ran the side of his finger along her cheek. "But I would never again force someone to marry me. And so, if the rumor spreads, I'll call all the men here together and tell them that if they ever hoped for either my political favor or my financial aid, they will not utter a word of this slander. If I hear they have—and I hear a great many things—I will grind them into the dust. And they all know I have the power base to do so."

The Great Hall was an appropriate place for Duncan's pronouncement, for a medieval knight stood before her, filled with power but loath to use it for his own aggrandizement. It was obvious, however, that for someone he cared for, he would unleash the hounds of Hell. For someone he cared for... was it possible?

"I never said I objected to marrying you," she said. "I just thought your offer was the only honorable solution you could think of. You've given no indication you've previously felt differently."

"*I've* never given any indication? Good Heavens, woman, when it comes to making your thoughts clear, you are the Sphinx. And honorable? What I feel is not honorable."

His caressing hand suddenly cradled her chin, turning her face toward him as he lowered his mouth to hers.

Chapter Ten

Duncan had not intended to kiss Sophia, but it suddenly became imperative he do so. He thought he'd take another little phantom kiss, such as they'd already shared. It wasn't all he wanted, of course. He wanted to lean her back onto one of the refectory tables and feast on the lushness of her lips. He wanted to explore the softness of her breasts, his fingers tracing the hills and valleys until she moved against him, desiring him as he desired her. He wanted to skim his palms along the tight roundness of her derriere and press her woman's core against his rigid erection.

But he'd learned he didn't always get what he wanted in life. So he would settle for a brief, honorable kiss.

Only that was not what happened.

When he turned her face up to his and gently touched his lips to hers, she did not remain quiescent. Her hands came up to touch his chest and then slid to his shoulders as she leaned into the kiss.

He had no choice but to drop the hand he had on her chin and run it along the graceful column of her neck until it rested at her nape. His other hand wrapped around her body and pulled her to him until their bodies touched. He didn't exert any pressure, but he was still very conscious of her breasts pressed against him.

The kiss itself turned into something very different from what he'd intended. When he ran his tongue along her lower lip, she relaxed her mouth and let him in. The desire that simmered through him could no longer be held in check. He kissed her as he'd imagined, as he'd wanted—no, as he'd needed.

Her initial response appeared to be surprise, and then she fully participated, her tongue following his lead, matching his movements. But her hesitation had been long enough for him to realize that this exquisite woman had reached her fourth decade and had never been passionately kissed. A sense of waste washed over him, and he suddenly felt like weeping. How much of his own life had been wasted? A waste not of kisses, since he'd had his fill of those, but of connection.

He'd been a good father who loved his children and who was loved in return. This love now extended to his sons' spouses and his grandchildren. But all this caring was paternal. There was no one not a relative whom he loved or who loved him. His late wife certainly never had. Other relationships were possible, but, dear Lord, he'd arrived at his fifth decade and hadn't found any. He and Sophia had both wasted so much potential.

He was dizzy with the taste of her, the feel of her. He'd thought he wanted her in his bed. But that wasn't enough—not any more. Certainly, he wanted the passionate Sophia, the woman he was sure could bring him soaring sexual delight. But he also desired the one who sat with him in earnest conversation before a fire and completed his day. He suspected she would complete his life, that she was the connection he'd waited so long to find.

Self-preservation, however, held him back from investing in something that might not come to fruition. He'd not again delude himself into thinking a relationship existed when it did not.

He pulled back slightly and broke the kiss, but neither of them moved apart. He moved the thumb on the hand that rested at the base of her skull and caressed her cheek. The pupils of her eyes were wide with arousal. He'd tumbled locks of her hair from her careful coiffure. The need for her pierced him.

"Would you come upstairs with me?" he asked. "There's something I want to show you."

For a moment she looked confused, then smiled. "If this is the prelude to a seduction, it's been handled well, but I feel our movements will be noted, particularly among the servants who are privy to the gossip about us."

Damn. She was right. He hadn't considered the possible repercussions when he wanted to take her hand and lead her to his chamber and produce Jane's note. He'd thought to show Sophia how wrong he'd been once and hope she could understand his fear of being wrong again.

Yes, that wonderful, sparkling kiss could be considered a sign of her regard, but since he'd once again initiated the action, he could never be sure.

"You're right," he said. "If you'll wait here, I'll go get what I wanted to show you."

"It's important then?"

"I think so."

"Then by all means, go get it. I'll be here." She gave him a Madonna's smile that warmed him to his toes. But would the expression remain when he showed her proof that he was oblivious to the emotional needs of someone who should have counted the most?

❧☙

Duncan was surprised at how heavy the small piece of paper felt riding in his pocket as he hurried back to Sophia in the Great Hall. There was such importance for him in those five words.

He'd almost made it to the hallway that connected to the Great Hall when he was haled by Roland St. Clare who was sitting in the library with his daughter Katherine and David Marsh. "Lord Marle, do you have a minute?" St. Clare called as Duncan passed the door.

No, he didn't have a minute, but he swung into the room anyway. He remembered the need to keep to his regular schedule to avoid appearing guilty if word of a potential scandal became known. And since he would normally join in any discussion if asked, there was no avoiding what he hoped would be a brief detour.

"Miss St. Clare, gentlemen, what's the topic of conversation?" Duncan asked with a smile.

For an awkward few seconds, there was no reply. Katherine St. Clare seemed intent on creating a pleat with her fingers in the skirt of her dress. David March looked at Roland St. Clare as if seeking guidance. It was, therefore, Roland who cleared his throat and looked directly into Duncan's face.

"My daughter overheard something disturbing that I thought you should be made aware of," St. Clare said. "When she went upstairs to the family wing to retrieve her drawing supplies, two housemaids were gossiping in the next room. What they said, eh, seemed to suggest that you and Lady

Lyndon were, eh, conducting a clandestine affair."

St. Clare's face had turned a startling red, but his honest eyes had not wavered.

And there it was. What Duncan had feared was laid out before him. All his thoughts on how to handle the situation disappeared—and he lied. "Thank you," he said. "I'm acquainted with this malicious rumor. It was started by a young man from the village who had been hired as a temporary footman for this week. Winthrop, my butler, admitted he could find no motivation for this calumny unless it was the man's effort to appear more important than he was. Needless to say, the butler immediately terminated him. There is, of course, no basis for this gossip."

A good lie always had some basis in truth, and Duncan felt this was a solid lie, or perhaps prevarication would be a better term, since he'd taken the truth and distorted it. He doubted it would hold up if the evidence of the wandering decanter and the connecting door were added to the tale, but evidently that had not been part of what Miss St. Clare overheard. Or, if it was, the young woman had chosen not to share it.

"I assumed there was an explanation," St. Clare said. "I just wanted to make sure you'd heard what is evidently circulating below stairs."

Duncan held his earnest expression. "I appreci—"

"No... Stop!" A woman's scream ended all conversation and brought everyone to their feet.

"What? Where?" St. Clare threw the words into the sudden silence.

But Duncan was already moving toward the door. He knew the voice and could guess the location and the cry chilled him to the bone. "Great Hall," he called over his shoulder. Then he ran.

He dashed down the hallway, the other two men running just behind him. He slowed to make the turn into the Great Hall and what he saw spurred him to greater speed. A large man—Isiah Harding—had Sophia pushed up against one of the tapestries. One of his hands covered her mouth and the weight of his body held her in place as he leaned into her. His other hand tried to control her flailing arms as she reached for his face.

Duncan ran directly at the man and with a strength born of desperation and fear, grabbed the back of Harding's jacket and jerked him away. Sophia slid down the tapestry to crumple on the floor. Duncan knelt beside her and pulled her into his arms. She was trembling and sobbing. Behind him he heard the scuffle as St. Clare and Marsh none-to-gently subdued Harding.

"Sophia, did he hurt you?" Duncan asked.

She shook her head, then muttered, "He mostly scared me." Her voice was uneven but grew stronger. "He said vile things about the two of us and attempted to kiss me. When I resisted, he grabbed me and pushed me into the wall."

"It will all be well now," Duncan assured her. "If you can stand, I'll carry you to your room, where you can clean up and rest."

Her head came up, the look of fright and shock overlaid with a flicker of pride. "*Carry* me? There's no need to carry me."

"There's every need." This was not the time or the place to explain he wanted to keep her in his arms as long as possible, that if he had it his way, he would never let her go.

He helped her stand and immediately put an arm under her legs and picked her up. She clung to him like a limpet. He could feel the slight tremors ripple through her. Her pride had been unable to overcome her fright.

He turned around to see much of the staff and many of the guests hovering near the door. Harding sat in one of the side chairs, St. Clare standing on one side and March on the other. He spotted Katherine St. Clare near the front of the crowd.

"Miss St. Clare, would you please find Lady Amelia and meet me in Lady Lyndon's suite," he said. "Winthrop..." he looked around.

"Here, milord," came from the back of the group.

"Winthrop, would you please clear this room with the exception of Mr. Harding. Please station two footmen at the door to make sure he stays here. I'll be back shortly to take care of this matter."

"You've already *taken care* of me, Lord Marle," Harding said in a sarcastic tone. "You refused to help me, but you were happy to support Henry Phillips. But then, of course you'd back Henry, since you've taken his stepmother as a lover. You can't blame me for wanting a taste of the light skirt who made sure I didn't get preferment. I—" Whatever other venom Harding thought to spew was cut short by David Marsh driving an elbow into the side of Harding's head. Duncan decided he quite liked the young man.

"I think we've found the source of the scurrilous rumors," St. Clare said, glaring at Harding.

"Indeed," Duncan said. He carried Sophia to the door, where the crowd parted like the Red Sea before Moses. Sophia turned her head into his chest, hiding from the curious stares, and they made their way to her room in silence.

≪≫

After settling Sophia, Duncan strode through the corridors in the east wing until he brought his hot, bright anger under control. When it had become compressed into cold fury, he sought out his butler.

"Winthrop, please locate the footman assigned as Mr. Harding's valet. Tell him Harding will be quitting the property within the next half hour. He should pack up everything and have it waiting in the entry hall. Also inform Harding's coachman that the coach should be prepared for immediate departure."

"Certainly, milord." Winthrop gave him a slight smile that indicated what had transpired in the Great Hall had made a villain of Mr. Harding and those below stairs were anxious to see him gone. "And if the equipage is not yet in place when Mr. Harding appears?"

"Then Harding can wait for his coach in the rain."

This gained a full-fledged grin from his butler. "It will be so."

Duncan nodded and made his way to the Great Hall. He signaled the two footmen standing guard at the door to leave and entered.

Harding leaped to his feet at the door's opening and glared at Duncan. "How dare you detain me here?" he asked, all indignant bluster.

"How dare I not?" Duncan was pleased that his voice didn't show any of his fury. "I was protecting you from Henry Phillips. I fear had the two of you met, the young Mr. Phillips would have insisted on a dawn meeting, and I try to avoid such contretemps at my house parties."

"I'm not concerned about the one-armed pup."

"Well, you should be, since I suspect the hand at the end of that one arm is quite accustomed to holding a pistol and making the bullet go where he wants it to. Fortunately, Mr. Phillips' accuracy will never be put to the test."

"He would have no call to take offense anyway," Harding said. "Lady Lyndon led me on and then pretended offense when she heard people in the corridor. Since you've been sampling what she has to offer, you know what these hot widows are like."

"Actually, I don't." Duncan shrugged out of his coat and draped it across the arm of a chair. "Do you box, Mr. Harding?"

The man looked confused by the change of subject but straightened as if his manhood had been called into question. "Yes, I enjoy sparing at Jackson's when I'm in town."

"Oh, good," Duncan said, adding his waistcoat and cravat to the pile of clothes. "It's not particularly satisfying to thrash a helpless opponent, although in your case I would have made an exception."

"What in the Hell are you doing?" Harding asked.

"I would have thought it was obvious. I'm stripping to the waist. My valet becomes quite vexed when I get blood on my linen." Duncan pulled his shirt over his head and added it to the heap on the chair. He flexed his shoulders. "I'll be happy to wait while you do the same if you like."

Harding gave a short, choppy laugh. "You, the infamous Gnome of the North, are going to best me at boxing? You fool. I have a good six inches and three stones on you."

"Three stones? Goodness, you must have a fine tailor.

Your pudginess doesn't show at all." Duncan moved two chairs back against the wall.

"You little runt!" Harding began jerking off his coat and shirt. When he was bare-chested, he moved to the now-cleared portion of the room and assumed the classic boxer's pose with his fists held before him.

Duncan smiled. This was going to be enjoyable. He wondered if he should tell Harding he'd learned to box at the colliery, and miners didn't always follow the proscribed rules. Then he remembered the look in Sophia's eyes when he pulled the cretin off her. Confusion. Fright. Shock. No, he'd keep his counsel and teach the man all the ways he could hurt.

He moved to the open section in the room and mirrored Harding's awkward stance. He'd just taken the position when Harding swung at him—a powerful punch aimed at his head and intended to put him out with one blow.

Duncan shifted to one side and let the strike slide past his face. He used Harding's forward motion to add power to his own blow. He buried his fist in the man's midsection, felt the air leave his lungs and his balance fail. Duncan shifted back and watched Harding fall to his knees.

"Down already," Duncan taunted. "I should have known a lumbering ox like you would provide no sport. You can only *pretend* to be a man by attacking a smaller, weaker woman."

Harding came off the floor with a feral growl, his arms wind-milling. Gone was any discipline he might have learned at his elite boxing club.

Smiling, Duncan danced away from the larger man's crazed assault. This was the fight Duncan had been seeking. He methodically set about punishing Harding with calculated blows. Strikes to the ribs strong enough to bruise but not break. Punches to the face intended to close eyes and reshape the nose.

Harding fought with desperation, his knees wobbly, his breathing labored.

Duncan laughed aloud, the blood singing in his veins. Political battles were by their very nature long termed and constrained. But this wild exultation of power... this was man at his most primitive. This was primal male defending his woman.

His woman. The realization of this truth put too much strength into an uppercut to Harding's jaw, and the man went down in a heap. He tried to push himself up, but his arms failed, and he collapsed back to the floor.

"Are we done, then?" Duncan asked his fallen opponent, although the answer was obvious. The man's face was a bloody mess. He was conscious, but barely. Duncan poked him with his toe. "Are we done?"

"Yes." The word sounded more a moan than syllable.

"Good." Duncan walked to where his clothes lay on the chair. He picked up his cravat and wiped the sweat from his face. His right cheek hurt where one of Harding's blows had gotten through. It would bruise, but not badly. His knuckles were another story. They were already swelling and stiffening. His penmanship would suffer for a while.

But the satisfaction was worth it.

He dropped his shirt over his head and turned to the man still slumped on the floor. "Your carriage is being brought around and I expect you to leave immediately. I think you would be smart to give up on any sort of political career since I have the resources to make your way very difficult. I would not want to embarrass Lady Lyndon, so I will not give others any specifics of your behavior here. But if I'm pressed, I will say you are without character and honor."

Duncan slipped on his waistcoat and coat, leaving both unbuttoned. "So, get dressed and get gone. I hope to never hear of you again."

He opened the door and was unsurprised to see Winthrop and a brace of footmen nearby, acting as if they had not been eavesdropping. "I'm sorry I left things a bit of a mess in there," he said, "but I'm sure you can quickly remove the trash and put the room to rights."

"It will be done." Winthrop gave him a broad smile, and Duncan continued on to his bedroom, feeling ridiculously pleased with himself.

Chapter Eleven

Sophia finally managed to chase Katherine St. Clare and Lady Amelia out of her room by claiming she wanted to nap in front of the fire. Their kind fussing had become more irritating than helpful. She would never have said so, of course, since the two young women were trying to be solicitous. And their concern *had* helped her overcome the shock of Harding's attack right after it had happened, but what she now really wanted was to be alone.

Saying she would nap was easier than doing it, however. Her mind continued to race. Most of the people in residence had been in the Great Hall when Harding had accused her and Lord Marle of being lovers. This meant Harding had either heard the rumors or spied them kissing. Their embrace had been stupidity on their part, but at the time, it had seemed as necessary as breath.

She was loath to think of the gossip swirling in the common areas of the castle. Duncan's efforts to contain the rumor to the staff would mean nothing with this new accusation on everyone's mind. The solution, of course, was simple. Duncan had asked her to marry him—and as she'd told him, the idea was not repugnant. In fact, it was most appealing. But...

Oh, yes, there was that tedious but... One of many.

But... She didn't think any type of forced marriage had a chance of being a happy one. Financial necessity and the need for security had forced her into marrying Viscount Lyndon. She knew she'd upheld her part of the contract and had done her duty until his death, but happiness had never been part of the equation.

And happiness was what she now sought.

She'd thought she could be happy carving out her own life, spending her efforts on her house and her step-grandchildren and her charities. But...

She was lonely. She hadn't realized this was the case until Duncan dropped into her life, or more specifically, her bedroom. Those hours, sitting by the glowing fire in the dark, had given her a connection she'd unknowingly craved. But...

Had Duncan felt the same connection she had? He'd seemed to actually want to marry, but there still seemed a lingering hesitancy. The conflict in her own feelings, the contradictory signals she felt she was getting from Duncan, and the irregularity of the situation all led to a disturbing string of buts.

And then the connecting door opened. There had been no knock, no warning. Duncan was just suddenly in her room. His hair was messed, his clothing in disarray. Yet he filled the room with masculine power. She leaped to her feet. Only with difficulty did she manage to keep from running forward and throwing herself in his arms.

He held up a slip of note paper. "I've retrieved what I wanted to show you," he said, as if the conversation in the Great Hall had not been interrupted by a drastic series of events. "I hope it will explain what I believe you perceive as my reluctance to marry you."

He hurried forward and thrust the paper into her hand. Then he stepped back, his expression one that might be seen on a prisoner awaiting a verdict.

Sophia unfolded the page, noting it appeared old and well-handled. The central fold was fragile and in danger of tearing. There were only a few words, and they made little sense.

I have always loved him. Jane.

"Without context, I'm not sure what I'm reading," she said. "And so it explains nothing."

"That's the note my wife left me when she ran away with a man she'd known in her youth. He hadn't been considered an acceptable suitor by her parents, since he was a younger son with few prospects. Instead, her parents arranged with my father for Jane to marry me."

"So, you and your late wife didn't know each other well when you married?"

Duncan gave her a rueful smile and ran his fingers through his already disheveled hair. "I thought we knew each other *well enough*—whatever that is. I thought we could find a comfortable life together. And what is even more germane to this discussion, I thought Jane felt the same."

"You were both very young when you married, weren't you?"

"We were both eighteen. Old enough to know our own minds. I'd been working in the mines since I was sixteen when my father pulled me out of school to give me what he thought was more practical experience. He believed that to successfully manage the collieries, I needed to personally experience all the jobs involved in mining. After working there, I definitely considered myself a grown man."

She smiled. "As the parents of adult children, I think you'll agree that being eighteen is hardly a guarantee of maturity."

"In my case, it was more a matter of focus than maturity. I was busy learning to run the mines and the farms and, on my father's death, I became involved with politics. I probably didn't pay as much attention to Jane as I should. She seemed happy to me. Good Lord, we'd been married nearly ten years when she left. We'd had four children together. I thought I knew her—but I did not."

Duncan looked so bereft that Sophia had to touch him. She needed to let him know she sympathized with his distress. With just a few steps, she was able to wrap her arms around his waist and lay her head on his chest.

"We never really know what another person is thinking," she said. "You can hardly feel at fault for not being able to look into her mind."

His arms came around her, but he held her lightly, as if giving her the opportunity to pull away. "I've always prided myself in my ability to understand people. I'm seldom surprised at what either a political ally or foe will do. I'm *good* at reading people. But that note shows I'm not good at understanding the finer emotions."

Sophia pushed back so she could look him in the eye. "And from the condition of the paper, you've reread this note frequently."

"Of course, I have." He sounded angry. "Those five bloody words are a reminder of my worst failure. Over all those years, Jane must have indicated she wasn't happy, but I was oblivious. She was my *wife*, for Heaven's sake. She was the person with whom I had the most intimate of all relationships, but I still missed all the signs of her discontent."

Sophia was well acquainted with feeling guilt for things not done, but she had also learned most of these missed opportunities would never come again and worrying about them was a waste of time. "Sometimes we just have to chalk our mistakes up to experience and realize that interpreting the non-verbal signs others give is often hard to do."

"Hard? More like impossible." He made a grating sound that might have been a chuckle. "Amelia thinks I need a sign as explicit as the Christmas Star."

"Well, I'm having trouble interpreting your Christmas Star reference," Sophia said, feeling adrift with this odd change in the conversation, "so I must have problems understanding verbal references."

Duncan laughed, a wonderful sound after his apparent distress. "Amelia was referring to my contention that the wise men who brought gifts to the Christ Child were not really all that wise. Since the stable was illuminated with a light from the heavens, anyone would have been able to tell it was a special place. And I need a sign that's equally obvious to be sure about what it means."

Without conscious thought, she abruptly leaned closer again, wrapped one hand around the back of his neck, and pulled his head down so she could kiss him. When her lips touched his, Sophia felt like she was coming home, and she knew all the *buts* she could conjure had nothing to do with the way she felt about this man. She pulled back before waiting to see where this delicious kiss could go.

"That's a sign," she said.

"Of...?" Duncan cocked one eyebrow.

She chuckled. "Now you are being purposely obtuse."

"I hope it means you will marry me."

"It means I'm interested in talking about it. Come, sit down." She took his hand and led him to his customary chair. She then sat in hers.

"Why do I feel sitting here is a sign we're about to enter into negotiations?" he asked. "I want a marriage based on mutual affection, not a business agreement. I think we've both already had a businesslike marriage and don't care to revisit those circumstances."

She nodded. "I agree. I'm looking for a relationship based on respect and hopefully love—although right now I can only say I care for you. I think real love comes with greater understanding."

He nodded and then flashed her a wicked smile she felt to her toes. "I think your list is missing passion, and for me, this is a requirement."

Sophia laughed aloud. "If you can't tell that is already in evidence, you really are terrible at reading signals."

"I was hopeful," he said with a grin. "And I'm also hopeful this means you don't want a long engagement."

"Of course not, although there are logistics to take into account. My two married stepsons live in the south and your children all live in the north. So the *when* for our wedding is dependent on the *where.* And then, where would we live? Here? At another of your residences? I know you've eschewed London for years, but would you consider taking me to Town on occasion since I have friends there? And if so, would you like to dwell at my house—and I use the word 'my' since I would insist that any moneys and property currently mine continue to be so. By the same token, I would not want to impinge on your children's inheritance should you predecease me. And—"

"Stop!"

She did, and for an indefinite number of fast heartbeats, silence filled the room. She was chagrinned. Somehow, in the middle of agreeing to a short engagement, the specter of lost independence had appeared and she'd reacted poorly.

"This is sounding a great deal like a business negotiation, which we both wanted to avoid," Duncan said. "I much preferred contemplating passion. But I understand most of your concerns and since neither of us has a father to arrange a marriage settlement, I guess it is up to us. So, to address your concerns…

"I would like us to wed sometime between Christmas and Hogmanay, which would be about two weeks from now." He gave her a quick smile. "You can tell I definitely don't want a long engagement. I was hoping we could leave here in two days' time and go to Brackenfel, my house on the edge of the Pennines. One of the advantages of Brackenfel, besides the house being more easily heated, is its location, which is less than four miles from the Scottish border. I figured we could slip into Scotland and get married at the small kirk in the nearby village of Alliburn. I assume Henry will come with us to Brackenfel and three of my children should be there, so we will have a small, family group at the ceremony. Then we can take a leisurely wedding trip back to London, stopping to see your other two stepsons on the way. Do you have any problems with these basic arrangements?"

"Eh, no. But—" Duncan held up his hand. It occurred to Sophia that his plan must have taken shape long before she'd asked her questions.

"And now to your other concerns... I have no problem with living in Town for part of the year, although if we do, I will have to attend the House of Lords. And you'll have to get used to having your husband lampooned in the newspapers, since I doubt my ideas will suddenly have become popular and the cartoonists have perfected the caricature of the Gnome. You will also have to be willing to host occasional political gatherings. We can maintain a residence either at your house or at Marle House in Mayfair. The latter has been in the family for a couple hundred years and is an imposing pile of rocks in need of redecorating. But the choice of domicile is yours. Do these suggestions meet your approval?"

"Yes." This time her voice held more conviction.

"Good. So we are down to the basic marriage settlement. I agree whatever is yours should remain yours. In addition to this, of course, I will make property and monetary arrangements if you should be left a widow. Don't worry that you will be taking anything that should belong to my children. There is more than enough to go around. If the basics of this are agreeable, Henry and I can work out the particulars between now and the wedding. Does this sound workable to you?"

Once again, all she could do was nod and say, "Yes." This all seemed to have been well planned. But she found his rather distant recitation of the information unsettling. She feared she'd offended him with her questions and concerns. Duncan had wanted passion—and she'd given him a legal sounding proclamation.

He suddenly stood and bowed to her, all formal and proper and definitely not to her liking.

"Then I will go change and make your excuses until

dinner. No one will fault you for taking tea in your room after the trying day you've had, and this will give you time to arrive at a decision."

He turned and walked to the connecting door. She suspected she'd handled the situation badly and had bruised Duncan's pride. She was somewhat relieved when he stopped and turned and gave her a brilliant smile.

"I hope you decide to marry me," he said, "for it is something I desire with all of my being."

And then he was gone, leaving her alone with her chaotic thoughts.

ಸಂಡ

Nan entered with a heavy tray and a happy smile. Sophia was delighted to see both. She was beginning to feel peckish and was heartily tired of her own thoughts.

The maid placed the tray on a side table and began removing dish covers. The enticing odor of scones fresh from the oven remined Sophia of how hungry she was. Nan uncovered one large plate of assorted sandwiches and another of a variety of biscuits.

"Good Heavens," Sophia said. "Is this all for me or is cook expecting an invading army?"

Nan gave her a saucy grin. "All for you. An abundance of food is cook's way of showing her appreciation." She poured a cup of tea, added the amount of milk and sugar Sophia preferred, and handed her the cup.

"Why is cook thanking me?"

"For reminding Lord Marle of his proud warrior heritage, of course."

"I still don't understand," Sophia said.

Nan's expression mirrored the one often seen on the

face of patient tutors when they were explaining something to particularly dull students. "Our village has huddled on the leeward side of Norsham Castle for hundreds of years. For all that time, the people of the village have looked to Norsham's lord for protection from invaders. Most of the staff here is from the village and our families have lived there for generations, and so the expectation that the Earl of Marle will defend what is his is bred into us. Now, in this modern day, the earl's protection usually involves solicitors and laws, and so it was gratifying to see the earl physically chastise the man who had attacked his lady."

Sophia was trying to get her mind around what *physical chastisement* entailed when Nan continued. "Oh, my lady, it was wonderous. That odious Mr. Harding was a bloody mess, his nose all crooked and his legs wobbly, when two footmen helped him to his carriage. We have you to thank for reminding Lord Marle that there are times when only a sound thrashing will remedy a situation."

Nan grinned as if she'd been a party to what transpired, but she'd given Sophia the basis to vividly imagine what had happened. Sophia hadn't lived in an all-male household and remained ignorant of how men sometimes behaved. But the idea of Duncan being involved in fisticuffs, of defending her honor by placing himself in the position to be physically harmed... it left her feeling breathless.

Isiah Harding was much younger and much larger, yet Duncan had prevailed. Sophia remembered being transfixed by the sculpted musculature of Duncan's chest when she had inadvertently burst into his room. She'd felt the power in his arms when they'd protectively circled her. Of course, he'd prevailed.

And when he'd arrived in her room earlier, disheveled and flush with victory... Heaven help her, she'd responded to his unknown gallantry with questions and demands as if she were a barrister. Because she'd been afraid to take a chance on a future that was different from the one she'd planned.

No wonder the poor man couldn't understand how she felt about him. She kept giving him conflicting signals.

"Nan, is Lord Marle in his room now?" she asked.

"No, milady. Hocking said the earl would be involved with the last of his interviews this afternoon."

"Good! Then will you help me with a project?"

"In any way I can." Sincerity shown from the young woman's eyes.

Sophia gave her maid a happy smile and said, "You need to get us some paper and scissors. Oh, and some sewing thread. I have a few things I want to make and place in Lord Marle's chamber. And you'll need to convince Hocking to leave our surprise in place until the earl arrives. Can you do this?"

"Easily," Nan said, and then she began laughing. "Oh, I think this is going to be such fun."

Chapter Twelve

Duncan walked up the stairs without the usual bounce in his step, caused, no doubt, by a morning of physical exertion and an afternoon of serious discussions. He was tired, but it felt good to have the last of the interviews finished. On the whole, this year's crop of hopeful politicians was a good one. He'd only had to completely reject the request of three of the men, and of them, only Isiah Harding had been refused because Duncan had serious reservations about the man's character.

Since he'd rejected Harding long before his despicable behavior toward Lady Lyndon, Duncan's reaction to the man reinforced his confidence in his ability to weigh intentions and character. Unfortunately, it also made him even less sure of his ever understanding what was going on in Sophia's mind. He concluded he must have a blind spot when it came to women.

At least there was no longer the threat of a forced marriage. Harding's actions made him a convenient scapegoat. The consensus now was that he'd paid the dismissed footman to start a false rumor in an effort to discredit Henry Phillips' receiving preferment. There was now no need to marry to avoid social scandal.

Duncan should be relieved. The realization that he was

not nearly caused him to miss a step. No, he very much wanted to make the Dowager Lady Lyndon his wife. The reasons for this chased through his mind and could find no one place to land. He just knew that she was the one woman he wanted by his side forever.

Was this feeling, which careened between lust and contentment like a ball on a billiards table, love? Duncan had no experience with romantic love—he had no idea *what* to call the emotion he felt. But he knew it was there. He knew it was strong.

Unfortunately, he had no idea if it was reciprocated.

He was still milling over this problem as he pushed open the door to his room, expecting to find Hockings waiting to help him dress for dinner. But his valet was absent. The room, however, was not empty. Instead, white paper stars lay on most of the horizontal surfaces, were tucked into the edges of the frames on mirrors and pictures, and hung from thread from the chandeliers.

The largest of the stars hung on the connecting door to the adjoining bedchamber.

He immediately walked to the door, pulled the paper star free of the thread looped over the top, and entered Sophia's room. She stood at the window, looking out at the darkening landscape. She wore a pale blue dressing gown and her silver hued hair flowed loosely to the middle of her back. When he had first seen her, he'd thought she looked like a fairy. Now she seemed to be moonlight personified.

"Is this a sign?" he asked, holding up the star, his voice suddenly husky.

She smiled and did, indeed, seem to glow. "It's a representation of the Christmas Star. And a wise man would know it means *yes*."

He slowly moved toward her. "Yes, to what?"

She also walked toward him. "Yes, to everything. Yes, I want to marry you. Yes, the living arrangements are agreeable. Yes, I trust you and Henry to come to terms that will protect my independence. Yes, I hope we can marry at the earliest possible date in the most convenient location. And finally, the most important... yes, I love you and promise to always tell you what I'm thinking and feeling."

Like filings attracted by a magnet, they had pulled together in the middle of the room. He reached out to cradle her face in both his hands. "Yes, you've made me the happiest of men. Yes, I will always love and honor you. And yes, we will be quite late to dinner tonight."

Her eyes reflected laughter. "I don't remember a question about going to dinner."

"Well, I took your mode of dress and the style of your hair to be a sign that you would be amenable to a delay in our arrival."

Sophia's low laugh circled the room. "You are improving with understanding signs and portents. In this case, I may have arranged for Nan and Hockings to stay below stairs until we ring for them."

"I like confidence in a woman, but did you lock the doors?"

"I wasn't that confident," she said. "Besides, some of the work should be yours."

He dropped his hands and backed up a step. "At your command," he said with a bow. Then, feeling younger and more alive than he had in years, he quickly locked the hall door and the one connecting to his room. As he hurried back to where she stood, he began loosening his cravat.

"You're definitely reading the signs correctly," she said, reaching up to help pull the fabric off his neck and drop it to the floor.

"This is what happens when one becomes a wise man." He lowered his mouth to hers and knew that after years of looking into a dark sky, he had finally seen the Christmas Star.

Epilogue

Edinburgh
September 1821

Harold Ashe heard the carriage and hurried to his friend Parker's room. There were already three boys crowded around the window. Parker's room had the best view of the Glenhurst School's front drive, an advantage since today was intake day for new students and everyone wanted to see them arrive. Even though it was difficult to judge much from two floors above, it was a bit of a game to guess what any given boy would be like.

Harry pushed in beside Burnage.

"I say, Ashe, can you back off a bit?" Burnage said, using his unusually sharp elbows to good advantage. "You've weeded up enough over this break to see over us."

"Which would be much easier had you not let your hair grow into a bush." Harry used his own pointed elbows to move his friend aside. While it was true Harry was growing up, he had yet to master the ability to grow out.

Burnage raked one of his hands though his wildly curling locks. "It's the current style, you dolt, which you'd know if you didn't live in the back of beyond."

"My father is currently Viscount Churchwell and his seat is in Northumberland, so that is where we live." Harry didn't point out that the rest of the year, his family lived in London where his grandfather, the Earl of Marle, was active in Lord Liverpool's government. By comparison, anywhere in Scotland could be called the back of beyond.

"The carriage door is opening." Parker whispered as if they could be heard, which was unlikely at this distance. "Stop squabbling."

Four pairs of eyes now fixed on the slowly moving door.

"What? Is old Talbot now taking six-year-olds?" Burnage asked.

"No, that's a first term boy. He's just a..." Parker was obviously accessing his feeble memory, "Lilliputian," he proudly said.

Harry closed his eyes and stifled a groan. He knew what was coming.

"I say, there're two of them. Just alike." Burnage caught Harry with another elbow in his enthusiasm to lean closer to the window.

"Two Lilliputians?" Parker asked.

Harry wished the headmaster had not made them read Swift last term. He also wished he'd remembered that this was the year that Balthasar, Melchior, and Gaspar would start at Glenhurst. But he hadn't, so he'd not planned what he was going to say when they appeared.

"My God," Burnage said, falling back from the window. "There are three of them. It's a litter of Lilliputians."

Needs must, Harry would have to just blurt out the embarrassing truth. "They're not Lilliputians," he said. "They're my uncles."

"Uncles?" Three voices seemed to say this in chorus, and all eyes were now focused on him.

"How is it bloody possible you have Lilliputians as uncles?" Parker seemed fixated on the only literary reference he'd remembered in the three years Harry had known him.

"For the last time, they are *not* Lilliputians or anything else that's fictional. They're just... not very tall. And they're my uncles because they're my father's half-brothers."

Burnage wrinkled his face in a way that usually indicated he was in deep thought. "How did your father get brothers who are younger than you?"

"The usual way, you dimwit. They're younger because they were born after I was. My grandfather was a widower and he remarried after my father was grown. I was still young, but I remember when the triplets were born." Good Lord, this was hardly a difficult concept. All of them had learned where children came from years ago.

"Oh, the devil," said Easterly, frowning like a disturbed badger and speaking for the first time. "If the Lil... eh, new boys are your uncles, this means you'll pound on us if we, eh..."

"Try to make their lives miserable," Parker supplied. It was tradition that incoming boys were subjected to various humiliations and were expected to do chores for the older students. The organized cruelties practiced at some other schools were not allowed, but this rite of passage was still difficult.

Harry shook his head. "No, I'll not be pounding anyone. Bal and Mel and Par will have to stand on their own. And the important word is *their*. You may have success in harassing one at a time, but they *will* retaliate, and it will be together. I can tell you from experience, this retaliation will be inventive and extremely uncomfortable. All three are wickedly smart. They will bide their time and when something hideous happens to you, they will look like innocent angels. They're bloody good at looking angelic. But when they look at you, their faces will leave no doubt they're the instigators."

"Something hideous happens? Truly? Have they taken revenge on you?" Parker showed better sense than usual with his alarm.

"More than once. The worst was the time they stuffed a pillow with stinging nettles and used it as a replacement for the one on my bed. When I put my head on it, the stingers came sliding through the fabric. The back of my neck and left side of my face felt like they were on fire. And then that area itched something fierce for most of the next day."

"Cor, what did you do to deserve that punishment?" While apparently indifferent to the triplet's arrival, Easterly was eager to hear Harry describe his defeat.

"I'm not going to say." Harry also *couldn't* say, since he no longer remembered the cause. He was sure it had been something for which the triplets thought they were responding with commensurate punishment. The three boys were frequently diabolical but were also intrinsically fair.

"But there's a good side to their being so smart," Harry continued. "If they like you, they'll help with your school work. I know it's hard to believe, but they think it's fun to do Latin translations."

Shocked disbelief was evident on every face that looked at him.

"I'm serious. Remember the long translation of Caesar's Commentaries we were assigned last winter break?"

"Ruined all of Christmas for me," Parker said.

"Well, it took Balthasar and Melchior and Gaspar less than an hour. And they seemed to have a great time doing it." In the process, they had also purposely included some incorrect words intended to embarrass Harry—his Latin master had asked him if *Roman fortifications* would have not made more sense than *Roman fornications*—but that was a small price to pay for not having to slog through the assignment. Of course, Harry was then beholden to the demon spawn.

The triplets had learned early on the art of creating obligation. The family swore the boys' father, Harry's grandfather, was a master of this.

"So, if we're nice to them, they'll be nice to us?" Harry could see Easterly weighing the odds.

"Yes, that's how it would work. I'd be sure they knew you all were their friends and impress on them that you would want some help on occasion."

Harry's three friends looked at each other, and then there were smiles all around. "That works," Parker said.

Feeling some need for ceremony, Harry stuck out his hand, which his friends dutifully shook in turn. Having the triplets here at Glenhurst might be an advantage after all. He would tell his uncles that he'd promised violence unless his friends were nice to them and point out that they would now owe him favors. He would manage to be repaid from both sides.

"Since we can't bedevil them," Parker said, "at least tell us why they have such strange names."

"They're not strange; they're Biblical. The triplets were named for the Three Wise Men."

"Why?" asked Easterly. "Were they born on Epiphany?"

"No, they were born in September. The only reason for their names that I've ever heard from my grandfather is the three of them arrived because they followed the Christmas Star."

"Now that makes no sense," Burnage said.

"I can only tell you what I've been told." Harry waited for the next question and when none came, he felt himself relax.

They would all be at Cambridge before the girls were presented to society and his friends realized he also had younger twin aunts. He was quite sure his friends would describe them as fairy princesses rather than Lilliputians.

About Hannah

Because Hannah Meredith's father was a career military officer, her early life was a somewhat gypsy existence. She'd attended eight different schools in different locations by the time she graduated from high school. She learned early on that friends she made in books could be packed up and taken with her.

She continued to add to the number of these portable friends as she attended college, received two degrees in English, married her high school sweetheart, had a family, taught at the high school and college level, and had a successful real estate career. During all this time, she continued moving as her husband's job required.

She and her husband of over fifty years have now retired in a charming North Carolina town. Hannah's book friends have come with her and live in a multitude of bulging bookcases and on assorted electronic devices. It is unsurprising, however, that new characters about whom no one has written have popped up in her mind. She is now trying to write their stories in the hope that she will create friends that others will want to pack up and take with them.

Under another name, Hannah sold over a dozen speculative fiction short stories to major Science Fiction and Fantasy magazines. She now concentrates on historical romance. She currently has five romances available: *Kestrel*, *Indentured Hearts*, *Kaleidoscope*, *A Dangerous Indiscretion,* and *Song of the Nightpiper*, a fantasy romance which was a

2018 RITA® Finalist and a 2018 PRISM Finalist. Hannah's novellas have also appeared in the four previous *Christmas Revels* anthologies.

If you'd like to keep up with Hannah, you can find her at:
http://www.hannahmeredith.com
http://www.facebook.com/HannahMeredithAuthor

A Perfectly Ridiculous Christmas

by

Louisa Cornell

Chapter One

December, 1817
Somerset, England

Desperate times call for desperate measures. Add a woman into the mix, and desperate moves quickly to frantic. Add four women, even if three of them are quite small, and frantic gallops into the realm of utter madness, never to see even a hope of sanity again.

His entire house was in chaos.

After years spent on battlefields, and worse places, in service to king and country, Valerian, Viscount Keynsham, hated nothing more than chaos. He'd hoped for a peaceful Christmas with his two best friends, William Collins and Viscount Thynne. He'd been looking forward to spoiling Thynne's three young daughters, Esmerelda, Celestine, and Estella. He'd imagined greenery and songs and wassail and... well, the making of memories to hoard against the years when his makeshift family would no longer be available. But Lady Catherine Chastleton's unanticipated arrival put paid to those dreams

When another packed portmanteau sailed past his head to land with a distinct *thunk* on the worn marble floor of his slightly battered country home, Valerian turned towards the first-floor landing from whence the luggage had been launched. His best friend's daughter, Esmerelda—ten years of age and a force of nature—dusted her hands together and offered him a defiant tilt of her chin.

Thynne, in spite of being the child's father, seemed unmoved by her behavior, Valerian decided to at least try and intervene. "Was that completely necessary, Esme?" he asked.

"*Humpf!*" With a negligent curtsy and a toss of her head, she stormed down the corridor towards the back of the house.

"Handled that well, *Lord* Keynsham," Thynne quipped from the safety of his negligent sprawl at the bottom of the wide staircase. "It is clear who is master here."

"Of a certainty, it isn't me." Valerian studied the landing in the hope the child might reappear. Her anger was justified. They'd all suffered these last three years, perhaps none more than Esmerelda. "She's *your* daughter, Thynne. Can you not at least attempt to take her in hand?"

Thynne would never reprimand any of his daughters. And Valerian knew why.

"After three months of blissful betrothal-at-a-distance," Thynne said with much hand waving and dramatic flair. "my fiancée has chosen Christmas, of all times of year, to make the pilgrimage from Edinburgh to become better acquainted with her future husband. Trust me, this way is best." He attempted to toe the portmanteau towards the mountain of baggage on the other side of the stairs. "What the devil is in here, an anvil?" He struggled to his feet and handed the item off to one of the footmen scurrying back and forth from the foyer to the traveling coach just beyond the open double doors and across the quarry-stone terrace.

Valerian hefted two more bags under his arms and started for the coach. "If it is Esme's, it is books."

"And if it isn't?" Thynne subsided onto the stairs once more.

"A live cat or dead fossils." Reverend William Collins, the local rector and another of Valerian's permanent house guests, announced as he strolled into the foyer from the front parlor. He handed Thynne a bottle of brandy and a tumbler. Which the man promptly put to use.

"Must the cats be included in this exodus?" Thynne asked.

Valerian paused as Dedham, his butler, relieved him of the baggage he'd been attempting to take to the carriage. "If you intend Estella to participate in this holiday exodus of yours, they must," Valerian assured him. Even at a mere five years of age, Estella was the most dangerous of Thynne's daughters. She had mastered the art of getting her way before she turned three. There wasn't a chance in hell of her leaving Keynsham Hall *sans* the half-dozen or so cats she preferred over dolls or the company of her sisters. "And I refuse to manage hiding *your* daughters, entertaining *your* betrothed and a house full of guests, *and* herding those furry, four-legged feline menaces."

Some days, Valerian wondered how he, a devout bachelor and preferred hermit, ended up making permanent houseguests of his two best friends, not to mention the three young daughters of one of said friends. Most days, it did not bear contemplation, as it induced stomach pains, a headache, or both. After three years, acceptance was the best tact to take.

"I doubt Miss Esmerelda would launch one of her sister's cats at you, Keynsham," Collins observed. "At her father's head, yes. At yours, probably not."

Valerian's stomach tightened and then began to roil. His friends' voices blended into so much noise. What the devil was he doing? This was a bad plan and wrong, for so many reasons. Still, it was not his decision to make. He'd given up making decisions for other people. The consequences of his previous decisions had led them to this pass.

"You did explain to dear Estella that she and her sisters will be spending Christmas at your hunting box, didn't you, Keynsham?"

Thynne might be one of Valerian's closest friends, but the man was rubbish at presenting all the facts when hatching one of his *perfect* plots. Especially when it came to the presentation of those facts to his own daughters.

"As I recall, you keep that monstrous pack of hounds at your hunting place," Collins said as he stacked a few cases together and handed them off to one of the footmen parading in and out of the house. "Hounds and cats, not a good mix."

"The cats are definitely not a wise choice," Thynne agreed.

Valerian rolled his eyes. "How long are you sending your daughters into exile? It looks as if you plan for them to stay—"

Collins interrupted. "Surely the woman won't visit more than—"

"Travesty!"

They turned as one to see Keynsham Hall's housekeeper, Mrs. Gilhooley, march into the foyer with a large food hamper in her arms. She'd come from Barbados over ten years ago with Thynne's wife, Melisande, and had stayed with them, following the drum, all through Thynne's military career. When Thynne had decamped from his father's estate these three years past and moved into Keynsham Hall, Mrs. Gilhooley had come as well. Valerian was most assuredly no longer in charge of his home. This imposing Creole woman was. Thank God.

"A travesty is what it is," she declared. She handed the hamper off to a groom, who staggered under its weight until a footman rushed to his aid. "Throwing your children from their home to impress a rich, white *hairless* you hardly know."

Valerian kicked at Collins, who was trying not to laugh. "She is an heiress, Mrs. Gilhooley, not hairless."

"The only way I have to know her is in the biblical sense." Thynne cleared his throat. "Once I do, I will tell her about the girls, and we will all move to Lavender Hill and leave you here to keep Keynsham and Collins in order."

"Don't think I won't stay here and do just that." She turned and lumbered towards the back of the house. "You and those girls aren't the only ones who need looking after."

"Now you've done it." Valerian snatched the bottle from Thynne's hand. Thynne, who'd promised to stay sober today, promptly took it back and poured himself another drink. "She'll blame me for this. I'll be sleeping on damp sheets, eating cold food, and lighting my own fires for months once this is all over. That woman is frighteningly creative when it comes to expressing her displeasure."

"I'll be doing the same. Isn't that some compensation?" Thynne downed his drink and poured yet another.

"A man half seas over most of the day doesn't give a damn about comfort. I do. You are certain you want to do this?" Valerian owned some guilt at what was transpiring. He'd set this in motion by finding his friend an heiress in need of a husband. Thynne was heir to the Earl of Taunton. The old miscreant had banished Thynne and cut him off financially, but he couldn't disinherit him.

"It's only one Christmas." Collins favored them with a resonant belch. "It is the fact he hardly knows her that necessitates this holiday adventure. Tricky thing, an heiress's sensibilities, especially when she is the daughter of a duke."

Thunk!

Valerian, Thynne, and Collins flinched and turned their attention to the oversized satchel which had landed in their midst. By the time they raised their heads to search the landing, the only sign of the culprit lay in the patter of slippered feet.

"You are certain you must remain here, Keynsham?" Collins eyed the landing as if expecting a French cavalry charge.

"It is my house," Valerian reminded him. "House guests expect a host who rises before two in the afternoon." Collins and Valerian cut their eyes towards Thynne, who promptly saluted them with his glass.

"Tell me again." Collins sounded afraid. With good reason. "Why am I the one who has to remain in exile with the girls whilst you two spend Christmas with the adults?"

"I found myself a wealthy heiress." Thynne leaned back against the bannister and propped himself up on his elbows. "I did not spend a great deal of time investigating her character, only her fortune. Trust me, springing three daughters on her all at once will undo all of my hard work."

Valerian flexed his shoulders to shake the sudden irritation that slithered up his spine. "Your hard work? I am the one who found her. And made the introductions. Her name is Lady Catherine, not *wealthy heiress*."

Collins snorted. "Should have looked for one a bit more fair-minded, Keynsham."

"I am the one who trekked all the way to Edinburgh to find him a reasonably comely lady who'd inherited a fortune from her rich, childless aunt. I am the one who learned she was in need of a husband to gain full control of all of that lovely money. Money he is sorely in need of if he is to have a hope in hell of salvaging that ruin of an estate his mother left him."

"Lavender Hill is not a ruin," Thynne declared indignantly.

"Damn near it," Valerian and Collins said together.

"Ruin or not," Valerian continued. "I am the one who offered him up as a likely candidate on account of his being pockets to let."

"Thank you for putting it so succinctly." Thynne fairly oozed sarcasm.

The rector grinned at their all too familiar sniping. "I suppose his being a handsome devil, heir to an old and revered title, and quite charming most days had nothing to do with her accepting his offer of marriage."

"Thank you, Collins," Thynne said. "Perhaps I should marry you."

"I can't afford you, not on a poor rector's income. Besides, I am married to my profession."

"Pity, that." Thynne cackled like an old woman.

"You are married to brandy." Valerian took Thynne's glass and placed it on the post at the end of the bannister. "And you, Collins, are married to your books."

Collins shrugged. "Thynne has the right of it. He needs to wrap Lady Catherine up fair and tight in holy wedlock. Then tell her about the girls."

"It's deceptive. *Reverend.*" Valerian had given in to Thynne's plan. He had no say in the matter. He didn't know Lady Catherine well enough to decipher what her reaction to Esmerelda, Celestine, and Estella might be. And it infuriated him… with himself.

"It's diplomatic," Thynne corrected. "Once we are married she will have no choice but to accept my daughters. Until then, mine is the perfect solution."

"When women are involved there is never a perfect solution." Valerian had learned that lesson the hard way. They all had.

"Perhaps once we are married, Lady Catherine won't mind their heritage." Thynne's innocuous attempt to temper their lunatic solution to his bride's imminent arrival set Valerian's skin to crawling.

"It isn't about their heritage. There is nothing wrong with their heritage." Fury, constantly simmering just beneath the surface of Valerian's every thought when it came to the girls, swept over him. "They are your children, born of your lawfully wedded wife. If Lady Catherine Chastleton has an issue with that she can—"

"She won't." Collins handed Valerian the tumbler, bearing a fingerful of brandy. "Once they are married, she won't."

Valerian turned to find his friends eying him with the

same wariness one might award a rabid dog. Or a man whose guilt and indecision had got the best of him. He downed the brandy in one long swallow. He'd made so many rash decisions since his father's death three years ago. Even the right decisions, when made for the wrong reasons and with no thought to the consequences, especially for others, might end in disaster. Or death.

An ungodly yowl—something between a dying goose and a banshee on a highland winter's night—rent the baited silence.

"What the devil is that racket?" Collins, eyes wide and mouth agape, paled to his hairline.

"Cuthbert," Valerian and Thynne replied as one. Their shoulders shook with suppressed laughter.

The three of them turned their attention to the besieged footman at the top of the stairs. The brave fellow carried, in arms outstretched to their limit, a specially constructed tightly-woven basket. From small openings on the sides, two orange cat's paws wind-milled in an effort to either escape the basket or eviscerate the bearer. The vessel nearly leapt from the footman's hands, so violent were the cat's machinations. And all the while, the ear-splitting caterwauling carried on with no sign of waning.

"Absolutely not." Collins dogged the footman's every step as the servant made his way outside to the coach. Thynne's youngest followed close on his heels. "I am not listening to that all the way to Wedmore Lodge. Estella, have mercy. Keynsham, tell her."

Valerian made to chase after Estella when Thynne cleared his throat and pulled him out of the way. A veritable parade of footmen, grooms, and maids trooped down the stairs past them, laden with what appeared to be half the contents of the house. Pillows, bed linens, boxes of fossils, five more baskets with disgruntled feline occupants and… the small pianoforte from the music room?

"Who told you to load the pianoforte?" Valerian asked the grooms at either end of the instrument. They bowed from the neck but did not reply. The upstairs maid, piano stool in hand, offered him a curtsy, but had no better answer than the grooms.

"Esmerelda did." Celestine, Thynne's seven-year-old middle daughter, announced as she flounced down the stairs. "She cannot possibly go into exile without it." This last delivered in a quite credible imitation of her elder sister. "Are you coming with us, Uncle Val? Or must you stay and help father land on his rich *hairless*?"

"Your father and I will accompany you to the lodge and see you settled in, but we must return to Keynsham Hall," Valerian explained, cutting his eyes at Thynne. "To entertain your father's rich *hairless*."

"Good Lord," Thynne groaned. He went down on one knee and took his daughter's hand. "Sweeting, it isn't like that at all."

"Come with me, Celestine." Esmerelda, dressed in her favorite dark green velvet ensemble, snatched her sister's hand from her father's grasp and half-dragged her towards the door. "We wouldn't want Papa's new wife to see us." They tripped out onto the front terrace.

Thynne eyed the tumbler on the inlaid hall table, apparently thought better of it, and took a swig of brandy straight from the bottle. At this rate he'd be irrevocably in his cups before they reached the inn between Keynsham Hall and the lodge.

Collins and Thynne had come up with this scheme, but Valerian had put it in motion. He was the one, against every instinct in his body, sending those girls away at Christmas. Valerian took the bottle away. Again. And handed it to Dedham.

"Dammit, Thynne, talk to them. Make them understand." Valerian pushed him towards the door.

"I've tried," Thynne assured him. "They are too young to understand. They're good girls. They'll do as they're told."

"You're their father."

"I am aware of that, Keynsham." Thynne pushed him away. "And I'm aware of how you feel about it." He crossed the terrace without looking back.

Valerian followed. He did what he always did when Thynne spoiled for a fight. He summoned the icy façade that had been his salvation these last three years.

"Esme." Thynne wrapped his arm around her shoulders and took her sister's hand in his once more. "I explained all of this to you."

Valerian refused to allow his face to show it. His heart, however, stuttered and limped along in his chest. No ten-year-old girl should know the pain and betrayal brimming in Esmerelda's amber eyes.

"We have obligations to the people at Lavender Hill. My marriage to Lady Catherine will help us to—"

"Fulfill our obligations," Esme blurted. A single mahogany curl escaped her braided hair. She tucked it back into her bonnet. "She has paid for the new roof on the dairy and for the drying barn for the lavender crop. Why does she have to come here for Christmas? Why must she come to live at Lavender Hill with us?"

"Unfortunately, Lady Catherine's money was not given without a price. She and I must marry, which usually works better when the bride and the groom are in the same county."

"Not always," Collins muttered from behind him. Followed by *"Umpf!"* when Valerian elbowed him in the chest.

"Your father is quite the matrimonial prize, Esme, dear." Collins gave Valerian a wide berth and paced to the front of the terrace where he took his horse's reins from the groom and used the height afforded him by the parapet to mount the animal. Thynne and Valerian's horses danced away from Collins's fractious mare. "He'll sort this out and we'll be back here before Twelfth Night. Where is your governess? It is time we were off."

Esme linked her arm through her sister, Celestine's, and marched to the coach, where one of the footmen helped both girls inside. Estella, already ensconced therein, lifted one of her cats into her lap and raised its paw to wave at Mrs. Gilhooley as the housekeeper crossed the terrace.

"They will be fine once we reach the lodge," Thynne murmured and took a step towards the coach.

"The governess, Keynsham?" Collins snapped his fingers in front of Valerian's face. "Where is she?"

"On her way to Hertfordshire," Thynne offered. "Keynsham gave her a few weeks holiday as her sister is in anticipation of an interesting event."

The servants continued to traipse back and forth between the house and the baggage cart with bits and bobs and ever more baggage. Thynne stared at the carriage, where his daughters pointedly ignored him and the chaos on the terrace.

"An interesting event?" Collins fairly shrieked. "How am I to survive the holidays alone with three little hoydens? This was not part of the plan. Why is your housekeeper putting a chamber pot into Keynsham's traveling coach?" Collins dismounted, handed his horse's reins off to a groom, and went to intercept Mrs. Gilhooley. Unusually tall for a woman and equally wide, she reached over Collins's waving arms and handed a second chamber pot into the coach.

"Estella will only use her own chamber pot," Thynne said softly. "Since her mother died... Keynsham, tell me I am doing the right thing." The carriage lurched into motion. Collins swung up onto his horse, still arguing with Mrs. Gilhooley. To no avail.

"You did the right thing in Barbados." Valerian took the reins from the groom and mounted his horse as the caravan of coach and baggage cart and riders made its way down the drive towards the gatehouse. "Now your daughters may have to pay for it. Right or wrong." He adjusted his stirrups. "I did the right thing in Spain three years ago, and your wife paid for it. So far, doing the right thing has been a costly affair." He started down the drive. Was it regret that made him speak so or a need to strike at his friend for putting three little girls through so much?

Thynne, mounted on his big grey, came up beside him. They rode in silence down the long drive and past the gatehouse before Thynne spoke. "Why two chamber pots?"

"What?"

"Why did Mrs. Gilhooley load two chamber pots into the coach?"

"Estella does not suffer coach travel well. Remember?"

Of course, he didn't remember. Whether by accident or design, Thynne hardly knew his children.

"How long before Collins waves the white flag and sends a footman to fetch one of us?" Thynne tugged a flask from the inside pocket of his greatcoat. "I give him a week."

Valerian flipped up the collar of his greatcoat against the sudden onslaught of the December wind. "Your girls will have him tied up and locked in the privy in three days. Four at the outside."

Chapter Two

She'd slept. In a moving carriage no less. So soundly, her own travel coach rocking to a halt before the Horse and Hound had not disturbed her. Only the arrival of a mail coach in the innyard had awakened her. Even now, the thick velvet squabs called her back to the arms of Morpheus. Reluctantly Lady Catherine Chastleton sat upright and attempted to brush the wrinkles from her new red and black carriage dress.

"Have we arrived?" Jenny adjusted her cap and adopted the hands-in-lap, perfectly erect pose of the ever-alert lady's maid. The wrinkled texture of her cheek, identical to the pattern of the padded side of the coach, gave her away. And Catherine could hardly blame her.

A well-sprung coach stood as one of God's greatest gifts. Blasphemous? Perhaps. Catherine had not spent a great deal of time in contemplation of the spiritual. Recently, however, she'd spent more than a little time in contemplation of comfort. Traveling from Edinburgh to Somerset in the chill of December did that to a lady. Of all the worldly goods Aunt Beatrice had left her—in addition to an obscene amount of money, and even more money once this last... inconvenient task was accomplished—the richly appointed travel coach had proved the most immediately useful. And the most decadent. At twenty-eight years of age, Catherine was very nearly free, and decadence had a definite appeal.

"Beg pardon, milady." Hamish O'Hara, Catherine's inherited coachman, came to the window and doffed his hat. "The innkeeper says it's no more than two hours to Keynsham Hall, but the leader has a loose shoe I'd like seen to before we continue."

"Of course." She leaned out the window to assess the inn. "How long will it take?"

"Long enough for you to have a cup of tea and refresh yourself, my lady." He opened the door and offered her his hand.

Catherine smiled. "You read my mind, Mr. O'Hara." She allowed him to hand her out. "Tea, Jenny. And perhaps a bite to eat." She strode across the innyard. Jenny scurried behind her, her pace a half run in order to keep up. Catherine, tall for a woman—and didn't the entire world take every effort to remind her—slowed in consideration of the maid.

"The quality of coach stopping here is better than at the last inn." Jenny caught her up and nodded across the yard. "Perhaps the tea will be too. The tea at the last place wasn't fit for dishwater, let alone for a duke's daughter."

"How does an inn keep tea for the express use of a duke's daughter? Is there a special tin or caddy, do you think?" Catherine followed Jenny's gaze to the handsome coach, even larger than her own, across the yard. An overburdened baggage wagon stood behind it. Half a dozen uniformed grooms checked the harnesses and ropes of both conveyances. The crest on the coach door pricked at her memory.

"You should pay more heed to your consequence, my

lady." Jenny sniffed and minced into the inn.

"You pay it enough heed for both of us." Catherine gave the elegant travel coach one last look and entered the inn's crowded common room to find her maid, already in high dudgeon, berating the innkeeper.

"My lady is the daughter of the Duke of Wharram and requires a private parlor. She does not share." Jenny was in rare form, which did not bode well for the innkeeper. There were earls and even a marquess or two who quailed in their boots at the mere thought of confronting Miss Jenny Ransom, Catherine's lady's maid of the past twelve years.

"That's as may be, miss, but his lordship and his party are in my only private parlor." The innkeeper, a short wiry man with a florid face and an impressive shrub of white hair, planted his hands on the long oak counter before him and leaned towards Jenny in an attempt at intimidation. "I'll not roust a brace of lords for the havering of some jumped up lady's maid, especially for the daughter of a duke I've never heard of."

Jenny reared back and filled her lungs, ready to launch a full-scale attack on the man's heritage, wits, and very likely his religious inclinations. A crash of crockery and raised voices issued from behind the closed private parlor door.

"Thank God for that, sir." Catherine looped her arm through her maid's and tugged her back a step. "If you knew my father you would no doubt ban us from your elegant establishment utterly." She offered him the beatific expression her ten-year-old niece, Lily Rose, used when she wanted to get her way. "Pray, tell me, who are the lordly guests wise enough to afford you their custom? Or is it a secret?" A sudden thud, punctuated by a plaintive *meow*, sounded from the direction of the coveted parlor.

Jenny snorted. Catherine brought the heel of her half boot down onto the maid's toes.

"No secret, milady. It's Lord Thynne and—"

"How fortuitous." Catherine gripped Jenny's elbow and dragged her along in her wake. "Lord Thynne and I are betrothed." She reached for the latch to the parlor door and raised it. "He is expecting me at Keynsham Hall for Lord Keynsham's Christmas—" The door flew open. "House party."

Apparently, the festivities had started without her. The room was, for lack of a better word, a shambles. As were its occupants. Lord Thynne knelt on the floor gathering broken crockery. Another gentleman, a clergyman by his mode of dress, armed with a large handkerchief, dabbed at the tears of a girl of five or six years of age. Two more girls, no more than ten years of age, held the crying child's hands and spoke to her in hushed tones. Sisters, perhaps? All three had the ebony hair, dark eyes, and honeyed caramel skin of exotic places Catherine had often dreamt of visiting.

Beyond a few overturned benches and chairs stood the last man she expected to see in such mayhem. "Good afternoon, Lady Catherine." Lord Valerian Keynsham executed an obscenely crisp and elegant bow. Quite a feat as he held at arm's length a large, orange tabby cat— a cat covered in what smelled very like a hearty beef stew.

"Good afternoon, my lord." She gave the room a slow perusal. "Am I interrupting something?"

Lord Thynne leapt to his feet and dropped the broken dishes onto the oak dining table. "Not at all, Lady Catherine." He gave the startled clergyman a look only describable as frantic and then grasped her hand to bow over it. "What a pleasure to see you again."

Tall and lean, with a mane of guinea gold hair and enviable green eyes, Viscount Thynne had charm and wit to spare. Heir to an old and wealthy earldom, he'd been the catch of the Season, especially in the limited society in Edinburgh. Catherine, however, harbored no illusions as to their decision to marry. She offered him a much-needed fortune. He offered her a means to an end and the promise of a malleable husband. The thing she needed most in the world. *Needed. Yes.*

"You were expecting me, were you not?" Catherine divided her attention between her somewhat nervous betrothed—he'd sprouted an unlikely sort of configuration of beads of sweat across his upper lip—and the low hissing of the whispered tête-à-tête at the round table in the corner to which the clergyman and the three little girls had retreated. This entire encounter defied description. She'd settle for an explanation.

"No. I mean, yes, of course." Lord Thynne's behavior grew more curious by the moment. The clergyman's more frantic. And the children's more unhappy and silent. Only Lord Keynsham remained unchanged. He still evinced the cold, composed demeanor he'd displayed in Edinburgh. It irritated beyond reason. He'd not taken his eyes off her. A spot between her shoulders itched.

Keynsham had divested himself of the cat. How such a large man moved quickly and quietly enough to do so gave her one more reason to take him in dislike. "We expected you at Keynsham Hall, but you were not expected until after four. I believe that is what Thynne meant to say," he said solemnly. Tall and broad-shouldered, Lord Keynsham was not a handsome man. Beneath thick black curls styled in a longish Brutus cut, his saturnine features rested on a sharply carved face which accented a broken blade of a nose, a mouth ever fixed in condescension, and silver-grey eyes capable of freezing the sunniest of days. Catherine suppressed a shiver.

"I was on my way there when the lead horse nearly cast a shoe. Had I known I was violating your schedule, Lord Keynsham, I'd have instructed the horse to take better care."

Keynsham tilted his head in an annoying combination of benediction and affront. "And I am certain he would have obeyed."

"He didn't mean that at all, my lady." Thynne turned on his friend with a fulminating glare. "Did you, Keynsham?"

"Of course not. A lady must always be allowed to arrive precisely when she pleases." He hefted a large wicker basket under one arm and gave Catherine another of his supercilious bows. "Collins, fetch the girls. We must be on our way if we are to reach the lodge before dark."

The rector mumbled a few words to the children and began to herd them towards the door.

She'd grown up with one of the most incorrigible, scheming brothers ever born. These three gentlemen were up to something. She'd bet her newly inherited travel coach on it. Catherine touched her hand to her betrothed's arm. "Thynne, dear, I should love to be introduced to your friend and these lovely young ladies."

Never had a silence descended so swiftly. Nor had one ever been so loud. From the three unmoving gentlemen to the three girls attending each of those same gentlemen with wide-eyed unasked questions, a great deal was being said without a single word. Which meant there was a great deal to be said. Catherine raised an eyebrow and gazed at Lord Thynne.

"Of course, where are my manners?" Thynne drew her arm through his and patted her hand. The faint scent of brandy wafted from his skin. Faint. Perhaps he'd cut back in honor of her visit. Which might explain his flustered demeanor. In the six weeks of their courtship he'd displayed many aspects of his character. This level of nervousness had never been one of them. "May I make known to you, Reverend William Collins, one of my oldest friends. He has the living on Keynsham's estate."

"Reverend Collins." Catherine offered him her hand. "What a pleasure to meet another of Lord Thynne's friends."

"Lady Catherine." The poor man tripped over a chair, but still managed to bow over her hand without falling to the floor. Barely. "The pleasure is all mine. How on earth was our raggedy friend able to win so fair a lady?" Of a height with Thynne, the Reverend Collins had one of those faces that would appear youthful well into his sixties. With gangly limbs, unruly chestnut curls, and ill-fitting clothes, he put her in mind of a character in the farce before the play, save for the flash of faded sorrow in his eyes. She knew that look, no matter how fleeting. She caught it in her brother's eyes from time to time.

"Your friend can be quite charming," Catherine assured him.

"When he chooses to be," drawled Lord Keynsham, one hip propped on the thick oak table.

She pursed her lips and narrowed her eyes at him. To which he reacted not at all.

"I taught him everything he knows." Reverend Collins

slapped Thynne on the shoulder, and all the while, behind his back, his free hand waved like a single-winged dove in an attempt to hasten the girls' departure.

"Except how to introduce your beautiful companions." She stepped around the clergyman and positioned herself between his diminutive charges and the door. "I am Lady Catherine Chastleton." She looked at each in turn, making certain to smile as she did. "And you are?"

"Actually—" Lord Thynne started.

"You see, Lady Catherine—" Reverend Collins interrupted.

"They are my mine," Lord Keynsham declared. He had done it again. He'd placed the basket on the table and moved on silent feet to stand next to her before she knew it.

"I... I beg your pardon?" Catherine wanted to stamp her foot in exasperation. Why did he unnerve her so? *Wait. What did he say?*

"Allow me to make known to you, my daughters. Esmerelda, Celestine, and Estella. Girls, this is Lady Catherine Chastleton. Her father is the Duke of Wharram, a very rich and powerful man." The introduction, delivered in his cold, dark baritone sent a chill down her spine.

The miniature beauties stood stock still and gawked from her to Lord Keynsham and back, and who could blame them with such an introduction. Their father cleared his throat. As if on cue, they delivered three curtsies worthy of any lady at court.

"I am very pleased to make your acquaintance, girls." They blinked up at her, silent and uncertain. Perhaps they were merely shy. Or perhaps they feared their father's displeasure. She had at their age.

"Collins, take them out to the carriage." His orders were for the reverend and the girls. His gaze, however, remained on Catherine.

"What about Cuthbert?" the smallest child asked. Estella, was that her name?

"I will bring him. Go with Uncle William." His voice changed. She did not know how. It simply did. His daughters shuffled out of the room, glancing over their shoulders the entire time.

"An excellent idea, Keynsham." Thynne took her arm. He and the Reverend Collins jumped as soldiers ordered to take leave. "Let me escort you to your carriage, my lady."

Jenny, who had stood in uncharacteristic silence through this entire scene, stepped to Catherine's side and whispered, none too softly. "I thought Lord Thynne told you his friend was a bachelor."

Catherine stifled a groan and closed her eyes.

"And so I am, Miss Ransom." Lord Keynsham gave the maid a negligible nod. "Lovely to see you again. Thynne, I will see you back at the Hall once I deliver Collins and the girls." He retrieved the basket, from which issued a highly indignant *meow*, and with a frighteningly pointed look at his friend left the room.

"Shall we?" Lord Thynne swept his free hand towards the door.

It struck her, a faded memory instantly so visceral as to tumble her stomach. "Why is Lord Keynsham sending his daughters away?" She pinned Lord Thynne with her gaze and swore he squirmed and looked to the doorway for help, if only for a moment.

"With your visit and the house party to follow,

Keynsham felt they would do better away from all of… that." His lips curved in a half-hearted smile. "They will spend Christmastide at his hunting lodge in Wedmore."

"Quite right, my lord." Jenny adjusted her bonnet and gloves. "Children should be seen and not heard. Especially those born under such unfortunate circumstances."

"I suspect there are a great many unfortunate circumstances in Lord Keynsham's daughters' lives." Catherine pushed past Lord Thynne and Jenny. "Being evicted from their home for Christmas will not be one of them."

"My lady."

"Lady Catherine, I assure you—"

Even as they followed on her heels, she barely heard them. Christmas had never been a happy time for her and her sisters. Perhaps her brother had enjoyed Christmas, although he never spoke of it. He'd spent Christmas with their father and mother, trotted out to guests and visitors. She and her four sisters had stayed behind on a little visited country estate, with only servants and the occasional elderly relative with whom to celebrate. And it hurt, dammit. It still hurt.

She spotted the girls deep in conversation with their father. He stood, hands clasped behind his back, bent low to attend the three children. They huddled next to the handsome travel coach she'd seen earlier. At least he intended them to journey in comfort. He appeared his solemn, immovable self. They appeared sad and confused, and the eldest addressed him with a belligerent tilt to her chin. Good for her.

To her surprise he stuck his hand out and each girl shook it in turn. What a singular thing for a father to do. Then again, how would she know? She lengthened her strides to catch them before they entered the coach.

"Lord Keynsham, a moment please."

He turned, his expression surprised and then questioning. From the corner of her eye she saw Lord Thynne wave at him, hand out and palm down. A signal, no doubt. Reverend Collins leaned out of the coach, wide-eyed and pasty-faced. Oh, these three were rubbish at subterfuge. What were they up to?

"How may I help you, my lady?"

She ignored him and came to a stop before his daughters. He cleared his throat. They curtsied. *Oh, for heaven's sake!* "Where are you and your sisters accustomed to spending Christmas, Miss Esmerelda?"

"At Keynsham Hall, our home these past three years." Rather than direct her answer to Catherine or Lord Keynsham, the poor girl directed it to Lord Thynne. Perhaps she blamed his invitation to Catherine as the cause of their eviction. She was obviously afraid to address her father. Catherine ground her teeth. A man passionate enough to have not one, not two, but three daughters out of wedlock surely had enough warmth in his blood to conduct himself with his daughters so they did not fear him.

"Then that is where you shall spend Christmastide this year." She raised her gaze just enough to meet Lord Keynsham's. He flustered her, those icy eyes and that stone-carved face. "I could not possibly enjoy my visit nor plan my wedding knowing three *children* are put out of their home for such a flimsy cause."

"They are my children, my lady." At Lord Keynsham's terse reply Lord Thynne surrendered to a brief coughing fit.

She'd never understand her betrothed's friendship with such an austere man, the complete opposite of Lord Thynne.

"All the more reason for you to allow them to spend Christmas at home. With you. Their father."

"The lodge is a jolly place, my lady. A full staff and Collins here is a master of Christmas revels and felicity. You love your Uncle William, don't you girls?" Lord Thynne explained, his voice taking on a wheedling tone. Catherine abhorred wheedling. She'd break him of that once they were married.

"To be sure, but I insist. They will spend Christmas at Keynsham Hall. I have heard it is quite a large home. Surely the nursery is far enough away from the rest of the house to ensure your children do not interfere with my visit or the adult festivities."

Lord Keynsham folded his arms across his chest. Six childish feminine eyes flitted from Catherine to Lord Keynsham to Lord Thynne and back again. Hopeful eyes. Wary eyes.

"Keynsham?" Reverend Collins prodded.

"If that is what you wish, Lady Catherine, I can do nothing save obey."

Insufferable man. "I doubt that, my lord. However, I came here wishing for the loveliest of Christmases. Children cannot help but aid in that."

With a few quiet orders he set everything in motion. Lord Thynne would ride his lively grey gelding. Reverend Collins elected to ride in the travel coach with the girls. He and Lord Thynne were engaged in a furtive and intense conversation, although she could not make out what they were saying. One of the liveried grooms had already left the innyard at the gallop. Lord Keynsham insisted on escorting Catherine and her maid to her coach. He intended to ride his own mount, a tall, handsome bay, back to Keynsham Hall. He handed them into the carriage, his looming presence all the more disturbing for his silence. First Jenny and then Catherine entered the travel coach. Once he shut the door, he covered her hand, draped over the open window frame.

"You are used to having your every wish fulfilled, Lady Catherine. I would be careful what I wished for, were I you."

Chapter Three

"Have you taken leave of your senses?" Thynne peered over his shoulder at the parade of coaches and baggage wagon just in sight behind them.

"I am not quite certain, but the topic is certainly up for discussion." Valerian urged Mercury into a trot. "One might say I took leave of my senses the day I moved Collins, you, and your daughters into my home. Or perhaps I took leave of my senses the day I met you. I definitely took leave of my senses when I agreed to this ridiculous scheme of yours."

"No need to worry about it now. You have bolloxed my plan up utterly."

He had. And he had no idea why. Nothing unnerved him, at least nothing had until today. However, something about Lady Catherine Chastleton unnerved him. Was that why he had claimed Thynne's daughters as his own? Thynne needed to marry the woman. Whether guilt over all his friend had lost or an abiding need to protect those three little girls from the cruelty society would eventually inflict upon them, Valerian had acted out of character. He'd spoken on instinct alone. Something he had not done in over three years and had vowed never to do again. Thynne needed to marry, and Valerian would see it done. Even if it was to the most irritating, managing, high-in-the-instep woman in England.

"This is a disaster." Thynne kicked his grey into a trot to keep up.

"Consider it training for your marriage."

"Dammit, Keynsham, I am serious. What do we do now? How shall we pull this off without Lady Catherine finding us out?"

"She's a woman, Thynne. They always find out. We can only hope to control when she finds out. Once you have bed her and wed her it won't matter." Valerian's hands fisted around the reins. An odd spark of anger settled beneath his right shoulder.

"You mean wed her and bed her." Thynne evinced remarkably little enthusiasm for consummating this marriage if his tone of voice and expression were any indication. The man looked almost glum.

"Whatever order works to our advantage, do it, man. You have a fortnight."

"What?"

"That is all the concession I managed to beg from your eldest." Valerian fought a grin. The girl was her mother's daughter. For the first time in a long while he thought of Melisande without the usual sting of grief. Singular, to be sure.

"You negotiated with Esmerelda? My Esmerelda?" Thynne removed his hat and wiped his brow before donning it once more. "You *have* taken leave of your senses."

"Our only hope is that in ten years or so, she finds some poor sod besotted enough to negotiate with her for the rest of her life."

"He'd better not be poor. My Esme has expensive tastes." Thynne glanced back at the carriages and then took a swift nip from his flask.

"Whose fault is that?" Valerian urged Mercury into a trot and Thynne followed. The man had to put aside his love of brandy if he ever expected to get around Lady Catherine. She was nobody's fool.

"Yours, not to put too fine a point on it," Thynne replied. "Since the pater cut me off, I cannot afford to spoil her. I can ply them with a dozen gifts a day, but eventually they will find out you have paid for it all."

"Only if you tell them. You will have plenty of money once you and the Duke of Wharram's daughter are wed." Which was the point entirely. Or at least Valerian hoped it was.

Thynne needed a wife, someone to manage him and with luck, bring him back from the brandy-filled hell to which he'd consigned himself. The girls needed a woman with connections to the highest in the land if they were ever to overcome society's scorn. Valerian owed them all that much and more. He'd make this work. Somehow.

The wind picked up. The clouds sank lower, covering the late afternoon sun with a grey wool shawl of shadows and gloom. Rain on the way, or worse, snow. Somerset seldom saw a great deal of snow, but if the day continued as it had started, Fate would likely send them a blizzard.

"She'll hardly marry a penniless lord, a mere viscount, if this plan of yours—you do have a plan, don't you—blows up in our faces." Thynne dropped his flask back into his pocket.

"Ah, but you're not a mere viscount," Valerian reminded him. A mere viscount himself, he ignored the unintentional slight. He'd learned to live with his place in the *ton*. He'd learned to live with his place in life. A handy skill when life afforded constant reminders of who and what a man was and would always be. "Once your father sticks his spoon in the wall, you will be an earl. Master of a large estate, an old title—"

"Old devil will outlive us all, if he has his way." Thynne reached over and pulled at the reins in Valerian's gloved hands. "You do have a plan, don't you, Keynsham?"

"Absolutely not." He tugged the reins free and kicked his horse into a gallop. "But I will by the time we reach the Hall."

"Damn you, Keynsham," Thynne shouted behind him. "What the devil have you done?"

୨୦୧୧

Thank God for fast horses and servants loyal to a fault. Valerian had only half lied when he told Thynne he had no plan. The moment he left the inn he'd sent the groom, Jem, as fast a rider as Ireland had produced, with a message for Dedham and Mrs. Gilhooley. They stood on the steps to the terrace as Valerian and Thynne raced up and slid off their horses, handing their lathered steeds off to the waiting grooms.

"Did you do as I asked?" Valerian took the steps two at the time. The others scurried to catch up.

"Of course, my lord. The entire staff has been informed to… well, to play along with this… with your…" Dedham drew himself up as they entered the foyer.

"Scheme," Thynne offered.

"Farce." Valerian believed in calling a spade a spade.

"Lie." Trust Mrs. Gilhooley to cut to the heart of the matter.

"Are you for me or agin me, Mrs. Gilhooley?" Valerian was not above doing a bit of cutting himself. The housekeeper's late husband, an Irish ship's captain, had used those self-same words on many an occasion to get round his fiery Creole wife.

"For ye, my lord." She rolled her eyes. "As are we all." She moved close enough only he might hear. "If my girls are hurt by you men's schemes, I'll kill you."

"Understood."

The entire household staff had assembled in lines on either side of the entrance hall. Valerian valued his privacy. And his fortune. He had servants sufficient to run his household with efficiency and fairness, but without the numbers many lords felt necessary to keep to emphasize their wealth.

"You all understand what you are to do?"

"Yes, my lord." They punctuated their responses with bows and curtsies. Valerian did not want to contemplate whether it was loyalty to him or fear of Mrs. Gilhooley that drove them to agree to the madness he had unleashed. He still had not sorted it all out himself. He was doing two of the things he'd vowed never to do again—act on impulse and manage the lives of others.

"They're coming up the drive." Thynne stood in the open double doors. He wore his trepidation like an ill-tailored coat. An improvement on the shroud of grief and self-pity he normally donned daily. Perhaps this might work out after all.

"Very well." Valerian signaled Dedham, who set the servants in motion. He joined Thynne and they walked across the terrace to meet the coaches at the steps. "It isn't too late to tell Lady Catherine the truth."

"We have only two weeks to play at this," Thynne said and nudged him with his shoulder. "No worse than pretending to be rich merchants in Spain."

"That was for king and country, we were spying on the French, and it did not end well for all of us." Valerian pondered his friend's ability to speak so lightly of the very worst time in all their lives. Had the brandy finally managed to erase Melisande's memory from her husband's mind?

"At least here no one is shooting at us." Thynne started down the steps as Lady Catherine's carriage rocked to a stop before the terrace.

"Not yet," Valerian muttered.

ಸಂಲ

Catherine was not surprised at the loveliness of the suite of rooms to which she was shown. Coming up the drive she was at once entranced by the golden limestone Gothic structure. The setting sun drew out the many shades of biscuit, tan, and sand of the soaring walls. A long balustraded wall surrounded the front terrace court. The lancet windows, finials, and cupola topped turrets lent an old-fashioned whimsy to the home of a man who would not know whimsy if it walked up and bit him on the—

"Watch what you are about with my lady's trunk, you great lummox." Hands on hips, Jenny held court in the middle of the commodious bedchamber, directing footmen and maids in making Catherine's rooms *fit for the daughter of a duke*.

Catherine strolled from the bedchamber, done in shades of primrose and green, into the small sitting room decorated by Adam in blues and white. The noise of servants at work mixed with childish laughter drew her to the door which opened onto the second-floor corridor. Lord Thynne had hurried her up the stairs and into these chambers with such alacrity she had not had the chance to see Lord Keynsham's daughters return to their home. From the sound of the chaos in the corridor, it was a happy but noisome event. She opened the door.

A ferment of servants, baggage, and children filled the space between the pale blue silk papered walls. Who knew three little girls needed so very much… everything? Catherine watched, fascinated and more than a bit amused. Maids hurried down the thick Turkey carpets, their arms laden with dresses, spencers, and coats. Two footmen carried wooden boxes piled high with shells and fossils. Four more struggled to carry a small pianoforte up the stairs.

At the far end of the corridor, another set of stairs led up to the third floor, or so Catherine assumed. At the foot of those stairs, the imposing housekeeper Lord Thynne had introduced her to on entering the house gave instructions as to where the servants were to deposit their burdens. She wondered at her relationship to Lord Keynsham's children as she was unmistakably Creole, despite the unlikely name of—

"Mrs. Gilhooley, we're to spend Christmas with you." The middle child, Celestine, ran down the corridor into the housekeeper's arms. "Isn't it wonderful?"

"Of course, it is. Christmas would not be Christmas without my girls, now would it." The housekeeper bent her head to listen as the little girl chattered on about Christmas puddings, and sugar cookies, and presents.

The eldest girl, her arms loaded with sheet music, offered Catherine a brief curtsy, an expression devoid of emotion, and continued down the corridor to join her sister with the housekeeper. Not quite the cut direct, but very nearly. Once she was enfolded in the housekeeper's embrace her entire demeanor changed. She smiled and handed the music to one of the footmen who was headed upstairs.

"Do you like cats?" a sweet voice at Catherine's elbow asked. The smallest of Lord Keynsham's daughters gazed up at her. Filling the child's arms to overflowing was the large, orange tabby Catherine had seen at the inn.

"I don't know." Catherine lowered herself to her knees. "I have never had one."

"Never?" The little girl's eyes widened in disbelief.

"Never. My father did not allow us pets, but my sisters and I would have dearly loved one." Catherine reached out hesitantly and petted the cat. After a moment, he arched into her hand and began to purr.

"He likes you."

"I like him, too."

As only a small child could, Miss Estella—Catherine finally recalled her name—suddenly saw the housekeeper. "Mrs. Gilhooley!" She ran as swiftly as possible, considering the hefty cat in her arms, and joined her sisters in the housekeeper's bountiful embrace. All around them servants went about the task of moving them back into the house. Servants who smiled indulgently and spoke with the girls with affection. Here they were loved and safe, just as any girl should be in her own home.

Children, especially those of the female variety, had so little control in their lives. Right down to deciding where they might spend Christmas. They could not choose their parents. God knows, Catherine would not have chosen hers. They could not choose their heritage or how society might treat them because of it. Growing up, Catherine had been afforded the most deferential of treatments by those outside her home. Within the walls of the many homes of the Duke of Wharram, she and her sisters had been treated as nothing but a commodity, surplus livestock, with no say as to when they might be led to slaughter. She did not envy these girls the censure their mixed race would bring. Until recently, however, her own lot had not been much better.

The chattering children and laughing housekeeper were a foreign land to her. A song she'd never heard, and it had nothing to do with their Creole blood. Catherine had to marry to gain access to her complete inheritance. She'd chosen Lord Thynne for all sorts of reasons that had nothing to do with love and everything to do with how she wanted to live her life. And that was a song with which she was all too familiar.

"Why has Lord Thynne brought you here for Christmas, my lady?" Jenny peered out the sitting room door and wrinkled her nose. "All of these children and that heathen housekeeper. Why did he not invite you to spend Christmas at Lavender Hill?"

"His house is being renovated." Catherine spared the happy scene at the end of the corridor one last look and stepped back into the sitting room. She settled into a comfortable chintz chair before the roaring fire one of the maids had lit.

"For three years?" Jenny prepared a cup of tea from the generous tray that had been sent up. She handed it to Catherine. "He has been living with Lord Keynsham for three years."

"These things take time." Catherine sipped her tea. Jenny did have a point.

"More like that mad earl of a father of his has burned it to the ground." Jenny settled onto a settee and drank her own tea.

"Well, there you have it. Would you want to invite your betrothed to spend Christmas with a madman in a burned down house?"

"Really, my lady." Jenny perused the offerings on the tray like a governess checking a Latin translation. "I cannot like his friend. What sort of man has his by-blows in the house with respectable people like Lord Thynne and the rector?"

"A good father, I should think." Catherine put down her tea and rose to stroll to the window which overlooked a walled-in garden with a maze. Three men stood around an ornate sundial. Night was falling, but she recognized Lord Keynsham's powerful frame at once. "Not that I know a great deal of good fathers. Lord Thynne and the rector do not seem to mind."

"You should not have insisted they remain here for Christmas."

"They?"

"Those girls." Jenny sniffed.

"Oh, for heaven's sake, Jenny. Lord Keynsham is not the first man to put the cart before the horse and end up with a child for his troubles."

"Yes, but three carts and still no horse? He will never marry if he insists on keeping those girls with him." Jenny came to join her at the window. "He has little to recommend him. His title is not a high one. His fortune is not known. This house is quite old. And he is not a handsome man."

"I suppose not." Catherine studied him as he stood, hands clasped behind his back, looking into the setting sun. An annoying flutter settled in her stomach. Lord Thynne and

Reverend Collins appeared to be arguing over something. Lord Keynsham turned and silenced them with a few words.

"I don't know how you will face the other guests when they arrive, my lady. Lord Thynne—"

"Is hiding a secret. They all are." She continued to observe the occupants of the garden. "And you, my dear Jenny, are going to help me discover what it is."

Chapter Four

Valerian ran his finger beneath his neckcloth and started down the carpeted corridor towards the stairs to the first floor. Life had turned inexorably complicated in the last twenty-four hours. Not the least of these complications was the need to dress for dinner. In the last three years, he and his friends had fallen into bachelor habits—dining in the small dining room *en familie*, often in their shirtsleeves and waistcoats, and usually with Thynne's girls at least one meal a day. Tonight, with a duke's daughter to entertain, full dinner regalia held sway as did the use of the best china in the ridiculously ornate formal dining room.

Jesus wept.

"I heard that." Collins, followed by Thynne, stepped out of his chamber and closed the door. "Your neckcloth is a mortal sin, Keynsham. When are you going to hire a valet?"

Valerian stopped in front of the large gold-framed mirror at the top of the stairs. "Why should I when you insist on valeting me and Thynne?" he asked.

Thynne elbowed him over as he checked his appearance in the mirror. "I think he has missed his calling. I may have to steal him away from your parish once I am married."

"As I continue to inform you, you cannot afford me," Collins replied and quickly retied Valerian's neckcloth. "I charge far more for making a viscount presentable than I do for saving his soul."

"Very egalitarian of you, Collins, considering one task is difficult and the other is damned near impossible," Valerian said as he threw the mirror a final glance, scowled, and started down the stairs.

"Which is which, I wonder," Collins inquired and grabbed Thynne by the arm to pull him along in Valerian's wake. "And to which viscount do you refer?"

"Don't ask," Thynne suggested "Speaking of damned near impossible, how did you manage to persuade the girls to dine in the nursery?"

"I renegotiated the terms of our agreement," Valerian informed him with a shrug.

"Dear God," Thynne groaned and ran a hand over his face. He'd shaved at least. Or, more likely, Collins had persuaded one of the footmen to shave him.

"Agreement? What agreement?" Collins shot his cuffs and smoothed down his hair, which immediately went awry once more.

"Keynsham negotiated with Esmerelda," Thynne said with a grimace.

"Are you mad?" Collins's horror was palpable.

"As a March hare," Valerian agreed. "Dedham, did you restock the sideboard in the dining room?"

"Yes, my lord." Valerian's butler had served the Keynsham family for fifty years. As any well-trained butler would do, he had fulfilled Thynne's request for a full complement of spirits in the dining room. A request Collins had informed Valerian of earlier. As a man loyal to the death to Valerian, Dedham had replenished the supply in the dining room with watered down brandy.

"I want to know the terms of this agreement," Collins demanded even as he looked to Valerian who nodded ever so slightly. The idea to water down the brandy had been the rector's.

The sound of female voices from the second-floor landing drew their attention back to the stairs.

"The terms were simple," Valerian explained with barely leashed patience. "Thynne has two weeks to *land on his hairless* and if the girls keep up this charade for the entire two weeks, I told them their father would allow them to have a puppy." Valerian stepped to the foot of the stairs, drawn by the music of feminine laughter. Lady Catherine's laughter.

"You what?" Thynne's question was a strangled whisper as his betrothed appeared at the top of the stairs.

"The new agreement is," Valerian said with a quiet grin. "You will allow each of them a puppy."

Valerian ignored the choking sounds behind him as the duke's daughter glided down the stairs. She wore a deep green velvet gown, the lines of which clung to her long-limbed curves like a lover's caress. The neckline revealed her collarbones and stopped at the soft curves of the tops of her breasts. The pearlescent beauty of the ivory skin bared to his view was emphasized by the long sleeves covering her arms, ending in points from her wrists to the tops of her delicate hands. A single strand of pearls with matching earrings served as her only adornment. Her amber hair, the same whisky color as her eyes, had been piled artfully on top of her head and fixed in place with pearl combs. He did not want to look at his friend's betrothed like this. And he did not want to stop.

"You look lovely, Lady Catherine." Valerian took the hand she offered and bowed over it. Her fingers, warm and remarkably strong, curled around his.

"Thank you, Lord Keynsham. How fortunate am I to have three such handsome dinner companions?" She slid her fingers free of Valerian's to place them on Thynne's offered arm. The two of them proceeded to the dining room. Valerian and Collins fell into step behind them.

"Did you really promise those girls three puppies?" Collins inquired softly.

"Uhm hmm." Valerian forced himself not to fix on the exotic swish of Lady Catherine's skirts.

"He's going to kill you."

"Uhm hmm."

"I know the lady is Thynne's betrothed, but shouldn't we have a chaperone here until the other guests arrive?" Collins took two steps to Valerian's one and was already out of breath.

"You mean besides the local rector?" Valerian caught Lady Catherine's eye as she stepped into the dining room. Something in her gaze set the hair on the back of his neck aloft.

"Well, yes, actually."

"Quite so." Valerian stopped and waved Collins into the dining room. "That's why your sister will be joining us tomorrow."

"My—Betsy?" Collins gasped, his face going white. "Thynne won't have to kill you. I'm going to kill you."

"Get in line."

෨෬

Catherine had no memory of a more... enlightening

dinner than the one she presently attended. The food, of course, was delicious—a mixture of English and Creole fare. Lord Keynsham's servants waited at table with efficiency and grace. And they smiled. Their master spoke to them very little. His stoic, solemn demeanor held firmly in place. But they served with a confidence and warmth she had seldom seen in *ton* homes, especially those of her father and his cronies.

The dining room was large, with a number of sideboards and commodes along the walls. The wall hangings of pale blue blended with the dark blue and gold of the Aubusson carpet beautifully. The furnishings were of walnut. Chippendale, if she was not mistaken. The crystal and china, edged in gold, but not overly ostentatious. The table linens were Irish, embroidered in white silk thread with the crest she had recognized on the travel coach.

Then there was the company. The three gentlemen had grown up together, almost as brothers. The Reverend Collins had a way with a story and had no qualms about embarrassing his friends with tales of their childhood misadventures. As turnabout was fair play, Lord Thynne regaled them with an account of the rector's unfortunate outing with a vicar's daughter on the Cherwell during their Oxford days.

"Defend yourself, Reverend," Catherine implored as she struggled not to laugh. "Surely you would not dump a lady, new bonnet and all, into the river."

"He did indeed," Lord Thynne assured her. "Collins joined the Church because he failed miserably as a sailor." And what failure, after a mere thirty years on earth, had driven her betrothed to draw his imitation of merriment from a bottle? He'd smiled, and laughed, and cajoled, and flirted all evening. Just as he had in Edinburgh. And, as then, none of it rang true. She glanced at Lord Keynsham. What did he see when he looked at his friend? A man who studied everyone as if they were some ancient text to be translated, what did he see when he looked at her?

"Alas, it is true, Lady Catherine." Reverend Collins pushed his dessert plate away and sighed heavily. "Had Keynsham here not leapt into the river and saved her, I might very well have been banished to live as some lofty lord's hermit. Doomed to live in a cave and provide amusement for ladies like you."

"Thank goodness for Lord Keynsham then, for I would have missed your wonderful stories." Catherine turned her attention back to the man at the head of the table. He'd not participated in the storytelling, save to add a comment here and there. Not precisely taciturn. He'd enjoyed his friends' remembrances. She'd seen it in his eyes. Pensive, perhaps that described him best. And when it came to Lord Thynne, watchful.

"The lady is a flatterer, Thynne. A wise man would marry her."

"Quite right, Collins. I think I shall." Lord Thynne saluted her with his wine glass.

In a carillon of clattering china and clinking crystal, Lord Keynsham erupted from his seat. "It has been a long day. Lady Catherine is no doubt weary from her journey."

Startled, his friends stared at him. Catherine dabbed her serviette to her mouth, taking far more time than the task required. She took one last sip of wine before she placed the serviette on the table and allowed Reverend Collins to pull out her chair. Lord Thynne lurched to his feet.

"Allow me to escort you above stairs, my lady." He came around the table and offered her his arm.

"Thank you... Gregory," she said, deliberately using his given name as she touched her fingers to his sleeve. "Perhaps we should see Lord Keynsham safely to his chambers after such a long day." She turned to fix their host with her most vapid society smile.

Reverend Collins coughed. He covered his mouth with his fist and continued to cough. Lord Thynne threw back his head and laughed. Lord Keynsham's face never changed save for the tiniest of quirks at one corner of his mouth. He inclined his head in the barest of acknowledgements. With a wave of his powerful arm, he indicated they should leave the dining room before him.

"Is he always this managing?" Catherine leaned in to ask Lord Thynne as they all climbed the stairs to the second floor.

"Oh, yes. You would never know he is the youngest of us. He has been in charge since we were children."

"I deserve neither such credit nor such censure." Lord Keynsham came up behind them, close enough that the scent of his cologne, sandalwood and some exotic musk, wrapped around her back like a cloak. "These two are perfectly capable of getting into mischief all by themselves."

"Ah, but who gets them out of said mischief, my lord? Who orders them to bed after a long journey?" She stopped before her chamber door and turned to face the three of them. "Or is that a privilege afforded only to lady guests and children?"

Reverend Collins snickered. "Oh, well done, Lady

Catherine."

"I never order children to bed, Lady Catherine." Lord Keynsham's dark voice carried an undercurrent of something hot and dangerous.

"Wouldn't do you a whit of good," Lord Thynne said, a barely-there slur to his words. "Those girls heed no man. Least of all their father."

"Mrs. Gilhooley." Catherine spotted the housekeeper's approach from the far end of the corridor.

"We all heed Mrs. Gilhooley. It is worth more than our lives should we fail to do so," Reverend Collins said and elbowed Lord Thynne who nodded with mock solemnity.

"You mistake me, Reverend," Catherine said as she motioned towards the woman bearing down on them. "Mrs. Gilhooley."

The housekeeper dipped them a brief curtsy. "Miss Estella is asking for a story and a good night kiss from her father. She refuses to go to sleep without one."

The door to Catherine's chambers opened behind her. Jenny cleared her throat. Catherine, however, did not move. The three men stared at the housekeeper, frozen in place as if waiting for divine intervention or Gabriel's trumpet, whichever arrived first. They did not look at each other, but dear Lord, it could not be more obvious they wanted to do so. And the housekeeper? Mrs. Gilhooley, never had a woman looked less Irish, appeared serenely amused.

"A story." Lord Keynsham finally spoke.

"And a kiss." This from Lord Thynne.

"That's what she said." The woman raked each of them, Catherine and her maid included, up and down, found them wanting, and continued down the corridor to the stairs to the first floor.

"You heard her, Keynsham," the rector said with a great deal of cheer. "Up you go." He pushed the viscount in the direction of the stairs to the nursery.

"Let us all go," Lord Thynne boomed. "I'd like to hear a story. Wouldn't you, Collins?"

"Indeed, I would."

Lord Keynsham's expression never faltered. Which took a bit of the wind out of Lord Thynne and the rector's sails. What on earth...

"I would enjoy a story as well, gentlemen," Catherine said as she walked past them and led the way down the corridor. "I will come with you and bid the children good night."

"That truly is not..." Her betrothed stopped when Catherine peered over her shoulder at him. "... Necessary, my lady." He tugged at his cravat and patted his jacket pocket, where he, no doubt, kept the flask he always carried.

Still Lord Keynsham said not a word. He prowled slowly down the Turkey carpeted hallway and up the stairs. The other two fell in step behind him, arguing in a rise and fall of whispers. Whispers of which the snatches she caught only increased her curiosity.

"Puppies..."

"My sister. Here!"

"Three puppies. Your sister? What?"

"Betsy. Here. Puppies?"

"Three. Dear God. Not Betsy."

Catherine resisted the urge to look back. Once they gained the third floor and traversed the Persian carpets a little ways, Lord Keynsham stopped at a set of double doors and pushed them open, his long muscular arms sending the doors wide. He moved to the side and, with a curt nod and sweep of his hand, invited her to enter.

The room was quite large. She surmised it might well stretch across an entire side of this wing of the house. Never had she visited a nursery so exotically decorated. The walls sported elaborate murals from corner to corner and top to bottom. Palm trees on sandy beaches on one wall, a jungle of ferns and exotic birds on another, views of the ocean, and a castle on high cliffs—to step inside was to step into another world. Pink marble floors peeked out from beneath Persian carpets and brightly colored woven rugs. Before a mantelpiece held up by dragons on either side stood a combination of fan-backed wicker garden chairs and comfortable damask covered tufted chairs and a settee.

Folding doors, pushed open across the far side of the sitting room, revealed an equally large, dainty bedchamber. Decorated in shades of pink and primrose, the room sported three diminutive canopy beds, draped in a sheer, fine fabric so delicate as to appear spun on the finest looms in India. The fireplace in this room, carved of black marble, consisted of horses emerging from the sea foam on either side of the mantle. Above the mantle, hung a portrait of the most exotically beautiful woman Catherine had ever seen. Petite, with ebony hair to her waist, fierce black eyes, dark caramel skin, and the figure of a pocket Venus, she wore a flowing gown of brilliant blue silk. And her face marked her as the mother of the three girls tucked up in their elegant beds more assuredly than any entry in Debrett's. Little wonder Lord Keynsham had made this beautiful creature his own.

Where is she?

"Papa, you came!" Little Estella slid off her bed and raced across the thick Aubusson carpets.

In two steps, Lord Keynsham intercepted her and tossed her high in the air. She giggled when she landed back in his arms. He held her close and whispered in her ear. Eyes wide, Estella gazed at Catherine and nodded solemnly. Once she was tucked back in bed, the other two girls crept over to climb onto the thick counterpane next to her. Catherine offered the girls a tentative smile and took a few steps closer to the bed. However, when she glanced over her shoulder, she saw Lord Thynne and Reverend Collins had stopped just inside the folding doors. Their expressions vacillated between highly amused and terrified. Curiouser and curiouser.

"Mrs. Gilhooley informs me you require a story, Miss Estella." Lord Keynsham sat on the side of the bed, one foot on the floor and his other leg cocked up on the fluffy mattress. He had no choice but to perch in such a fashion as the bed was now replete with little girls and an assortment of large, fluffy felines. "My repertoire of stories is sadly lacking. What would you like to hear?"

"The siren story," Estella begged and clapped her hands. Her sisters nodded in agreement.

"And how does the siren story start?" Somehow, Lord Keynsham smiled without moving a muscle in his face. What a ridiculously fanciful notion. His eyes, his voice, the way he leaned in close to the girls—perhaps it was merely the way he drew smiles from those around him. He gifted smiles to others, but seldom kept one for himself. Catherine shook her head.

And he was entirely too clever as well. In response to his

question, Celestine launched into a story of a brave, beautiful siren who sang lullabies to children and swept their nightmares away. Each of the sisters in turn added bits and pieces to the story, an obvious much-loved favorite. The siren befriended three soldiers, men who crept behind enemy lines to discover the evil emperor's secrets. The soldiers' adventures grew more grand and perilous as the story continued until one day they became trapped at the edge of a cliff overlooking the sea. Before the evil emperor's henchmen discovered the soldiers' hiding place, the beautiful siren appeared and lured them away with her song. The soldiers were saved.

"What a lovely story," Catherine exclaimed. "What happened to the siren?" A pall fell over the room, swift and vicious in its suddenness.

Reverend Collins finally answered her. "The siren's song was so beautiful the angels in heaven insisted she join them."

Catherine turned to look at him and Lord Thynne and found them solemn and a bit pale. When she directed her attention to the storytellers once more, they had turned their gazes on the portrait over the fireplace. The heavy gilt of the frame glittered like sunlight on water. And Lord Keynsham, as he too settled his attention on the painting, conveyed only an icy sadness, difficult to decipher and even more difficult to see.

"She is an angel now," Estella explained. "And she watches over us from heaven."

Catherine flinched at the wave of chill and sorrow that eddied around her.

"She does." Lord Keynsham pushed to his feet. "And what she sees this moment is three young ladies who should be in bed."

Esmerelda and Celestine scurried to their beds and snuggled under the counterpanes. Lord Keynsham banked the fire and set the guard before it. He snuffed the candles on the mantel and the ones on each girl's bedside table. Catherine retraced her steps towards the folding doors. Lord Thynne and the rector had made quick work of the candles and lamps in the sitting room. When Lord Keynsham moved to turn out the lone lamp sitting in the window, Esmerelda, who had added only a little to the story and even less to the conversation and laughter, protested.

"Please, uhn… Papa. Not that one."

He raised an eyebrow but stayed his hand.

"That one is for Mama," Celestine explained. "So she can find us in the dark to watch over us." She curled her hands around her counterpane. The opaline interior of a nautilus shell on her bedside table caught the lamplight.

"Your mama loves you," Lord Keynsham said softly. "When you love someone, you can find them even in the darkest night."

Catherine touched her knuckles beneath her chin to keep her mouth from dropping open. She nearly checked to see if perhaps Reverend Collins or even Lord Thynne had expressed these sentiments.

"But I will leave the lamp on, just in case. Good night, ladies." Lord Keynsham bowed, marched past Catherine, past his friends, and out of the nursery as if his hair were on fire. By the time Catherine and the remaining two gentlemen had bid the children good night, come down the stairs, and stood once more in the second-floor corridor, their host was nowhere in sight.

Catherine took comfort in her betrothed's and the rector's bemusement at Keynsham's abrupt departure. She despised being in utter confusion alone.

"Well, good night, my lady." Lord Thynne kissed her hand and fled down the corridor and around the corner.

"Good night, Lady Catherine. Pleasant dreams."

"Good…" She stared as the rector trotted a few doors down and nearly slammed his hand in the door in his haste to enter his room. "Night."

"My lady?" Jenny stood in the doorway to the pretty sitting room. "Is everything alright?"

"You tell me, Jenny." Catherine swept past her, toed off her slippers, and collapsed into a fireside chair. "What have you learned of this household? And it had better be good."

Chapter Five

He'd awakened to discover the blizzard he'd anticipated had not arrived. Yet. And now he stood—hid actually—in his library, still contemplating the weather like some stuffy country gentleman. The view afforded Valerian from this particular first-floor window showed the occasional flurry of snow fluttering by like petals shaken from white wisteria vines. Good Lord. Acting the father had turned him into a sentimental sapskull.

Valerian had once eaten an entire trifle by himself. The trifle had been intended for at least six people, and Valerian had been all of nine years old. The sweetness had been marvelous at first, then cloying, and at last, truly sickening. In fact, he'd been so ill, he thought, as only a young boy could, he might die. Only after three days' time, much of it spent over a chamber pot in the nursery, had he recovered fully.

Watching Thynne woo Lady Catherine Chastleton over the past five days put him in mind of that experience. He'd found his friend the perfect wife. Yet, when the man managed to get out of bed and spend time with his betrothed, it irked Valerian no end. And seeing Thynne and Lady Catherine stroll in the gardens or sit in the drawing room together made him sick at his stomach. The question of his recovery from this two-week spectacle was in serious doubt.

Infuriating.

Worse, they still had no idea how Lady Catherine might react to the knowledge her husband-to-be came with three children whose mother was a Creole freed woman, daughter of a former slave from Barbados. The lady's maid, however, left no doubt as to her opinion of *Lord Keynsham's unfortunate daughters* and what they might expect from life. If her mistress shared the maid's harsh, unhelpful insight, and desire to see the girls rusticating in the country for the remainder of their lives, Thynne was in deep trouble.

Then again, if Valerian's visceral reaction to Lady Catherine's presence in a room—in his house, in Somerset—continued, Thynne was not the only one in trouble.

Speaking of trouble, the squeals of girlish laughter, which had drawn him to the long French windows at one end of his study in the first place, echoed from the gardens below once more. The chill of the December weather did little to deter the girls' daily forays into Keynsham Hall's now dormant gardens. The tall maze and sculptured shelter of the ancient yew trees shielded them from the cruelest winds. And the upstairs maid, Annie, who had been persuaded to supervise them, made certain they always wore their warmest coats, hats, and mittens.

The case clock in the corridor struck eleven. Perhaps he should find a reason to send Lady Catherine into the gardens. In the last five days, she'd not spent ten minutes alone with the children. Anytime she came the least bit close to them, Thynne did his damnedest to shepherd her away, as if the girls had some dread disease he feared she might contract. How was the man to discover how she felt about *his* daughters if he insisted on keeping them as far from her as possible? Did he really intend to marry the unsuspecting lady and announce at the wedding breakfast— "By the by, those three lovely girls aren't Keynsham's daughters, they're mine. Congratulations, you're a mother."—?

Knowing Thynne? Highly probable.

His friend's problems and decisions were no longer Valerian's concern. The two dozen guests to arrive in a little over a week, after Christmas but just in time for the festivities leading up to Twelfth Night, were Mrs. Gilhooley's concern, thank God. Valerian had only to maintain this grand deception and stand back when the entire thing crashed down around them. A simple enough task if it did not involve a lady who smelled of summer roses in the dead of winter and three little girls who enjoyed torturing him, making demands of him, and stealing into his heart to leave crumbs of dreams of a wife and children of his own.

Valerian tapped his forehead against the now frosted window panes. "Shoot me now," he muttered.

"Do not tempt me, Valerian Keynsham."

He nearly jumped out of his skin. He banged his head on the window and whirled to find the owner of the voice that put sergeants barking orders at Waterloo to shame. "Betsy. What the devil." He took a breath and executed a bow. "Miss Collins, how might I help you?"

Of medium height, with brown hair bent towards frizzy in inclement weather, brown eyes more discerning than the most exacting governess, and a figure with more angles than curves, Miss Betsy Collins terrified nearly every man she'd ever met. With good reason. Her own brother had turned a perfectly nice rectory over to her three years ago. Which had resulted in Collins visiting Keynsham Hall. Permanently. If

Valerian weren't terrified of her himself, he'd get even with her for that little gift.

She snorted. "Don't you *Miss Collins* me, Lord Keynsham. We've known each other far too long for that nonsense." With an incredible lack of grace, she marched across his study and grabbed his arm at the elbow. "If you want to help me, you will talk Lord Thynne out of this ridiculous scheme."

"I have stopped making decisions for my friends." He stumbled out the door, dragged by the rector's determined sibling.

"Yes, I know. Fine time for you to decide to stop." She pulled him down the stairs to the foyer and snatched his greatcoat and gloves from a remarkably unflustered Dedham.

Valerian managed to dig in his heels once they crossed the terrace and stood on the steps leading to the drive. "Betsy, where am I going and, more importantly, why?"

Arms akimbo, she blew a stray wisp of hair from her eyes. "I just came from the foyer. The duke's daughter insists on riding over to Lavender Hill to inspect the house and property. She cannot go alone."

She shoved his arm into his coat and spun him around to try and force his other arm into its sleeve. "She is Thynne's betrothed. Why is he not accompanying her?" Valerian drew the line at allowing her to put his gloves on as if he were some clumsy, forgetful child. He took them from her with none too little effort.

"It is eleven o' clock in the morning, Keynsham. You know why he is not accompanying her." Sadness, anger, regret—all in evidence in her regard. He did not look away, though his every instinct cried for him to do so.

"Her name is Lady Catherine, not *the duke's daughter*."

He kicked a stray pebble down the stone steps. "You've spent a great deal of time with her since you arrived. You have been cordial and appear close to becoming bosom bows. What has caused you to take her in dislike?" Had he imagined Betsy's approval of Catherine? And why was it suddenly so important?

"I do like her." Betsy gazed up at the second-floor windows behind which Thynne lay in a brandy induced stupor as he did every day until the late afternoon. "Very much. She is capable, managing, the ideal woman to be wife to an earl, and she is utterly wrong for Thynne and you know it."

"Wrong? Nonsense, she will take care of him and the girls. Thanks to her late aunt, she knows a great deal about lavender farming and has a good head for business." *She is beautiful, too clever by far, witty, tart, and has a body that calls to me all hours of the night.*

"*Hmpf!* You and William have taken care of him these last three years. Which is why you must ride out with Lady Catherine because her betrothed is incapable of doing so." She looped her arm through his and thereby forced him to descend the steps and walk towards the stables.

"Unfair, Betsy. He is a grown man. We are not responsible for his drinking." Valerian's defense was half-hearted at best. Their boots crunched on the gravel of the path, covered with a light dusting of snow. They walked in silence for a dozen or more paces before she spoke again.

"There are many sorts of responsibility. What reason does he have to stop when you and William live his life for him?"

"Live his life? Now who is talking nonsense?" A flash of

heat crept up his neck and flushed his cheeks.

They stopped a ways from the stables. "Those girls are in for a very difficult life and a sot for a father will not aid them in surviving it. They have been happier this week with you as their *father* than they have been since their mother died. But you are not their father, and when this farce is over, they will have to live in the rubble you, William, and Thynne have created."

"Don't mince words, Betsy. Do give me your full opinion." The girls had been happy? What did it say about him that he took a bit of pride in those words?

She pulled her brother's faded blue wool coat more tightly around her. "You say you will not make decisions for your friends any longer, but you have. You have decided Lady Catherine will make Thynne a good wife and his daughters a good mother." She waved away his attempt to interrupt her. "You will accompany her to Lavender Hill and seek to discover her true feelings as to the girls and their futures. When he is sober, our friend, Thynne, can defend himself. The children cannot."

Valerian pulled on his gloves and buttoned his coat. "How would you suggest I do so without revealing our *farce*, as you so kindly put it?" He glanced up to see the grooms leading out two saddled mounts—his own Mercury and the lanky gelding, Allemande, he'd bought at Tattersall's the last time he'd visited London. Seated atop the black gelding, in a very fetching dark green riding habit and a far more sensible hat than he'd ever seen on a lady, Lady Catherine tilted her head and perused him with a mix of curiosity and humor.

"You will hit upon a way to winkle it out of her." Betsy patted his arm.

"I do not *winkle*, Miss Collins." The very idea.

"Of course, you do. It may well be the thing you do best. Your talent for winkling saved me from running off to Gretna with that horrid Lord Fallow." She rose on her toes and kissed his cheek. "Thank you for that, by the way." She shoved him towards the waiting horses and strolled back to the house.

Valerian snapped his gloves into place and shook out the capes of his greatcoat. "Lady Catherine does not strike me as the *winkling* sort," he muttered. "But it might be a great deal of fun to find out."

ೞಣ

One of the first skills any child of the Duke of Wharram acquired was the ability to recognize an inquisition. Catherine had not asked for an escort for her trip to Lavender Hill. She was not surprised when Lord Keynsham elected to provide it. He was an imperious, managing man. To her delight, he assured her it was not his idea at all.

"When Miss Betsy Collins asks one to do something, it is understood one will obey. Arguing with her is an exercise in futility at best and the shortest route to Bedlam at worst."

They rode down lanes devoid of company with high hedges on one side and high rock walls on the other. He divulged the foibles and secrets of the Collins siblings—Betsy was in charge and William tried his best to stay out of her way. Which explained why she lived at the rectory, and he lived with Lord Keynsham. Catherine regaled him with the latest tales of her brother, the Marquess of Winterbourne's, adventures. Keynsham knew her brother from when they were at school together and had kept company with him in London from time to time.

After the first hour, as they drew nearer to the border between Keynsham lands and those lands attached to Lavender Hill, the viscount directed the conversation into more personal avenues. Thus, the inquisition began and his true reason for agreeing to accompany her came to light. Miss Collins had a great deal of determination, and Catherine appreciated her no-nonsense approach to life, but Lord Valerian Keynsham did not take orders from anyone.

"Are you sincerely interested in assessing the renovations on the house, Lady Catherine, or is inspecting the estate's ability to support you the reason for this ride on a bitter December morning?" At least he did her the honor of asking a direct question.

"Both, actually. A lady is seldom afforded the opportunity to check these things for herself. Most of the time she is handed off to her husband at the altar and expected to accept it all with a simper and a smile."

His bark of laughter frightened a flock of magpies into flight. "You? Simper? Surely that would be one of the signs of the Apocalypse."

"My aunt left me more than money, Lord Keynsham. She left me years of knowledge and research on the farming of lavender. I have high hopes for the estate."

He turned his horse from the lane and guided him through a gap in the rock wall. Catherine followed, and after a brief time threading through a grove of trees, they entered an open field asleep beneath a thin blanket of snow. "This is where Lavender Hill's lands begin. Shall we commence the inspection here?"

"Hmm." Catherine urged her mount up the hill. From the top the view consisted of acres of fallow fields waiting for spring.

Lord Keynsham rode up to join her. "You are fortunate to know so much about lavender cultivation. I may well throw myself upon your mercy in raising my own crop this year."

"You said this will be your second year with lavender. Your fortune was built on other endeavors was it not?" Two could play at an inquisition. Jenny had discovered very little about the goings on at Keynsham Hall, but what information she'd gleaned from the servants Catherine fully intended to use.

"My family's fortune was built on many things, Lady Catherine. Until three years ago it was built on the profits from sugar plantations in the West Indies. Barbados and Jamaica, primarily." The wind stood as nothing when compared to the sudden change in the viscount's tone.

"Until three years ago?" Catherine had no fear of cold-hearted men. She'd lived under the thumb of one the first sixteen or so years of her life.

"I sold them. The expense of running them was no longer equal to the profit. My father, who inherited them from his father, had little knowledge of how to run them and allowed others to do so. I find a landlord must at least attempt to pay attention if he wishes to make a profit. I took what I made from the sale of the plantations and invested in a fleet of ships. Shipping is a more profitable endeavor. Not very proper of either of us to discuss money and how it is made, but I am a mere viscount and needs must when the devil takes the reins."

"Barbados. Is that where you met your... your daughters' mother?" Jenny had passed on the few pieces of information she'd gleaned from the conversations of the servants.

"It is. Thynne, Collins, and I went down to the West Indies ten years ago, before we purchased our commissions."

"I see." She didn't, actually. He'd bought and sold land and people for profit. People who might well be related to his daughters.

They rode down a well-worn bridle path into the stable yard of a large red brick mansion. Only half the size of Keynsham Hall, but a more than adequate country home. Even on this wintery morning carpenters and brick masons swarmed the house, making good use of Catherine's money. A couple of the workers came to take the horses as she and the viscount dismounted.

"What would you like to see first, Lady Catherine? I will answer any questions you have if I can." Lord Keynsham fitted his hands to her waist and lifted her from the sidesaddle with ease before slowly lowering her to the ground. He indicated a path away from the house towards what appeared to be a large barn.

"Your daughters, Lord Keynsham, what do you intend to do about them?" She had not meant to be so blunt. Disappointment did that to her. She was disappointed in him, with no idea why it mattered so much.

"Do, Lady Catherine? What do you mean, do?" He opened a small door set within the double doors across the front of the barn-like structure. Once she stepped inside, he closed it and lit a lantern hanging by the door.

Lavender. Catherine unpinned the smart little hat she'd worn and closed her eyes to soak in the soothing scent. The air fairly shimmered with it. Once he turned the lantern up, she saw the plants hanging on drying lines from one end of the barn to the other. The scent was heavenly, like a field in full bloom. For a moment she forgot his question, and hers, and all thoughts of marriage and money. Here was something she knew. Something she trusted. Something she might depend upon to always be the same and to look after her, so she need never depend upon or be disappointed by a man ever again. The years she'd spent learning the mysteries and many secrets of lavender from Aunt Beatrice had paid off in more ways than one.

"What should I do with my daughters, Lady Catherine?" His dark voice rumbled so close it resonated up her spine and settled against her shoulders. She turned and took a step back from his large, intimidating frame.

"I am certain I do not know. They are intelligent, happy children. You appear to have provided them with an excellent governess. I am certain she will turn them into accomplished young ladies worthy of taking their places in society when the time comes." She paced the aisles of the drying barn, inspecting work tables and the other tools necessary to turn lavender growing in the fields into blooming plants in June and July and then harvestable crops in August.

"But?" He stood on one side of a worktable fiddling with tools and all the while watching her like a hawk.

She, however, was no mouse. "What places will they be offered in London society? They are their mother's daughters. They are beautiful. When they are grown they will be stunning. You will make certain their manners are impeccable. They will be women any man of sense would be proud to have in his home. But, tell me, Lord Keynsham, how many men of sense do you know in London? And how many do you know who will be far more inclined to offer your daughters a place in a discreet little house on Bruton Street—an exquisite, exotic prize to make him the envy of his fellows?"

"You have a hard view of the men of the *ton*, my lady." He was leading her down a path, and she was powerless to step away from it.

"The men? Shall we talk of what the women will do to your daughters? The gossip. The shunning. The hateful stares and unkind words. Skirts pulled to the side. No society mother will allow her son to court an illegitimate girl of mixed blood, no matter how large her dowry. And should a man be desperate enough to brave society's censure, how will he treat a woman he has married solely for her money?"

"What, then, is my solution?" His eyes narrowed. He gripped the lip of the wooden work table so tightly his knuckles were white. "Keep them here in the country, hidden like all dirty little secrets?"

"If you think so little of me, one wonders why you would recommend me as wife to your closest friend." A sharp pang pulsed just beneath her ribs. His stone face revealed nothing, but his eyes burned with condemnation.

"You think I do not know what faces them as they become women and attempt to take their rightful place amongst the vicious, vacuous ranks of *good* society?"

Catherine laughed, a long bitter sound. "You have no idea, more's the pity. If men understood the place in which a woman must live her life, perhaps they might take better care than to produce daughter after daughter for which they have little use and even less understanding. Your daughters are lovely, but did you give even one thought when you were having a ripping good time creating them as to how unfair their lives might be for no reason save the circumstances of their births and the fact they were not born men?"

Shouting at each other? Perhaps not, but Catherine and Lord Keynsham were well on their way. She'd started the conversation, but she'd fully expected him to cut her off or change the subject as he was wont to do when they'd conversed in Edinburgh. Why would he even solicit her opinion concerning his daughters?

"Would it be better had my daughters not been born, my lady?" He fixed her with the oddest stare—questioning, but more.

"Never, my lord. They are beautiful, loving, magnificent girls. Surely you see that?" Catherine did not understand. What did this man need from her?

"I do. But what shall I do, to give them a chance in life?" His eyes blazed with a frightening, seeking light. How had she ever believed him to be cold?

Catherine squared her shoulders and made herself look back into that fiery gaze. "Educate them to within an inch of their lives. Teach them to take care of themselves—of their fortunes, their property, their hearts, and their minds. Tell them they bow to no one. And send them to France where magnificent women are appreciated. They will have the men of Paris on their knees. An excellent position from which to judge the contents of a man's heart." She refrained from covering her mouth with her hands. Never had she spoken so boldly and honestly with a man. She'd done so for those little girls, or so she did her utmost to convince herself. She'd said too much. Dear Lord, let him change the subject. Or climb onto his horse and leave her to find her way back to

Keynsham Hall. Or back to Edinburgh.

A slow half-smile curved his lips. "Thank you, Lady Catherine. Shall we look over the improvements to the dairy?"

"I beg your pardon?" Had he read her thoughts?

He came around the work table and offered her his arm. "The dairy. Most women are far more interested than you, my lady, when it comes to items they have purchased. Then again, most women don't purchase dairies or drying barns."

It took a moment for his words to sink in. Who was this man? She gave herself a sharp mental shake.

"Most women cannot afford to do so, and those who can do not see the necessity in it." She curled her gloved fingers around his arm. He doused the lantern and led her from the drying barn across a cobblestone yard to a newly constructed dairy.

"Necessity?" He looked down at her, one eyebrow raised in consternation.

"If a woman wants the independence never to have to measure her worth in the eyes of a man and be found wanting, dairies and drying barns may well be a necessity." Drat him! He'd tricked her into revealing too much. How did he do it, over and over again? Catherine disentangled her arm from his and marched into the dairy. She needed a bit of distance and a few moments to cool her temper.

"Does it meet with your approval, my lady?" Ah. The cynical, superior Lord Keynsham had returned.

"I hardly know. Lavender I know. Dairies and cows are beyond my understanding."

"Somehow, I am certain very little is beyond your understanding." That quirk of a smile played along the lines of his lips once more.

"I will take that as a compliment. I should like to see the house now." Catherine marched past him out of the dairy.

He fell into step next to her, hands clasped behind his back. A pose he maintained as they toured the half-renovated house, floor after floor. Jenny had not been far off the mark. The house had not been burned down but had been neglected to the point perhaps a fire might have been merciful. Prowling along next to her, the viscount said nothing. Catherine made notes in the little notebook she carried in her reticule. Still he said not a word, not even to inquire as to what she was noting. The silence did not disturb her so much as the way he studied her, constantly and with an air of something warm and seeking.

Once outside, the chill of the late afternoon air indicated they'd spent the better part of the day together. Something she and her betrothed had yet to do. Had she enjoyed the day? A question for which she had no answer.

"You appear to have misplaced your hat." Lord Keynsham lifted his hand towards her head, but at the last minute let his hand fall to his side.

Catherine pressed her fingers to her hair as if to assure herself he had not touched her. Only a touch could account for the shiver that meandered through her.

"I took it off in the drying barn." She set off towards the barn. And, of course, he followed her. She flung the small door open and stalked to the table. For some reason her fingers shook. The pins refused to hold the hat in place.

"Having trouble?" he murmured from just behind her.

"How do you do that?" She turned and caught herself before she stamped her foot in utter exasperation.

He took the hat from her hand and placed it back on the table. "Does Thynne see your worth, Lady Catherine? Does he measure it in pounds and pence or in beauty and wit and an irritating tendency to say what you think?"

She looked into those icy grey eyes, a stormy winter sea, and was dragged beneath waves of astonishment and anger.

"You would know that better than I, Lord Keynsham. This marriage is a means to an end for both of us. Your friend—"

"Is a fool." He curved his hand around the back of her head and drew her to him. He pressed his lips to hers—warm, soft, and searching. He withdrew, then touched their lips together once more. Then again. "Catherine."

And then, dear God, she kissed him back.

Chapter Six

"More tea, Lady Catherine?"

"Hmm?" Dear Lord, she must stop this. Young Esmerelda had asked her a question.

"Do you think it will snow for Christmas?"

"Shall I play the pianoforte?"

"Would you like more tea?"

Catherine had no idea of the question as she'd spent the last few days in a state of stunned amazement. All for one kiss. One very passionate, soul searing, heart pounding abrupt kiss. Abrupt in that Lord Keynsham had groaned, pushed her away, jammed her hat onto her head, dragged her from the lavender barn as if it were on fire, tossed her onto her horse and spent the entire ride back to Keynsham Hall saying... not a single word. An odd response and not very flattering at all.

She forced herself to sit up straight and look about without appearing to look about. As the child had the teapot already in hand, Catherine elected to go with the last question flitting through her scattered wits.

"Yes, thank you, Esmerelda. That would be lovely."

For three days Catherine's time had been carefully managed, she knew not by whom, but had her suspicions. Miss Collins entertained her every morning. She and

Reverend Collins joined her for luncheon and a stroll through the gardens, by which time Lord Thynne had arisen. He either took her for a drive to check the progress on the house at Lavender Hill or read to her in the first-floor parlor. By six in the evening, he had left her in the capable hands of Miss Collins once more who joined her in the nursery for a few hours with Lord Keynsham's daughters. They had tea and cakes or worked on their embroidery together or listened to Esmerelda play the pianoforte.

It was all very civilized, just the sort of visit one might have with the family of one's betrothed. Save, these people were not Lord Thynne's family, not really. He had only his father, the Earl of Taunton, from whom he was estranged. She knew not why. When they talked, it was of Lavender Hill, of people they both knew in London, of their time in Edinburgh, or of the irascible Miss Collins, who annoyed him to no end. They never spoke of his family or hers, and they certainly never spoke of his friend, Lord Keynsham.

In fact, she had barely seen the man since their precipitous return from Lavender Hill. He dined with them every evening and immediately withdrew to his study whilst the rest of the party adjourned to the drawing room for tea and card games. He was all that was polite, after a fashion. His own fashion, which consisted of listening to dinner conversation, commenting very little, and gazing at her when she least expected it.

"He likes you, Lady Catherine." Estella, sitting cross-legged on the floor with a cat draped across either knee, blinked up at her with those fathomless dark eyes.

Catherine looked down to find Cuthbert, the large orange tomcat, sprawled in her lap once more. She stroked his fur and smiled. Everyone in the house *liked* her. It would be nice to know why. She'd spent so much of her life trying to discover why her father disliked her so, until she finally decided it did not matter. It would be nice to be liked and to know why, beyond her money and relation to the most despicable duke in England.

"I like him too, Estella. He is a very likeable gentleman."

Miss Collins choked on her tea. "In a pig's eye," she muttered.

"Lady Catherine never had a pet, Miss Betsy. Never in her whole life."

"That is a pity, Estella. Every girl should have a pet."

The little one beamed at Miss Collins and then at Catherine.

"Just not six pets."

Esmerelda and Celestine rolled their eyes and nodded their agreement with the rector's sister.

"I think Estella must have a great deal of love to give to keep so many companions faithful to her." Catherine continued to stroke the big orange lump who had gone limp in her lap and had begun to purr.

"Do you like our papa?" Celestine asked as she rearranged an impressive array of fossils on a child-sized work table next to the tea service.

Thank goodness Catherine had not been sipping her tea. "Your papa... your papa is a very fine gentleman."

"Yes, but do you like him?" Esmerelda handed her a plate with a lemon cake on it. Catherine's favorite.

"I like him because he is Lord Thynne's good friend. He looks after him and all of you, and I think he is quite kind, even if he is a bit stuffy."

This sent the girls into peals of laughter, just as she had intended.

"Well done," Miss Collins mouthed. "Ladies, I am afraid Lady Catherine and I must leave you now. The dinner bell will sound soon, and we must go and dress."

The girls scrambled to their feet. Catherine lowered Cuthbert to the floor, stood, and brushed out her skirts. Curtsies accomplished, Esmerelda and Celestine went back to what they were doing. Estella tugged on her skirt.

"Yes, dear?" Catherine bent down to attend her.

"I think Unc—Papa likes you almost as much as Cuthbert does."

"Good night, Estella." Miss Collins hurried the child towards the nursemaid who sat in the rocking chair in the corner. She grabbed Catherine's elbow and tugged her out into the corridor.

"They are charming creatures, are they not?"

Catherine had to lengthen her stride to keep up with the rector's dynamic sister. His sister who was up to something. As was everyone in this house. Jenny had had no further luck with the servants. The children's mother had died in Spain three years ago. The same number of years Lord Thynne and Reverend Collins had lived with Lord Keynsham. The three gentlemen had gone to war together. Lord Thynne and Reverend Collins had sold out three years ago. Lord Keynsham had stayed on through Waterloo. Something had happened three years ago, and it was still happening in this house.

"Miss Collins."

The young woman stopped at the top of the stairs to the first floor. "Yes, my lady?"

"Two things. I should very much like for at least one person in this house to call me Catherine, if I may presume and call you Betsy."

"I should like that very much."

"Good. And second, will you come into my sitting room for a moment's conversation out of the hearing of men, children, servants, and feline companions?"

Betsy laughed, a very light and musical sound. "We have done our best to ensure you are not lonely here, have we not?"

They stepped into the sitting room attached to Catherine's bedchamber. Someone had built up the fire, and the room was warm as toast. She took one of the fireside chairs and Betsy took the other.

"You have questions."

Catherine did like a woman with wit and no patience for small talk.

"The girls' mother died three years ago. How did she die?"

If she was put off by Catherine's bluntness, she did not show it. "It is not spoken of in most circles, but Wellington engaged a great many officers as spies during the wars. My brother and his friends did a bit of spying for him from time to time. Three years ago, they were asked to discover where Napoleon was receiving supplies in Spain."

"Dangerous work. I have never understood how doing something for king and country could be considered dishonorable."

"Men and their honor, Catherine. You can pry them away from nearly anything, save their precious honor."

"What does this have to do with—"

"Melisande. The girls' mother was Melisande. Her portrait hangs in the nursery. She was with them. In Spain. She looked Spanish enough to carry off a ruse or two. Until she didn't."

Catherine started. "The story the girls tell at bedtime."

"Yes. A fairy tale wrapped around the truth. They sought to lure a French officer into a trap, so they might question him. The trap was sprung on them instead. Had it not been for Melisande, they would have been captured, perhaps killed. Keynsham has never forgiven himself. None of them have."

"I don't understand." Her heart ached for Keynsham, who took the blame and responsibility for everything and everyone around him. It was not fair, to him or to those around him.

"They were all in love with Melisande. They adored her, and she them. But she only fell in love with one of them. Keynsham was in command. He gave the order for the mission to go forward, and Melisande lost her life. Estella was two years old." Betsy reached for the poker and gave the fire an unnecessary stir.

"My God. I cannot imagine. No wonder he tries so hard to be cold and unfeeling."

"Indeed. A helpful trick when one is in pain and wants no one to know. Each of them has their method of hiding. Makes me want to knock their heads together at times."

"That, I can imagine." Catherine laughed and shook her head. Another thought came to her. "I do not understand a man who sold his slaves and plantations to another taking the daughter of a former slave as his mistress, having children with her."

"He told you he sold them? You are fortunate. He is not fond of speaking of it at all."

"Why not? Half the families in Debrett's have interests in the West Indies. I abhor the practice, but society does not agree with me, at least not in private."

"His father and grandfather owned the plantations. God knows how long they were a part of the Keynsham fortune. I knew both men. They were not bad men. They were men of their times, raised to believe things you and I know to be untrue. It is not an excuse, merely an explanation. Keynsham's father sent him to the West Indies to see to the properties and to learn of his responsibilities. Of course, nothing would do but for my brother and Thynne to go along."

Catherine snorted.

"They did not like what they saw, but then the war came along and there was little they could do until Keynsham's father died and he became the master."

"But to sell them, like property." Catherine did not want to believe this of the man who haunted her dreams and made her doubt her very reason for being in his house.

"He is such an *arse* at times," the rector's sister declared.

"I will not argue with you on that score."

Betsy leaned forward in her chair. "He did not sell the plantations. He turned them over to the slaves. The slaves he freed now run the plantations and share the profits amongst themselves. He helped them to set up a company. The man who held the living here before William went down there to make certain all is fair and equitable. They are doing quite well from all reports, especially since Keynsham handles the shipping of their goods to market. The East India Company wanted nothing to do with shipping crops raised by former slaves so..."

"Keynsham ships it for them." Catherine sat back in her chair with a huff. "He bought ships after he sold the plantations," she said softly, remembering what he'd said. "Because ships were more profitable."

"Oh, he charges them for the shipping, a reasonable rate and more than fair, but he does make a profit. Val isn't a saint, by any stretch of the imagination. None of them are."

"Val?" Catherine raised her eyebrows.

"The four of us grew up together. I am not certain they knew I was a girl until I put my hair up. Even then it didn't matter." She stared into the fire. "Mores the pity."

"You were fortunate. You grew up with men who respect and protect you. I have one brother and four older sisters. My brother was kept separate from us for years. By the time he was of an age to protect us, we'd already seen how ugly the world could be for a woman."

"It is indeed, Catherine, but we don't have to let it stay that way. And there are good men to be found. One would hope your brother is one of them."

"He is. He took us from our father when he was still a young man, a child really. And he has stood between us and him ever since."

Betsy rose and went to the commode beneath one of the windows. She poured two glasses of sherry and came back to hand one to Catherine. "Shall we drink to good men?"

"By all means."

They sat in silence for a few moments.

"Catherine, may I be so bold as to ask you a favor?" Betsy placed her empty glass on the table between them.

"Certainly. We are friends, are we not?"

Betsy tilted her head. "I think we are well on our way. In that spirit, I would ask you to try and understand these three men and find it in your heart to be forgiving."

"Forgiving?"

"They often do… ridiculous things in the name of love, or worse, in the name of the greater good. And those ridiculous things nearly always blow up in their faces. Should you be caught in the blast, try to be forgiving." She stood and went to the door. "They truly are good men. I will see you at dinner."

The door clicked quietly behind her. Catherine stared at the door and wrinkled her brow. "What the devil was that about?"

ಸಿ೦ಬ

Dinner was a disaster. The last three days had been a disaster. Hell, every moment from the time Valerian had laid eyes on her at the coaching inn until now was a complete and utter disaster. How had he let Thynne and Collins talk him into this? If he spent one more evening sitting across the dinner table from a flirting, chatting Thynne and his betrothed he might run mad. If he spent one more bedtime reading a story to three little girls and tucking them in with a kiss all under the intense observation of Lady Catherine whilst Collins and Thynne stood in the shadows and chuckled, he'd murder them both. And then kiss the lady senseless. Again.

Thank God for efficient servants and roaring fires. He'd been cold for days. Ever since he'd pushed that amber-haired siren out of his arms and ridden back to Keynsham Hall like a dog leaving the butcher shop. Three days later his body still ached with a chill that refused to leave him for even a moment.

Tonight, he'd dispensed with his duties as host and supposed father in record time. Once he gained the sanctuary of his chamber, he shed his dinner clothes and stepped into the huge copper bathtub before the hearth.

All through dinner she'd gazed at him with a half-puzzled smile on her face. He'd scowled at her, ignored her, and conducted a determined conversation with Betsy. All to no avail. He knew Catherine was there. And she knew he knew it, damn her. She was for Thynne. Valerian had already taken one wife from his friend. He'd be damned if he took another. As if he could. Lady Catherine Chastleton was as far from his touch as the earth from the stars.

Which meant, of course, he had relived that kiss a thousand times. He breathed in her scent, studied her form as she walked in the gardens, and listened for her voice in every room in the house. Worse, he'd had dreams. Dreams of stripping her bare and learning every inch of her ivory skin in exquisite detail. Dreams of her crying out his name in the throes of passion. Dreams of her holding his child in her arms and smiling at him. Christmas was a time of miracles, but he'd given up on miracles long ago.

Christmas. Tomorrow they would gather greenery to decorate the house. The pudding had been stirred up on Stir Up Sunday with great ceremony. The girls had insisted Lady Catherine stir in the sixpence. They had even invited her into the kitchens with Mrs. Gilhooley to help bake Christmas sweets and pies. In two days, Christmas would be over. The other houseguests would arrive soon after, and when they did, he had every intention of slipping away to the hunting lodge. The house party was to celebrate Thynne and Lady

Catherine's betrothal and marriage. She would know the truth about the girls and would, if they were fortunate, blame him for the deception. And he did not want to celebrate that. If he stayed away long enough, Thynne would be married and living at Lavender Hill with his wife and family.

Family.

"Shoot me now." He scrubbed his hands over his face and sank beneath the warm water of his bath.

Splash!

Valerian came up spluttering. And found a large, wet, orange, irate tornado spinning in his bath water. "What the hell—" He attempted to stand up.

"Lord Keynsham, I beg you, don't!" Lady Catherine, dressed in a filmy, floaty night rail and wrapper skidded to a halt at the foot of his bed.

"Don't? I am being attacked by this feline monstrosity and I am naked." He attempted to lift the cat from the bath water. He was promptly swatted across the arm and the knee.

"I can see that you are naked. If you rise from that bath I will see even more that you are naked."

"You can? You will?" He mustered a grin and then a hiss as Cuthbert, the fiend, swatted him once more.

She rolled her eyes at him, which made her face an impish delight to see. "Do stop. Let me have Cuthbert and I will leave you to your bath."

"My bath has left me, madam. A cat being dumped into it will do that."

"Dumped?" She took a few steps forward and stopped. "I didn't dump him in there. He leapt into your bath because I was chasing him."

"Do you have that effect on all male creatures or just cats?" He was sitting naked in his bath and flirting with her. What the hell was wrong with him?

"Estella has let me borrow Cuthbert as I have never had a pet of my own. He has been sleeping in my room but ran out when I heard a knock on my door and went to answer it. I do not want him to wander about and make her think I do not appreciate her gift."

"That is very kind of —Jesus wept, Cuthbert, that is my…" Valerian erupted from his bath and flung his furry tormentor onto the bed. He snatched his banyan from the fireside chair, but not before Lady Catherine had perused his form at least twice. She did not look away, which made him happy for some ridiculous reason. Some parts happier than others.

"Cuthbert!" she shouted and sprinted into the corridor.

Valerian wrestled into his banyan, belted it, and went in pursuit. For some reason, the door to the attics was open and, of course, Cuthbert bolted up the stairs.

"Where does this lead?" the deliciously disheveled Lady Catherine asked.

"The attics. He will be fine. There is no need to…"

She started up the stairs, hitching her wrapper and night rail up enough to reveal a splendidly formed ankle. He sighed, picked up a lamp from the cherrywood table, traversed the corridor, and headed up after her. Only when he reached the top of the staircase did he hear childish laughter, a great deal of shushing, and a door slam. As he'd much rather investigate Lady Catherine than the goings on behind him, he started into the maze of rooms that comprised Keynsham Hall's attics.

It took only a few minutes to find the lady sprawled across a large four poster bed peering underneath it and calling Cuthbert's name. The view of her shapely rump through the silky fabric of her nightclothes was well worth a trip to the attics. It was worth a trip to Egypt if truth be told. He was still standing there staring like an idiot when she sat up with an exasperated sigh.

"He ran under this bed, but I cannot find him. Estella will never forgive me if I lose her cat."

"Why are you marrying Thynne?"

Chapter Seven

"I beg your pardon?" Catherine had not recovered from seeing him in all his naked magnificence and now Lord Keynsham asked her the most idiotic question ever posed her?

"Why are you marrying Thynne?" He came slowly across the creaky attic floor and placed the lamp on the table next to the Holland covered bed. "I know why he is marrying you. Why are you marrying a drunkard who has made no attempt to set his estate in order until his betrothed provided him the money?"

He stood over her in a green silk banyan embroidered with tropical birds. On another man it might look silly. On him it looked... enticing. "He is your friend. How can you speak of him so?"

"Because he is my friend and I know him all too well. He is a good man, but he is taking a damnable long time to remember it. I had hoped you would encourage him to do so."

"A woman would be unwise to try and change her husband before he truly is her husband."

"I don't think you want to change him, Catherine." He drew a finger down her cheek. "I think you like him the way he is. Manageable. Willing to concede all control to you.

Willing to let you do all the work. That is why you are marrying him."

"Perhaps that is what he needs," she said softly. His eyes never left her face, even as he traced her eyebrows, her forehead, her chin, and finally her lips.

"That is what you think you need, Catherine. He needs a woman who will make him take responsibility for his own life. Someone to heal him. You cannot heal him. You can't even heal yourself."

"How dare you?" She half rose and raised her hand which he caught and then kissed. "Lord Thynne is willing to take what I have to offer. I don't expect more of a marriage with him. And he doesn't expect more of a marriage with me."

"Thynne is a fool," he murmured against her lips.

"And you are a fraud, Valerian. A complete and utter fraud." She kissed him. Catherine gripped the lapels of his banyan so tightly the silk squeaked. She pulled him down onto the bed and kissed him some more. His shock turned to amusement and then to something not funny in the least.

"Why am I a fraud?" He stripped the ribbon from her braid and sifted his fingers through her hair, spreading it over the white cover on the bed.

"You want everyone to believe you are a cold-hearted bastard." She kissed his chin, his ear, and the line of his throat. She was out of her mind and did not care. What had he done to her?

"I am ravishing my best friend's betrothed and I do not intend to stop. Still think I am a fraud?" He propped himself on his elbows over her, eyes ablaze, chest heaving.

"Then we are both frauds, Valerian, because I do not

want you to stop."

He struggled out of his banyan. His body was just as magnificent in the dim lamplight of the attics. Slowly, so slowly she wanted to scream, he removed her wrapper and night rail and kissed each portion of her body he revealed with burning, tantalizing kisses. When she finally lay bare before him, she began to consider what they were about to do. He saw it in her face.

"Are you certain, Catherine? There will be consequences and questions and doubts tomorrow. But it isn't tomorrow yet. And I want you so badly I may die from the wanting."

"I don't want you to die." She pressed her fingers to his lips when he started to speak. "I do want this, with you, tonight."

"Thank God." He kissed her so tenderly she thought she might weep. And then his kisses moved down her body and she did. He kissed his way to each hip. He trailed kisses across her belly, which made her laugh as his hair tickled her. He took her mouth, plundered it and seared it. Their tongues met in a slow sensuous dance she'd never imagined possible. He caressed her breasts, kneaded them gently and then cupped first one and then the other for tender kisses and playful nips before he drew a nipple into his mouth and suckled so deeply she felt it in the pulsing core between her legs. He must have sensed the need there. His hand moved to caress her, to part the folds and circle parts of her body she'd only ever explored alone. He slipped a finger inside and then two. As he started a rhythm of gentle strokes, he found her mouth once more and set up another rhythm with his lips and tongue.

She could not keep still. Her legs moved in an attempt to

urge him to do something, she knew not what. She ran her hands over his shoulders, his arms, his chest. His body was hot, smooth, powerful... beautiful. Mindless now as Valerian's hands and mouth worked a strange building magic over her senses, she strove to draw in every essence of him. His scent was soap and heat. His eyes fired with a passion she'd never seen. The sound of his breathing, punctuated by deep groans, rose over the sleet pelting the windows and the roof above them. And there were other sounds. Sighs, moans, soft cries in a voice she knew and did not know. Her voice as she'd never heard it, free and unafraid to show this man what she was thinking, feeling, and being in this moment.

When she could stand it no longer. When her body was bowed to reach for something just out of reach, Valerian whispered her name and in exquisite increments joined their bodies together. When they lay hip to hip and he throbbed inside her, a sense of such completion washed over she sobbed aloud. When he withdrew, even the slightest bit, she pulled him back. He was a part of her, and she did not want it to end.

"Shh, my love," he murmured. "Let me show you. Let me." He withdrew completely and slid home once more. The next time she rose to meet him. In a few strokes, their bodies found a rhythm, and with each stroke, it increased until she knew not where he began, and she ended. The tension built higher and higher. She strained against him until the tension exploded in sensations she'd only imagined in her darkest dreams.

"Valerian!"

He stroked once, twice, and with an inarticulate cry, threw his head back as she felt a rush of heat deep inside her body. He lowered himself atop her. Breathing in her ear.

"I love you, Catherine Chastleton. God help me, but I do."

Her breath froze in her lungs. What had he said?

He rolled to his side, his face more relaxed and open than she'd ever seen it. Perhaps it was the lamplight. Perhaps he'd said what he said because she'd just given him her virginity, not nearly as painful as she'd been led to believe. Did men say such things to deflowered virgins? How had she allowed this to happen?

"There you go, trying to decide how to manage this, the single most unmanageable event on earth." He ran a finger down her nose.

She batted it out of the way. "I am not trying to manage this. I simply got carried away."

"I see." His face began to return to its normal impervious mask. "And now that you are no longer carried away?"

"That isn't what I meant." She sat up and covered herself with her wrapper. "This cannot be managed. Damn you, Keynsham, I think I love you too. How the devil did this happen?"

He laughed. He laughed long and loud, and it was the most wonderful sound in the world. "If you discover the answer to that question, do let me know. I have no idea."

"Perhaps you only think you love me."

"I know I love you. I feel as if I have been struck by lightning, but I know that lightning is love. And I know I will probably love you until the day I die."

"Why?" Catherine nearly wailed. No one loved her, save her brother and sisters. People liked her, cultivated her friendship, toadied up to her, or cast her aside as useless because she was not a son. It had not bothered her, until she saw Valerian standing in that inn with that ridiculous stew-covered cat in his arms.

"You are irritating, intelligent, managing, beautiful, stubborn, magnificent, alluring, and unfailingly kind. And I don't think I can live without you."

"Thank you. I think." She lay back down, her entire body aglow. If he was lying, she would kill him in his sleep.

"And?"

"And what?" She smiled.

He pinched the underside of her breast. "Why do you think you might love me, minx?"

"You are a complete fraud. You care about the people around you. You are a good landlord and a good master, according to the gossip my maid was able to winkle out of your servants. You are not so vain you refuse to deal with cats covered in stew or little girls in search of a bedtime story." She turned on her side to face him. "You gave your plantations away and gave your slaves a way to new lives."

"They were never my slaves. One man has no right to own another. I did what was right." Even in the dim light she saw him blush.

"You don't fear my need to be independent or my need to manage."

He chuckled.

"You are arrogant, annoying, and controlling, and I love you in spite of it. I have no idea why," Catherine finally admitted.

"It is frightening." His voice whispered across her skin. He laced their fingers together. "To fall in love so quickly and with such passion. It frightens me more than Napoleon's entire army, cannons blazing."

"But you have been in love before, haven't you?" A question niggled at the back of her mind.

"Once, a long time ago. And not like this." He cupped her chin in his free hand and turned her to face him. "Never like this, Catherine." He kissed her with a fervor that swept all questions away. And when he moved over her, she forgot every possible way this was wrong and might end badly. She wanted him, and he wanted her. Nothing else mattered.

ℬℭ

Valerian awoke with a start. He'd gone to bed with an incredibly beautiful woman who'd said she might love him. And awakened with a corpulent, orange tom cat perched atop his chest. The other side of the stored four poster bed lay empty. He snatched up his banyan from the foot of it and went in search of Catherine.

There were a thousand troubles ahead of them. Not the least of which was her betrothal to Thynne. He wanted to believe it would all come to the good. He'd never asked for much of life. The one time he did, he'd been denied in the gentlest way possible in favor of his best friend. Perhaps this time, as a once in a lifetime Christmas gift, he'd receive the one thing he'd wanted all his life. Perhaps.

"Catherine, where are you? The sun is coming up. We need to decide how we are to go on from... here." *Oh Hell.*

She had donned her night rail and wrapper and wandered into the one part of the attics he'd forgotten. He'd forgotten a great deal since she had come back into his life. But this instance of forgetfulness might well cost him everything.

"I am certain there is a perfectly reasonable explanation for this, Valerian." She stood before him like an avenging angel. Behind her, he saw the portrait of Thynne, Melisande and their three daughters painted just after Estella was born.

"Yes, *Valerian*, please regale us with the perfectly reasonable explanation for this." Thynne stood at the top of the stairs taking in the entire scene with bloodshot eyes. Collins stood on the step behind him, a pry bar in his hand.

"I will explain this," Catherine waved from herself to Valerian. "If one of you will explain this." She waved her other hand towards the painting.

"Your maid went in to wake you and could not find you," Collins started as he stepped between Valerian and Thynne. "Esmerelda finally told us they had locked you in the attic with *Papa*. I thought..."

"You thought she was locked in here with her betrothed. One of my wives wasn't enough, you blackguard?" With a roar, Thynne tackled Valerian to the floor.

The last thing he saw before Thynne socked him in the eye was Catherine stepping over them and descending the stairs whilst Collins clutched the pry bar and swiveled his head from the scene before him to what was assuredly about to be a scene behind him.

※※

A few hours later, Valerian sat in his study with a piece of steak over his eye and a few bruises on his chest. The fight had not amounted to much. Thynne, pulled from his bed at eight in the morning, was still half seas over, and Valerian had only tried to defend himself from permanent injury. He had no desire to fight his friend. Collins had let them go at it a few minutes and then slapped them apart with the pry bar and the most pertinent announcement of the day.

"Gentlemen, we have far more important catastrophes to

sort out this morning."

So far, nothing had been sorted at all. It was Christmas Eve. Betsy, Catherine, and Annie had taken the children and a battalion of footmen and grooms out to cut greens to decorate the house. They'd returned an hour ago amidst much laughter and noise. Thank goodness Esmerelda, Celestine, and Estella had enjoyed themselves. Christmas in the place they'd come to call home, after so many years of living like gypsies, had been the whole reason for this debacle.

Catherine had said she loved him. Now an errant portrait and a few hours later, he had more doubts than Prinny had debts. This had happened to him before, but this time he was not sure he'd survive it. He'd lost Melisande twice, but the loss of Catherine…

"Get your *arses* in here. Not you, Catherine. I asked them to bring their *arses* because that is where they seem to be keeping their brains these days."

"Betsy, for the love of God, will you stop barging into my study like the bailiff in search of the rents?" Valerian glanced up and immediately stumbled to his feet.

"No." Betsy dragged Thynne to the settee to the left of the desk and shoved him onto it. She performed the same service for her brother at the other end of the same settee. Catherine entered the room and took one of the comfortable leather chairs before the fireplace. Betsy took the other.

Catherine's cheeks were flushed with the winter's cold air. She wore a crimson wool dress trimmed in black and gold. It covered her from neck to the floor, and she had never looked more alluring.

"Well." Betsy looked from Thynne to Collins to Valerian.

"Which of you is going to start this confession?"

"I didn't—"

"He was—"

"I cannot begin to—"

"Oh, for pity's sake, stubble it! Catherine, would you like to begin?"

"Thank you, Betsy, I would." She rose and paced the floor, an Amazon warrior in all her glory. "I believe I have managed to piece together this scheme, with dear Betsy's help."

"Dear Betsy, my *arse*," Thynne muttered. Catherine fixed him with a golden-eyed stare. He shrank into the cushions of the settee.

"You three *gentlemen*," she turned that gaze on Valerian, "decided that whilst I was good enough to marry Lord Thynne, I might not be good enough to accept his daughters. His daughters born of his lawfully wedded wife, I might add. Apparently, my money made marrying a snooty aristocrat who would cast children aside for the color of their skin or the circumstances of their birth more palatable."

"That isn't what we thought." Valerian knew it was a lie even as he said it. Worse, so did she.

"When your first plan, to ship those girls off to a hunting lodge for Christmas failed, then *you*, Lord Keynsham, took it upon yourself to come up with the second ridiculous idea— to pass the children off as yours until you could assess my fitness to be their mother."

He opened his mouth and then closed it again. She had a full head of steam and she was right, dammit. No good came of trying to interfere with a woman in that state.

"You forced this entire household, and your dear sister,

Reverend Collins, to participate in this farce and you bribed those children into living a lie as well. Have I forgotten anything?"

"You forgot the part where you spent the night in bed in the attic with my best friend," Thynne groused, arms folded across his chest. He glared at Valerian, who glared right back.

"Not polite." Betsy slapped Thynne across the back of the head.

"Dammit, Betsy, I'm a viscount. A little respect if you please."

"You will have my respect when you start acting like a viscount, put down the brandy, and become a father to those girls before it is too late." Betsy's declaration had the virtue of bringing the entire moment to stultifying silence.

Catherine took in the room in one slow, painful perusal. "Lord Thynne, you don't love me and that is as it should be. I cannot marry you. I have discovered where my worth lies, and it does not lie in managing you whilst you slowly kill yourself. Your daughters are brilliant young ladies, and they need a parent. As much as I have come to love them, I cannot be that parent. I will stay through Christmas for their sakes. Do not worry about the money. Consider it my Christmas gift to your girls."

Thynne struggled to his feet. "Lady Catherine, I beg you to reconsider."

"That was very nicely done, my lord," Catherine assured him. "Esmerelda, Celestine, and Estella are expecting you to help them supervise the decorating of the house. Do not disappoint them. They are expecting you as well, Reverend Collins. Apparently, Uncle William hangs a superior mistletoe." She smiled, ignored Valerian utterly, whispered something to Betsy, squeezed her hand, and quit the room.

"I told you this would never—"

"I need a drink and—"

Two loud smacks rent the air. Valerian repressed a chuckle as Collins and Thynne rubbed the backs of their heads.

"You two stop squabbling," Betsy ordered. "Thynne, if you touch another bottle of brandy, I will beat you to death with it. William, if you come up with one more idiotic, ridiculous, imbecilic scheme and drag me into it, you great looby, I will tell every unmarried lady in the county you are in search of a wife."

"Well done, Betsy." Valerian dropped the steak onto the butcher paper, wiped his face with his handkerchief, and started around his desk.

"And, you, Lord Keynsham," she poked her finger into his chest. "go after her. She is in the conservatory in search of flowers for our Christmas table."

"My intention all along." He kissed her cheek. "Thank you for that, Betsy-belle."

She swatted his arm and blushed, a rare occurrence for her.

Valerian stopped before his friends. "I know I cost you Melisande, Thynne. And I know I can never make amends for it."

"She… my wife died saving all our lives, Val," Thynne said quietly. "I have always known that. It was easier to let you take the blame than to acknowledge my own. Do you love Lady Catherine?"

"More than I ever thought possible. It sounds ridiculous." Valerian shoved his hands into his pockets.

Thynne laughed. "I knew I loved Melisande the moment I saw her. There is nothing ridiculous about love. It will find you in the darkest night, remember?"

"Or," Collins added. "in the most ridiculous Christmas farce ever performed."

Taking a page from Betsy's book, Collins and Thynne grabbed his arms and dragged him out the study door. "Go after her," they said together.

Valerian ran. He ran through the house, past servants draping greenery over doorposts and window frames. He ran past Mrs. Gilhooley, who squealed when he spun her about and bussed her cheek. He ran past Esmerelda and Celestine making bows of red, gold, and white ribbons. He ran past Estella riding a footman's shoulders as she pinned pine cones and sprigs of holly to the greenery. He ran past Dedham who pointed in the direction of the conservatory in case Valerian had forgotten the way.

When he reached the French windows into the conservatory, he stopped, terrified. What could he say to make up for the lies, the schemes, and worst of all, for ever doubting the kind of woman she was? And a voice whispered down the corridor or perhaps he merely imagined it.

"You English men will use a thousand words to avoid saying the words a woman most wants to hear. It is truly ridiculous."

Melisande. Still watching over all of them and booting them in the *arse* when needed.

"Thank you, cherie," he murmured. Valerian pushed the doors wide, not caring about the loss of heat. He followed the marble pathway to a long table of potted begonias. Catherine heard him. She had to with the boisterous tattoo of his hessians on the heated marble floors. She continued to cut the fullest blooms and place them in a basket.

"I'm sorry, Catherine. Please forgive me. I love you."

She slowly turned, a lovely red flower clutched in her hand. "What did you say?"

He stepped closer and slipped the flower from her fingers. He placed it behind her ear and stroked her hair into place. He dropped to his knees, eliciting a very unladylike snort of laughter from her.

"I am sorry I ever doubted you. I am sorry I lied. You can run to the ends of the earth. After what I've done I would not blame you. But I will always find you. Even in the darkest night."

She cupped his cheek and brushed away something wet with her thumb. "How on earth did you know exactly what I wanted to hear?"

"You'll think it ridiculous." He leapt to his feet and pulled her into his arms.

"You darling man, ridiculous appears to be what you do best." She curled her arms around his neck.

"If that is a yes, I'll spend the rest of our lives improving on ridiculous."

"That is a tall order, Lord Keynsham."

"I am yours to command, my lady. I am ever yours to command."

And for all the years to come, he was!

About Louisa

Louisa Cornell is a retired opera singer living in LA (Lower Alabama) who cannot remember a time she wasn't writing or telling stories. Anglophile, student of Regency England, historical romance author—she escaped Walmart to write historical romance and hasn't looked back. A two-time Golden Heart finalist, three-time Daphne du Maurier winner, and four-time Royal Ascot winner—she is a member of RWA, Southern Magic RWA, and the Beau Monde Chapter of RWA.

Her first published work, the novella *A Perfectly Dreadful Christmas* in the anthology *Christmas Revels*, won the 2015 Holt Medallion for Excellence in Romance Fiction. Her first full-length published novel, *Lost in Love*, was a Golden Heart finalist. She recently released *Stealing Minerva*, the introductory novella in her *The Brides of Lord Creighton* series. Her first novella for Scarsdale Publishing, *A Lady's Book of Love*, was released in May.

Louisa lives off a dirt road on five acres in the middle of nowhere with a Chihuahua so bad he is banned from vet clinics in two counties, several very nice dogs, and a cat who thinks she is a Great Dane and terminates vermin with extreme prejudice.

http://numberonelondon.net/
http://www.louisacornell.com/
https://twitter.com/LouisaCornell
https://www.facebook.com/RegencyWriterLouisaCornell

Our Thanks

This is the fifth in the Christmas Revels series, and each new edition has been more successful than the last. For this, we would like to thank our readers, many of whom have said they look forward to the arrival of each new collection. We do our best to offer you thoughtful stories with Christmas at their heart and hope to continue to be worthy of your interest. Do we guarantee that you will "love" each and every story? Of course not. We all have different tastes. But we *can* guarantee that we have all taken great care to present the best tales possible.

We hope you enjoyed our efforts and that they have enhanced your Christmas spirit. If you missed any of the earlier volumes of *Christmas Revels*, be sure to check them out—*Christmas Revels, Christmas Revels II, Christmas Revels III,* and *Christmas Revels IV.* Each contains totally different, but equally delightful, novellas.

Also, please consider leaving an honest review at any of the purchasing sites. This helps other readers decide if this book will meet their needs. We're glad you chose to visit with these pieces of our imaginations.

Thank you,

Kate   Louisa   Anna   Hannah

Made in the USA
Middletown, DE
06 November 2018